IVAN AND PHOEBE

Ivan & Phoebe

OKSANA LUTSYSHYNA

Translated by Nina Murray

DEEP VELLUM PUBLISHING

DALLAS, TEXAS

Deep Vellum Publishing
3000 Commerce St., Dallas, Texas 75226
deepvellum.org · @deepvellum

Deep Vellum is a 501c3 nonprofit literary arts organization
founded in 2013 with the mission to bring
the world into conversation through literature.

First US Edition, 2023

LIBRARY OF CONGRESS CONTROL NUMBER: 2023007570

Library of Congress Cataloging-in-Publication Data available upon request.

Support for this publication has been provided in part by the National Endowment for the
Arts, the Texas Commission on the Arts, the City of Dallas Office of Arts and Culture, and
the George and Fay Young Foundation

ISBN (TPB) 978-1-64605-262-2 | ISBN (Ebook) 978-1-64605-283-7

Cover design by In-House Design International

weareinhouse.com | @weareinhouse

Interior layout and typesetting by KGT

PRINTED IN CANADA

I owe many humble thanks to:

All those who fight for Ukraine, men and women, named and unnamed, alive and dead;

Markiyan Ivashchyshyn, Ihor Kotsyuryuba, Rokslyana Shymchuk, Taras Prokhasko, Andrian Klishch, Oleh Kuzan, and Maria Mayerchyk—participants in the Revolution on the Granite whose reflections and insights formed the idea of this novel;

Solomiya Pavlychko, whose book started it all;

Marianna Kiyanovska, Oksana Zabuzhko, Zhanna Sloniovska, and Maryana Savka, who were there at the origins of this idea and inspired and supported me through the most difficult times—words are inadequate to express my gratitude;

Solomiya Chubai, Svitlana Odynets, Bohdana Matiyash, Diana Garda, and Nabil Khan for their invaluable assistance, in matters large and small;

Ihor Markiv, Dmytro Lendyel, Vasyl Shander, and Oleksandr Havrosh for our many conversations and the information they so generously shared;

The Department of Slavic and Eurasian Studies at the University of Texas at Austin and Mary Neuberger personally for their unfailing support;

Baltic Centre for Writers and Translators on the island of Gotland and the library of the Gotland campus of the University of Uppsala, where most of this book was written;

My parents, Olha and Petro Kishka, without whose kindness and love none of this would have been possible;

Marin Marais, Antonio Vivaldi, Tomaso Antonio Vitali, Johann Sebastian Bach, and especially Jean-Baptiste Lully and Michel Richard Delalande, whose music was my lifesaving thread in the darkness.

He is an elongated candle, he is a spruce . . .
—Petro Midianka

If my lady has her armor,
let her wear it ever tighter.
—Lesya Ukrainka

Just make sure to keep our wine safely kept—
We will taste it one day. That time will come yet.
—Kuzma Skryabin

PART ONE
THE GLOAMING

HAD THE KNIFE IN HIS FATHER'S HAND NOT SLICED THE TENDONS IN his arm that Monday, Ivan most likely would have run away from home. He stood there listening to his mother, Margita, and Myron Vasyliovych and comprehended nothing, as if they were speaking a language he did not know. "We'll make beef stroganoff," Margita was saying, her smile beaming at Ivan, "and mix a bit of it into the *holybtsy*, right, honey? It's good to mix up the pork in the *holybtsy*... and let Ondia keep an eye on the hired cooks 'cause when the pharmacist's son got hitched one stole their best ham they bought from the Slovaks."—"You got cabbage?" Myron Vasyliovych asked. "We sure do, Ildia's brought plenty!" Margita answered, smiling now at her in-law-to-be, who was, as ever, well cologned, handsome, clean-shaven, and dressed in a blindingly white shirt. "Come on, come inside! You've been standing here for half an hour already! Come in! Come in for a bit at least."

Myron Vasyliovych was the one who brought the calf that morning. Freshly slaughtered and wrapped in a length of thick industrial plastic, it lay on the small island of cement in the yard, surrounded on all sides by the lush riot of June vegetation. Somnolent young wasps buzzed above it. The summer had only just begun but the ground emanated heat like a busy oven. One could feel the noontime swelter ripening slowly in the fresh morning air. The fruit trees in the orchard had already bloomed, and the heads of peonies drooped brownish like dying embers, but the roses Margita cultivated with special affection were just beginning to bud. It was too early for anything to bear fruit, except the raspberry bushes dotted with a few red berries. "There I came, they said go pick one, so I picked it, and the next thing I see—they've got its head on a pole," Myron Vasyliovych related his impressions from the trip to the village.

While Myron Vasyliovych conferred with Margita, Ivan and his father carried the carcass to the cellar to butcher it. The cellar was cool; the single light bulb under the low ceiling gave off a dull glow. Massive jugs of wine lined the wooden shelves along the walls, and the smell of the aging liquid seeped through their thick glass. The men went to work but before they had a chance to get far, the knife in his father's hand slid along a slippery pink joint and, instead of plunging into the muscle and stopping there, kept going. The knife reached Ivan: it slipped along his bare forearm piercing sharply at the elbow. Ivan yelped in shock and grasped his arm; the cut was small but deep. He felt faint. Multicolored circles floated before his eyes and, leaning against the nearest wall, Ivan slid slowly to the floor as his legs no longer appeared to obey him. It must be the wasps, he thought, the wasps from outside came in and the biggest one, the one with an iron stinger, bit into his living flesh instead of the carrion.

Later Ivan lay on the concrete outside under the vine trellis, while Margita rushed into the house to fetch him a clean shirt. He could not recall how he got out of the cellar—did someone carry him? His arm hurt so much he wanted to scream, and he bit down on his lip: he wasn't about to make a fuss over a tiny little cut! There was hardly any blood—so why was he in so much pain, such terrible pain? Ivan got up cautiously, his father supporting his back, and Margita came with the shirt and water to wash his hands; he could only move the good one. He felt he was about to faint again and leave himself to be changed like a doll. Myron Vasyliovych said he would take Ivan and his father to the doctor's, dashed into the house, called someone, and made arrangements.

The clinic on the hill—a white-hot rectangle of glass, concrete, and metal—appeared peacefully asleep in the sun. There were no patients to be seen, as if the breath of summer had restored the whole city to perfect health at once and people, instead of languishing in sickrooms, were luxuriating along the river or in the mountains that massed on the near horizon. Flies buzzed between the panes of glass in the windows that, given the recent vintage of the construction, were not made to be opened, and bored reception nurses behind tall wooden counters fanned themselves with fans they made out of newspaper. It was so quiet you could hear someone open and close the door a floor above; the clang of small instruments tossed into a metal dish pierced the sleepy air like a nail driven through flesh.

The old surgeon spent a long time examining Ivan's aching arm and probing here and there with small needles while Ivan's father breathed heavily in the background, slumped on a stool after he climbed the stairs. "Hurt here?" the surgeon pressed on a spot which made Ivan hiss. The world went dark for him again. "I see," the doctor continued. "The boy wishn't get wed, eh?" Ivan's father chuckled. "Won't sign the form at the registrar's, eh?" the surgeon said, now to Ivan. "Girl got you trapped, is that right?"

Ivan said nothing. The pain was so great he felt he was on a different plane of existence altogether.

"Well, it's nothing," the surgeon, who had to be bored and in dire need of company, finally concluded. He could not keep this patient any longer. The doctor sighed, fixed Ivan's arm in a sling, wrote out a prescription for a painkiller, and patted the young man on his good shoulder. "It'll heal up fine. The tendon is not severed, just nicked a bit. You'll be moving the arm by Saturday."

Back at home, Ivan went to bed and lay facing the wall, his forehead pressed against it. Serves him right. He could almost laugh at himself: he was so set on running away, he even saved up some cash, but was so torn—it's no small thing, to skip one's own wedding! He'd thought so hard about it all: where he could go, with whom he could stay . . . And it was all over now. No need to plan, to wonder—he wasn't going anywhere. Who in the world would take him in with a sliced-up arm? He couldn't even sit through a train ride, let alone heave himself onto the third berth in the overnight train to Lviv. And the worst of it was he wasn't capable of defending himself. Which meant his running away would do nothing. He would just have to go with it. Drift along the flow of his own life.

Ivan shuddered. He thought of going to confession with Phoebe, as was customary before a church wedding. Myron Vasyliovych dropped them off downtown, and from there they walked uphill to the church, along a narrow street paved with round cobblestones. The same street Ivan had walked the year before, when he followed Myron Vasyliovych to hear the choir practice at night. This time, it was morning, and the plaster creatures on the reliefs that adorned the old building followed Ivan and Phoebe with their sightless eyes, sun across their faces. Sunlight didn't quite fit into the narrow street, and the parts of it that remained in the shade were pregnant with mystery and stillness that pooled over the old stone like clear and treacherous water. A young woman came around the corner and walked toward them. They watched her and couldn't believe their eyes: she was dressed exactly like Phoebe, in a long skirt, white top, and cork-platform sandals that were high fashion at the time. She walked like an airy sprite, and the skirt whirled around her ankles just as it did around Phoebe's. A doppelgänger. Another bride, sent to him by the old city. It shouldn't have been a surprise—everyone bought their clothes at the same market—and still the sight of the other girl sent chills down Ivan's spine. The confession did not take long. The Holy Father asked questions automatically, in a routine tone, showed no reaction to Ivan's answers, and did not ask for details. Ivan, on the other hand, would have liked to have a conversation. He wished ardently to be told, like a small child, what was sin and what was not. But there was no conversation. The priest must have been just as brief with Phoebe, who knelt for confession with her back to Ivan, so all he could see were the light soles of her platform sandals, already scuffed and dusty. By the time they left the church, the sun was high and the day had turned hot, and they still had to shop for white shoes for Phoebe to wear with her wedding dress. She and Kateryna Ivanivna had bought everything else, but had no luck with the shoes, and Phoebe worried there were none to be had in the whole city.

They found a pair in a bookstore. It was a time when one could buy the most unexpected things in formerly clearly intentioned places: milk in plastic bottles at the post office, or church calendars at the bakery, pinned up for display among the shelves smelling of cookies. At the bookstore, stacks of shoeboxes towered under the saleswoman's desk. Someone from this or another employee's family shuttled to wholesale markets in Poland or Turkey. Or perhaps Romania, another common destination. Phoebe tried out the shoes in the middle of the store; no one else was there. Coloring books flashed their cheerful covers from the shelves. There were few other books, some esoteric titles and the leftover Soviet editions, unsold for decades.

Across the street from the sixteen-story apartment block, the tallest building in the city at the time, was a hamburger stand, a new and exotic thing. The street here was noisy, with cars thundering by on their way to the river bridge, but they decided to eat outside. Tables on the sidewalk, à la Paris, fit in well in the old city, on the right bank of the river, where a few old streets knotted into the historic core. Here, on the left bank, among new construction, sitting outside felt more awkward, but that's what Phoebe wanted. She put the shoebox with her wedding shoes on her knees. Ivan could not take his eyes off her and did not notice a stranger coming their way until the man was right next to them. The man spoke hoarsely and before Ivan had a chance to hear the words, the smell hit him—*that smell*.

The smell of soldiers' boots and humiliation. The smell of prison, prisoners, and guards.

Ivan's first—and preposterous—thought made everything glow red-hot in front of him: Who sent this man? Where did he come from? Why did he approach them at this very moment? Had he followed them from the bookstore or all the way from the church? Did he keep them in sight, did he hide in doorways when he got too close and they could have spotted him? How many more are there? What do they want? Is this guy a new version of the crazy Sashko who tailed him in Lviv? Run all you want, Ivan, but you know you can't hide forever! They can find you—and did, on the eve of your own wedding!

Ivan pressed his hand across his forehead to calm himself. Quiet, he told himself, the man looks too worse for wear to be a snitch. His face was pale, cadaverous even, and you don't get like that in a week, or even a month, without the sun, it takes years. Tattoos covered the stranger's arms and neck; his clothes were worn and laundered so much you could not tell their original color. And he was thin—not like the provincial skinheads in their eternal tracksuits and leather jackets.

Phoebe, meanwhile, was staring at the man in utter horror, and he grinned back at her in a manner that was meant to be friendly but was spoiled by missing teeth. He did not look old, forty at most, so he must've had the teeth knocked out.

"Dude," the man said again, in Russian, with a lisp, "be a pal, buy me a drink."

Ivan, a touch less anxious, gave in to the rush of gratitude he felt—not so much toward this ex-con as to life itself that once again took mercy on him, Ivan—signaled to the young man in the booth to come out. Ivan ordered a tenth of vodka for the stranger and paid for it right away. It was fine. He wanted everything to be fine, for everyone.

The man, however, downed the drink in one gulp, standing up, and then casually pulled up a chair and sat down at their table— undeterred by the fact he was clearly not invited. His movements were smooth and surprisingly quick.

"That was nice," he stated, his affect visibly transformed. There was a confidence now, a surety in his words and gestures. "Don't be mad at me, pal, I just got out. It was still the Soviet Union when I went in. I got a little lost. I'll smoke, okay?" He didn't wait for a response, pulled out a lighter and a pack of cigarettes from his pocket, lit one, and inhaled deeply. He sucked on the cigarette again with pleasure. Ivan thought it was odd the man had his own supply and didn't beg for one, and on top of that, where did he come by a whole pack of fancy smokes?

Doubt crept back into Ivan's heart. The smell of this man tore at his insides—even the good, strong cigarette smoke could not mask it. The ex-con kept his heavy, prickly eyes fixed on Ivan and instantly registered Ivan noticing his cigarettes. His pupils suddenly shrank, gleamed like liquid fire. Smoke rose around his face. The man gave his cigarette another pull and went on, in a different tone now, coy and dreamy, and completely inappropriate:

"I see you have a nice missus here, pal . . . Or is she a fiancée? She's nice anyhow. Mine, you know, didn't wait for me. Can you believe it? I show up, with nothing, and she didn't even let me through the door."

Now Ivan was angry. He might have put up with the man's cigarettes and rudeness if he'd been by himself, but not with Phoebe!
Whoever this man was, this talk of women signaled nothing but
trouble. Ivan stood up, lifted the shoebox from Phoebe's lap, took
her hand, and they walked away. The stranger clearly didn't expect
this.

"Wait!" he shouted at Ivan's back. "Tell me, what's this independence we got going on now? How am I supposed to live? I don't
know!"

Ivan half expected the ex-con to chase after them, but evidently finagling a seat at someone else's table was the limit of the
man's alacrity.

. . . and now—the arm. Another omen, on top of the earlier
two . . . Ivan felt beset by omens. What next? A roof to cave in
on him? Will the icons in church crack and collapse to the floor
during their wedding? What was he supposed to glean from these
messages? *And if thy right hand offend thee* . . . His arm lay inert,
a narrow, painful drain for his blood, a river, immobilized in the
vise grip of bandages, and somewhere on the shores of this aching
river, eerie visions lay in wait for him, faces more terrifying than the
most frightening masks. The river slowed, went shallow, baring, it
seemed, the very bottom of human existence; hideous marsh creatures smeared in black silt rose from it.

Thoughts ceased obeying Ivan's will, mixed freely in his mind.
Now and then he fell asleep. At night, he woke often, parched,
and tiptoed through the room where his father slept and into the
kitchen, intent on not waking anyone else, especially his father,
but still he disturbed the old man, and his father groaned in half-
sleep and turned over, pulling the quilt over his head. Ivan drank
water from the tap, no matter that Margita kept asking him not to
do it because, here on the right bank of the river, water came from
the municipal pipes, which meant it was brackish and loaded with

bacteria, not like on the left bank, where they had artesian wells—
Ivan did not care, he pushed his face under the tap and drank, drank
for what seemed like hours, only to be roused by thirst again, later,
and go to the tap again. The thirst would not leave him, it whipped
him out of bed, it pursued him, and he kept trying to outrun it.
He'd shudder awake and not be able to recall if he'd been asleep.

By Wednesday, he started to feel better. On Thursday night, he
and Phoebe even went for a walk and then sat in Margita's kitchen
drinking tea from the old tall mugs, chipped a little but decidedly
cozy. Margita joined them for a bit, she exuded smiles like myrrh
and spoke to them in a honeyed voice. Those were their last peaceful hours.

On Friday morning, pandemonium descended. There were
people everywhere. Ivan could not turn without bumping into
workmen in freshly stained overalls or women from his and Phoebe's
families who were moving pillows, bedding, or china. Both floors of
the house, even the half-finished second one, were abuzz. Kateryna
Ivanivna, Phoebe's mother, cleaned the second-floor bedroom,
while workmen laid tile in the not-yet-functional kitchen. The tile
and the workmen had been ordered by Myron Vasyliovych, and he
was paying for both, but that did not mean Margita wasn't pulling
out her hair. *She* would have fixed the renovations at a much better price, albeit a slower pace, but why wouldn't you just go a little
slower for the sake of a good deal, and Dusi's godfather would have
done everything just fine, and wouldn't have charged a lot. Among
all the ruckus and Margita's kvetching, Phoebe was ordered to sit at
the kitchen table with a large bowl of warm soapy water and wash
the stemware. Phoebe sat there with her head down, and her long
wavy hair cloaked her delicate shoulders. Goblets and glasses made
small squeaky sounds under her fingers as she rubbed the golden
rims and the tender crystal stems.

Margita, indefatigable, dashed to and fro, and her sisters, Ivan's aunts Ildia and Ondia, flew at her heels. They polished surfaces, scrubbed floors, baked the sweet *sütemény*, and moved mountains with their bare hands, like three giantesses, primal mothers of the world born themselves for superhuman tasks. There was nothing they did not know, could not or would not do—they were of a hundred eyes and hundred hands. They made the bed for Ivan and Phoebe, polished the just-laid tile in their new kitchen on the second floor, cut roses in the garden and made them into bouquets for the living room and bedroom, and bottled tart homemade wine. They came into the kitchen carrying lengths of linen and scissors and cut through the thick fabric, making shapes. They asked Phoebe to hold one end. Ildia creased her angular, wrinkled face into a smile and talked to Margita, who was not yet quite as old, but already touched by time. Ondia, the eldest, called to them from the stove—that's where she was, starting to bake and cook, she wouldn't leave all of it to those thieving hired hands. Ondia was thinner than her sisters but had the same mouth and called out in Hungarian, over the crackling of the lard in her pans and the ruckus overhead. Ondia arrived the day before from Hungary, where she'd lived for many years and from where she brought her sisters magazines with pretty homes and gardens, smoked chicken thighs, good spices, Erős Pista chili sauce, Vegeta seasoning, and jeans. And now there she was, in the center of the kitchen, pumping at the air with the spoon she was using to stir her cooking, and rattling her old dry bones. Snips of thread fell to the floor. They'd better be done with the linens soon, before the fabric absorbed all the kitchen odors.

Every now and then, Margita popped up next to her son, put her hands on his shoulders, and said to him—or, perhaps, to herself—"God knows we old folks put enough into this, let you young 'uns deal with this construction now."—"Just wait and see, we'll put a third floor on this house yet," Ivan answered through his teeth. "Maybe," said Margita, with a coy wink, and instantly looked younger for she was still beautiful: black eyed, raven haired—it would go gray over the next three years, her hair and even her eyebrows. She moved things around on the table, and said something like, "Just you wait, we'll have a skyscraper here! Let the neighbors sue us because their tomatoes get no sun!" That's the kind of mood she was in.

On the chosen Saturday everyone got up at five—both the hosts and the guests, of whom quite a few had been put up in Margita's house. The Lviv party came in the morning—everyone Ivan dared invite, everyone except Mysko, Mysko was already in Canada. Ivan could not allow himself to think about Mysko, because that name meant Lviv and the last summer, which he had forbidden himself to remember since it separated his existence, like a floodgate, from a completely different world: Ivan's other life, another dimension.

And Rose. Rose was another one he forbade himself to remember. He asked no questions about her, did not send regards. He did not write and did not call, although he had her number. He did his best not to think about her even when he contemplated his escape plan; she was no longer his. How could he possibly present himself to her? What would he say to her husband? He didn't even know whom she'd married . . . Okay, he might come up with something to say to the husband, provided, of course, that said husband didn't knock him out then and there, which would have been completely appropriate. But what would he, Ivan, say to Rose?

He exhaled, wanting to expel memories along with air. He brought the guests into the house and handed them over to Margita and Ondia, who fussed happily: made thick, strong coffee, Hungarian-style, poured it, steaming, into the festive white bone china (bought in Slovakia), and fried eggs.

Styopa and Christina came, Ivan's brother-in-law and sister.

Finally, everyone finished drinking everything they'd been poured, sorted themselves into cars, and set out for the new development to pick up Phoebe. Ivan was squeezed between two guys from Lviv, Mykyta and Andriy Groma. They parked in front of the nine-floor apartment block which looked shabby and unkempt, despite the fact that the neighborhood was still referred to as "new." The high-rises were planted without an apparent order, close enough for residents to see into each other's windows, and the wind blew constantly in the gaps between them, sending waves of dust down the cracked sidewalks. They rang Phoebe's doorbell and were answered by the stately, festively dressed Myron Vasyliovych who inquired how he could help them. The ritual began.

Choking with laughter, the party presented Serhiy Kovach, aka "Seryi," Ivan's best man, and said he was the groom who'd come to collect Phoebe. Curious neighbors peeked from their apartments. Myron Vasyliovych bantered and haggled, apparently, because finally the negotiated "bride" came out of Phoebe's apartment— this was the broad-shouldered, gangster-like Mykyta, wearing a veil and adorned with lipstick. It wasn't clear how he found his way into the apartment, since he came with Ivan's party.

"My love!" Mykyta squealed and grabbed Kovach into a bear hug. Kovach made as if to pick up his "bride," but instead Mykyta lifted the spindly-legged Kovach off the floor and spun him around. Kovach made puppy noises, and Mykyta went on in his falsetto of the fairy-tale wolf who's pretending to be a goat, "My love! My love!"

Eventually, Myron Vasyliovych made a sign like an expert ringmaster, and the scene fell apart. The bride's honor attendant, a distant relative of Phoebe's, stepped out of the kitchen and thundered his welcome in a bass. Ivan thought the man must be a good entertainer with a ridiculously low voice like that, and his enormous height, and his hands as big as spades, which moved nonstop. They entered and arranged themselves in the living room, the same room where Ivan had spent so many evenings with Phoebe and Myron. Mykyta went to wash his face; Kateryna Ivanivna brought out sandwiches and a bottle of vodka for the guests. Then, and only then, did they call for Phoebe. She came out of her room where she'd been dressed by her bridesmaids and friends. Phoebe's large dark eyes seemed still moist from crying. Ivan hugged her and felt the stiff lace of her dress, the wreath that held the veil, and more fabric. Only her hair touched his hands, softly, like silk.

After the civil ceremony, people came up to congratulate them. Ivan was surprised to see Yura Popadynets and Kreitzar in the crowd of guests. He did invite Yura, but did not expect him until the reception in the evening. He didn't dare invite Kreitzar, and went as far as to avoid him, only sending messages through Yura, who would stop by to see Ivan at the bank now that he was sober more often. But Kreitzar came. He was dressed simply, despite his good job—he laid brick for rich people's homes, so he was probably making more than Ivan. However, he gave all his wages to his mother and sister, and left himself nothing, not even enough to buy a new shirt. He stood there with his perennial smile that could be interpreted as, "Please excuse me for taking up this space, I'm sorry, I'll just be a minute." He held a bunch of flowers, not store-bought but common, delicate flowers, just picked, and likely from Kreitzar's own garden: a few small roses of different colors, bluebells, some red herb of grace. The smell of roses filled the room. Ivan felt his heart fill. He went and hugged his friends. He could not love them more in this instant, they were his dearest guests.

Everyone fell quiet in the church. No one spoke, no one laughed, you could only hear an occasional cough, modestly muffled, and a baby mewling, then hushed by a mother or a grandmother.

They waited for a while. Ivan and Phoebe stood before the priests, and behind them the best man and maid of honor stood just as still and solemn.

"The servants of God, Ivan and Maria, are now being joined to one another in the community of Marriage . . ." The words fell onto Ivan with the full weight of their real names. There he was, this eternal Ivan, wedding this eternal Mary to be his wife. Suddenly he felt like laughing, he remembered all the stupid jokes along the lines of "My wife is an angel—Lucky you, mine is still alive," here you go, Ivan, 'fess up: you ran so far that you ran all the way to this here church where they are about to marry you without you really being here. Laughter tore at his lips. He stood in the middle of the church, surrounded by people, his family, but they were all strangers to him now. He remembered Yarema saying to him, "Hold the perimeter." They did hold it, didn't they, back then at the square. . . . But now he was alone. The crowd swallowed Mykyta, swallowed Andriy Groma, and maybe Ivan himself, just as well. He felt beached. Cast away.

And then he heard the choir.

The sopranos sang first, at first softly, and then with great reach and urgency, as if delivering a prophecy, but then again, after a few measures, they would turn soft and vulnerable. The men's voices slowly entered after them: the baritones and basses, a low tremor, an expectant pause, a lull before a storm. The sopranos did not stop but instead called back with an extended and, as it felt to Ivan in that moment, desperate "Ame-en!" to the priest's every phrase until the men's voices would drown them out as if to say, Hush, no need to cry, everything will be okay. Ivan felt cold, as if his face were covered in snow. It was also cold behind him and around him, a wintry draft swirled around him, but then suddenly Phoebe's warm hand came out of that cold and clasped his, and he squeezed it tightly, grateful. Perhaps everything will indeed be okay. Why wouldn't it, after all? He didn't have to listen to the voices, did not have to look behind him at the church full of people. He had been given this one woman, and this woman only, and as long as they were together, everything would be okay.

The priest gently pressed down on Phoebe's shoulders and she knelt. There were many times when they had to kneel, but in this one instance Ivan was to stay standing. He didn't know how he managed to step on Phoebe's luxurious dress, so that when she had to stand up she had to yank her hem sharply from under his foot. All the blood rushed to Ivan's face, he was so ashamed. Just a moment ago she was holding his hand, helping him through this, just as alone as he was in the midst of this ritual, this city, this temple of the Lord; and now there he was, pinning down her dress, as if to signal the arrival of the ancient tyranny, and all because the ritual itself had the oppression forever built into it: the wife was to obey her husband "as Sarah had." He didn't know this, didn't make the effort to learn the details of the rite, he just agreed when people told him to be wedded in church. Now the thought scorched him, he wanted to extinguish it, was afraid to follow it to its logical conclusion, like the thread that was supposed to be his lifeline—except the only thing from which it could save him was his own cowardice. "Rose!" The name flashed inside him as a hot flower of pain blossomed in his heart.

He did not hear being asked to exchange rings, just did what he was expected to do, spoke the words he had to speak. He did not remember leaving the church, or the bells ringing. At the restaurant, the room smelled of slightly faded flowers. First there were toasts, the guests wished the newlyweds much love, many children, and material wealth, while imbibing, of course, wine and *pálinka*.[1] The tables bent under the dishes. Time after time someone would

---

1. Hungarian vodka.

start chanting, "Bitter, bitter, bitter is the hooch, let the bride and groom fix it with a smooch!" Others would join in, and then Ivan and Phoebe would have to stand up and kiss publicly. Eventually, there was chaotic shuffling and motion as the guests traded seats to be closer to whom they wanted to talk to or drink with, and the occasion lost its formality—now Ivan could go chat with the guys or step out for a smoke.

The musicians arrived. The vodka went to Ivan's head, but he preferred to believe he was not drunk, that he would momentarily regain his ability to move gracefully. Someone from the Lviv party stood by the band, Andriy; the musicians touched their instruments, tightening and tuning things, played one note, then another, like a cook testing a simmering stew. They laughed. Andriy went to the center of the dance floor and raised his arms as if to give a special signal. The band played rock'n'roll. Everyone rushed to dance, including the oldest and youngest, and kept at it until the next entertainment, traditional wedding games. For a while, Ivan even forgot about his arm—the wound no longer hurt as badly as it did the first couple of days, but it still hadn't closed. Perhaps everything will, in fact, be okay? Perhaps he had not, in fact, been sent any signs.

They got home around four; it was light already.

Margita and her sisters were sitting in the living room. They spoke Hungarian to each other; Ivan did not understand the language very well, and did not feel like focusing, so only picked out individual words, *Hát . . . természetesen . . . !*[2] He left Phoebe in their bathroom, which had no way of locking—Margita intended to continue with the renovation and did not believe there was an urgent need to fix anything perfectly at the moment, and she was the only one who made any decisions in the family—went to the

2. Sure, you bet!

kitchen, opened the window, and lit a cigarette. A while later, a loud and desperate scream shook him out of his stupor. Ivan dropped the cigarette and ran out of the kitchen.

All three sisters crowded in the bathroom door, Margita and Ondia in the front and Ildia hanging back. Ivan pushed them aside to reach the source of the scream, which was followed by another, and then one more. Phoebe, completely naked, stood under the meager shower, attempting to cover herself with her hands. The concept of a shower curtain was foreign to the household.

"What is going on here?" Ivan shouted. Phoebe started sobbing.

Understanding nothing, he looked around and saw that his mother and both aunts had no notion of leaving, but instead edged closer and kept looking at Phoebe over his shoulders.

"*Has*,"[3] Ondia said quietly to Margita, and this time Ivan clearly knew what she meant.

"Mom, the guests must be really tired," he spoke firmly, blocking Phoebe from view. Margita merely twitched. She, along with her sisters, was somewhat drunk. Ivan pushed and shut the door in her face, then turned to face Phoebe.

"They just came and stared at me," she complained.

"To hell with them. They're drunk."

He waited for Phoebe to rinse off and get dressed.

"Go upstairs," he told her, then pulled at his own shirt, dry now but soaked through with sweat. He worked at it gingerly, so as not to disturb his arm. Phoebe left; he turned on the shower, climbed in. Again, he heard voices. Carefully, without turning off the water, he stepped back onto the bathmat, shuffled to the door, and listened.

"You gotta get him away from his pals," Ildia was saying. "You

---

3. The belly.

just work him like my Onika worked her Iovzhiy, and look at him now! He doesn't even touch drink, doesn't go fishing and stuff, just stays home and works. You just stay home and keep it nice, and the husband will keep to you, too. It's no use fooling around."

"You've got to finish the construction," Margita added. "You've got to lend a hand now, Father and I are not what we used to be. Sure, you've got to get Ivan away from his pals. I don't want no Yura Popadynets in this house 'cause he is one washed-up drunk."

They said more things, but Ivan stopped listening. He could have gone out there, naked as the day he was born, shooed the womenfolk away, and rescued Phoebe. But instead, he lowered his skinny body into the old, peeling bathtub, mottled in black spots, turned off the shower, and opened the faucet. Just to sit there in the warm water.

He clasped his head with his good hand. He didn't have it in him to go interrupt. Or to get up. Or to open the door. He could only feel how terribly tired he was this week.

How terribly, terribly tired.

•

That summer, it was Mysko who rescued Ivan from the outskirts of the city, from the stifling streets Ivan kept wandering like a maze. Around every corner, he was seeing spies, or rather, men sent to follow him everywhere because, of course, they were not employed as spies anymore. The best way to refer to them was to call them men who never gave their real names. The Soviet Union had collapsed, but they, these men, persisted. They told him so themselves, mocking him, as they always did: "Don't you go thinking you'll get away from us."

But Ivan was ashamed to share this with his gang. The gang may well not have understood, not seen what he saw—after all, there were plenty of people who came and went from the orbits of youth organizations then. Any organization, really; those were the years of revolving doors, people seemed to have woken up, all at once, from a long hibernation. After that extraordinary summer of 1991, when the old regime finally fell, and hundreds and thousands of people stood in the squares, chanting, breathing with a single pair of lungs, "End to K-P-U!" And then heaved, like a moan of pain, "In-de-pen-dence!" When the parliament stood to read the document that proclaimed the nation's independence, when the parliamentarians, some of whom had been political prisoners, sang "Oh the Red Viburnum in the Meadow" everything changed, and the country caught on fire.

To be fair, Yarema Goshchyshyn had warned them a long time ago that they must not ever let themselves be suspicious of each other. He prohibited them from playing that favorite game of Soviet students, spot-the-spook, telling them it was a hopeless and harmful idea that destroyed trust. And trust, he told them, was the most precious thing we had. No, scratch that: *Trust is the only thing we have.*

Yarema was right. Not every young man who did not come back to a second meeting was a rat. Yarema might not even have recognized the two men, "Sashko Petrenko and his friend," whom Ivan introduced that one night as "good guys." Patriots. Ivan didn't even bring them to the office; they just dropped in on a dorm party. The girls were still fixing things up in the kitchen, putting food on plates, spooning the usual potato salad—generously slathered in mayonnaise—from jars. Yarema stood in the kitchen doorway talking to someone else when Ivan arrived. They greeted each other, and Ivan nodded at his protégés and felt, in that same instant, the graveyard chill that emanated from them seize his back. Yarema nodded back, they shook hands, and the rest was a whirlwind, and Ivan did not see whether Sashko Petrenko (or, rather, "Sashko

Petrenko") spoke to Yarema or any of their other leaders. He did
not see "Sashko" later at that party at all; he even went out on the
balcony to check if the two men had gone there or were smoking on
the street below, but they were gone. One could reasonably believe
they had a drink and went back wherever they came from, their
sole motivation having been a chance to get a free dinner. Yarema,
quite possibly, never found out who they were. In fact, that's most
probably what happened, because he did not treat Ivan any differently afterward; other guys would have told Ivan if anything was
wrong. Except, of course, if they had all agreed to keep silent and
walled him off with that silence so he would go on thinking everything was just fine, and who could have blamed them: they would
not have told him they suspected him *especially* if they did, in fact,
suspect him to be the traitor.

Ivan had some standing in the group; they'd known him for
a while. He was one of the guys, he went to the protests and got
arrested along with everyone else. He joined the one-day hunger
protest in support of the Chinese students, the ones in Tiananmen
Square, the ones who were later arrested en masse if they were
lucky not to have been run over by the tanks. Ivan went to the
celebration of the Unification Act[4] in January of 1990, when the
human chain stretched from Kyiv to Ivano-Frankivsk. That was a
celebration of Ukraine becoming whole in 1919 after being torn
apart by foreign powers. What faces he saw that day! Ivan could
never forget them; they were so suddenly, newly alive, grown men
had tears running down their cheeks. They linked, held hands, and
stood there, in Lviv and in Ivano-Frankivsk, in the cold wind and
the freezing drizzle, men and women, dressed in indistinguishable

---

4. The Unification Act is an agreement signed on January 22, 1919, by
the nascent Ukrainian People's Republic and the West Ukrainian People's
Republic on St. Sophia Square in Kyiv.

clothes that could only have been manufactured in the Soviet Union. They laughed and they cried.

It was around that time Ivan's group came to understand how they would fight. That was it: standing *together*, being together—it would be enough. As long as they remained organized.

On a spring day, they came together after lectures in an empty classroom that smelled of warm chalk dust. Yarema listened impatiently to Bodya, "the Afghan." Bohdan Melnyk had come back from fighting in Afghanistan a year before and advocated for armed guerrilla resistance. A few other guys were inclined to support him.

"What guerrilla tactics?" Yarema finally said. "We cannot do it in the middle of a big city. Do you intend to pry cobblestones loose from the downtown streets?"

"We could hide in the basements," Bodya countered, unwilling to give up. He had anxious eyes, sudden gestures. His black hair was peppered with gray. "And if you are worried we won't have weapons . . ." He let his voice trail off.

Yarema got up and went to the window. The sunlight, refracted through the thick panes, held a pillar of sparkling chalk dust. The particles danced slowly in midair.

"We cannot have weapons," Yarema said in the same slow, level voice. He always put things like that: simple, short—and then everyone spoke at once, interrupting each other, all trying to get out the same point: that weapons were irrelevant, no one had weapons in Tiananmen Square.

"And where's that Tiananmen now, huh? They all went to jail, and those who didn't got butchered for their organs. You want to be a pile of organs?"—"What about Gandhi, did he just get arrested, too? And didn't ever do any good, did he? The whole of India protested, folks just sat quietly, and see what happened? The British couldn't hold on!"—"The British didn't hold on because they were fucking done with the place! They'd have never left if they could still use it!" Someone brought up Jan Palach, and then Vasyl Makukh. Self-immolation kept coming up for months, the idea of it terrified but also inspired them; they thought it would only take a few suicides, even just a single one, and everything would change, the single martyr's life redeeming the whole nation, and then . . .

Andriy Groma sided with Yarema. By then, Ivan had gotten to know Andriy well: they spent a lot of time walking around Lviv together, Andriy telling Ivan the history of the streets they took and buildings they passed. There was nothing, it seemed, that Andriy did not know about the city and he was passionately devoted to every stone, doorway, and stained glass window. He had a habit of speaking very fast, as if he were worried he would not have the chance to make his point.

"Yarema! What are we waiting for?" Bohdan Melnik spoke again, eyes flashing. "You know this: they will only listen when our guns do the talking. All right, okay, maybe not the kind of guns I have in mind. We don't mean to kill anyone. But we must be . . . forceful. People will support us."

At the next meeting of the Students' Brotherhood, two members of the Rukh[5] movement joined them, both formerly imprisoned dissidents, Myroslav Hnativ and Orest Ostapenko. Ostapenko had been released very recently, in 1989, and in such poor health that people doubted he would manage to travel home from the labor camp near Perm where he had been serving his sentence. He practically had no kidney function. There were heavy shadows under his eyes, his eyelids were swollen, and his joints were beginning to swell as well. Everyone expected him to die, but instead, miraculously, his kidneys healed. Now he stood among the young

---

5. Initially organized as the People's Movement of Ukraine for Reconstruction (i.e., for perestroika), Rukh was founded in 1989 as a civil-political movement as the Communist Party was the only political party allowed in the Soviet Union.

people, straight-backed, sinewy, strong, with a luxurious mustache he'd cultivated since his release and no shadows under his eyes. Ivan had never been so close to the man, and could not stop marveling: What kind of people were these dissidents that neither prisons nor labor camps could break them?

Ostapenko and Hnativ asked questions about the "underground" work, promised assistance. Bohdan hinted at weapons and the older men said nothing, but Ivan got the feeling they approved of the idea. They clearly liked Bohdan.

"Underground!" Andriy snickered. "There is no underground. It's just us, and we are common citizens, we do not see ourselves as different in any way from the rest of the people. We are the people."

"The people?" Ostapenko challenged him. "And for whose sake, young man, did we rot in the gulag? And what do you think we have on our minds now? Retiring to a quiet dacha? If I say you have to be underground, that means you have to work with us, and under our leadership . . ."

There was more he meant to say, but Yarema did not let him. He stood up, tall, with his mess of black unruly hair and faced Ostapenko:

"The time of hiding has passed. Everything has changed. What Bohdan is calling for, and what you appear to welcome, is terrorism, not civic action. What is our aim? To be seen. To be seen as part of the nation we want to represent. When you face a defenseless man and look him in the eye, can he really be an enemy? You are looking at yourself. That is us. We will be the mirror the people look in and see themselves. Then they will be together, with the same goal."

Yarema spoke about the awakening. About the realization that you have power that comes when you know you are not alone, that there are brothers at your sides, lit up by the same ideas and aspirations. And as long as you are together, you are invincible.

"Consider," he said, "how many wars the Soviet Union has fought. And how many it is still fighting. Do we benefit from them in any way? If we were, as some would suggest, to blow up a building, what is it that we would be destroying? A historic site. And what if there were people in it? This would be a sure path to self-elimination. We want the opposite: we want to be present and seen. If Kyiv rises with us, and the country follows, who would be left for the regime to rule? The regime relies on the majority's silence. We must take away this silent majority."

Yarema, for one, was easy to picture with an automatic rifle in his hands. Or with a sword. He held himself like a warrior, was broad-shouldered, powerful. But he would have neither a rifle nor a sword. He just stood there, face-to-face with Ostapenko, who was clearly irate. Yarema grew up in the mountains and must have taken something from them: he knew how to be immovable. He knew the power of fortitude.

"All right," said the other dissident, Myroslav Hnativ. He was a tall man with pale blue eyes. Rumor had it that he was adept at yoga and Asian martial arts. In prison, he became famous for his ability to debate any topic with no preparation at all, legal issues especially. He knew the Soviet Constitution by heart. "All right, boys, I understand: you've got Gandhi, you've got nonviolent resistance. This is laudable. But if you read your *Bhagavad Gita* as carefully as I assume you did, you would recall Krishna's counsel to Arjuna."

The young men fell silent. No one knew who this Arjuna was, not even Yarema.

"You don't recall it at the moment?" Hnativ went on. "Well, Arjuna sees the enemy army and realizes it is led by his own uncle, the warriors are his kin. He asks Krishna, 'How can I wage war on my family? There's my grandfather there, and my uncle.' Krishna tells him he is to fulfill his duty—in this case, his warrior duty. I'll tell you another thing, too. Nonviolence is great when you already have an army, when you are strong. When you have a choice. When you are the oppressed and call for nonviolence, you are nothing but a coward. So you, boys, are about to have some serious egg on your faces with your so-called actions. Instead, you have a chance, if you would just listen to your elders, to serve your country. You'll be rabbits preaching nonviolence to the python who is swallowing you as you speak."

The room became uncomfortably quiet. Hnativ had a point. A few young men looked down, discouraged. Bohdan looked triumphant. Yarema then spoke to Hnativ:

"So you believe us to be cowards, do you?"

"No, I shall believe you to be whomever you show yourselves to be," Hnativ spoke decisively. This was his element; he could strike like lightning. "If you behave like cowards, you'll be cowards. So what do you say, boys," he asked the group, looking beyond Yarema. "Shall we fight together? Tell me!"

He looked charged, ready to dart around the room, to look into each man's face, ask each one of them separately. And then Yarema put a stony hand on his shoulder.

"What is this?" Hnativ sneered. He survived had the camps, the interrogations, the snitches, and the traitors; he feared no one, least of all one of these boys.

"You called us cowards," Yarema said. "But we could also call you something, a demagogue, for example." His voice turned steely. "You better leave."

Hnativ laughed in Yarema's face. He jerked his shoulder free and challenged:

"Who do you think you are?"

Andriy Groma and Ivan stepped up to Yarema's sides. Yarema pointed to the door. Everyone spoke or yelled something at once. Orest Ostapenko lost his poise entirely and turned beet red in the face:

"How dare you!" he yelped. "You're turning against your own! You are the reason we lost the nation! The people won't follow you."

In that moment, Ivan truly did not know what to do. The men who were their guests, unbent and invincible, represented, because of the suffering they had endured, a different category of human beings. They carried the memory of pain and struggle, they were anointed by what they had survived, they had no fear. And they were also honest, utterly open, and did not—could not—hide the bitterness that was eating at their hearts like hungry worms. Righteous wrath erupted from them. Until then, Ivan had only seen these men from afar, at marches in Lviv or Kyiv, or on TV—they were legends to him: Ostapenko, Iryna Kalynets, Vyacheslav Chornovil, Lukyanenko, Antoniv, Sverstyuk. All straight-backed, full of dignity. Could Ivan and his friends really match them? What if they could not?

And now Ivan was alone. Summer dragged on without an end in sight and he did not want to go back to Margita. He could not remember how he managed his last set of exams, how he gradu- ated. It had been a year since he was officially a student. Sashko, his torturer, had disappeared, but warned him others would take his place. Just when it seemed the worst was over, Ivan lost him- self to panic. Everything scared him: people, dogs, old buildings. He stopped going to the old city. He lost his sense of time. Ivan only knew it was summer because the asphalt turned gummy in the heat, and the suburbs stood dusty and dry. It was hard to breathe as if the air, poured mercifully into the clay bowl of the city at night, evaporated as soon as the sun rose. Lines of poetry about a suicidal city swirled in Ivan's head, but he could not recall who wrote them.

Mysko Bilyak, his best friend, found him; he just turned up one day at the apartment Ivan shared with two roommates. Ivan barely knew these guys and avoided his own crowd—he was afraid of the silent wall, afraid it would grow taller and thicker, and just as afraid to ask whether it was there at all, afraid to let it be seen that he lived holding his breath, afraid to ask about things that were not there. Mysko appeared at the door of that wretched apartment like a fiery angel. The air, already palpably hot, seemed to turn to flames around Mysko's bright red hair. He had a wide, flat face, a sharp jaw, and a full, sensuous mouth, a Klaus Kinski lookalike. A Klaus Kinski with very red hair. One dreaded to think how much kids must have bullied him in school and what he must have done to them. Mysko Bilyak was fit to be cast in that German movie *Aguirre, the Wrath of God*. Except he had emerged that day from the waves of infernal heat to effect a deliverance.

Mysko moved Ivan into his own room in the dorm that belonged to the Sports Education University, where, in exchange for a small tithe to the warden woman (Mysko called her Baba Yaga), one's utter lack of affiliation with sports or education could be overlooked.

"You'll work for me," Mysko told Ivan. "I'm starting a business."

Mysko was making his own way in life, a path that had nothing in common with Yarema's or the one taken by the boys who'd come back from Afghanistan.

The dorm, dilapidated like all Soviet dorms, was wormed through with dark, endless hallways with greasy, long, unpainted walls. When Ivan arrived, a skeletal cleaning woman was banging around with a mop and a bucket. She came occasionally, and otherwise it was quiet, the kind of quiet that dwells at the edge of a large city. Water ran on a schedule during limited hours, ceilings peeled, murky windows hadn't been washed for decades. Cockroaches darted along the walls and tables. The windows looked out onto the woods.

For the first few days there, Ivan just slept on the narrow, uncomfortable bed pushed against the wall; for the first time in what felt like forever he felt safe. The neighborhood was simple, semirural—women kept their eyes down and sold slightly rotten vegetables on the sidewalks; men came to the nearby convenience store drunk and placed themselves in the line for bread or pickles so that they could hold on to something with one hand, forestalling a fall.

Mysko was the only person Ivan really trusted. If Mysko told him to follow him to hell, Ivan would have gone without a second thought. In a way this was odd because Mysko, of all of them, was the most skeptical. He questioned everything—the revolution's aims, its strategy, its tactics. Ivan listened to Mysko argue with Yarema and Andriy countless times, and yet, in the end, Mysko did go to Kyiv with them, and slept on a cot in the Maidan with them during their hunger strike.

One day Mysko asked Ivan to go downtown, to print something at Yarema's office. Ivan's jaw dropped. He couldn't bring himself to say anything; he didn't know where to begin. Naturally, he did not make it to Yarema's office downtown. In fact, he didn't even make it downtown: he only got as far as the streetcar terminus. He waited for the number 2 and his heart thundered in his ears. It felt wrong, his heart, it was working too hard, it raced, what if stopped? *A streetcar stop where your heart stops*, ran a self-composed cheerful ditty in Ivan's head. Vague shapes floated in front of him, as if in a fog: the small crowd waiting for the streetcar, individual people, the sunflower seeds they chewed, spitting out the shells straight onto the sidewalk, the tram itself when it appeared, its steps Ivan could not bring himself to climb, and then another and another . . . Ivan stood and watched and listened to the bells of the old-model trams and could not move a muscle.

Back at the dorm that night, Mysko asked for the printouts. Ivan just stood there defeated. He could hear nothing except the heavy thumps of his own heart and the noise of blood in his ears. Mysko studied him for a moment, then sat down on a bed and gestured for Ivan to sit, too.

They still said nothing. Mysko held his green, gold-specked eyes on Ivan's face. Finally, he said:

"It's not like I haven't noticed you barely leave the dorm."

"Yes, I do."

"Oh yeah? Where do you go? To the store?"

They sat a bit longer.

"I saw Bohdan, before he went to live with his mother," Mysko said. "I've seen others like that. I see what's happening to you. You have to do something about it."

"What?" It was the only word Ivan could squeeze out. "What . . . *can* I do?"

What could he do? Tell Mysko everything? And what would Mysko do then other than lose the last shreds of respect he had for Ivan, as well he should? But how could Ivan have done otherwise? Back then, in '91, they weren't wasting their time threatening him or arresting him, they simply told him they would kill his mother.

"If you want me to help you, tell me everything," Mysko said. Then he waited.

Ivan took in their room, the two beds, the dusty floor, the rectangle of the window, already dark, unprotected by curtains.

"I'll tell you what," Ivan said slowly. "Let's talk about it tomorrow."

This was a trick Ivan learned back then: to ask for another day, the blessed *tomorrow*. He had asked for it of the man he knew as Sashko Petrenko, and he had asked Rose; he asked without a thought for the consequences, for the actual tomorrow, he brushed away the fact that he was merely postponing the catastrophe—and only for a day! He uttered the plea automatically by then, without hope, at least without hope for anything specific.

Mysko agreed. He nodded, smoothed down his red hair, and went to bed. Ivan, on the other hand, did not sleep a wink that night as he lay in his bed and tried to puzzle out what to do next.

At one point he slipped out of the room and went to stand by the open window in the shared kitchen, where he could smoke. What was he to do? Did he have it in him to tell Mysko everything? He could barely own up to it all himself—let alone share with another . . . Because was there, really, a place for him in Lviv?

For the first time in a very long time, he had to admit it: He could not live in this city.

Which meant, this was the end. The only thing he could do was run. Add his name to the ranks of those who could not bear it, didn't have it in them, who ran. Thank goodness, he thought suddenly, he could still run. He still had money and the physical strength to do it. And the will to act. He could still *go* home, instead of being delivered, like a piece of refuse, from some loony bin. Or as a bloody mess scraped off a pavement under a seventh-floor window. Or a body to be identified after being shoved off a speeding train.

Ivan was so used to mourning his lost life, the incredibly successful career he had once imagined having in Lviv, the incredibly beautiful life he would've had here, full of beautiful things and refined feelings, that he realized he was overlooking some simple but genuinely good things. He was alive and generally sane, as long as he resisted the urge to think of "Sashko Petrenko." He would run and live somewhere else. Where? At Margita's of course. At home. In Transcarpathia. He still had a home and a family that would be thrilled to see him.

Compared to others, he was a lucky bastard.

Ivan finished his cigarette and exhaled the smoke. Tomorrow he would tell Mysko he was going home.

He only had to come back to their room and climb under his thin blanket, however, to sink back into black despair: What would Mysko think of him? This much was clear: he'd think Ivan a coward. A traitor. He would have to conclude that Ivan did not believe in him, Mysko, his best friend, his talent and pluck, his dream of running a business. That Ivan did not want to help him. If only someone else could make the choice for Ivan, if only circumstances just sort of miraculously conspired to force him to go home . . . For example, if Margita called him at the dorm, and Mysko just happened to hear Ivan's side of the conversation. Margita used to call the check-in desk at his old dorm, and whichever old woman was manning the desk would send someone to fetch Ivan from his room on the seventh floor, and he'd come running downstairs while Margita waited, and would snatch up the receiver, gulping for air, out of breath. But Margita did not have the number for this new dorm. Well, he thought, it didn't need to be hard for her to find out. He could call her and tell her the new number. Then he could ask her to give him a call here at the dorm. Sometime in the evening, when Mysko would be home.

Ivan tried to dismiss this idea. He tossed and turned on his narrow bed like a sinner on a roasting pan in hell. Lies and more lies. He wasn't about to undertake such a scheme.

But then again, why not? He would go to the post office and call Margita—just to give her the new number, so she would know how to reach him, nothing wrong with that, a mother should have a way to get a hold of her son, if she needs to. In fact, he had neglected Margita lately, it was high time he called. So he would make sure she had the number. And then suggest she should call him—at night, in the next few days. She would be happy to do so. Mysko would see him run downstairs to answer. The doorwoman would back him up; yep, a call from home, she took it herself. And then he could tell Mysko that . . . that he, Ivan, was needed at home . . . because . . . because someone is sick? No, better not fabricate something like that. Because they just want him back, that's all. His parents want their son to get a job, help them out, even support them. They are not getting any younger after all, and they've got a lot to manage, the pigs, the chickens, Margita's vegetable garden, and they need money to pay for the things they can't grow. The whole chain of events occurred to Ivan casually, as if unbidden, until suddenly he knew this was not just an idea—he had a plan. This was exactly what he was going to do.

The next day, the weather turned. Daylight faded in the early afternoon; a storm was coming. Ivan opened the window, breathed in the moisture in the air. He still had to go to the post office, the one downtown, to make the long-distance call. He closed the window, put on his shoes, grabbed his raincoat, left the room quickly, and ran downstairs. Outside, he heard thunder. People ran for cover in advance of the imminent downpour. Ivan, instead, bravely charged into it. The storm caught him on Lychakivska Street and in a few seconds drenched him to the bone, raincoat notwithstanding. His shoes—old and worn but comfortable and therefore beloved—instantly turned into a pair of slippery little boats.

Closer to downtown there were more people in the streets. Ivan had to step into a roofed doorway next to the Vynnyki Market and he felt suddenly weak in the knees, as if about to faint. It was cold; he shivered in his wet coat. Two other men and three women sheltered under the same awning; the two older women carried grocery bags, and the younger one had terribly exhausted light eyes badly made-up with thick black eyeliner. The tint had run into the small wrinkles around her eyes. No one spoke even though they stood very close together. The woman with the eyeliner kept sighing. In this huddle, Ivan felt comforted and no longer irredeemably alone. He looked out at the street, at the streetlights' smudged reflections in the puddles and sensed his heart lift for a moment: here was a respite, a bit of dry ground in the great flood. Here he was safe. No one would come looking for him in this deluge.

And even if they did, they wouldn't find him.

Ivan let himself luxuriate in this wonderful sense of safety for a quarter of an hour, watching bubbles rise and burst in the puddles.

Still, he had to go on. Stepping out from under the awning felt like a plunge into an icy lake. It was not far to the central post office from there, but things felt risky—there were too many people out, even in the rain. The streets grew narrower in the old town, so passersby caught at each other with their open umbrellas as they sloshed along the narrow sidewalks. Streetcars, clanging, tore through the scrim of the downpour. Their long metal bodies instantly took up the width of the street. Light bounced off the glistening cobblestones. The flashes left Ivan blinded.

Suddenly, he froze; he saw a shadow out of the corner of his eye. Someone was following him. Ivan stood for several seconds in the middle of the sidewalk, waiting—perhaps the person, whoever it was, would pass him by. No one did. Ivan started walking again, and the shadow moved along with him.

Ivan's heart raced, beating so hard he had to stop again—he just could not go on. They must have found him after all. Someone was tracking him, which meant someone wanted to know the routes Ivan took, his routine. Who could it be? Why? Could it be "Sashko Petrenko" again? Could it really? Or was this someone new? Of course, this would be someone new . . . he had come to know "Sashko" quite well. "Sashko," disgusted as Ivan was to admit this, was almost family.

And what on earth possessed him to think he would be safe at home? Did he forget what they threatened to do? Had he no pity on Margita, his own mother? He wished he were dead. A dead man, at least, has the assurance he won't be used for someone else's purpose . . . although, come to think of it (and here his heart seemed to flip itself over again, nearly bringing Ivan down), how could he be sure of that? What if they employed a whole cabal of skilled psychics who could summon dead souls from oblivion, like Gogol's antichrist, to be tormented again? What if they fielded armies of spies in every possible world and dimension, every city and town, and there was no place—absolutely no place on this earth—where he, Ivan, would not be visible and therefore vulnerable?

He wondered if he could die right there; the tension he felt was inhuman, unbearable. His throat felt as if it had been filled with broken glass. Ivan could not breathe. Lightning tore open the skies, mutely, the thunder arriving moments later. The thunder, paired with the sharp flash of light, brought Ivan back, as if both the thunder and the lightning had boomed inside him, deep in his soul. What was it Yarema used to say? *Don't go looking for rats.* Don't look for shadows behind your back. Don't believe everything you see happening around you. Don't be afraid, because fear, Yarema used to say, is just an idea. An idea can be dismissed. An idea can be replaced.

Ivan breathed out. He turned around sharply and saw the shadow dart into the nearest doorway. This gave him a chance to change course. Ivan turned a corner, and then another. Finally, around another corner, he saw him: a tall, skinny man in a green raincoat. Gotcha! You won't catch me now! Ivan thought, and laughed nervously to himself. If this was a game, he would win it. There were plenty of doorways that led into dark buildings of old stones that smelled of age and mildew, where one inhaled the air of boiling cabbage that seeped from under doors covered with rotting fake leather. Ivan had learned that most doorways in the Old City led to passages through the building to the courtyards; one used to be able to traverse old Lviv without taking the streets, one courtyard to another, until the Soviet authorities locked up most of the throughways to make it easier to catch people.

Ivan dove into the first available passage, but the back door, the one to the courtyard, was locked. Or . . . did he have the right door? There was another one right next to it, and Ivan yanked the handle. The next moment he was inside someone's apartment. He could hear laughter in one of the rooms. The place smelled of old rugs,

Ivan and Phoebe • 45

warped furniture, tobacco, and something else—urgent and titillating. Ivan walked gingerly along the worn-out floorboards and peeked into the room; there was a table, with mismatched, worn chairs helter-skelter around it. A vase holding red glass tulips stood on the table.

Suddenly, another door—Ivan glimpsed the kitchen beyond it—opened, and a half-dressed woman ran out, laughing. Her dress was unbuttoned to the waist. She wore old-fashioned stockings with a girdle, oddly arousing. A man came chasing after her, cigarette in one hand, and it was clear that the chase had nothing to do with escape, all of it a game. Ivan barely had a chance to step aside. Neither the woman nor the man paid any attention to him, as if his appearance in the apartment was fully expected. It was a peculiar place indeed, full of laughter, full of glass tulips.

Ivan turned to leave and came face-to-face with a petite, sinewy woman. He did not hear her approach, and now she stood in his way. She looked straight at him. Ivan was overcome with shame; only now did he notice he had dripped, and kept dripping, rainwater all over the floor. His hair lay plastered to his skull.

"I'm sorry," he said. "I got the wrong door."

"Who is it?" someone called from the depth of the apartment. The woman opened her thin, thickly carmined lips and answered, in a regular voice, as if addressing Ivan himself:

"Must be a student . . . quite lost."

Ivan squeezed by her to the door, pushed, and ran out of the apartment. What the hell was he thinking? Could he not tell a courtyard door from an apartment door? It's not rocket science! Angry now, he fished for cigarettes in his pocket, but of course his pack had turned to mush in the rain. Then he heard a squeak, someone else entered from the street.

Instantly sure it was the man in the green raincoat, Ivan dashed up the stairs. Of course, nothing said the man could not follow him all the way . . . but then Ivan heard the man ring the doorbell of the apartment he'd just left, a peal of laughter through the open door, then music. Then the door closed again.

Ivan stood on the landing, next to an open window. No one else came from the street. No one was chasing him. For some reason, he felt certain of it now. He smelled the air about him: wet sawdust and rotting trash. The window opened onto the courtyard, one of those narrow stone wells where the air sits thick and torpid, and grass roots through the chipped flagstones. He was looking into a black hole, from a landing in a strange building, in the middle of a strange city where all he had were Mysko and his dorm room.

A rebel, right! An underground operative. An eternal revolutionary. There he was, chased up these stairs by rain and fear, disgraced by the surveillance, unnerved by an illicit brothel, and utterly broke except a few fifteen-kopeck coins he had brought to call Margita. He was ridiculous. The Soviet kopecks were out of circulation, but people held on to these particular coins because they were the same size as long-distance telephone tokens. And what was it he was going to talk to Margita about? Of course, he needed to ask her to call him at the dorm tomorrow, so that he could manufacture an excuse for his best, and apparently only, friend, because he was too scared to tell him honestly that he, Ivan, was exhausted and wanted to go home.

The rain fell harder. Drops, whole strings of water splashed onto him through the window. Ivan had to go. The self-loathing he felt turned into anger. Enough of this chicken shit! He hit the peeling windowsill with the heel of his hand, not too hard, but Lviv continued to regard him impassively with its wet eye of the open window. He had to leave the building. And the city. He wasn't going to call Margita—no need to pretend. He would just go back to the dorm and tell Mysko he was leaving.

But he did not.

He pretended to be asleep early. At five in the morning, Ivan slipped out of his bed and found his duffel bag—his one bit of luck was that he never did unpack properly after he moved to Mysko's room. Ivan grabbed a few other things, dirty clothes that were draped over the back of the chair next to his bag. His wet clothes from the day before went on top; he wished he could put them into a plastic bag, but that would have made too much noise. Time to go. Mysko was asleep. Ivan placed his key on the pillow. Later. He would explain everything, later. Now he just had to go to Margita's, shake off his troubles. He would get better, and then he'd be able to tell Mysko everything.

In the dark hallway, with the weak light of a cheap flashlight he found in his bag, Ivan scribbled a note for Mysko, short as a gunshot: "I'm going back to my parents because I have to. I'll call later. Ivan." He thought about it and crossed out "I'll call later." Then wrote the same sentence again above the crossed-out words.

•

It took him most of the day to get home. He took local trains that served small towns—he had very little money.

Ivan walked through the city, and his entire body, not just his eyes, recognized the streets. He walked lightly, as if air itself lifted and aided him on his way. At his parents' fence, he stopped. The narrow back gate was locked, but he knew where they kept the key: in the mailbox, in the inside of the gate. He could reach it by squeezing his hand between the pickets.

Ivan got the key, opened the gate, and stepped into the yard. The smell of night-blooming flowers overwhelmed him. The doors to the glassed-in porch were also locked, and he did not have the key. Ivan knocked gently on the glass. He waited, but Margita must not have heard him: they must have been watching

TV. He had to go back to the gate and ring the bell, then return to the porch.

Finally, the door to the house opened. Margita came out, caught sight of him, and clasped at her heart in the dusk.

"Son!" her black eyes flashed with delight. "Why'd you not say a thing, I'd have asked Dad to go fetch you at the station . . . Goodness, I've got nothing made or baked, if I'd known I'd have . . ."

"I don't need anything, Mom," he said, barely audible.

His father came to greet him, all a smile, and out dashed the Raptor twins—his sister Christina's kids. The boys launched into a dance around him, hollering, "Uncle's here! Uncle's here!" and he didn't even have anything to give them. All he brought was himself and his laundry, and they were still so happy. Ivan's head spun, either with anxiety he didn't realize he had felt or because he was hungry.

Margita took him to the kitchen to eat. His father and the Raptors sat with him and demanded stories, "So, how are things? What've you been up to?" until Margita, laughing happily, tsk'ed at them, and said, "Let him eat!"

Later they all sat in the living room. The Raptors were supposed to go to bed, but they wouldn't, they were too excited. Christina and Styopa arrived. Styopa, Christina, and the Raptors were living at Margita's temporarily because Styopa, in the process of fixing or improving something at his place made a large hole in his kitchen and could not find a way to cover it. Margita put Ivan's head on her lap. She used to do this when he was little; she would tousle his hair and kiss him on the temple. Poor Margita, she had waited for him so long! Poor, lonely, overworked Margita, what was her life like? She wore the same pair of beat-up sandals for the third summer. Ivan let the sadness he'd felt for her, all the compassion he'd amassed over the years, rise and flow toward her. He did not resist or deny his complete failure. Margita looked at him, as he lay there quiet, comforted by her affection, and quietly sang an old song—*Winter's over, winter's gone, of the snow there's none*—until he fell asleep. When he woke up, the Raptors were in bed, the TV had been turned off, and Margita was making a bed for him on the other, wider couch. Sheets rustled, pillows were being fluffed. A single lamp under a faded shade glowed in the corner. A folded striped blanket lay on the chair.

•

The Raptors had just been born when Ivan left home. Back then, Margita and Christina fussed in the kitchen every night, heating water for the babies' baths, filling the tiny bathtub placed on a pair of chairs, and bathing the Raptors, as their father called them. Sometimes Styopa also called them the Falcons: he'd heard the folk song about the falcons and named his children after raptor birds because he wished for an independent Ukraine. When hungry, the Raptors demanded attention with loud cries. Warm steam curdled in the kitchen, a figure in a bathrobe—through the dusky glass in the door Ivan could not tell whether it was his sister or his mother—scooped the water out of the bathtub. "A-a-aah, a-a-aah," Margita sang as she stomped around the dinner table where the Raptors lay prostrate on warmed flannel sheets, and Christina unbuttoned her robe, wet with milk. After they nursed, Margita would rock the babies to sleep while Christina leaned over a bowl which she would scrub and sterilize later, just like every other thing in the house, and squeezed her breasts to wring out the last of the milk.

And now the Raptors were six. They were big boys, hefty balls of above-average weight, and no one could really manage them. Their father Styopa, savage with alcohol, skinny, and beset by poor digestion and chronic lack of money, would sometimes chase them around the house while blasting his song from the old tape player of the pretentiously named International brand. "Hey, hey, hey, my raptors!" Styopa thumped, after another day at work where someone yet again had made him mad. "You damned butterballs! Some provisions you fed 'em, woman," he'd shout at his wife, "that you'd grown 'em so!" And then he'd pick up the song again, commanding the boys, "Fly away from mountains and valleys!" and chasing them until they started to sweat and were covered in a thick, abundant sheen. Margita would then step in with a "Let the kids be now!" Christina never stepped in. She worked in the kitchen silently and served Styopa dinner. Styopa was a very picky eater. Whenever he had to put something spicy into his mouth, he'd gulp a glass of vodka first.

Someone would turn on the TV. The Raptors wanted to have their milk from bottles as if they were infants, and Margita could not refuse her beloved grandsons. "Who else'll spoil them if not their nan?" she said. "They'll be grown in a blink, off to make their way in the world." The Raptors perched on the couch, looked wily, chewed on the rubber nipples and drank warm milk under the adoring gaze of their grandparents. "Go sit with them," Margita would tell Christina, and Christina would go to the couch and sit with the boys and hold their bottles for them. Margita would take her place in the kitchen, chopping and stirring. The TV murmured along, and Margarita sang, "Sheep, my sheep, if I should die, who will be your shepherd?" She endured, though, she watched and watched over her flock.

Ivan spent the first few weeks as if asleep. He feared he would feel awkward at home; giving up on Lviv felt like a complete and utter defeat. But once he was there, he had to laugh at himself. He'd forgotten that the place he returned to was not a godforsaken village lost to the world, but a real, elegant city. The river emanated coolness and the waterfront was as charming as ever; no other

city in Ukraine could boast a waterfront that felt so European—
so Parisian!—carefully landscaped, with a mature alley of lindens.
The residential buildings of the Galagov neighborhood, developed between the wars by Czech architects, stood soothing in
their well-proportioned geometry. The downtown was as lively
as ever—the main promenade, Korzo Street, was full of people at
every time of the day, and the first cafés to get a permit for outdoor service set up tables under tents and umbrellas. Sparks flew
under women's heels on cobblestones, orchards bloomed with
abandon, small green grapes budded along the trellises, and above
it all shone the indefatigable Transcarpathian sun. Lviv was cavern-
ous, gray, full of spires, squeezed between the hills into a hard sting
that pierced the lead-colored sky above the cross-stitch of streetcar wires in the perennial fog. And here, the colorful land lay open,
hospitable, and even the mountains that loomed in the distance
seemed to be lounging on cloudy pillows, as if abundance itself, the
opulent goddess, chose to inhabit the verdant bodies of these valleys and forests and the very air.

Ivan walked the city that was supposed to be his perdition and
instead felt born anew. The scent of blooming lindens filled the ripening orchards. Here, this was his terra firma; let his friends from
Lviv or even Kyiv think him a complete loser if they wished. He
wanted to tell them—the friends he spoke to in his head—this and
more, something he felt deep in his bones and for which he had no
words, something that had everything to do with the wind over
the Uzh River and the old trees, the courtyards of the stately inter-
war developments, their clean minimalist lines, and the geometry
of the cobblestone streets. And the Japanese cherries that, like a
pink flood, washed the city in bloom every spring.

Margita went through Ivan's clothes and fretted, "What happened to the shirt I got you . . .? And the one that Christina gave
you for your birthday? And how do you manage to ruin all your

jeans so, it's like they burn on you! We have to get you new things."
She dragged him to the stadium that had been converted into an
enormous market, full of people, stuff, and dust. The stadium was
a ways from downtown, and everywhere people were grilling meat
over logs burning in rusted steel drums so that any T-shirt or jeans
one bought smelled powerfully of oil and burnt gristle. There was
no shelter from the sun. Half the population of Ivan's high school
was here, making a living by selling shoes, women's outfits of artifi-
cial silk, plastic dinnerware, and Turkish soap. Underfoot, the broken brackets that used to support the wooden stadium benches
protruded from the concrete. Women wore white shoes with
incredibly thick platforms and chose garnet lipstick and dyed their
hair raven black. Ivan could not meet their eyes, such was their
great height, and instead faced their dark mouths. He inhaled the
smells of this Babylon and feared his city's spell would break. But
the spell held fast.

The summer surrendered itself to heat. Ivan's eyes ached
and he walked without seeing, guided by memory, by smells and
sounds. His body had its own sense of the city. Here the cobblestones ended and asphalt began, it smelled of tar; here was the frail
breeze from the river, so he must be on the waterfront; here was a
great waft of even hotter air from the ancient industrial-sized coffee machines still employed in a few cafés. Much shallower now,
the river struggled along its bed, and at the bridge, exhausted, split
into two smaller streams, leaving in between a dry island covered
in yellow grass. Heat filled the streets. The basement rooms of the
restaurant At the Uzh, which used to be wine cellars, stayed cool
and sheltered swarms of thirsty men with beer steins.

Ivan's father liked to drink as much as anyone else. He went to
At the Uzh with friends, laughed heartily, turned visibly red, and
returned home in good humor. Ivan studied his father, the way he
watched TV at night, the way he laughed unprompted—regardless

of the jokes on the broadcast, but in response to the turns of his own internal narrative—and wondered, Why was he like this? What happened? Ivan remembered little of when he was young. But there had to have been something—a beginning. Did his parents fall out? Or did something happen at work? How does a man come to choose to remove himself from the world? Was it possible his father, too, was called into an official room where he was told to sit in front of a Borovik[6] or another man named after a mushroom?

Ivan's father seemed to have come alive since Ivan returned. He waited for Ivan to get home for dinner and would not start without him; afterward, he told entertaining stories. He even seemed to be drinking less, not turning to the homemade red wine to cloud his eyes quite as often. Margita kept wine under lock and key in the house, but his father still managed to find it, and if he couldn't, he went over to the neighbor who would share his. He promised to help Ivan find a job; his friend Mytio Klovanych was a manager at a bank. He gave Ivan money to buy cigarettes—Ivan had long since run out of his own savings. He even paid for him to make an inter-city phone call to Mysko in Lviv—this could not be done from the house lest the ever-curious Margita overhear the conversation. Instead, the two of them went to the post office. Ivan's father walked slowly, his bad leg gave him trouble, and Ivan begged him to stay home—what's the fun in going to the post office anyway!—but the old man insisted and seemed to glow with joy as they walked. There was something poignant in their quiet progress together through the midtown; they stayed under the trees, in the shade.

Ivan made himself call Mysko. What if Mysko was mad at him? What if he didn't want to speak to him at all? "Let me just explain everything," Ivan said, knowing he could not possibly do so.

Mysko laughed.

---

6. *Borovik* is the Russian name of the *Boletus edulis* or porcini mushroom.

"No need, I get it. Things just didn't work out for you in Lviv," he said.

"And what about you? How are you?"

"I'm great! Looks like I might get a chance to go to Canada. If it all works out, I'll go."

"Forever?" Ivan asked.

"Nah, what would I do there forever? I'll just stay as long as I need."

"And what about your business?"

"That's why I'm going, to find clients in Canada. So don't be a stranger!"

"And you, too! Call me."

Ivan gave Mysko Margita's landline number and they said goodbye.

Now Ivan belonged only to his homeland.

·

Ivan went to see Yura Popadynets and Korchi Vash. One day his legs just carried him to the apartment building where Yura lived, a place he'd known since he was a child. Close to the ground, the walls of the building were nearly black. It was a standard five-story Khrushchev-era housing block, very near the city's main street, and still it was surrounded by tall, wild grasses. Ivan climbed to the second floor and rang the doorbell. A shirtless man opened the door. Bright sun backlit him, and Ivan could not see his face.

"Yura?" he asked, stepping into the sunlit hallway, into that void, and the man stepped up to meet him, bent down to see Ivan's face, close enough almost to tickle him with his black, unfamiliar beard, and finally grinned.

"Vanya!" he exclaimed and grabbed Ivan into a sweaty hug. Yura smelled of drink.

Yura made his living writing code. It had been two years since he graduated with a degree in physics, but there was no work—only small piecemeal jobs. His mother yelled something at him from the kitchen. She had just brought home humongous bags of apricots and was about to boil them down into jam. Margita made jam, too, but at least Margita lived in a house—this poor woman was obliged to work in a tiny kitchen where, in summer, the heat got downright infernal.

Yura was interested in Ruthenian politics, which, seemingly overnight, had sprouted several warring factions. He studied the Ruthenian dialect and butchered it mercilessly when he tried to speak; he had no rural family who would have spoken it as their native language: he grew up in the city, and his parents had come from Vinnytsia, in central Ukraine. None of this bothered Yura. He informed Ivan that Ukrainians were a minority here in Transcarpathia, and he, Yura, also belonged to a minority because Ruthenians were the actual majority, and they had their own language and their own culture, and therefore were entitled to their own state. Yura cited the authority of an American expert who came often to lecture and distribute books.

"Their own state, is that so?" Ivan asked, so as not to laugh in his friend's face. Their own state! That's what one always heard when bigger powers were about to tear Ukraine into bloody shreds.

Despite the heat that made him feel like his brains were melting, despite the sickening smell of sugared simmering fruit, Ivan tried to explain things to the slightly drunk Yura. He told him it was wrong to fixate on the interests of a single region, they must see the broader context of history, they must remember the endless frozen tundra of Siberia, must stay aware of the global geopolitics. He wished for Yura to be able to imagine Ukraine not just as a small bit of land under his apartment building but as something immeasurably larger. Could Yura really not see that it was precisely

the nation's independence that so many complained about so readily and viciously that had given them the freedom to entertain
their Ruthenian and suchlike ideas? Had Ivan and his comrades in
arms not sat in protest on the Maidan, had people like Vyacheslav
Chornovil, Oksana Meshko, and Levko Lukyanenko not gone
to jail, had our people not fought their people back in the forties
and then through the fifties from the underground hideouts in the
Carpathian forests, what would it be like now? The Soviet Union
would have been alive and well, and Ivan and Yura would be standing here talking about completely different things: the black market, jeans, records, the music they all ached to hear—only there
was no music in the Soviet Union except for patriotic songs. That's
what they would have talked about, whether they spoke Ruthenian
or not. In the best-case scenario.

Later, when Yura's mother was done with the jam making, they
sat in the kitchen and sipped warm beer. Rather, Yura did—Ivan
did not want any. He couldn't have drunk even ice-cold beer, he felt
so hopeless. He had forgotten the place to which he had returned,
forgotten to what isolation he had doomed himself when he came
home. Until that moment, he didn't realize that to keep Ukraine
inside of him—all of it, the nation—was an effort of will and constant work. He had to keep thinking of the Maidan all the time.
He wasn't angry at Yura; Yura couldn't know better. Ivan told him
stories, not about the politics but about one of the Vyvykh[7] festivals, about other parties and festivals, about artists, musicians, and
the long conversations they had had. Yura listened. Maybe, Ivan
thought, some of it might get through.

The next day, Ivan went to see Korchi Vash. Korchi lived with

---

7. *Vyvykh* (Вивих) means "displacement," "a bone out of joint." Vyvykh
was the name of two alternative culture and nontraditional art festivals
held in Lviv in 1990 and 1992.

his parents in a private house, like Ivan's. He spent his days at a research institute where he sat in an office that was quiet as a tomb while the cleaning lady worked her way up and down the hallway. The cleaning lady appeared to be the only person doing any work at the institute. Korchi's father used to be a professor but retired a long time ago—both he and Korchi's mother were of advanced age; they had their son late in life. Their home was full of books, and the old man, before he started drinking, loved nothing more than a long philosophical conversation.

"All of our guys have gone to work at the border," Korchi told Ivan. "Iovzhiy has even bought his own apartment already."

Apartments sold for anywhere between three and ten thousand dollars. Korchi, unlike Yura, did not drink, appeared nearly unchanged, held up his end of the conversation, and did not need to be lectured about Ukraine. Only Korchi's smile had turned sadder, and his shirts threadbare. He had patches on his elbows.

"I have a dog," he said. "His name is Billy. He is a real Labrador retriever. I bought him in Hungary, very expensive, he's got the pedigree. Every day I take him for a walk in the park."

They went out of the house into the yard littered with old bicycles (Korchi's father told everyone he would fix them, but he never did because he drank) and came to a good-sized doghouse. The dog came out.

"I'll insulate it for the winter, don't worry," Korchi said, scratching the back of his head. "Billy won't be cold. He spent last winter in the house, but my mother won't let him stay again. Look how fine he is! Good boy!"

The dog was indeed, as Korchi said, very fine: large, black, perfectly muscled. Korchi pulled the retriever close and petted him.

"Have you seen Yura much?" Ivan asked.

Korchi smiled his sad smile and looked away.

"Why would I? I don't drink. Did you go see him?"

"I did."

"And?"

"Well, I didn't know, did I? I barely got out of there."

"My point exactly. What do you think you'll do next?"

"I've no idea. And you?"

"I'm at the lab for now. As far as the future . . . maybe I'll go get a wife!" Korchi joked.

"Do you have a candidate?"

"Nope," Korchi said and spread his arms wide. The elbow patches glimmered. "We could go to the park if you'd like. Billy and I are about to go anyway; he likes it there, when it's a little cooler, at night."

"And Kreitzar? What about Kreitzar?" Ivan asked preemptively, he didn't want to put himself through a repeat of the Yura experience.

"Kreitzar's good. He works construction, makes good money, but his mom takes it all to run the house and support Yerzhia[8]. He herds goats, too," Korchi smiled. "Right there, by the suspension bridge on the river, the old woman sends him out when he comes home from work."

"Goats?"

"You bet! Let's go to the park, and then take a walk along the river. I bet we'll run into Kreitzar there. I haven't seen him in ages."

They walked down the long street to the park along the river, past people's fences. The heat let up a bit. Behind the fences, front gardens stood verdant and full, dotted with flowers, mostly roses. The rosebushes sent their new branches reaching through the chain-link, like hands through a prison-camp wall. Very young women sat on the grass in the yards, nursing babies.

Ivan ought to see Pavlo Dankulynets, too, a Rukh member he

---

8. Short for Erzsébet, the Hungarian version of Elizabeth.

had met on the Maidan. Pavlo gave him his number, Ivan could call him, and say what? He could not imagine himself at a political party's office, nor as any kind of a community activist.

Styopa, his brother-in-law, called Ivan nearly every day.

"So, is our food good enough for you today?" he'd ask on the phone and Ivan would have to come over, take a seat at the table, eat and drink.

"In five years, I'll have servants slaving over here!" Styopa would boast of his future affluence.

By then, Styopa and Christina had moved from Margita's back to their own place. Styopa puffed on a cigarette, and his breath smelled of drink. Christina spent her time in the greenhouse, tending to the tomatoes. She now always had black dirt under her fingernails, and her face was tanned a dark shade. Christina smoked a lot, cooked a lot, and carried sacks of cement whenever Styopa's rheumatism caught up with him. They would sit down to dinner—Ivan, Styopa, the Raptors, and Styopa's father, the widowed Paikosh, who lived with the family—and Christina would serve them. "Bring me some bread! Get 'im a clean fork. Pour the kids *kompot*[9] to drink," commanded the Paikoshes, junior and senior.

The kompot stood cooling on the stove after dinner; one or the other of the Raptors would run into the kitchen, scoop up a cupful, and toss it into his hungry maw.

"You rug rats!" Styopa yelled at them. "Get lost!"

"We ain't rug rats!" the boys called from behind a door. "We are Raptors! Ukraine's not dead yet!"

"There, see that?" Styopa snickered. "I'm the one who taught them that. Ukraine's not fucking dead yet!"

He'd pour vodka for himself and Ivan, take a long drag on his

---

9. *Kompot* is a sweet nonalcoholic beverage made by boiling fruit in a large quantity of water drunk hot or cold depending on the season.

cigarette, and talk as fragments of him emerged from the smoke—now it was his voice doing the talking, now only the body.

"Why aren't you putting up a house, eh? Why'd you come back if not to do something? Do something real, enough of that book stuff; look at my pal Dyuri, he's putting the roof on his place before the rains."

A house? What house? Ivan had come back to live, not to work construction, but Styopa's words made him aware of all the little signs he was trying not to notice: the talk at home of reinforced concrete, the cost of framing and brick laying. Margita managed her household like a powerful spider presiding over an extensive and ever-growing web. She got her shopping and her cooking done, and the pigs and the chickens taken care of all before lunch, then would pour herself a cup of coffee, spread jam on a slice of bread, and sit down alone at the table. The oilcloth threw brilliant sunshine back at her. Margita ate her bread, drank her coffee. Sometimes she'd wink at Ivan as if there were things she knew about his life he had no inkling of yet. She spoke to him with her back, the way she moved. When he asked her why she smiled like that, she only shrugged.

Unsettled, he went to see Korchi again. He rang the bell at the garden gate but no one came. Was Korchi out at the park? No, it wasn't the right time. The sun set late, there was plenty of daylight yet.

"Korchi!" Ivan called over the fence. For a long time nothing happened and then Korchi's father, very drunk, made his way out of the house unsteadily and informed Ivan over the fence:

"If you've come to see Korchi, he's gone. Gone over to the Czechs to dig ditches. Some . . . someone stole his dog yesterday. So he left. With Lotzi."

"How come he didn't tell me?" Ivan asked, several times; he was stunned.

"I don't know, son, why this or that." The old man sighed loudly. Suddenly, he looked over his shoulder to check if his wife was watching, pressed his head against the pickets, and whispered, breathing hot into Ivan's face, "You wouldn't by chance . . . have some money? I'd pay you back?"

Ivan made his way home and just sat there on the couch in the living room. He refused to accept the news. He felt as if he'd stepped on a broken foot. For the first time after his return, perhaps, he fully grasped how long it would take him to heal. His father was speaking to him, but Ivan did not hear him. Margita came to the living room and said something as well. Ivan nodded in agreement, because why shouldn't he acquiesce to whatever his parents were saying? He had no one else in the entire world. Tears boiled up in his eyes, and his throat caught.

It was the tears that brought him back.

"Your father spoke to Klovanych; you're to come to the bank tomorrow," Margita was saying. She did not see Ivan's moist eyes, so he wiped them carefully, pretending to be sleepy, nodded to Margita, and leaned his head back.

Right above him, he saw a crack that stretched across the ceiling. The weight of the second floor was making the joists sag.

•

Volodya, the head of accounting at the bank, was only a few years older than Ivan. Whenever the weather permitted, he biked to work and came into the office smiling and sweaty, rolling up his sleeves. In a previous life, Volodya was a well-known athlete, a ski jumper. Eventually, he broke a leg and that was the end of his career. Whenever he told stories of his ski jumping days, girls hung on to every word. However, Volodya was married and the girls did not interest him. The bank, on the other hand, interested him very much indeed. Volodya studied banking and accounting every day with real dedication, and now Ivan and blond-haired Tolya, another new hire nicknamed D'Artagnan for his exceptional zeal, studied along with him. Sometimes, Volodya would indicate that they might start a business together one day—he didn't know what kind of business yet, but for some reason Ivan believed in him. Ivan found his old bicycle in the garage, tinkered with it, and started riding it to work as well.

Everyone loved them: the clients, the boss, the guards, and the accounting department, which was staffed entirely by women, slightly overweight and dressed in cheap cardigans bought in Poland. Whenever Volodya, Ivan, or Tolya D'Artagnan came into the large room—the biggest in the bank—where these women worked, they would all look up and watch them with affection. Everything depended on these boys: the delivery of electronic transfers that were the latest innovation being introduced into the national banking system, the computers, and the temperamental printer that was, in those years, firmly beyond the control of simple mortals. All these things saved loads of time, and the bank, one could say without hesitation, thrived.

The boss, Dmytro Dmytrovych, or Mytio, was a short, middle-aged man, puffy with drink and chronic kidney trouble. He had odd habits at the office. He smoked out of the open window—which in summer meant blowing smoke directly into the fanned leaves of the large plane tree that grew next to the building—smoked prodigiously and loudly, and could be heard yelling at people on the phone equally loudly. Yet he navigated the banking sector effectively and the clients trusted him.

They saw all kinds of clients. One day Volodya and Ivan had just come back from sorting something out at another bank and barely had the chance to get off their bikes when a rather imposing gentleman with a Vandyke beard and dressed, despite the warm

weather, in an expensive suit, shirt, and tie, came up to the two of
them, sweaty and panting as they were, and asked:

"Are you the head accountant?"

He sized up Volodya, who stood there in his shorts, smiling
with disgust. Volodya, however, simply did not know how to be
embarrassed.

"Himself!" he said, happily, and pointed at Ivan: "And this is
our head of IT!"

The "head of IT," also wearing shorts and just as sweaty, with
hair plastered to his forehead, nodded in a welcoming manner. The
client hesitated. He held his chin in his hand and said nothing while
he must have considered whether he could trust these hooligans.

"I have a Visa," he finally pronounced, proudly.

"To where?" Ivan blurted, but Volodya knew what the man
meant and laughed.

"You mean a Visa card?" he asked.

"Yes, a card. A platinum card. Do you . . . Where could I put it
in here?"

That made everyone, guards included, laugh, except the client
himself.

"I could tell you where you could put it," Volodya finally managed to say. "But I'd probably be fired if I did."

The server facility—that was the aspirational name of the room
where they worked—was small, cramped, and nowhere near com-
pliant with any health and safety regulations for accommodating
such delicate but not necessarily salubrious equipment as PCs or, as
the boys affectionately called them, *machines*. The machines heated
when they ran, and by the end of the day the climate in the room
was such that everyone at the bank referred to it as Africa. In summer, they brought in large fans. In addition to Ivan and Tolya, a
young woman named Vasylyna worked there; she was hired at random when the boss's niece, who was meant to be employed instead,

refused the job at the last possible moment. Vasylyna practically lived at the bank; she brought tea bags and a portable water heater. She was distinguished by having the virtue of speaking very little.

At night, the guys—Volodya, Tolya, and Ivan—often stayed alone in the building, except for the guards. They would pour cognac into espresso cups they had borrowed from the women in accounting, drink it in tiny sips, and talk. They made fun of whatever happened at the bank that day, their jobs. Such as the time the boss told them they were not making themselves particularly useful and would go without a bonus that month. In response, they stopped working altogether until first the printer and then the PCs refused to obey anyone else, and the whole operation ground to a screeching halt. Or all the times well-heeled clients rolled into the boss's office, threw the keys to an Audi or a BMW onto his desk, and demanded a loan with the car as the collateral, telling him he could keep the wheels if they failed to pay.

Ivan would come home to Margita and her low lights late at night. It was quiet then, his father asleep, snoring vigorously. Margita stayed up, watched Hungarian soap operas on TV, waited up for her son. She took him to the kitchen and served him dinner, reheating whatever the family had eaten that night. She stood at the stove, stirred sticky rice porridge or flipped thick slices of fried pork with onions and hot red peppers, and asked her questions:

"Honey, you can't work yourself to the ground like that. What are you doing there at work until the small hours?"

"What else would I be doing?" Ivan said, not catching the hint, or rather, pretending not to catch it.

"Well, we have to finish the house. With your wages, we could buy rebar!"

"Sure, go ahead. I never said you shouldn't."

He said that and saw everything in a flash: The bank wasn't real. Only the night outside and Margita were.

·

Ivan was living through his second autumn at home. Leaves had fallen, October quietly turned into November. Pale plumes of smoke rose above the houses in Maly Galagov—people were burning firewood in their old-worldish tile stoves. Faded plants still held on to the earth with their weak roots, grew yellow, and prepared to fall into the moon-cold crater of winter. This was grape harvest time. Margita and Christina climbed up ladders and snipped off dark clusters of fruit; then Margita piled them into zinc tubs to ferment. The sharp smell of grapes mixed with the wood smoke and flowed above the neighborhood like a heavy, black river—this was the smell of days passing. It stung one right in the heart, shocked one awake, and Ivan saw his life clearly for a few nearly unbearable moments around noon. The first frost was just around the corner, and the air held very little of the late warmth, only during the day and only in the sun, just enough to pour the last drops of sweetness into the grapes and quince; after them, the only thing to ripen and fall was snow. The pallid sky drew closer and closer to the roofs as if it intended to lie down on them and fall asleep for the long winter.

It was at that time, during that second autumn, that Ivan's torments began. In the dark, Ivan listened to the wind and the night make someone a bed of iron sheets, make and remake it, and the intolerable, constant rumble of this work filled the universe. The rumble put Ivan on edge.

"What was that racket in the night?" he'd ask Margita in the morning, but she just looked at him uncomprehending.

"How would I know, honey, I ain't heard anything . . ."

"How could you not, Mom? I couldn't sleep all night!"

Margita would have no answer to that; all she could do was shrug and go back to making coffee or porridge for Ivan's breakfast.

Ivan had to walk to work; he was too dizzy to get on his bike.

At night, he came home and fell into bed exhausted, and then lay there all night under the weight of that incessant rumble, as if under many feet of water, on the bottom of a heavy sea, and the bottom was also lined with iron. He felt how hard it was, how it tilted under him this way and that, making him sick, and tried to get up but could not because above him the sky was very low and ironclad as well. He listened to the rumble intently, but whenever he did this, the noise grew quiet, stole away like an animal, or rather, the hunter, only to emerge again in a little while, first distant, and then closer, closer, until it filled all the space around Ivan. What was it? A warning? But who would be trying to warn him? And of what?

Ivan would leap up from his bed and look around him wildly, searching for the enemy in his own home.

In the morning, every muscle in Ivan's body hurt, his joints creaked; he would down several cups of coffee in Margita's kitchen, to be followed by more at work, and run out of the house as soon as his heart started to race.

The weather turned to rain. In the evenings before leaving the bank, Ivan would dash to the small market next door to buy cigarettes. He didn't smoke much at all, and could have quit altogether—he had the good fortune of never becoming dependent on nicotine—but he did not want to. Smoking gave him something to do, a way to keep his hands busy. He liked to watch the dark square in front of the bank as the headlights of passing cars flashed in the wet pavement and the glow of streetlamps refracted in a million sparks.

On one particular night, he had almost finished his cigarette and was about to go back to the bank. He and Tolya had promised to walk Vasylyna home; she was renting a room from a crazy old lady who liked to yell at her in Hungarian and routinely locked the gate "for the night." "Night," for Aunt Andreia, or, as she was known in Hungarian, Ondi-néni, meant eight o'clock, or often five in winter, so the guys had to give Vasylyna a boost to climb over the fence. To accomplish this, Vasylyna would take off her shoes and stand on their hands, her feet in thick ribbed hose on their palms. And then Ivan had to go home, where Margita and his iron bed waited for him.

That night, Ivan was contemplating these actions that constituted his most immediate future, but the persistent lack of sleep had made it difficult for him to contemplate even these simple things. He saw a car pull up to the bank, it was Dmytro Dmytrovych, the boss. This was odd because the boss never came to the office at such a late hour. A passenger got out of the car. Ivan did not recognize him; the man was of an average height, slim, and moved in a manner that implied great physical strength. The man said goodbye to Dmytro Dmytrovych, glanced at his watch, and walked away into the darkness roiled with lights. Ivan dropped his cigarette, ground it with his foot, and followed the man, not at all cognizant of why. He was not inclined to cloak-and-dagger stories, and it's not like there was any mystery to the man at all. So the boss gave someone a ride to the bank, so they didn't see Ivan under the awning where he was smoking in the dark, what of it?

The boss's guest walked with a beautiful, buoyant gait, at times he seemed to float above the ground, barely touching it with the soles of his shoes. Ivan kept just close enough not to lose sight of him. When they crossed a crowded square, a whole swarm of people suddenly swallowed the man, and Ivan almost lost him, but got lucky again when the man stopped to say hello to someone. Ivan saw him start again and walk around the corner bakery. On the other side was a steep cobblestone street that led to the cathedral. Ivan made his way through the crowd and ran, panting, around the bakery, but could not find the man. He had disappeared. He could have gone into any of the doors on the street, and they all had locks for the residents only. Such a small city, and yet how easy it was to melt away in it! This was a prestigious old neighborhood, inhabited by old Hungarian families and widows, so many widows, dressed forever in black. The windows of the music school up the hill were open despite the weather, and Ivan heard a cacophony of sound: students were tuning instruments, a violin and an oboe, or perhaps several oboes, a small orchestra concealed in the dark.

Ivan caught up with the man at the top of the hill, where he went into the cathedral through the back door, and Ivan just caught a glimpse of the people inside, men and women, a choir. The choir faced a cantor whose hands drew complex figures in the air. They were lit by church lights. Piles of coats lay on dark wooden pews, their sleeves intertwined.

Then the door closed.

Ivan stepped quietly inside, climbed the stairs to the empty mezzanine. He peeked cautiously from behind a wall. Below him, in the church proper, there were only a few people, a handful of heads in the front and a couple more in the middle, most covered with black headscarves, some, the men's, bare, gray, or graying. The man Ivan had followed here was in the choir. He was not insubstantial at all, but rather athletic; Ivan could just see his high cheekbones and black hair.

The evening mass began. Everyone who had been sitting stood up. The delicate cantor raised his hand, and the choir slowly sang, "A-a-a-a-men!" What came after that, Ivan could not recall.

He lay down on a hard pew and plummeted instantly through the sweet molasses of dreams to their very bottom, which was even sweeter. He stayed there for a long, long time, long enough for the mass to end and the choir to dress and leave. Ivan stirred awake barely in time to run downstairs and out the door before he would've been locked in for the night like Khoma Brut, that poor bastard in Gogol's horror story.

Afterward he went there every Tuesday and Thursday. He climbed straight to the mezzanine, which, luckily for him, remained unoccupied, lay down on a pew, and slept and slept. He did not think about God, wasn't in the habit of doing so. And would God really have chased him out? Would He think it wrong that an exiled soul had found shelter and the exhausted body, rest? Neither did Ivan think about the choir singer he had followed to the cathedral. The man didn't matter, did he? He was just a man in a crowd, an accidental messenger. Or so Ivan thought until, to his astonishment, Dmytro Dmytrovych introduced the man as the bank's new staff lawyer—he finally got around to firing the previous one, Grisha, who was constantly drunk and showed up for work only occasionally.

The man's name was Myron Vasyliovych, and everyone liked him immediately. The boss allocated him a separate office, which Myron Vasyliovych ironically called his "chambers" because the chamber—meaning, the bathroom—was right there, next to it in the hallway. His office became the destination for throngs of pilgrims: clients, people from other banks, people who were vaguely the boss's friends—he let these cut ahead in line. Something constantly tinkled in the cabinets, because the boss continued to store glasses and a few bottles of liquor in the lawyer's office. The lawyer—always finely dressed, in a thoroughly ironed white shirt, perfectly shaved, and wearing cologne—did not drink, but made jokes, laughed. No one ever saw him in low spirits.

One day the boss asked Ivan to come to Myron Vasyliovych's office. Groggy with lack of sleep (it was a Wednesday), Ivan hesitated but could not find an excuse. He tried to keep his eyes on the floor so that no one would see how puffy they were. He said hello. The men answered. Ivan focused on their feet: the lawyer's pressed trouser cuffs and his shoes, cordovan, generously shined. The boss's shoes were black; his toes bulged inside and stretched the leather.

"So, how are all things PC?" the boss asked.

"Fine. Great!" Ivan said.

"I need you to help a young woman, then," the boss followed.

"A young woman?" Ivan was taken by surprise. "What woman?"

"Thank you," a quiet voice said, and it was only then Ivan realized there was another person in the room. Eyes still down, he glanced around a wider circle on the floor and indeed saw a pair of women's booties on sensible heels, with zippers on the side. The black booties, still wet from the slush outside, showed white salt lines where the leather had begun to dry.

"Do introduce yourself!" the boss commanded.

Ivan finally raised his head. The girl stood beside Myron Vasyliovych. She had unbuttoned her terra-cotta-colored coat and held her beret in her hands. She had dark chestnut, wavy hair. Her skin was pale. Big brown eyes, open wide.

"This is my daughter, Maria," the lawyer said.

"She is in need of a computer," the boss explained. "She needs to print something out. I thought you'd help her. Ivan is the smartest one we have, graduated from the Polytechnic in Lviv. I know his dad well, we studied together in Lviv, way back when. It's a good family, strong one. Good people."

The second half of Dmytro Dmytrovych's speech sounded suspiciously as if he were praising a potential bridegroom.

"You're a student too, aren't you, Maria?" He turned to the girl suddenly.

For a second, she didn't know how to react, and her father waved her off and answered before she could open her mouth:

"Linguistics, and you know what it's like for a girl now, that degree is only good for catching a husband."

The girl looked at the floor just like Ivan did.

"I'm working on getting her a job at a bank," Myron Vasyliovych went on.

The boss interrupted:

"Go ahead, Ivan, take Maria to the computer room. We have stuff to talk about here . . . and Myron, I won't take no for an answer this time," he added, pulling glasses out of a cupboard, completely at home in the lawyer's office.

Ivan didn't realize he had no idea what to do until they came to the "server facility." He had to turn his back to Maria and could feel her eyes on him. Briskly, he moved Vasylyna and her work from one machine to another (Vasylyna raised an eyebrow, but did not object), closed whatever windows she had open, and started up a new document. Finally, he turned back to his guest. She still had her coat on, despite the heat in the room.

"Go ahead," Ivan said, pulling up a chair for her. She sat, but still did not take off her coat.

"Oh, come on, take your coat off! You're not going to last a minute here," he insisted.

The girl perched on the edge of the chair as if she were going to ride it sidesaddle. She nodded vigorously and began to wiggle out of her coat, still sitting. This looked incredibly awkward, but she silently continued wrestling with her sleeves like a drowning man with the sea.

Finally, she spoke:

"I brought my own floppy disk."

"All right, give it here," Ivan requested.

Maria spent an hour or two at the computer. She typed, carefully, words that appeared on her screen in a narrow column. Ivan prohibited himself from peeking, either at her or at her work, although he desperately wanted to. Something about her pale face, her delicate, sensitive shoulders that shuddered at every sudden noise or unfamiliar voice. Was she really so skittish? Vasylyna went home at five. Then, Volodya appeared.

"Oh, hi! What are you typing?" he asked from the door. Unlike Ivan, Volodya was not embarrassed by anything, or anyone.

"Some poems," Maria said softly.

"I'm Volodya!"

"I'm Phoebe."

"What do you mean, *Phoebe*? Your dad said your name was Maria."

"Because . . . Phoebus was the Greek god of poetry," the girl said, even quieter.

So the text went in a column because it was poetry, Ivan caught on. He snickered inside. Sure, she's the goddess of poetry now!

"Phoebus Apollo, Greek," Ivan said. "But Apollo was a man, and you are a woman," that came out with Margita's well-practiced barely-there sneer in Ivan's tone. The kind that the other person couldn't miss but could do nothing about, since the words did not exactly mock. Maria, meaning Phoebe, blushed ferociously. The more astute accountant made desperate signs at Ivan from behind her.

"So what," she finally said, beet red. "A woman can be a poet, too."

"A lady poet, then," Ivan countered.

The awkward pause that followed didn't last long, since Volodya, thankfully, was still there.

"All right, boys and girls," he said. "Enough of this. Phoebe, nice to meet you. Poetry is a serious business. We should drink to that!"

Tolya D'Artagnan, who came from a highly educated family, could not take his eyes off a real-life poet. Volodya produced a bottle of wine, uncorked it, and poured four glasses.

"To poetry, then?" Ivan said, still sarcastic. He could not look at Phoebe. Volodya made another face to communicate, *I'm doing this for you, you idiot, shut your trap already!*

After that, she came a few more days in a row, and just like on that first evening, perched quietly at the edge of the chair, her thin legs crossed, click-clacked, click-clacked something in a column. She would start at a simple question or at the sound of someone's steps in the hallway. She never spoke to Ivan, except to say hello, goodbye, and thank you. But one time, when she caught Ivan looking over her shoulder, she abruptly, and without so much as a hint of shyness in her voice or motion, offered to let him read what she was writing. She raised her eyes at him, and they, too, in that moment, were neither pleading nor misty.

"I'm not a poetry fan," he muttered.

"No one said you have to be," she answered calmly. "Just read."

Ivan was taken aback. He'd gotten used to the skittish version of her, had a particular and rather solid image of her in his mind, but with those one or two sentences she shattered it to pieces. He felt angry at her for it, and at the same time surprised at the unexpected intensity of his reaction. Was it possible that he . . .? They were basically strangers, so what would make him so certain that she . . . that she . . .

Ivan was drawn and attracted to her. He could not walk indifferently past her chair, her screen, her hair. When he saw her shy and skittish, he felt confident and did not need to be near her because he felt he had the situation under command, but as soon as she would raise her eyes at him and say something in that different voice of hers, Ivan would go mad. How did she learn to be so serene, to write her most certainly very silly verses, because who's ever gonna read them, except maybe him, Ivan, because he is a nice guy, he'll read them and say kind things about them, he is the lord and king for her and her scribbles, and she ought to worship him for it, worship him and avert her eyes like a slave girl in a harem instead of staring at him like that, shameless, as if he were a circus display! Instantly, he was shocked at himself. What's gotten into him? What slave girl in what harem? Phoebe was the daughter of Myron Vasyliovych, his colleague, his employer's lawyer, Mytio

Mytiovych's good pal (of course, Mytio Mytiovych counted most
of the city among his pals), a philologist-to-be from the local university, and, most likely, not all that bright, if we're being honest,
no wonder her parents haven't married her off yet, that's why she
has no job to go to, so instead she begged her daddy to let her come
here and even deputize a peon to serve her, the peon being Ivan,
but what the hell, why does he need to be looking at her legs, and
her hair, damn it, what's happening to him? What's happening?

"So, would you like to read?" she repeated, and Ivan was ready
to fall at her feet. What he said instead was:

"I'll print my own copy and take it home. I'll have more time
at night."

"But it's night already!" she said, laughing, and good Lord,
who knew she could laugh? But then again—did he forget whose
daughter she was? Ivan came to stand behind Phoebe and read her
screen over her shoulder. Fine. He'll see what galactic foolishness
she's been typing and get his peace back. *Sunlight falls, a lacework
/ but no longer for me,* he read and snickered in his mind. What
did I say, he thought, this makes no sense, might as well stop now,
but his eyes stubbornly followed the lines down the page: *I am
interred—I'm not alive / I'm in a cell, I'm buried,* and now he could
not shake off the words, the rhythm of the syllables. *I am a subterranean tree / I grow my branches deep.* One of her uneven, irregu-
lar lines suddenly grabbed him and dragged him somewhere dark,
into an abyss. And collapsed under him like a bridge that is no longer required.

"Listen," he said to her, without any anger, or mockery, or
thoughts of slave girls. "This is really good!"

Somehow he knew he no longer needed to defend himself.
Her poems had released them both from their protective cara-
paces. They looked at each other in that moment as they were, real,
and smiled—and later would remember it for a very long time,

this sudden connection. Eventually, in a different time, when there was so much more between them, and later, when it was all over, this moment glowed undiminished from the very bottom of their existence like a self-fulfilling promise, and this would give them strength—both of them.

"How do you know anything about poetry?" she asked.

"I studied in Lviv," he said.

Ivan then started to tell her about the Vyvykh festival, the poets Andrukhovych and Irvanets and Dovhan and Pozayak and others.

"If only you could be there," he said. "*There* would be the people for you to talk to."

Then the conversation turned to the revolution.

"The Revolution on the Granite, you know, when we . . ."

As a rule, Ivan avoided talking about the Maidan, he did not want the truth of what he'd done to find its way to Margita. While he was there, in Kyiv, he always sat with his back to the TV cameras, and, of course, refused to be interviewed, but now he could not help himself.

"Do you remember those days? What was it like here? Did you support the revolution? Did you strike? Protest?"

Phoebe could only shrug.

"If only. I was still in school. We went AWOL from our classes, but that was about it."

"Did any organizers come to speak to you?"

"Yes, from the university."

"So the university had our backs!"

"I don't know. I just remember we were all happy because classes were canceled and the weather was so beautiful . . . I'm sorry, I'm just telling you the truth, the way it was for us. We went and got ice cream, those who had any money."

"I don't mind," he laughed. "I know the way things are in this town." He did indeed. Who would go to a protest? Margita? When would she do that, before caring for the pigs and chickens, or after she got her chores done?

"When do you clock off?" Phoebe asked suddenly, and he fell back to earth from the sky.

"Well . . . I've got lots of work to do yet," he grumbled, and walked away from her.

"It's okay," she spoke to his back in that imperturbable voice of hers. "I'll wait for you."

•

Phoebe's mother, Kateryna Ivanivna, generously peppered her speech with folksy sayings. These almost invariably featured an animal, most often goats. "You've plenty of time to take your goats to market," she would say when someone was being impatient. "You'll be whipped like Sidor's goats," she jokingly chastised her family. "Ah, there's the goat come back to the barn," she'd say, with a smile, when Phoebe brought Ivan home. In addition to goats, Kateryna Ivanivna's language accommodated slinking cats, leaping hares, and barking dogs. "Lordy lord, the tomcat's gone and the kitty can't go on," was her way of describing what she thought was a hopeless situation. "You've got as much use for that as a hare for a stop sign!" she would say about something not very useful. "Said the man to his dog, and the dog to his tail," she'd say to dismiss the latest local politics. If she ran out of sayings and proverbs she knew, Kateryna Ivanivna did not give up—she just made up her own.

Myron Vasyliovych would come home after the rest of the family, sometimes even after dinner—to which Ivan was, by custom, welcome—take off his shoes in the hallway with great relief, settle into an armchair, and stretch his legs. The fine fabric of his dress socks hugged his flexible feet tightly, throwing into high relief the knots of muscle, chiseled and sharp, and his high arches.

This always made Ivan think about Taras Shevchenko's paintings, in which people's bare feet were rendered with attention and precision. Kateryna Ivanivna would come out of the kitchen, careful to maneuver among the furniture in the tight living room. Phoebe would sit on the floor, on the rug, and whenever she lowered her head, Ivan could see the vertebrae in her neck—he thought they looked like a string of large pearls—and her sharp shoulder blades.

Every once in a while, Kateryna Ivanivna would serve dinner on the table in the living room, reserved otherwise for special occasions, saying, "It's not like we're eating stolen food, are we? We pamper our guests all the time, why not treat ourselves special for a change." This, one understood, implied that Ivan was no longer considered a guest. After dinner, Myron Vasyliovych would make himself comfortable in his chair and launch into a story, but only at the dinner table because if he moved to an armchair or the couch he would fall into a sudden, instant, and inescapable sleep—he had a form of narcolepsy. He could wake up just like he fell asleep, in a flash, but at that point he would take himself to the bedroom and there were no more stories to be gotten out of him that night.

"Honest men can't get ahead nowadays, and cheating doesn't get you far either, unless you're good at it," he liked to say. That was his own personal proverb.

"We used to go to Romania to trade, remember?" Myron Vasyliovych reminisced one day. "After Ceauşescu. I bought winter boots for everyone there. You couldn't get your money exchanged, you had to take something over there and sell it for leus. So I cut big plastic bags into smaller pieces, filled them with candy, ran an iron over the edge, and voila! I had these nice tidy packets, as good as out of a factory. We sold a ton of those at ten leu a piece. Shoes sold better, though, the regional head of urology sold seven old runover pairs right next to me."

"So did you make good money?" Ivan asked, entranced by the serene cynicism of Myron's stories.

"Are you kidding?" the lawyer laughed. "What money? With a country as crappy as ours, you can't make crap!"

Or he would talk about the apartment block where the family lived; he referred to it as a "slab heap." Concrete slab housing blocks, most of them nine floors high, were built on an enormous field and looked irredeemably ugly: despite their relatively recent construction, the external paint had peeled, revealing gouges and scratches in the walls; the elevators, the size of a cage, were filthy and broken; and the stairwells were covered in graffiti.

"In the kitchen, the plumbing works fine, and we have hot water, but in the bathroom we don't. So I rigged a hose we can attach to the kitchen faucet and run to the bathroom, and cut a hole in the bathroom door to run it through. Where else would people do that? An American, if he saw our system, would have a conniption. Do you know who else sold stuff at the market in Romania, next to me and the head of urology? A university professor," and Myron Vasyliovych named a luminary of the academic world. "He was trying to sell a water pump, you know, for drinking water. But no one would even look at it, people didn't know what it was. Soldering irons, no problem; shoes, no problem; candles sold like hotcakes, but no bites on the pump. He tried everything, waved his hands at them, made water noises, and still no one bought it," Myron laughed. "He went around asking if anyone knew how to say water in Romanian, but none of us there did. Nobody thought to bring a dictionary either, we just mimed everything. Then he remembered he had studied Latin, and someone else told him that 'for' in Romanian was '*pentru*.' So there he was, calling customers in with his, 'Pentru aqua, pentru aqua!' Damn classicist."

Kateryna Ivanivna, by contrast, never said much. She had a stern gaze and kept her lips pressed together tightly, which made

Ivan subconsciously expect her to say something terse, but she never did. She never said anything disagreeable and would just get up to bring another dish or more bread or water to the table. Sometimes Myron Vasyliovych and Kateryna Ivanivna sang duets. Myron Vasyliovych played the guitar quite well.

Phoebe never joined in when they sang, only made herself smaller, as if their voices scared her. And she wasn't Phoebe at home, anyway—she was Marichka.

With Ivan, she could be Phoebe, but then something would shift in the space around them, and Phoebe would fall out of her serene self-possession and turn into Marichka again, a mute fawn with large dark eyes, the maiden of black lace. He glimpsed the lace she wore for the first time in a park, when they were kissing and he undid the buttons on her cardigan, and then her shirt, and from there the filigreed blackness that hid the pale nakedness of her body overwhelmed him. She would not have aroused him more if she had been completely naked. With Rose, everything had been different; Rose did not wear lace, or even bras. Rose was like earth itself, open everywhere and therefore irresistible. Phoebe, by contrast, held many layers. The lace appeared to shield her vulnerable soul, and there was a certain charm in that, but the much more powerful spell lay in the fact that this armor was no armor at all, it could not have stopped or warded off anybody. The thought made Ivan blind with ardor.

Naked, spent, she was his, and he would kill anyone who dared so much as to touch her, he would gladly die himself before he let anyone else come near here. But then she would emerge from the froth of her nakedness, the froth of her lace, her serene eyes and serene voice would emerge—no, that was not right, it was not serene but rather full and deep, as if her voice were a river, as if her voice could turn anything else in the world into water, meaning, as Ivan knew with the most primitive fibers of his soul, into words.

Ivan, who yearned to possess this incarnation of her, too, this one first and foremost, with time would become frightened. Confusion overwhelmed him. Where did the defenseless, mute girl he had sworn to protect go? This other one, with her voice like a river, had done him no wrong, and yet fear sparked inside him and tightened around his body.

It would be easier to love someone simpler, Mysko would have told him. Ivan closed his eyes, and half asleep saw Phoebe as a magnificent city with lush gardens, he could see it so clearly on the horizon, but he had so, so far, to walk to reach it. There were no shortcuts. Ivan stumbled and staggered along the well-traveled road that seemed to have neither a beginning nor an end, and the chimeric city hovered right before his eyes. Worse, the city was not a mirage; it was Ivan who turned out to be such a slow traveler. What if someone else reached it first? Fear again wrapped him in its bony arms, fear ached inside him, like a sick organ. Phoebe would leave him. She would not be able to wait long enough for him. But Phoebe was here, *here*! All he had to do was undress her down to her lace . . .

Seryi, Ivan's schoolmate who was not exactly a friend but someone Ivan cherished in memory of their childhood friendship, invited Ivan and Phoebe to his dacha. Everything there was well made and solid; Seryi's father had been the head of an important agency. Back in his schooldays, the proposition would have seemed to Ivan a dream come true, to be alone with their girlfriends at the parents' dacha! But now, after everything that had happened between him and Phoebe, Ivan found being at this house and the company of Seryi and his girlfriend oppressive. He could hear them wrestle loudly on the other side of the wall, the noises of their love. He thought of the concrete slab apartment blocks, the space inside them sectioned off into hundreds and thousands of tiny cubes, people in each of these doing the same thing he was, aping his every move just as he was repeating theirs. You are all moving in unison, a totalitarian unison, after you get out of your pants, skirts, boxers, and socks. Everyone can see you; everyone knows exactly what you are doing in that very moment. Everyone is just so happy to have another idiot join their cohort, another fool who cannot control his own instincts.

That night Ivan entered Phoebe so sharply, moved inside her so quickly and mercilessly that he caused her pain. He had this desperate urge to get out—out of himself, out of her—that at first, he did not even register that she was protesting, trying to stop him, pull him out of herself like a noxious weed. That she was crying.

Later, he turned on the bedside lamp and studied Phoebe as she lay next to him. A shadow lay on her face. It was as if he had touched the very bottom of his love and desire and then realized he should not have done that. He had nowhere deeper to go, and he would not be allowed to turn back. If he knew how to talk about this, he would talk and talk, but he did not. He embraced Phoebe and held her, without passion, but full of love.

Still, she did not seem to understand him. Or did she? She also did not know how to talk about such things. Perhaps no one in the world did, how would Ivan know?

Now she will definitely leave me, Ivan thought, knowing full well that the thought would revive his fear and his whole body would ache. Let it hurt. Maybe the pain was his penance.

For several weeks afterward, they did not go to the dacha even though Seryi kept inviting them. Instead, they spent time in Phoebe's room. Phoebe had put posters of movie stars (David Duchovny, wasn't it?) over the glass pane in her room's door and had her father make the lock functional. They could probably have made love there, too, and that might well have been what Phoebe wanted, but Ivan could not do it. He could not even hug her. Duchovny, unblinking, stared at him from the posters.

"Do you have a girl?" Margita asked him. She already knew he did because Ivan had been spotted in the city with one. Everyone always spotted someone, never mind there were a hundred thousand people in the city, it might as well be a village. On the pedestrian bridge across the river or down Korzo Street, you ran into your friends, your enemies, and a whole bunch of kin.

"So what if I do?" Ivan answered Margita's question with a question.

"Naught," Margita shrugged as if the news was of little interest to her, then narrowed her eyes and said casually, "Bring her here. You've got cabinets to put up in the second-floor kitchen, she can sit with you. That'll keep you at home at least."

At first Ivan thought this was Margita's way of making a joke, spiced generously with her unique sarcasm, but soon, and with great surprise, he realized she was serious. She was indeed prepared to tolerate a strange young woman in her home if that would tie Ivan down.

"I don't know her very well yet," he'd mutter.

"Sure, how could you?" Margita would counter. "You gotta live with someone to know them. No good wastin' time, you oughta settle down already instead of dancing at discos."

"Mom, we don't go to discos."

"Sure, sure you don't. How'd I know where you go?" Margita would shrug.

Ivan came home late because he spent his evenings at Phoebe's. His insomnia was long gone. Often, he'd eat dinner there as well, to the accompaniment of Myron Vasyliovych's stories and Kateryna Ivanivna's many proverbs, the ones with goats in them. So Margita could no longer have him all to herself in the evenings when Ivan's father slept and the TV in the living room was turned down low on the Hungarian channel. She could not pile his plate high with tasty food, pour melted butter over the freshly fried cheese balls and dust them with sweet breadcrumbs. He was not there when she fished out of the pot her delicate, finger-sized *tőltőtt káposzta*[10] in tomato sauce. Or when she cooked pork fat into brown curls to be mixed into her mashed potatoes, made with hot milk because you never put in milk colder than the potatoes, it goes blue and turns the whole dish blue. Now Margita was alone in these hours. She would leap to her feet when Ivan finally came home, run up to him, look into his face with hope: "Gosh, you're out late. Want something to eat, sweetie?"—"No, Mom, I ate already." —"Like their food is any good," she'd say under her breath and leave him alone, offended. In the morning she would talk to him the way only she could, with her back.

Ivan got no relief at home. Margita would not stop kvetching that they'd never finish the house, and when they could get rebar, and when this or that would be delivered.

"Mom!" Ivan would finally plead. "It's winter! Have you not been outside recently or what?"

"Gosh, honey, I can't even bring it up, you fly off the handle! I'd rather you got married instead, I'd have some help finally!"

The idea of Phoebe being of help to Margita was so absurd it made Ivan laugh out loud, something he had not done in a while.

"What's you laughing at?" Margita asked, offended. "You're a grown 'un, old enough to help his parents, and he's laughing. You've got some skirt you're chasing, so stop and marry her already, bring her over and make a home!"

"What if that's not what we want?"

"What do you mean, you don't want? Sure, I see, you'd rather free load off your parents. Well, I ain't going to let you ride my back to my grave!" Genuinely angry, Margita was shouting.

Christmas came and went through the din of her shouting; Ivan spent most of it at Phoebe's.

---

10. Hungarian for *holubtsi*, meat-stuffed cabbage-leaf wraps.

Once the winter holidays were over, Myron Vasyliovych invited Ivan into his office, shut the door behind him, and inquired when Ivan intended to marry his daughter. Ivan was so shocked that for a few moments all he could do was gasp for air.

"Why now?" he finally managed to say.

"Your mom called and asked Kateryna Ivanivna if you and Marichka are getting married or what."

"And?"

"Well, Kateryna Ivanivna was honest with her and told her we haven't had you propose."

"And what did my mom say?"

"Your mom said to expect one very soon. So I just wanted to ask you when you were planning to do it, so I wouldn't be out at the choir rehearsal."

"Well, I . . . Phoebe and I . . ."

"Phoe . . . who? You just make your plans with Marichka and let us know, and we'll get a proper dinner ready, so that come your proposal we'll have something to toast it with, and something to eat after."

What was he supposed to do now? Get married? And live. Live where, how? At Margita's of course, and to get on with the construction. "Got what she wanted, didn't she," he hissed to himself under his breath, and realized suddenly he wasn't sure which woman he had in mind: Margita or actually Phoebe. He thought of Phoebe's poems, on the floppy disk that, all this time, for whatever reason, he hadn't been able to make himself return to her. He didn't know why. Of course, he didn't believe that the disk was the only reason Phoebe was with him, since she could have easily gotten help with her project somewhere else. But then, come to think of it (and he really did not want to think about it, and yet the thought occurred to him, in spite of his intention to the contrary), what was she going to do with those poems? What were they good for? Okay, so she'd have them printed out. If only that's all she wanted, to print them out for herself. No, she wanted something else. Apparently she imagined herself to be a poet, one of those who organize launches and do public readings, and sit around in cafés, as they do in Lviv, reading something to one another. And what about Ivan? Who was he going to be with her, the lady poet? And which poetic luminary would steal her from Ivan?

He could not go there. That's where the pain lived. That's where the pain zone lay, a precipitous drop to the center of the earth through a fog-covered bog. Beyond the pain lay a sticky feeling, like mud under his feet, like earth itself, and just as ineluctable: this woman, this naked body, the body intended for his pleasure and for bearing and feeding his children, this body should not, must not, write poems. It must not write anything at all. It might not even be meant to speak. It ought to be its naked self and nothing else. Just so. Perhaps Margita was right: he should marry Phoebe. At least then it wouldn't hurt so much.

That night he came to Phoebe's angry. Tears brimmed in her eyes, sparkling like candles. Did she really want to get married? She? She must think that getting married is like getting to write poems together. She does not understand that Margita is waiting for her on the other side. And Margita's pigs, of course, can't do without them. And the rebar. And all the other stuff.

Ivan shook his head to rid himself of these wrong, angry thoughts. He had to find a way to talk about this with Phoebe, had to explain things to her (what things?), console her (how?). Just as soon as he thought that things could not get any worse, they did.

"What about my disk?" Phoebe asked. "Have you finally brought it?"

She had asked him for it before and he had made a joke of it, told her he forgot. But he had been forgetting it for several months. And Phoebe was not a child. She could very well approach her father, and him, Ivan, her father's son-in-law—damn, no, that's nonsense—she could very well insist on having her floppy disk right there and then, at once. And what would he, Ivan, say to her then?

"No, I haven't," he snapped back at her. His urge to console Phoebe evaporated. Let her cry. How could she not realize that now was not the time to ask for that disk, that they both had much bigger problems than a stupid floppy disk? Was she deaf and blind? Or was it that she could not forgive him that night at Seryi's dacha? And what's this challenge he heard in her tone? "My disk!" While he, Ivan, is trying so hard to calm things down, make her happy, and keep Margita at bay, convince Myron Vasyliovych to change his mind, she—*she!*—cares about no one but herself.

Somehow he endured the rest of that night with her, and left, but did not go home. He flagged a cab, paid the driver, and had him drop him off at the bank, where at this late hour only the guards were in the building. Ivan was on great terms with the guards. Vitya, a young police officer, was on duty. Ivan asked Vitya to disarm the alarm, telling him he had forgotten something important he needed for a meeting the next day. He went in, turned on his computer, waited for a long time for everything to load, and then enjoyed finding Phoebe's file and deleting it. Then he emptied all the files from the trash can, too. He found the floppy disk where he had put it many weeks ago—in the desk drawer. He shoved it into his jacket pocket, turned off his computer, said goodbye to Vitya, and flew out of the building.

He knew exactly what he had to do. She demanded to have her disk back, did she? He would tell her the disk got lost. They want him to get married, do they? Fine, he would get married. He stopped by the garbage container. He was downtown, but at the moment, with offices and stores closed for the night, the only people around were the homeless, dumpster diving. No one paid any attention to Ivan, and they could not have taken him for one of them, in fact, they would very much pay attention to him if they thought him a newcomer on their turf, the entire city was divided between different clans. They must have thought him a lost office dweller and not worth the trouble: his jacket was old and worn and he didn't look well-to-do . . . Ivan pulled out Phoebe's disk, dropped it to the ground, and stamped on it, again and again, then picked it up, broke it into halves, dropped it, and ground it into the dirt with his feet. He relished crushing it, crushing not just the plastic, but all of Phoebe's words, all her blackness, all her dreams, and her lace.

"Serves you right, serves you right!" he muttered under his breath, and then, without noticing, out loud, and pounded, pounded the thing with the hard soles of his boots, even when there was nothing left to pound, the plastic was dead and the words had flown to other worlds. He was out of breath. He stopped, panting. The disk lay under his feet broken, shattered beyond all recognition. "Why did I . . ." he whispered, realizing what he had done, in a flash. "What for?"

They set the wedding date for summer.

PHOEBE'S FIRST MONOLOGUE

to put down words fast I am put— (crossed-out) only some of the
words

Shut up.
Shut up, you, woman.
Such a little thing, and already a woman.
Freeloader.
Like anybody needs your stupid poems?
Shut up with your poems.
You are dumb.
What did I just say!
Take the trash out.
Make dinner.
We spend our entire lives working for you.
You ungrateful thing.
Pick up the kid from daycare.
You don't lift a finger at home.
You are dumb.
All you ever do is read books.
You are dumb.
You are lazy.
Nobody wants you.
You appreciate nothing.
You are a pushover.
Crybaby.

You don't have any character.
You won't ever amount to anything.
We used to think you might amount to something, but you never did.
Had a future, they call it.
Get out of here!
Shut your trap.
You don't know how to forgive.
You should be grateful.
Shut up.
You hold grudges.
You only remember the bad stuff.
Freeloader.
Shut up.
Why haven't you cooked the potatoes?
Why is the room so filthy?
Here, stuff your face.
I bring you grub, and you don't appreciate it.
What would you even do if you were hungry?
Freeloader.
Woman.
I'm going to slap you.
We are old now.
You never appreciate anything.
You were raised in a normal family, not in a cretin's school—that would've served you right!
Eat like you haven't eaten for years, don't you?
Shut up.
Show me what you are writing.
You know nothing, you are interested in nothing.
You are dumb.
You should be grateful.

Who, me? Hit you? You don't even know what a real beating is.

You hold grudges.

We are old now.

You should have seen your grandpa beat your grandma, now that was for real!

Or you should have seen my dad beat my brother, slammed his head right against the toilet, he did.

You have no idea what a real beating is.

Just you wait, he'll come home and set you straight.

Let him whip you.

Lie down on the bed, I'll give you a belt.

You got a C at school.

You missed your dance lesson.

Lie down, I said!

Freeloader.

Why haven't you cooked the potatoes?

Don't you dare talk back at me!

Such a little thing, and already a woman.

Oh, we've given up a long time ago.

Go make five hundred bucks to pay for your own wedding, then you'll talk.

No one ever beat you.

All you want is to eat, don't you? Chicken is what you like, don't you?

And what if we had nothing?

Shut up.

Shut up, woman.

Let's go over your homework.

You are dumb.

Trust me, you'd know it if someone really beat you.

We are old now.

You won't even bring us a glass of water to drink.

Shut up.

No one ever beat you here.

Gee whiz, nicked her for a nickel and she's crying up a ruble!

You've never seen a real thrashing.

You are going to stick to your grudges for the rest of our lives, aren't you?

Shut up, woman.

Shut up.

You want more? You want more?

Stop wailing.

You dare not wail at me!

Shut up.

Shut up, woman.

No one ever beat you.

You live in a normal family.

What if we'd sent you off to the cretin's school instead?

They never have any food there.

You make it sound like someone here beat you.

Do you know what they do in those schools?

Shut up.

Will you just look at her? Crybaby!

You don't appreciate us.

We are old now.

Freeloader.

You are dumb.

Running around with your stupid verses.

Shut up.

Shut up, woman.

•

By the time Ivan woke up on Sundays, Phoebe would be half sitting in their bed, awake and looking at him. He would have very much liked to hold her in his arms, but the weekend mornings, not to mention the weekday ones, when they each had to run to their respective banks, were not their own. Margita thought nothing of coming into their bedroom to give them jobs to do. Then Ivan would have to get up, start the car, and take Margita wherever she wished. Or, if it was a Saturday, go work in the vegetable garden, or fix something or other, so that Phoebe, who received her own pressing assignment from Margita, would dash out of the house to steal a kiss and look at him with longing.

Margita would summon Phoebe to the kitchen with her. She did not let Phoebe cook separately for Ivan and herself because that would've been a waste of food, and anyway, Ivan preferred his mother's cooking to the cardboard little sausages with rice, because what else could this newly minted wife of his feed him? She didn't even know how to buy sour cream—never from the village women but from the farmwives, they have the good stuff, it might look thin, but it settles good and thick like butter, you can stand a spoon up straight in it, whereas the cream from the village women just sours overnight. You never know what those wenches mix into it! How is it that Phoebe's mother didn't even teach her that much?

In the kitchen, they would talk, meaning Margita would talk and Phoebe would listen while she picked over buckwheat or peeled apples for Margita's obligatory apple-and-clotted-cream pie she baked every week to have with tea. Finally Margita had someone she could talk to, someone to whom she could complain about her husband who drank his entire life, her son who'd spent half of his God knows where, her son-in-law who ran a decent house, but, boy, did he have a temper on him and liked his drink, too, the government that kept cutting pensions and wages, the prices at the market and the dishonest women who put who knows what into their sour cream, the Colorado beetles,[11] the neighbors whose new cottages put too much shade on her vegetable garden, and the god-awful roads that made it such a chore to go to the cemetery to tend to her late parents' graves.

Never in her life had Margita been to a resort or on a vacation. She might not have even seen the sea. She wore the same clothes year after year in the name of thrift, because, really, what's an old wench like her to want new clothes for? Her coworkers once bought her a bottle of Red Moscow perfume as an office present, and she would never use it but kept it, along with an ancient tube of lipstick, in the drawer of her bedside table, long after the liquid had gone dark and the scent acrid.

Never was there in Margita's life an occasion or a festivity that would justify using up some of the spoiled but still cherished perfume: birthdays, Christmases, and Easters she spent at the stove, and the delicate scent would have been lost among the aromas of smoked sausages and fresh aspic, evaporated from her sweaty skin. Only when she and Ivan's father were invited to someone else's home would Margita pull out her precious vial—and then put it back unopened because the occasion did not, after all, seem important enough, and if it actually did, then how would Margita look other people in the eye if they had never known her to smell of anything but clean clothes and bar soap and suddenly she showed up all perfumed, like a girl out to strut her goods!

When Ivan came home from work, Margita was all smiles and kind words. She fawned upon him, made his favorite foods, asked about his day, praised him. Whatever she felt she had to complain

---

11. The Colorado potato beetle is native to the American West and was introduced to Europe at the American bases in France during World War I. During the Cold War, the Soviet government said the beetle was a biological weapon brought in by the Americans to destroy Communist potatoes.

about she would've already unloaded on Phoebe. The old spider had the young one caught fast in its web. While Ivan ate, Phoebe would sit with him but could barely get a word in, since Margita did all the talking. Phoebe would then ask if she could do another chore, wash the dishes, say? Or take something down to the cellar? Or to give to the pigs? But Margita, who during the day readily took her up on every offer, in the evenings rejected Phoebe's impulses with, "Don't you fuss, honey, no need, I'll do it, you sit with your husband, talk to him, don't let me chatter away!" while she kept talking without pause or end, so Phoebe had no choice by to sit by that table like a lost bone.

Styopa, now Phoebe's brother-in-law, would get drunk and show up at eleven or even at midnight, holler from outside the back gate to be let in, and, once he was in, would climb the stairs to the second floor, where Ivan and Phoebe lived, where his shouting and arm-waving would send Phoebe, terrified, to hide in the bedroom, while Styopa gripped Ivan in his viselike grip and dragged him to the kitchen. They'd open the window and smoke, shaking off ash into the yard below while Styopa boomed his wisdom into Ivan's ears, "Be a man, already, what's that bank job of yours for, build your house, come back to reality!" Styopa's was the most superior reality, one you could touch. All these money transfers and the stupid internet were, for him, at best, marginally helpful in life, but they were not life: life was a field of potatoes to be harvested in the fall, animals raised for food, cucumbers in the greenhouse, and the house, the impregnable fortress a man could rely on in times of mortal danger. And the times, they would not be long in coming. Styopa had no need to read philosophy and no reason to believe any end-of-the-world doctrines. The end of potatoes was for him the end of the world, and the end of bricks, the end of history.

Once tired, Styopa would go home. He never stayed the night even though he would have been welcome to. Ivan would sigh with relief and exchange a knowing look with Margita, who always woke up and came out to check on the noise and let her late-night guest out. Afterward, they would lock all gates and doors—the house was indeed their fortress—wish each other a near-giddy "Good night!" and go to their respective bedrooms. Margita understood everything. Margita was his accomplice. Ivan was growing used to this different relationship with Margita, no longer felt he had to protect himself from her as if she were an alien force.

Which made it that much worse when he finally saw things as they were.

That night, he came home earlier than usual. Margita was serving dinner, silent. Phoebe was nowhere to be seen. Ivan said something; Margita did not respond. She was speaking to him with her back, as she alone could, and this felt weird; he had forgotten how to decipher this language of hers. "Mom, what's wrong with you?" he said finally. Margita only waved him off. "Did a pig die? Did father come home drunk again?"—"A pig! I'll show you a pig!" Margita exploded. "It's just pigs on his mind, is it?" Ivan, stunned, listened to his mother shout at him while his thoughts followed one another as if in an alternative time: Pigs? He had pigs? On his mind? But he could care less about pigs. "We done saw the story! Mariyka done told me!" Margita exclaimed. A story? What story? And who's Mariyka? It took Ivan a moment to realize she meant Phoebe; he was beginning to see double. "What story? About whom?" He suddenly thought of the pretrial detention facility in Lviv: Was it possible one of his guys got arrested? Which one? "You! On TV! A show!" Margita thundered. Ivan felt a bit relieved, at least no one had gone to jail. "How could there be a story about me on TV, Mom? I'm not a member of parliament or something!"

"Honey," Margita said, suddenly in a different tone. She sat down beside him and folded her hands on her lap. "Honey, why'd you not tell us the truth?"—"What truth?"—"That you done gone to that Maidan of theirs!"—"Mom," he croaked as he pushed down a mouthful of food, "that's so long ago, years!"—"Don't you try to confuse me! Years!" Margita shouted again. "Why'd you not tell me?"—"Because you wouldn't have let me go!" Ivan exploded, shouting, too. "You bet I wouldn't 'ave! They could've killed you all! Did you not know that? Why'd you mess with them? I done told you: never mess with politics!"

"Mom!"—"Sure, it's *Mom* now, and where was your head then?"—"Mom!!"—"Where was your head, I ask you!" and they went on shouting like that, each on his and her own, neither one listening to the other. Things wrestled, turned over violently in Ivan's chest; he would not have known how to name what was coming out of his mouth like black smoke. Was it fury, pain, fear, or contrition? Or guilt? Was it rage at himself for having trespassed? He had to fish out small black fragments of feelings from the dark well of his self, one at time, hold them up to the light, and study them for a long time before he could identify them, give each a name as Adam gave names to the birds and the beasts. But he could not—there was not enough time in the world, the world harried him, whipped him forward, drove him on like a tired horse. He was just as confused by what was erupting out of Margita, could only feel that her blackness was fuller and more potent than his own, that it was lava hotter than fire—a blackness compressed under decades of her hard life. This lava now flooded the kitchen, ran over the house, filled all the available space, it was about to drown the street, and bury them all in its path.

"You don't understand," he spoke at his mother. "If only Bandera and Melnyk had been different people, and Konovalets[12]

---

12. Stepan Bandera, Andriy Melnyk, and Yevhen Konovalets were political and military leaders of the Ukrainian nationalist movement in the pre- and post-World War II period.

had not been shot . . ." Margita startled, "Which Konovalets? Who was shot? Where?"—"Ah, Mom, in Rotterdam, back in the 1920s!"—"Pox on you! What's he got to do with anything? What did you have to do with anything? Why'd you gone messed with politics? What do you want? Do you not know that it's one bandit atop another in there? Murderer after murderer?"—"Mom, if not us—then who?"—"How am I supposed to know, who? I ask you, why should my own son have anything to do with it?"

"Mom," Ivan tried to speak calmer. "Mom, do you think we'd have our independence if we hadn't done it?"

He spoke the words out loud and froze. Time flowed past Ivan, great big clouds of time, they passed him, and he remained standing, invisible in their midst, unknown to anyone just like other men like him.

"Independence!" Margita boomed again. "Oy!" And then she spoke in the hot language of tears, the passionate tongue of passion, "You don't understand, honey, when the Russians came, they took our horses, and my, what horses they were, lithe as serpents, but they perished right after, the war was ending and they left them dying at the ford, I only came in time to see their hearts stop and they had tears in their eyes, because horses, honey, they do weep! So what? Did anyone care? New life, they said! A new life with no horses it was for us, and how we did love them! We raised them ourselves, you'd never been around horses, you don't know what it's like, but I do!" Margita was speaking softer now, which gave her words even more weight, Ivan could hear her barely contained sobbing in them. Ivan knew how to speak to his comrades, knew how to speak to statesmen, how to look the nation's first president in the eye. But to speak to his mother as she mourned her long-murdered horses—that he did not know how to do.

He shrugged, spat, and got up from the table. "Eat without me," he snapped at Margita when she tried to stop him, broke free, jerked his shoulder from her hand so roughly she startled and shied away from him, and went upstairs. In his bedroom, the unmade bed sat pale like a blind eye. Phoebe had stopped doing anything other than the chores Margita gave her downstairs. She did not stop to make the bed as she rushed to escape to work in the mornings and if she allowed herself a cup of coffee, she left the cup, the saucer, the spoon, and other small, tiresome things in the sink, she did not want to keep this house anymore. She told Margita she was tired. "Why don't your mother come over to help you?" Margita groused in return, but Phoebe only waved her off; Kateryna Ivanivna had plenty to manage on her own, with a teenage son at home, and she did not particularly care for Margita. She would stop by only when she knew Margita was not at home.

Ivan took a running leap at the bed, landed facedown on it, and remained still. What to do now? Where to go?

Phoebe no longer met Ivan downstairs when he came home from work, she stayed on their floor. And yet she found the time to tell his mother about the Maidan. *So whispered Phoebe, bitch, into his ear*—a version of Ivan Kotlyarevsky's line turned up in his mind and kept trying to get out, never mind that Ivan knew it was Hebe in the original, but who cares, Hebe or Phoebe, they were both bitches.

Now, Christina, his sister, would have thanked the good lord daily for a man like Ivan, Margita said: he worked hard, he brought home his salary, he didn't drink, and Styopa lately had gotten even more contrary and brought home some lunatic artists, said he was going to buy a house in the village and turn it into a café, and the artists would do the design for him, especially the one who was Styopa's favorite, an unkempt dude in track pants who went by Shoni.[13] Christina hated Shoni more than the others, because he

---

13. Hungarian, short for Alexander.

ate like four men, bragged about his talents, complained about being poor, and yet while taking advantage of her dinnertime charity, managed to open a whole gallery of his paintings in the city. Paintings for which, let's be clear, Christina wouldn't give a bent penny.

He could not go there. As much as Christina loved Ivan, she would not be able to protect him from the Paikoshes, not to mention Shoni the painter, they'd pin him down in the living room in a cloud of cigarette smoke, and Styopa would order Christina to put a spread for the guests on the table, and then Ivan would have to hear how stupid he was, how he couldn't manage in life, how he knew none of the things that a good man of the house should know.

Where else? Korchi was gone, he was still either on the Czech side or gone over to the Slovaks, and lately workers like him started going over to Russia, the very thought of which made Ivan's skin crawl with disgust and fear. What work could there possibly be up there, after their gulag? Yura Popadynets did, of late, abandon his Ruthenian obsession and got into photography instead, so he disappeared for long stretches into the mountains, where he took pictures of weddings and other memorable occasions, and was gradually building something of a professional reputation. He even quit drinking. Ivan could have gone to him, although he would not have told Yura any of his troubles. Yura wouldn't understand, Yura never had a house to keep or in-laws to deal with, he only had his mom and their two-room apartment.

Ivan did not realize he had walked to Kreitzar's house. He did love Kreitzar, had always loved him. Why did he hide from him for so long? Kreitzar was not at home. Yerzhia, his sister, told Ivan he had taken his goats to the river. Ivan found Kreitzar on the nearly deserted riverbank, far from downtown. An old overgrown park lay on the other side of the river, untamed green willows bent low above the water. The river had gone shallow in many places, and now only weak separate streams flowed in the once-full bed, barely climbing over the gravel. The grass was young, juicy, verdant. The day was not sunny; clouds hung over the city. Kreitzar was sitting on a rock at the edge of the water and smoking dreamily. The goats circled him, nibbled the grass. Ivan came up to his friend, sat down. Kreitzar smiled beatifically; he was drunk.

"So, here you are."—"Sure am," said Kreitzar. "What d'you want the goats for, anyway?" Ivan asked, shrugging at the animals. He pulled out a cigarette, too, and lit up. "The goats? They are the thing! The very thing," Kreitzar said. He kept smiling. "Don't you know?"—"No, I don't," Ivan agreed. What did he know, after all? Everyone had something to teach him: Margita, Styopa—Kreitzar might as well jump on the wagon, too. "Everyone needs goats."— "What do you mean, *everyone*?"—"Well, look how many money-bags we've got around here. Goat milk is healthy. All these big shots drink it and buy it for their kids, too." They were silent for a bit. "No kidding," Ivan said, as if he wanted to be convinced. In fact, he couldn't care less about the goats, their milk, and especially the "moneybags" in their matching colorful suits, since the moneybags, as far as he knew, drank vodka, not milk, at their fancy restaurants. "Sure thing!" Kreitzar said enthusiastically. A strange conversation this was, on the subject of goats, at the river, under the frowning sky. "D'you think they don't have kids? And what's the very bestest milk for a kid? The goat's!"

"They have kids?" Ivan repeated, thrown suddenly back to the time when he and Mysko read Yevhen Chykalenko, a great philan-thropist who had five children, none of whom had any interest in their father's work. *It would be better if all conscientious Ukrainians who fight for their country raised goats instead of children*, Chykalenko had once written in an angry letter. Meaning, maybe you shouldn't invest your entire soul in doing something that won't benefit the nation in the long run and will only be used up by your tiresome children.

Who are, as we all know, of great and glorious ancestors the unworthy seed.[14] Chykalenko would have liked Kreitzar very much. Even his nickname, if you think about it, was of the right era.[15]

Kreitzar was telling Ivan something but Ivan could not focus on the point of the story. "Svetka, Svetka," Kreitzar repeated. "Who's that?" Ivan finally asked. This prompted Kreitzar to deliver a long and convoluted story that was absolutely impossible to comprehend while sober, so they herded the goats home, and Ivan went over to Kreitzar's neighbor who, like Margita, grew his own grapes and sold homemade wine. The neighbor pointed his finger in the direction of Kreitzar's house and shook his head resignedly. "That there is how it starts. That lad's a goner," he said. "Far from it!" Ivan objected, because he had to object; he couldn't just give up on his friend. "That there is how it is, once a little, twice a little, and then it's over," the neighbor muttered, more to himself now than for Ivan's benefit. Ivan took the wine, went back to Kreitzar's, and they drank together, sitting in his messy yard, where his mother would come out at regular intervals to give them a tongue lashing. Ivan, made happier by the wine, found a spot on the top of a cold gravel pile and surveyed the street from the height of that improvised hill. Let them see him. Let them tell Margita they saw him, he didn't care.

•

Kreitzar, who had been Ivan's friend since the days of kindergarten and their first soccer matches, was actually also named Ivan. His name was Ivan Farkash, but no one ever called him that, and when

14. A line from Taras Shevchenko's poem "To My Fellow-Countrymen, in Ukraine and Not in Ukraine, Living, Dead and As Yet Unborn, My Friendly Epistle," as translated by Vera Rich.
15. The kreitzar, or kreuzer, was a coin of the Austro-Hungarian Empire.

all of the Galagov boys grew up and some became Ivan Ivanoviches or Vasyl Vasyliovyces, Kreitzar remained Kreitzar and nearly as small as he had been in seventh grade. He and Ivan used to spend a lot of time together when they were kids. Ivan remembered them going to the village to visit Kreitzar's grandmother and the massive snows that lay there on the slopes of the mountains like giant blankets, and going house to house with other boys at Christmas, an all-male *vertep*, their hats fringed with green tinsel, with a tambourine and an accordion, ten of them or more. Other singers came to their house, too, and sang:

> *New joy*
> *is on the world bestowed*
> *to the Holy Virgin*
> *a son has born*
> *here she birthed him*
> *here he lay swaddled*
> *she put down green hay*
> *for his bed to keep warm*
> *Herod the evil*
> *learned great frustration*
> *when the Lord eternal*
> *came incarnated*

The word "evil" and sometimes other words in the carol were pronounced with that Transcarpathian (Ruthenian) hard ı, almost as broad as the Russian ы, there was no sound like it anywhere else in Ukraine. The house smelled of freshly cut pine, delicious food, wine, and beeswax candles. The Christmas tree blinked its lights in the corner. Grandmother spent hours in her room reading the Psalms, while her son and daughter-in-law, Kreitzar's uncle and aunt, ran the place. Kreitzar's uncle was much older than his mother. And now Kreitzar's uncle was gone, as was the grand-mother; only Aunt Mykhailyna was left. Cousins had gone away in search of work. Kreitzar's father had left his wife and children for another woman, and the latest rumor was he'd been seen in Mukachevo. Kreitzar lived with his mother and his sister, Yerzhia, who was a year older than him and just as petite, but unlike him, was good-looking. Kreitzar loved her to pieces. It was for her sake that he did not drink, no matter how much he wanted to, and had learned the bricklaying trade, and spent years herding goats just so she would have clothes to wear. Kreitzar himself dressed like a pauper.

He recently let his hair grow long, this made him look like a very young Axl Rose, except an Axl Rose who could not sing or play the guitar. Finally, a third cousin once removed brought Kreitzar into his construction crew—the crew did new builds and renovations and was always busy—and now Kreitzar earned enough money to support his small family. They had plenty of work: rich people's houses rose one after the other in Chervenytsya, first piercing the ground with the stone bones of their foundations, then raising the ribs of the walls, and slowly growing layers of meat and fat until they were ready to conceal themselves completely behind the gleaming armor of wrought iron fences. Between the goats and construction work, Kreitzar had no free time whatsoever, and his house stood with half-finished walls and a yard in a state of permanent disorder, dotted with piles of sand. Goats roamed the tall weeds behind the fence. The goats smelled.

Kreitzar loved his job. The crew worked with an easygoing atti-tude and happily made fun of their employers' endless faultfinding and requests to redo something that just got done. They asked for a marble staircase up to the narrow standard-issue bathroom left over from the Soviet days? No problem! A window that spans two walls? Here you go! Not all crews were as agreeable—there were some honest sticklers for truth in the business who would argue until they foamed at the mouth that this or that whim of the client was utterly idiotic and that only they, the working people, the hands-on craftsmen, knew how to do things properly. Sometimes, such folks would not even be paid, but they found new jobs regardless, because construction was booming. Ishtvan, the foreman of Kreitzar's crew, was a very wise man. He taught his guys not to get too attached to any particular job, and to cultivate a broad, long-term view of things. As he said, we do the job right but we're not the ones living here.

Kreitzar's mother and sister did not touch the yard. His mother cooked and did laundry for all of them. Kreitzar bought a sewing machine for Yerzhia. She finished a tailoring course and now worked in tandem with a more experienced friend whom she paid a referral fee, making clothes to measure. Her clients would curve their lips in disgust as they climbed the porch: there were no railings, the concrete steps crumbled, and the yard lay around them like in ruin. But Yerzhia did fine work and did not charge very much since she was just starting out. The clients were happy about that. Kreitzar came home exhausted, but as soon as he washed and sat down to dinner he saw his mother's and sister's smiles, felt their loving warmth, and his fatigue evaporated. So what, the yard needed attention and the porch had no railing? They had bread and things to put on it, their goats, the goats' milk, and they had just replaced the roof; they were set for the winter. You can last a long time just on what you have. No one could bother them as they owned the house. Kreitzar basked in the comfort of home. The din of the forks sounded like music. He heard plenty of horror stories from the guys in his crew about pensions and folks not having enough to eat, but he was all right.

•

That spring, however, trouble came to their door. Their neighbor, Layosh, barged in, sobbing, and begged for money—he had run afoul of the "buzzheads." Who, as it turned out, were camped out at his place, waiting for him to come back with money borrowed from his good neighbors. Over his mother's objections, Kreitzar took some cash and went with Layosh. There he discovered the following: a handful of gangsters were, in fact, seated around Layosh's dinner table, just like in a mafia movie, and among them was none other than Kreitzar's father, in the flesh, the old (although he wasn't really that old) Farkash, whom everyone called Wolf.[16] He used to be a sambo coach. Kreitzar's money was not accepted; his father took him out to the mudroom, inquired after his mother and sister, and told him to go home, deputizing one of his squires/guards/ clowns, a particularly crane-like one, as an escort, despite Kreitzar's protestations that he only had to go next door.

Kreitzar left Layosh's house no longer feeling his legs. Layosh had to be left to fend for himself. Outside, as to be expected in March, the weather was foul. The snow had melted but everything was wet. Out on the street, Kreitzar realized he had forgotten his hat at Layosh's but had no desire to go back. To hell with that hat, his Mom will knit him another one. They have yarn. She's been meaning to unravel his old sweater anyway. He was distracted from this line of thought by the crane-like clown, who said, "What's up, man? I'm Sanya. You?" Kreitzar shuddered. He said, "Kreitzar."—"All right. Hey, why'd *Bácsi*[17] let you go like that?" Sanya probed. "How would I know?" Kreitzar muttered. He did not feel like talking.

At Kreitzar's, Sanya somehow managed to invite himself to tea and then succeeded in charming Yerzhia. Now, he was sort of going out with her, although most of the time she waited for him to show

---

16. *Farkas* means "wolf" in Hungarian.
17. *Básci*: Uncle (Hungarian).

up and he didn't. She waited in vain, but that's how things are when you are in love. Kreitzar himself fell for a girl, Svetka, whom Sanya vaguely knew. Svetka lived in the six-floor apartment building next to the post office. They had all been invited to Svetka's birthday party, and that's where Kreitzar fell in love with her. Kreitzar narrated all this to Ivan in great confusion with endless digressions. Making sense of the story was as about as hard as finding gold in river sand.

But the story was there, and it was, unfortunately, very simple: Kreitzar was fatally in love. Now there were two of them, the brother and the sister, and both ached with the same pain. Kreitzar insisted to Ivan that he only wanted what was best for Svetka—as if Ivan would have doubted him—and that Svetka lived poorly with her mom and stepfather in a small Khrushev-era apartment, and that he, Kreitzar, could give her, as it seemed to him, immeasurably more than that. Since that was the case, then how could Svetka not fall in love with him—she would fall in love with him, eventually, he just had to wait, right? He, Kreitzar, would have her move in with his family and would spend his evenings at the table with the three women his heart cherished most in the world. His mother, Yerzhia, and Svetka, all three, with him. Kreitzar was mad at Sanya, but let the Lord judge him. Kreitzar was even willing to give Sanya a seat at his family's table, just as long as it made everyone happy. He, Kreitzar, would then fix the porch, install railings, clean up the yard, and the goats would provide milk enough for all of them, and maybe with time, they'd manage to build a second floor, to have more room . . . He could see it all in great detail. He would build, he would paint. Love became for him the second floor on his life's home.

Ivan listened to his friend and sipped his wine. He stopped by Kreitzar's more and more often, sometimes coming there straight from work, forgetting Phoebe, forgetting Margita. No, not quite—he never, for a moment, forgot about them. It's just that he did not know what to do. He did not know what he was supposed to do with all that.

•

Late fall came. Margita was about to celebrate her birthday. Ivan's father stayed up late cooking a thick aspic, to be served with grated turnips and horseradish. The aspic was poured into deep soup bowls; the clear gelatinous layer quickly disappeared under the fat. Father was in the kitchen, marinating herrings: he deftly cut off their heads and fins, folded the fish into jars preloaded with rings of onion, and topped them off with oil and vinegar. "Our turnips are the best," he said to Ivan. Ivan looked into his father's light eyes with small red veins, studied his yellowish eyelids, the gaps left by the missing teeth in his mouth. Margita arrived, chopped meat into stew pieces, and started on her goulash. Phoebe was given the job of cutting up veg-etables for salads, and whatever else was needed for the cold appe-tizers. Margita had baked her *sütemény* the night before. She made different ones: with chocolate cream, with vanilla, and with whipped cream baked in the oven, in addition to the apple pie and the tiny rolls, *kikhlyky*, to be served with the very strong Hungarian coffee delivered in minuscule cups of Slovak white china at the end of the evening, strong coffee at a late hour to give her guests the boost they needed to get home after the lavish dinner.

Family came—Styopa and Christina with the kids, Myron Vasyliovych with his wife and son, the old Paikosh, Styopa's father—and a few old friends. They had to put the leaf in the table to make room for everyone. There was customary table talk, inter-rupted every now and again with Margita's pleas to "try this new salad" or "take more aspic, you've hardly had any." Christina was talking to Kateryna Ivanivna (finally they found something to talk about), but Styopa, who just had to have his wife only to himself, interfered. "Wife," he roared so the whole table could hear him, "you've got a mouth like a railway crossing: more open than shut!" Everyone laughed despite how unfair this was, Christina usually spoke very little, but Styopa must have heard the phrase somewhere and could not wait to try it out in public, even if it came at Christina's expense. She'd take it. Styopa was one of those who would say, "Look, there come people and wives."

Margita flitted to and fro, and Phoebe and Christina soon got up, too; there were plates to change and forks to wash for the guests to enjoy the entree better—never mind they couldn't even look at another bite, but such was the custom. In the interval between dishes, guests spread out, someone even went upstairs to Ivan and Phoebe's. Some went out to the yard to smoke, Ivan's father, Ivan was sure, disappeared somewhere to have a drink in peace, so that Margita would not see—she kept a vigilant eye on the contents of his glass. He must have had a bottle hidden somewhere, in his "stash spot," as Styopa called it.

That evening Ivan didn't see so much as a slice of Margita's face; she accepted his present—he did buy her a present—with a mutter instead of thanks. She might as well have been cursing him. Later, Ivan went into the kitchen, he wanted a bottle of sparkling water. Margita saw him, sent a look sharp as a knife across his face, and turned her back on him.

"Mom!" he called out, no longer able to take it. "Would you please let it go? Why are you so angry at me? It's not like I can change anything now."—"Oh, now it's I who won't let you be? Well, I told no lies to you! I don't go in front of machine guns!"—"Mom, there were no machine guns there."—"Sure! Right!" and Margita turned to spooning the gravy into a serving boat for the table. Ivan turned and went back to the dining room, and she dropped the ladle and chased after him: "Don't you dare! Don't you even dare!" She didn't get to say what it was he was not supposed to dare, because the only guest still at the table, the old Paikosh, who an instant before looked to be peacefully dozing over the not-yet-cleared platters of cold cuts and cheese, woke up abruptly and raised his gaze at Ivan and Margita.

"What's that you scolding him for?" he asked Margita.

"Ah, let it be, you have children, you know how it be!" Margita laughed. She knew how to laugh well. Perhaps that's why everyone loved her so much, her laugh with its dash of bitters. The old man grinned, too.

"What'd you gone done?" he asked Ivan warmly.

"I done naught," Ivan said, sending Margita into a fury again. Still smiling at the old man, she, like a two-faced Janus, barked at her son in a lower voice:

"You know you could've died there!"

"Where'd he go?" the old man inquired. "To talk to the mafia in Mukachevo, or what?"

"Gone to the Maidan mafia, that's where!" Margita exclaimed. She was no longer smiling.

"Tut, Margita, that's all done and gone, and our Ivanko's alive and well," Paikosh consoled. Ivan thought the old man would not know what Maidan they were talking about since it had been years. But he knew right away.

Styopa came back into the house, full of cigarette smoke and a little pissed off, as always, making lots of noise, and called for one of the women—he wanted a drink of kompot and was not accustomed to serving himself. Margita went to attend to him. Old Paikosh stretched his neck to see into the hallway, did not see anyone, shrugged, and poured Ivan and himself drinks. "Sit," he said. "Let us . . . a drink!" They drank. "Well. Warms you up, eh?"—"Yeah," Ivan said, because the stuff did, in fact, warm him up. "Well," Paikosh poured another round. They drank it, and then the old man leaned close to Ivan and asked, "So, you were there?"

Ivan stared at his unexpected companion in surprise, as if seeing for the first time this sinewy, small old man, with gray fuzz on his head, and his face grown ruddy from strong drink. His eyes, though, were perfectly clear. Ivan could never have imagined the old Paikosh as his coconspirator. They did not much care for each other, weren't really family. Paikosh, as small as he looked, had a heck of a temper, and had been a boss in the Soviet days.

"So you stood up for Ukraine?" Paikosh said, almost tearful. He'd already had plenty to drink, and the last shots with Ivan made him even more intoxicated. "You stood up for Ukraine! Didn't you?"—"I did."

They were silent for a bit. They felt close to each other, there were no chatty, intrusive wives sitting between them, diluting their strength like water with wine. Margita came back, observed their sudden brotherhood, and, instantly piqued, slammed down a plate of potatoes, or sauce, Ivan was too drunk to tell. Others started coming back to the table, the room grew crowded. Margita ignored them. Through tears, or perhaps boiling lava mixed with tears, she squeezed out, "Look here, what have we—you've banded with him, old man! I'd never have guessed! Why?"—"What do you mean, why? Mother!" Paikosh intended to deliver his *mother* with steel in his voice, as he would've done back when he was a boss, but his voice let him down, as, swollen and cracked, it poured out of his throat like the River Tysa, whose water had run with blood. "Ah, children! Don't be asking me, for I don't know why the Lord God sends us his trials . . . My own brothers, Vasylko and the oldest, Fedirtsio, both perished. How our old mom did grieve for them! Vasylko fell at Krasne Pole, and Fedirtsio, the oldest, he . . ."

"What's ya looking at, can't you see he's drunk witless, nothing to see here and naught to hear! Come eat, eat!" Margita bellowed, summoning those who weren't at the table yet. But the old man's lament cut through, "Children! Let me tell! Let me tell! Children!"

Paikosh talked and talked, he went on and on, undeterred by Margita, who kept trying to stop him. He told his tale different ways, almost in sobs and then abruptly in a dry, near-prosecutorial voice, telling them of the many thousands who had died and who they were, and on what days, and under what circumstances, and never stopped—just as if he had to unburden himself of it all: the tears, the numbers, the dates, and the names of the murdered.

"It started when the Czechs retreated in Uzhhorod, children, in September '38. They quartered themselves in people's homes, in schools, there were no lessons, and we, stupid little things, went happy, free. Who could have told what would come next! On November the tenth of 1938, the Hungarians reached Uzhhorod, and our dear Carpathian Rus retreated to Khust, they surrendered our three cities to the Hungarians and called themselves Carpathian Ukraine there in Khust, and Avgustyn Voloshyn declared our independence, and my brothers, they went to be there, and we had the Hungarians, and the *madyarons*[18] cried with joy . . . They greeted them with flowers, like liberators! And it all started when the Czechs appointed their own man as the minister of our autonomy, not one of us, a Czech, Lev Prchala. And the people . . . the people! Our people would not take it and called for elections. My brothers went, and I went to the meeting; people chanted:

> *We won't give them Carpathian land!*
> *We won't give our freedom to them!*
> *Neither the Poles nor the Hungarians*
> *will have our native land!*

"That's how it is, our Silver Land—it is Ukrainian! The Czechs gave

---

18. A *madyaron* is a derogatory term for a Transcarpathian who is believed to hope for a union with Hungary.

our boys no ammunition, no guns, and retreated, and just like they gave us up, they later gave up their own land to Hitler."

"The Czechs? What do they got to do with anything, if the Galicians were behind it all!" Margita exclaimed. The old man only spoke faster, to keep her from interrupting again:

"March 14, 1939! Thirty-nine . . . The Hungarian army crossed the border of our Carpathian Ukraine. On the fifteenth, Voloshyn announced the mobilization, and do you know, children, how many people signed themselves up? Three thousand! That very day! Men and women, we had the Women's Sich, too! Our people wanted to defend our land, oh yes, *we* stood up for it, not just our Sich soldiers! Let all those bastards hear that our Silver Land is Ukraine! Ivan Chuchka and Yakiv Golota, they led the march to Sevlyush and on to Khust. Our seminarians enlisted, dear boys! In the afternoon of March the fifteenth, the assembly elected Avgustyn Voloshyn president of Carpathian Ukraine. The German consul came and told them to turn themselves in. They did not. Voloshyn and Kolodzynsky surrendered nothing and no one. Mykhailo Kolodzynsky was killed in the battle of Krasne Pole.

"On the sixteenth, at nightfall, Voloshyn and his government left Khust.

"My brothers, and Stepanko Bidzilya with them, stayed with our aunt in Khust—Stepanko told me later, he was the only one left alive. My brothers! What they woke up to! In the morning, the mailman called up to their window. 'Rise up,' he said, 'Your Government fled! The Hungarians are near!' Downstairs in the street, there was a car, and men were giving out rifles and rations, so they all took one, Stepanko and my brothers, they did. They sang with the Sich troops *Ukraine is not dead yet*, and that other song they had, about Saint George and Saint Barbara, only where were those patron saints that day? Wherever they were, it wasn't with us.

"It was cold, really cold; Khust is in the mountains, and the cold rolled down the mountains into the valley. Freezing drizzle came down from the sky. Fog. The winds . . . It was morning, but dark as in winter, a gloaming. A gloaming, children! Five hundred Sich troops marched to Krasne Pole, and Vasylko with them. They held their lines for four hours under the Hungarian artillery barrage, the Sich troops and other Ukrainians, those who stayed behind when the Czechs left. They perished . . ."

The old man, overcome by memories, broke down in tears again. Styopa used the pause to step up to his father, put a hand on his shoulder, and draw him closer. "Now we don't want none of that," he said. "Let's go outside, get some air . . ." But, with sudden force, the old man shook off his son's hand like a feather, "I am not done telling you, children! Voloshyn . . . Voloshyn was not afraid. He had the courage not to bend to any of them. He was a patriot, a rare patriot! And what did the Russians do to him? Had him rot to death in jail. Our small autonomy, what a land it had been! We took care of people. The Hungarians, once they beat us, put four thousand men behind bars, the monsters. They cut off people's ears, gouged their eyes, beat them terribly. Bodies floated down the Tysa River, who knows how many? The river was full of the dead. The living . . . the living were in concentration camps in Varjúlapos. Some of our people, those who were not Ukraine-minded yet, there in the jails, they wanted to side with the Hungarians, welcomed *Magyarország*, but when our folks raised their voices and cried 'Glory to Ukraine!' those Ruthenians forgot their Hungarians—they were so impressed. Because Ukraine is and has always been in our land!"

Ivan shuddered. He and Mysko had only read about the Carpathian Ukraine, and once at Ostapenko's watched a documentary film sent from the diaspora about those events. The little country that, albeit for a short time, managed to exist, was doomed. The documentary footage showed Avgustyn Voloshyn, a Greek Catholic priest, calling the Slovaks and asking from his desk next to an expansive bookshelf filled with gold- and silver-titled tomes, "The Slovaks are about to declare their independence? What time? At ten?" Later, these words became for Ivan and Mysko a kind of inside joke, there was so much irony in them, obscured by the dark cloud of history, that the words emerged from it in a different context every time, in a different tone. "So, what time is independence?" one of them would ask, usually Mysko, who'd glance at his watch for the fuller effect. "As usual, at ten!" The other would answer.

"And Fedirtsio, the oldest, and Stepanko Bidzilya, they went with the Sich riflemen from the Polish lands, they all retreated. To the border. But the Hungarians struck a deal with the Poles to turn our men in, and there on the border . . . the Hungarians shot them, and our Fedirtsio, the oldest . . . Stepanko Bidzilya told it, he managed to hide. They lined the men up and fired, and then when the first line fell, fired on the second line, and they all cried 'Glory to Ukraine!' and the Hungarian sergeant couldn't stop wondering, Why'd they come to the Hungarian lands to build their Ukraine, asked them why they hadn't started from the middle of their own?"

"Some stories you're telling us for the night!" Margita wiped her tears with a tea towel. "It's all those Galicians who brought the trouble! They talked our boys into it! Our boys got shot and washed down the Tysa River, and they just vanished into their forests like they'd never been! You forget, you do, in your talk of Hungarians, forget how the Russians brought prisoners over from Hungary in '56! Remember the tanks in the streets? Hungarians beat you. Sure. And Russians, any better? The liberators, *pobyediteli,*[19] those drunkards! And in '64, remember? The mattresses in the jail were all black, those prisoners had set them on fire to send a signal, but who saw it or even heard of it?"

---

19. Russian for "the victors."

The old man no longer tried to answer, no longer talked. He lowered his head and sat whispering to himself. Silence fell. Everyone experienced it alone, separate from the others. Everything that had just been spoken and wept over was like the other side of the moon, incomprehensible and dark, and now that it was put before them, no one knew what to do next. One could not laugh about it. One could not drink to it. One could not live with it. The only sounds were the creak of a chair someone shifted on, the pop of the knuckles in someone's hand, someone's hesitant cough. Dark shadows, it seemed, ran across the walls of the room. The past, of which they knew so little, and now it manifested itself like a silent film, the long way of sorrows, from Avgustyn Voloshyn to Fedir Paikosh. The dead lay dead in the woods, and the living were silent above them.

The front door slammed shut; someone had come in from the street. A moment later, Myron Vasyliovych stood on the threshold of the mute dining room; he had gone to fetch something in his car. He took in the silent guests and hosts, and, intuiting things instantly, as only he could, said, "My dear in-law, much health and wealth to you and your home. May you live a hundred years!" And then he filled his lungs with air and began to sing "Mnohaya Lita" in his magnificent, resonant voice. "I-i-i-n jo-oy, and i-i-n he-alth!" he sang, and the others, one by one, joined in, at first quietly and then louder, and held "in joy" on to the song as if on to a lifeline. Many are dead, and the living are more in number yet, let us be living, let us sing glory to the living while we can.

"Ma-a-a-ny years, ble-e-e-e-ssed years!" They sang.

So much they put into their singing that even the old Paikosh forgot his sorrows and sat with his eyes closed, his face beatific, and Margita wiped her reddened eyes again and smiled—and then sang, wishing herself "Many years."

·

In November, power cuts began. The power would disappear for hours at a time nearly every day. Sounds faded with the lights. People returned to their ancestors' ancient daily rhythms, established back when everyone rose with the sun and went to sleep with the chickens, but people's minds were no longer ancient, they'd been poisoned by a different life, different laws of existence. You could have made a fire, but that required a different setting: not the urban landscape where a fire was associated with bundles of homeless men warming their hands over barrels, but a thick, old forest. You could have gone to live in nature, but for that you needed nature, not the concrete boxes of the new apartment blocks raised on muddy bogs, without order, with no thought given to their inhabitants' convenience.

Ivan's father would go to their neighbor's, where the two would play cards in the kitchen, and that's how they spent their nights, a pair of woozy old men. They had grown old and had nothing before them other than the table with the card game, but after a bottle of wine, this felt tolerable. They would not have been able to sit like that at Margita's, she'd be spitting fire at them. As soon as the lights went out, all domestic work stopped (and there was always plenty since Margita did not know how to sit still). Every time the electricity cut off, Margita cried out the way a martyr doomed to a horrible death might cry out in the moment when his sentence was delivered, a martyr who had known a long time that everything would go exactly like this and no other way, knew this and still hoped for a miracle, but the miracle never came. Margita would go sit by the window, where it was not much lighter than in the middle of the room, and start cursing the government, cursing it with words Ivan had never heard her speak before, all of them—the president's administration, the parliament, these newfangled politicians who yesterday were Komsomol activists—and the way she cursed them you'd think these people were evil incarnate, demonic spawn. Others were free to persist in the illusion that these were merely comical, incompetent people, but she, Margita, knew the terrible truth: their essence was of the Inferno born, they breathed death. Ivan would intervene, and be shocked that his mother, Margita, half Hungarian and half Slovak, was mourning the very body of Ukraine as it was being torn apart by dog-headed monsters. It was as if someone had taken old Paikosh's laments and translated them into a woman's tongue, a woman's tongue that spoke louder in darkness.

Phoebe felt nauseous all the time. Margita would listen outside the bathroom door, then ask Ivan, "Why's *your* wife throwing up again?" But he only shrugged, "I don't know." He wasn't touching Phoebe, hadn't touched her for two whole months since New Year's Eve, when they went to a party at Tolya D'Artagnan's, and Phoebe danced with men. She laughed. She was delicate, in a black dress with sparkles. Ivan had thought he no longer loved her, but his sudden jealousy surprised him. He grabbed her roughly, jerked her out of the dance circle, "Let's go home," he said, and they went, on foot, across the entire city, through fireworks and drunk shouting, through other people's fun. It was almost two when they got home. Margita must have woken up in her bedroom on the ground floor, she wouldn't have expected them so soon, would've thought the young 'uns would party until dawn as they ought to. The light went on in her window, then quickly went off. Ivan still had Phoebe by her hand, and he'd gladly have had her by her throat. He squeezed her hand so hard she yelped. Up on their floor, he went to the bathroom and ran the tap, thought of the gas heater coming on downstairs, listened to the measured hum of the pipes that could wake Margita again, she slept lightly, her entire body attuned to her house around her. Was she wondering, at that very moment, what they were doing? She could surprise them upstairs, so Ivan locked his door.

"Come here," he ordered Phoebe. He undressed her like a child. She did not resist, only looked at him with her humongous eyes. He recalled Margita telling him that Phoebe's eyes never laughed no matter how hard she was laughing. He could not look into her eyes now, he drew her into the bathtub, full now of warm, even hot, water, and switched off the lights, leaving only a night-light on in the hallway. He did not close the bathroom door—he would have his own wife in his own house!—climbed into the bathtub and there, in the water, turned Phoebe to face away from him and entered her, and did not leave until everything was over. Over for him, because nothing even started for her, and maybe that was for the better, let her get used to not expecting much from life, let her at least get used to being a woman like Margita, delighted with small things: preserves for the winter, an apple pie.

And now Margita was asking him, "Why is *your* wife throwing up? What do you mean, you don't know?" She stopped there, did not finish her thought because it wasn't decent for a mother to ask such a thing of her son. Since Ivan had no answer to give her, she kept talking to herself, muttered under her breath. She did not dare ask her daughter-in-law, such a delicate, apparently weak girl, but with eyes that never laughed. "Honey," she'd start on Ivan again. "Don't you be like those bumpkins from the village who can't tell when a wife's expecting. Don't you know?" Ivan would have very much liked to tell his mother he had no idea where children came from, but said nothing.

"All right then!" Margita would say, insulted. She was not schooled in the fine arts of polite conversation, was not at ease with talk. But she did teach herself to put the grievance in her voice, and this was a simple but effective weapon, like a log on chains that could break open the doors of any fortress had you failed to find a local willing to take you through the secret passage inside the walls for a price. "Sure, you'll just be bringing me children here and expect me to feed them!" she said, as if she'd forgotten all about the Raptors and her animallike love for them, about the bottles of milk, and the treats for those two overgrown louts. Perhaps she feared that Phoebe's children would be different, same as Phoebe: high-strung, aching, ever poised to leap into nowhere. Phoebe did not tell Ivan anything, only looked at him quizzically as if she expected him to open the conversation. Phoebe's eyes turned darker every day. Dark in the darkness, they gleamed and sparked with a hard edge, like knives.

Things came to a weird kind of balance. No one blamed Ivan for anything, no one spoke to him. Phoebe kept silent, turned inward. Margita cursed the government, his father got drunk at card games. Unlike the previous winter, Ivan did not have to trudge into a distant neighborhood to see Phoebe home or visit her. He did not even miss his conversations with his father-in-law. He missed no one, he only wanted to be left in peace, wanted everyone to leave him alone. He knew that this spell of peace would not last, that he would have to speak to Phoebe again, that he would have to tell Margita everything. But let it not be now, let it be just a little later. Every night when he came home, he prayed to the heavens: Let it not be today.

One night, just as he came in, Phoebe crawled down the stairs, came into Margita's living room, terribly pale, even in candlelight you could see how pale she was, and said, as she braced herself against the wall with one hand, "I am pregnant."

PART TWO
REVOLUTION

I shall clothe myself in Christ's shroud, my skin
is an iron armor, my blood is a vein of flint,
my bone is a sword swifter than an arrow,
more deadly than a sharp-eyed falcon. My armor is on me,
my Lord is inside me.

From Otaman Ivan Sirko's prayer before battle

IF IVAN EVER FOUND HIMSELF CALLED UPON TO DESCRIBE THIS autumn, he would have described it as light. Kyiv was made of countless cubes of light in all shades of yellow; they massed along the streets and in the city squares from the bright shades of fall foliage to the gold-tinged gossamer air. It was as if an artist had spared no paint and poured all of it into the chalice of the city, its hills and terraces, the steep bluffs along the river. Kyiv stood humming quietly in this glow like a taut string, while the threadbare, dry leaves of the trees let through glimpses of the gray walls of the downtown buildings and the white blazes of the delicate old houses on the Podil. The city brimmed with light.

Lviv was different. The light there was different: pale, almost northern mornings were followed by days filled with sharp-edged shadows like figures in a silent movie. Lviv was not a chalice, it was a tall, narrow flute carved of dark stone, and with the soul of the city locked deep at the bottom, tamed by its secret discipline. The light there flashed on steep roofs, sparked on red tile and steel-clad spires, and melted only to shoot up, become a needle, and then root under the ground where the River Poltva flowed, imprisoned. Lviv held a long, dark night deep in its heart, a night from which it could not bear to be parted. Lviv could never have summoned this much light.

It was October 2, 1990. Kyiv wrapped itself around them, clothed them in a protective cloak—many years later Margita would say it was near the Feast of the Intercession and the Holy Mother of God herself watched over them during those days. Margita, who had worked her entire life in a Soviet job, nonetheless lived by the liturgical calendar, as if in her own separate time. She had kept at least that much for herself. Ivan, on the other hand, lived like everyone else, in a fog out of which illicit festivities surfaced once in a while, strange occasions, and inexplicably important dates for which Margita always turned out well prepared; and while the KGB agents and schoolteachers hunted for those who went to church on liturgical feast days, Margita quietly baked Easter breads or set the ritual Christmas meal at home, lit candles, and muttered prayers.

Fifteen of them met up in the morning, right after getting off the train, in the *Dieta* cafeteria on Ivan Franko Street. Ivan drank sweet coffee out of a faceted glass; it was made weak with milk or water, he couldn't tell which. The place smelled of fresh dough, cinnamon, morning. Afterward, all of them, fifteen young men from Lviv, stood for a while outside the cafeteria, on the sidewalk, drunk on the warm air, light, and open space that pushed up here from the bluffs, from the Dnieper itself. Ivan was dying to see the river, but there was no time for that because they had to gather in the square at ten o'clock sharp. The Dnieper was nothing like the modest and tame Uzh—you could glimpse it from the hills—but its bed was cut deep and wide, and the steep trails down to the water were dense with bushes and trees.

Several men in riot police uniforms came into the cafeteria. Ivan turned to look at them. Was it possible they knew of the planned protest? But why now, this morning? Had the organizers made a mistake? How were they supposed to walk downtown to the square now? How would they reach the granite they intended to sit on? Would they even manage to sit? Or were they about to be caught one by one, handcuffed, and taken to parts unknown in black vans, never to be heard from again? After all, they did plan for such a scenario, and that's why other groups of five were scattered around the city, so that if indeed Ivan's group was detained, others would take their place. But they had to make it to the square at least! They had to do that much. Well-informed people reported that in Dnipropetrovsk, security forces had loaded dogs onto airplanes, specifically those perfectly schooled German Shepherds that were not so much trained working dogs as living weapons to be aimed at defenseless detainees and prisoners. The dogs were supposedly being taken to a dog show.

Tymish Gamkalo, nicknamed Gavkalo,[20] started laughing at the dog show ruse first thing in the morning when he and Ivan went out to smoke out by their railcar door. The train was approaching Kyiv, and they rode past the endless concrete platforms of suburban villages and stretches of forest where the autumn trees shuddered and flickered like candle flames in the wind. The dark space between the railcars was empty, and only the doors connecting them creaked open once in a while to let through an unfamiliar train attendant.

"Just think about it," Tymish had said to Ivan, "when they need to move armored personnel carriers they probably also take them to a trade show. They really should learn to lie better!"

Meanwhile, the riot policemen were peacefully drinking coffee. A pair of regular policemen chatted nearby, and Ivan thought they were even speaking Ukrainian. They did not look frightening at all, but rather domestic, perhaps because one of them had his face still crumpled from sleep, lines of folded fabric fresh on his cheek. Either he'd rolled out of bed a minute ago or had slept at the station.

---

20. From the word *gav* the Ukrainian onomatopoeic rendition of "woof!"

"Should we go to the Mariinska?" Ivan asked Bodya, "the Afghan," their head of security. Ivan was also in the security squad, it was made up exclusively of their own people, well-tested Lviv guys who had gone on more than a few protests and trips to clean up the graves of the Sich riflemen who'd fought against Russia.

"It's full of cops," was all Bodya said. His black eyes looked unblinking from under his furrowed brow.

Ten o'clock was coming fast. Ivan did not remember crossing the square or sitting down on its granite, and then there they were, on the black island in the middle of white-and-yellow Kyiv, on the granite quarried from the riverbanks that suddenly became their terra firma. They unfolded their signs: I'M ON A HUNGER STRIKE AGAINST THE GOVERNMENT, COMMUNISM IS SOVIET RULE PLUS NUCLEARIZATION PLUS BUREAUCRATIZATION PLUS IDIOTIZA-TION OF THE ENTIRE COUNTRY, NO TO THE NEW SOVIET BAR-RACKS! USU DECLARES POLITICAL HUNGER STRIKE, WE WON'T DRINK! WE WON'T EAT! TILL WE LIVE FREE! THE NEW UNION TREATY—LEG-IRONS FOR UKRAINE. They raised the big banner that listed their demands:

> *Young people of Ukraine! We, your peers, Ukrainian stu-*
> *dents, begin our hunger strike on October 2, at the Indepen-*
> *dence Maidan (the October Revolution Square) in Kyiv.*
> *We demand that the Supreme Council of Ukraine:*
> *Dismiss the Head of the Council of Ministers, Vitaly*
> *Masol;*
> *Hold new multiparty elections to the Supreme Council of*
> *Ukraine no later than Spring 1991;*
> *Adopt a resolution to nationalize all property of the So-*
> *viet Communist Party and Komsomol within the territory of*
> *Ukraine;*
> *Refuse to sign the Union treaty;*

Return to Ukraine all draftees who are performing their mandatory military service beyond the borders of Ukraine and guarantee future military service within the republic...

Around them, Kyiv's life swirled. Police came running but did not bother the students with their signs and banners. They milled nearby and spoke anxiously into their radios. Some time passed, and still nothing happened. Apparently, the police, for whatever reason, did not have orders "from the top"—quite possibly those "at the top" had no idea what to do with people who were just sitting on the granite pavement and going hungry. These people declared their hunger strike, and then did nothing else. Yes, they held up signs, black letters on white boards. Most slogan writers composed theirs in a serious tone, but there were also a few ironic jabs in the mix. Neither the police nor the passersby could grasp why these young people were sitting in the middle of the square—were they just common hooligans? No one in the Soviet Union, young people above all, was allowed to have a political opinion other than the one of complete and total approval of the Party and the government. The young were supposed to obey their elders.

At some point in the afternoon more signs were raised with names of supporting organizations: The Student Fraternity (from Lviv) and The Ukrainian Student Union (Kyiv). Someone started tearing sheets to make more white headbands for the hunger strikers, reinforcements came: a group of Kyiv students led by Ihor Rud' and another crew from Dnieprodzerzhinsk. Ihor Rud' and Yarema were friends and, rumor had it, came up with the idea of this protest together, and not just anywhere, but in Lithuania, where they had allegedly gone on Komsomol business.

Then everything began to spin, and Ivan's memory could only snatch and preserve separate pieces of what was happening. "What do you mean, home? You don't need to go home; you don't want to go home," he heard Yarema say to the student who had just helped Ivan tear a sheet into strips. The student stared at Yarema with round eyes, his mouth open. "My mom is there," he muttered. Yarema turned his entire body to face the young man, he was tall, a mountain of a man with a wild mop of hair. He put his hand on the student's shoulder and asked simply, without pathos, "What's your name?"—"S-slava."—"Listen, Slava, pal, we are here to make history and you want to run home and hide with your mom?"

Slava, naturally, didn't go anywhere. Passersby, meanwhile, began to approach them cautiously, and some came to stand by the rope that marked their perimeter. This was the perimeter that Ivan and other security squad guys were set to watch like hawks. No one was to cross it and enter the students' encampment itself. As things went, it was the security guards who were asked questions most often, about who they were, why they were doing this, etc. For the rest of the days on the Maidan, Ivan would speak in the coarse voice of a man with constantly overworked vocal cords.

"Now, who are you people?"

"See there, there's a sign that says 'Ukrainian Student Union' and another for 'Student Fraternity.'"

"Fraternity, eh?" the man shook his head and glancing at the cops over his shoulder, spoke rapidly, "You better get out of there, lads, with your fraternity. Don't you see you've got the dogs worked up!"

"We are not here to get anyone worked up. We have come because we have demands for our government."

The man looked at Ivan as if he were a three-headed alien, with a mix of shock, disbelief, and fear. His disbelief slowly took over the other two emotions, and the man snorted dismissively and left. Really, it was laughable. How could such small fry as this, say, Ivan, have "demands for our government"? That's absurd. The man might well have thought a studio was shooting a black comedy on the Maidan that day—except there was no camera crew yet.

Two elderly women, on their way past the encampment, slowed down and looked closer to read the signs, but as soon as they grasped their anti-Soviet messages, looked down and walked very quickly to get away. Ivan caught a snippet of their conversation, as one hurried the other in Russian:

"Come on, Irochka, don't look at them, they are parasites and freeloaders . . ."

"Sure," Tymish said. "Freeloaders who don't eat anything!"

Ivan remembered them discussing their demands: the point about nationalizing Party property had Gavkalo laughing for three days straight as he assured the guys this would be their ultimate downfall.

"This, specifically," Gavkalo told them, "this will get them up in arms! They would never accept this! What do you mean, you want to take away their special grocery stores? What are those honest Communists to eat then?"

•

It was the Lviv group that added the points about dismissing Masol and reforming the military service. "We have to be certain they have to give up something; they are too good at empty promises. We will fold up our tents only after we hear about Masol," Yarema told them, but no one really had any objections, especially when it came to the army. Later, on the Maidan, they would be joined by a few deserters, guys from different places in the Soviet Union who could not stand the harassment in the military and ran away from their bases. Bodya could only grind his teeth when he listened to their stories.

No one really knew how things went for Bodya in Afghanistan. He did not talk about it. Ivan pictured that country—its hot dust, its mountains, and its sun—but could get no further than that. Only once did Ivan catch a glimpse into Bodya's Afghanistan, when, after another protest, they all fell asleep at the small-town railway station where they waited for the train, and Bodya, asleep, started muttering in a foreign language. When they woke him up, he all but jumped to his feet. Someone asked him what language he was speaking.

"English. What did you think?" Bodya said.

"Get out of here!"

"Did you think I was friends with the mujahideen?"

"But who'd you have to speak English to?"

"The Americans, that's who," Bodya spat.

"What'd you talk about?"

"What do you think?"

That was the end of it. Maybe it really was English, Ivan was no good at it. Plus, the actual spoken language (if there had been, indeed, real Americans) could well be very different from what they had all studied in school, where they butchered both pronunciation and grammar and memorized wild tales about Lenin's childhood or heroic Young Pioneers, dead as doornails to the last man. Ivan wondered what Bodya could have talked about with Americans in Afghanistan. Weren't they the enemy? Or was it possible they were unfortunate drafted slaves, just like the Soviet soldiers?

Bodya made disapproving noises as he inspected the Kyivites. Bodya did not care for them and was against having them involved. He did not like their leader, Ihor Rud', who irritated him for ineffable personal reasons. He shrugged and walked away from Rud', thin as a beanstalk (Bodya: "In the army, they'd squash a mosquito like him dead on day two"), as Ihor spoke to his guys. The police detachments came closer. There were more of them, too. A few men in plain clothes arrived.

"Oh, look! The executive cadre!"

"Nah, they won't take us."

"And what if they wanted to?"

"Giya," someone was saying to Georgiy Gongadze, "We'll have to make sure to shove you out of here if they arrest us."

They had agreed that Giya would go raise the Caucasus.

Andriy Groma took the megaphone and began to speak:

"Friends! It is time to make a choice. Either we will win ourselves an independent, democratic Ukraine or we will remain a colony of the empire, a spiritually poor, robbed people. We don't want to be thinking later, as the poet said, 'And we stood by, and did not speak, and silent did we scratch our heads, we mute, despicable, enslaved.' This is why we call upon all of you to support our actions. The fate of our homeland depends on all of us. May God help us!"

There were almost no people around them now: the gawkers had left, and the passersby were afraid to stop. But one guy was so curious to hear what these strange students would say into their megaphone that he pretended to be tying a shoelace, stooped down on one knee nearby, and hid his face.

Yarema came back with someone from the city council that had, after all, issued them the permit for the event. A truck brought tents, blankets, and field cots.

They had won the first battle.

In a few hours, after nightfall, a tent city rose on the square.

•

When Ivan first came to Lviv in the last days of summer, he found that the spot in the dormitory he had been promised, and to which his right was documented on a piece of official-looking paper, had been given to someone else. Or not exactly given—how would he ever know? So his father, who had also been a student at one of Lviv's universities, pulled every string he could think of and found him a room to stay in. A bed in a room, to be precise, in an apartment in a building across the street from the lecture hall. The secession-era facades of the buildings on this street, incredibly neglected, shed bits of brick and plaster onto the cobblestones. Inside, there were series of rooms that opened onto each other and were thus ill-suited to family accommodations—these had once been requisitioned by the Bolsheviks from the original owners and subsequently repartitioned into bizarre dwellings. Some of these rooms were now inhabited by students—illogical, chimeric spaces, unpredictable as the turns of fortune in the time of epochal changes.

Life here was exciting and haphazard: conversations swirled, portable immersion heaters were lost and found, borrowed guitars were played, and something about which upperclassmen said "hot cannot be raw" simmered in pots in the communal kitchen. The place was irredeemably dirty; the old, rotten floors could not release the dust trapped in them, and neither could the walls, plastered here and there with bad wallpaper. The spirit that ruled these rooms, however, was one of genuine fraternity. There was a lot of laughter, a lot of talk about politics, and a lot of plans.

Once he got over the initial shock of living in this maelstrom, Ivan would look out of the window and brim with the happy sense of belonging, his head spinning. He would breathe in the cold, foggy Lviv air and survey his domain: the massive buildings of the Polytechnic University, almost all of which were located together here, not far from St. George's Cathedral, their patron saint. These buildings, these people, Ivan told himself, are a fortress, a literal city on a hill that knows how to take care of its own. The Polytechnic stood solid and confident, and stone lions kept watch over it.

Right away, it became clear to Ivan that folks did not pay much heed to Soviet rules here. The entire community had developed its own strategies of resistance and survival. The guys refused to be the gray, frightened shadows—the country was already full of them. Moreover, they refused brilliantly, with a laugh, probably exactly like the Zaporozhian Cossacks writing their reply to the Ottoman Sultan in Ilya Repin's famous painting. Andriy Groma, his roommate, a year ahead of him, asked Ivan the first week, "Why haven't you joined our Komsomol troop?"

Ivan made a face. Komsomol? Here? Of course, formally, they were all enrolled, but in practice . . . Ivan knew a few genuine career Komsomol people: his school's troop leader was in his class, and Ivan himself went to the dedicated room a few times. Every year, the school's Komsomol troop had a ceremony to induct new members; a fool's errand wherein the inductees had to recite the principles of "democratic centralism" from memory. After a Komsomol meeting, the upperclassmen would sit on the windowsills and smoke, so that the smoke wouldn't stay in the room.

The school was on the riverbank and was considered the "party school" for the regional elites. Just a bit farther, on the Post Square, kitty-corner from the Rock Garden, stood the eyesore of the City Party Committee building, where the school's Komsomol youth dreamed of landing. A job in the regional committee, then, represented the pinnacle of their ambition—that was housed in the White House, an elegant building of the Czech-rule time, in the heart of a manicured park.

"We run it here," Andriy clarified to the stunned Ivan, "on the Polish model."

This explanation did not help.

"The Polish model?" Ivan asked. Model of what, he thought, the tiny Fiat cars the Poles drove across the border to sell jeans?

"It's like this: the top is the top, and the Party is as strong as ever, but the grass roots are self-organizing. Like Solidarity, heard about them?" Andriy was losing his patience.

"Sure!" Ivan said, pretending to understand. He already knew that these guys traveled to other Soviet Republics and even other socialist countries on youth exchanges, but it was also clear they weren't exactly exchanging tips for Komsomol event management.

At first Ivan refused. He didn't need it. It's not like he had come to play at politics, he had to study. And on top of that, he was from Transcarpathia (this was not entirely true, as his father was born not far from Lviv). He tried these excuses on Andriy. Andriy wasn't exactly offended, only shrugged his shoulders, but almost in jest as if to say "Never say never; whether you're inside our Komsomol or out, we have a shared," he always used these same words, "*sense of grievance.*" Ivan waved him off, but he still went to a few meetings of the local organizations, the Student Fraternity and the Lion Brotherhood.

That was where Ivan met Yarema, who already was seen as something of a legend. The Student Fraternity was forever organizing something: they published a broadside, made posters, and demanded that the First Departments[21] at all universities be dismantled. They wanted military draftees from Ukraine only to serve in Ukrainian territory. This, Ivan thought, would win Margita's approval, because her greatest fear was to have Ivan fail entrance exams to the university, be drafted, and then get packed off to the end of the world, into the endless sands, or sent to fight someone else's war. Or stationed in Kamchatka. Or Sakhalin. Ivan remembered he laughed when she told him that, said, "So what, at least I'd see the volcanoes," and she cut him short.

It was also where Ivan met Tymish Gamkalo. Gamkalo—nicknamed Gavkalo—was smallish, had super-curly black hair, and always made Ivan think of a hedgehog. In addition to his analytic talents, Tymish knew how to "read" the newspapers—his family had

21. A cover for KGB officers whose job was to ensure the academic community's loyalty.

drilled it into him. He could read the front page of *Pravda* in such a way that everything fell into place: who was out of whose political favor and who failed to deliver on a promise and what that promise was. Often he'd go red in the face reading the Communist Party press, but to ignore it was beyond him. He was powerless against his twin yearnings for both outrage and Communist news media.

The first rallies in Lviv began at about the same time. Ivan wandered into one on his own, without Tymish. A woman spoke about her experience being imprisoned in Soviet camps. Ivan listened to her, stunned, looked at the crowd, which was quite large, and saw the long line of people who were still making their way to the rally spot at the Ivan Franko monument. He did not know what to think. He felt more lost and awkward than part of something important.

Later, he and Tymish went together. Different rallies were different, you didn't know what kind of speaker you would hear. Blue-and-yellow flags fluttered in the wind.

"Russia is an empire just like the USSR!" some people shouted.

"We are for a democratic Russia!" others exclaimed, which would send Tymish into convulsions, first with laughter, then with fury.

"What are they talking about, a democratic Russia!" he hissed. Another man climbed to the podium, hollered:

"Russia does not wish to be the big brother! We want to be a sister to you!"

"Bullshit!" Tymish spat.

"Well, wait, all right," Ivan tried to argue. "But why? There used to be liberals in Russia . . ."

He wasn't quite sure what he was talking about, something from the history classes tugged at his memory, *raznochintsy*, wasn't it?

"Show me one liberal of theirs who is willing to let the colonies go!"

"Colonies? Meaning, like, labor camps?" Ivan asked, and Tymish only whistled in response.

At night, Ivan returned to the labyrinths of his unexpected new life, where someone inevitably would be playing the guitar and singing, where sailors' noodles, the eternal student food, boiled on the stove. People read and talked. Above them and below them, to their left and to their right, in rented rooms and broom closets, roosted students just like them. Ivan studied his lecture notes, and since he had a good memory and a dependable dose of talent, he got decent grades even when he had to study amid utter chaos. He couldn't help but notice that most of his neighbors and friends were likewise doing fine academically; the chaos, apparently, was not a hindrance, as if these old, but not ancient, walls were imbued with a protective spirit.

Ivan's conversion happened a bit later and was so straightforward that if he'd heard it told as a story about someone else, he wouldn't believe it. That night, Tymish and Andriy planned to go visit a painter and invited him to come along, which Ivan did just to be in their company, not because he had any particular love for art.

The painter's place, a typical Lviv bachelor's flat (one room and a bath, no kitchen) on Rudnyeva Street, was thoroughly neglected and in this did not much differ from the digs where the Polytechnic gang dwelled. Dust covered every surface. It smelled like mold, and the dark parquet floor creaked underfoot. The floor was polished, or painted, with an unknown substance and covered here and there with striped woven Hutsul runners. Paintings and paraphernalia completely hid the walls: Japanese-style miniatures mixed with traditional Carpathian landscapes of mountains, meadows, thatched cottages, and churches on hills; there were large portraits of unknown women hung between abstract canvases. Everything in the apartment was smeared with paint. The easel held a work in progress—something that looked like a scene from *Ivanhoe*.

Andriy and Tymish listened while the painter talked about his favorite artists and teachers, showed prints, and pointed to paintings on his walls, and Ivan, who didn't very much like the painter because he seemed a weird character who struggled to put two words together and kept repeating himself, went to take a closer look at the canvas on the easel. The painting did, in fact, feature a knight, a bareheaded man dressed in chain mail and a long cloak with a lance in his hand. Above the man's head was a pennant with a coat of arms that featured a bird and something that looked like a smashed plant. There was a motto in Latin script, but Ivan didn't bother to read it because what could there possibly be, in this tired Walter Scott fan fiction? Ivan's eyes had all but slid off the painting when the letters suddenly came together into comprehensible words: "Knight Ivor Molybogovych."

Ivan rubbed his eyes. Why? How could he have understood the writing? Was it in one of the South Slavic languages? Or in Czech? He used to hear plenty of Czech; back home you could get TV broadcasts from Czechoslovakia and Hungary. Oddly affected, Ivan looked around him. Stacked against the wall, he found an entire series of paintings of knights and went to study them, lifting them carefully one by one. Here was the sturdy Dobroslav in a blue cloak and a blue-and-yellow coat of arms, a sword at his belt. Pylyp wearing chain mail and helmeted. Pylyp! Is that even a name in Czech? And finally, as if to dismiss Ivan's last doubts, there was "Volodymyr, Prince of Galicia," a royal figure in a blue ermine-lined cloak and a crown, with his coat of arms on his chest, a bird in flight in its center.

What *was* it? Ivan suddenly realized what affected him, why he felt the way he did. It was the look on their faces. He was looking at real knights, men who served as no one's entertainment, men whose faces were full of dignity and character. These were not the Cossack leaders of the Khmelnitsky times, guilty of every mortal sin. Nor were these the posturing tricksters of the silver screen who only cared about their power to infatuate the kind of women who stayed glued to their TV's night after night. Neither were these the ignorant poor peasants or near-paupers Ivan had been taught about in school by textbooks that held that "peasants and the land they work" inevitably meant serfdom and subjugation. No, the men in the paintings had lived in cities. Ivan read the captions: "Master of Zvenihorod," "Vasylko from Terebovlya," "Vsevolod from Przemysl." These were leaders of citizenry, commanders of troops, scholars.

Ivan searched his memory for what he had retained from his school history. Right, there was Kyivan Rus, once and never again, because the Mongols came and wiped it out, and then it was straight to Ivan Kalita[22] and the Russian tsars, with a footnote provided by an appropriately marginal, barely known principality of Galicia-Volhynia, hardly even worth mentioning, they were all penniless ne'er-do-wells who could only aspire to be a part of Muscovy, could never manage on their own.

Ivan asked the painter, pointing to the canvases:

"Who are these people? Were they really . . . ours?"

"Sure were," the painter nodded, pleased. "They're a commission I got for a dacha." Now Ivan thought the painter was joking. "It's kitsch. Have you heard the word?"

"But where did you get their names?"

"The names? Must've got them from a book; I couldn't have come up with them myself!"

"But the knights themselves, where are they from?"

"What do you mean, where? The Kingdom of Galicia-Volhynia, our early state."

"Our state," Ivan repeated.

---

22. Ivan Kalita, also Ivan I, Prince of Moscow, 1288–1340.

He burned with the *sense of grievance*, burned so hot he wanted to burst into sobs or punch a wall. How? Why? He knew nothing, he had been told nothing, he was never taught anything, anything at all. He had only been taught there was Moscow. And there was snow there. Even the winter festival in his native Uzhhorod was called, by the power of the local Communists, "Russian Winter." Whatever was Russian about it? And these, these men in the portraits had never been shown to Ivan's kind and, judging by how things were, never would be shown. Maybe, Ivan told himself, maybe it was because Transcarpathia was different, it had a different history, it had not been a part of Galicia-Volhynia but instead belonged to the mythical "white Croatians." All right, say that's true, but there were castles in Uzhhorod and Mukachevo. Why did he know so little about the men who had actually ruled from them? Was it because all kings and nobles were classed, by his textbooks, as "bloodsuckers of the people"? But bloodsuckers could not have eyes like these, faces like these!

Ivan thought of the Communist bosses he knew: they were all uniformly angry, doughty, ruddy-faced. He could not recall a single one who would carry himself with as much dignity as the men in the paintings. On the contrary, the bosses slumped their shoulders, grew big round bellies and triple chins, developed humps. They looked at you askance, did not even look properly but peeped at you, spied at you from under their furrowed brows. They shouted at their subordinates, and were shouted at by their superiors, exactly as in Taras Shevchenko's poem "The Dream," where Tsar-the-Father kicks his ministers, and they kick the lesser lords and their servants.

It occurred to Ivan that the painter was half kidding when he told him the portraits were for a dacha. Or not—a man with a dacha could, after all, have commissioned these if he had a taste for armor and heraldry. It would be very romantic.

The knights kept their own counsel. Their faces were enlightened, their spirit exalted. They held calmly onto their swords, wore their crowns and helmets dutifully.

It was Ivan's true history that faced him, and the very thought of it awakened his entire self, made his blood cry out from the bottom of its living well: This is I! This is mine own!

The painter turned to Tymish and Andriy, said:

"I see your friend is not too aware. Is he really one of ours?"

"We are working on him," Andriy answered without a hint of a smile.

•

The next morning, Ivan woke up to a new world.

The camp stood surrounded by a crowd of police. Were there, really, so many in Kyiv? Or had they been brought in from the rest of the union, to have an assembly right there on the square? But the square itself had been transformed: this place that had been so cold and inhospitable, with its field of barren granite, now swirled with life, buzzed with work. More than a hundred people had joined the hunger strike, most of them from Lviv. Medics walked between the rows of cots, talked to people, distributed drinking water. Someone was working on linking up with the press, others found cars to take organizers to the local universities, each accompanied by a striker with a white headband. Mysko, who did join the hunger strike, would later tell Ivan the hardest part of it was being nauseous all the time and having to drink volumes and volumes of warm distilled water.

The security squad was, of course, fed outside the camp, so as not to torment the strikers, God forbid, with the sight and smell of food. Ivan ate, standing up, along with Tymish Gamkalo and that Slava whom Yarema had talked out of going home, at a table in a typical Soviet cafeteria with no seating or table service, designed for people to wolf down their food and rush out, letting other proletarians take their spot, all of them too keen to work for the benefit of the Communist state to care about what they ate. Women in white uniforms ran the kitchen. The guys got blobs of unappetizing mashed potatoes slapped onto their plates and a steamed cutlet and a glass of tepid tea each.

"How are things here?" Tymish asked Slava, the only one of them from Kyiv.

"There was a rally. Several columns of people, tons of them. The Democratic Bloc came out to talk," Slava reported rapidly, in between gulps. "We carried our banner, but all Kravchuk did was yell at Mykhailo Goryn that he'll have *no consolidation with the opposition, never a consolidation with the opposition.* Goryn was all fancy, with his blue-and-yellow tie. Then Serhiy Konyev came out, he said, again, the parliament should be dissolved."—"And then what?"—"What-what? Nothing. It's still there."—"Yeah, it's still there, for now," Tymish nodded. "And the people sang, Kravchuchok, Kravchuchok, little bird, why don't you fly away to Moscow once and for all! It was very nice," Slava said and smiled as he finished his tea.

More reinforcements arrived: geography and geology students with their constant leader, Oleh, nicknamed "the Geographer." Everyone in this group was tall and rugged as if the land they studied imbued them with its own fortitude. "My Volhynia lads!" the blond Oleh called them, but not all of them were from Volhynia. But the name stuck. Ivan knew the Geographer a little, and he was, in fact, born in Lutsk, but had lived, along with his parents, in Lviv for a long time. Still, the region had not lost the significance it held for Oleh. It was there, he told them, that the Ukrainian Resistance Army began, and also there that it was most cruelly and casually betrayed. The Geographer's lads wasted no time in living up to their reputation of hotheads and daredevils and soon raised a sign that boldly read: "Volhynia does not want to be a part of the Union!" The Geographer laughed at this. Ivan liked listening to him; the man could talk to anyone, possibly even animals and birds.

Closer to lunch the weather got warmer, the sun came out and filled the square with light. Handfuls of locals filed into the camp, bards, poets, dissidents, there were so many of them! The actress Neonila Kryukova came. She was incredibly beautiful. She made a white headband for herself and joined the hunger strike. "If we do not become masters of ourselves, if we do not defend ourselves, no one will help us. This is why my first demand with which I join these students is complete sovereignty of Ukraine!" she said into the megaphone, and her voice and her beauty made the policemen, who stood bolt-upright and tense around them, loosen up a bit and come alive. Ivan admired and revered her. He'd never seen this woman before, neither on the stage nor in the movies. Something about her reminded him of Rose, but Rose could be prickly, she lurched and strove through her thorns, through the thorns of the world, while this woman appeared to be in total harmony with herself.

Yurko Galaida, Bodya's deputy, arrived, and Yarema announced a few changes: Bodya was to become a coleader of the entire protest, and Yurko would take over as head of security. Those who did not know Yurko might have thought this was, at least, a very odd decision to make, because how would this small, freckled man with a constant smile on his face manage such a machine? But Ivan had gone with Yurko to Zaporizhzhia to preserve Cossack graves and had had a chance to witness the steppe-dweller's endurance that lay behind Yurko's warmth and good cheer, the incredible power of concentration he had, how steely his voice could be. Ivan knew Yurko was a grandson of farmers who had been dispossessed and displaced by Stalin's dekulakization campaign. Yurko regarded the world as if it were a wall map, without fear. Life could drop him in the middle of anywhere on earth, and he would manage just fine.

In his new role as head of security, Yurko gathered the squad, inspected the perimeter ("Keep holding it"), and then stood to the side. He did not talk to passersby and casual visitors. Ivan and Mysko exchanged a look: Yurko, it seemed, had the valuable and rare gift of being able to analyze movement, even in a system; this was an important field for Mysko. Yurko did nothing superfluous, always saw anything that went wrong anywhere and went to address the problem. He reacted to the smallest irregularity. Yurko looked at the world through half-hooded eyes, as if not focusing on anything in particular. Such a look, Mysko had told Ivan, was often cultivated in martial arts.

Random Kyivites now stopped by the camp more often, but none stayed long, they went on their way. Someone had brought a bunch of warm sweaters and blankets, and a kind soul handed over a touching bag of small three-kopeck buns. The security squad refused all donations of food on the spot. Yurko Galaida paid particular attention to this. A gray mustachioed man reached in and lifted the rope that marked the edge of the camp. He dove under it. Ivan stopped him, "Where are you going? Please return to the other side."—"I'm Levko Lukyanenko," the man belatedly introduced himself. For a moment they stood facing each other: Ivan not sure what to do next, and Lukyanenko waiting to be let in. Then Oleh the Geographer ran up, and he and Lukyanenko embraced like old friends, laughing. Orest Ostapenko, the elder dissident, made his way toward them from the other side of the camp.

Mysko sat beside a grandmotherly old lady who wore thick glasses. The woman had already put on the white headband indicating she had joined the hunger strike. Ivan listened closely to their conversation: he was keeping an eye on Mysko, worried about him.

The woman was asking Mysko if he had started the strike correctly; it was important to follow a certain sequence to avoid an obstruction of the bowels. Mysko solemnly promised that he did, that he had worked very hard to do things properly. Ivan could barely help laughing, he had seen Mysko snarf links of sausage on the train the day before.

"Do you know who that is?" Ostapenko asked Ivan, pointing to the old woman. "No."—"That's Oksana Meshko. Not just any old lady."—"Do you know her?"—"I do, quite well. If it weren't for her, I probably wouldn't have been let out of prison." And Orest Ostapenko told Ivan that this was the seemingly ageless "Grandma Oksana, Mother of Cossacks," the woman who defended and worked for the Helsinki Group, a human rights organization that called out abuses in the dark Brezhnev days. For this, the KGB packed her, an already elderly woman who had been imprisoned in the gulag in her youth, off to Siberia for five years and took several months to transport her there just to wear her down in the process. They took her way out to the shore of the Sea of Okhotsk, where she was to live in a log cabin that was completely covered by snow in winter, so she could not go outside. And the old woman lived there alone, listened to the waves and the falling snow, lit a candle, and prayed. Eventually, she was released and went to Australia, at the invitation of the Ukrainian diaspora, where she proceeded to read off dissidents' names for the whole world to hear at a special session of the Australian Parliament. Then Grandma Oksana went to America. And then, just to spite her tormentors, she came back home. The KGB had hoped that the old lady had had enough of the hard life and would stay in the West. But she did not.

Ivan studied the old woman's face, so chiseled, so full of power it was not old at all. Where did she draw her strength from? She must have had a great power of love inside her, and another, just as great, the power of hate in order not to be broken. Most people are afraid of feeling hatred, Mysko had told him. They fear carrying it inside them, fear knowing it about themselves.

Stepan Khmara, member of the Supreme Council and another former political prisoner, came running—he was wearing a track-suit and a fake fur coat with its price tag still attached. He was in such a rush to see the students that he must've just popped into a store and grabbed the first thing that seemed useful in case of the weather turning cold. He had a striking face: stern, with high, sharp cheekbones, dark tanned. "You know, you're being a bit too cocky, boys," he said. "How is it that you have none of our peo-ple among your leadership? How dare you?" He spoke angrily. He was, in fact, angry at them and was not about to hide it. His deep-set eyes pinned down whomever he was talking to. His was a hard gaze to hold. But the young men laughed.

"They are on their own," Orest Ostapenko said to Khmara; Ostapenko had made his peace with the way things were. His face had relaxed, all frustration long gone, and now he all but glowed with joy. Khmara blinked at him, then again at the guys, and said nothing. He just sat down on the granite with them.

Later, they sang the old battle song "The Red Viburnum." Bards came, and Marichka Burmaka with them. Oleh Pokalchuk. They sang "The Student Squad Does Not Retreat." The exhilara-tion of the crowd did not let up. Ivan closed his eyes, and when he opened them again, Rose stood before him.

"You? But . . ." he could only exhale.

The girls were not supposed to come with them. This had occasioned a storm, the girls argued they wanted to be a part of the protest, but the guys, Yarema foremost, were implacable: no and no, because it was likely—guaranteed in fact!—to be danger-ous. Having any girls participate in the hunger strike was out of the question: they were future mothers and could not jeopardize their health. "My health? My, how did you put it, future children? You should be ashamed of yourself! You are a hypocrite!" Rose yelled into Yarema's face when he declared this position during the last meeting before they went to Kyiv. "Why should I be held hostage by my own body? You don't think there's anything wrong with this, do you? You don't feel I should be the one who decides what to do with my body? I and I alone, and not some phantom children that I might never want to have!".

Yarema said only that it was an order, it had been decided, and the point was not open to discussion. On their way back from the meeting to their dorms, Ivan kept trying to cheer Rose up: he genuinely did not understand why Rose could not accept the leadership's decision since it had been dictated by logic and a rational approach to things. "How do you not understand? It's discrimination!" Rose could barely breathe, she was so furious. "Wait, what? How?" Ivan asked. He felt insulted because he really, truly did not understand. "How is it discrimination that I was born a man and you a woman? Shall we be mad at evolution itself? For having us be born humans and not, say, pythons?"—"What do pythons have to do with anything!"

And Rose stood there in the streetlamp light, in the middle of the sidewalk, gasping and rushing, and not entirely sure how to put what she felt into words, shouted into Ivan's face that She! Would not! Be treated! As a body alone! Like a piece of meat! That she was a person and Yarema's order could mean only one thing: that the guys did not see her as an equal human being. That they dehumanized her. "You're wrong!" Ivan argued back, waving his arms at her. "You know full well it's not like that. It's just that we are different, and we have different jobs to do!"—"Who told you that? And if so, then why was it only in the twentieth century that women got the vote? Women fought in the Kengir uprising right along with the men!"—"What are you talking about, the vote? Why can't you see that we just want to protect you? And what's Kengir got to do with anything? Those were prisoners, it was totally different. And the vote—that's not fair, either. Men, serfs, didn't have the vote, did they? Plus, all we're talking about is one protest. A single event. You've gone everywhere with us before—to Zaporizhzhia and other places. . ."

"Right! We did. And what did we do there while you were busy with your all-important men's work? We'd get up, go get the water, boil it, make food, feed you, wash up, sweep, tidy, and then it was time to make lunch, and it was like that all day! Did you forget? Oh, I'm sorry, how could you forget? You never even noticed! None of it even existed for you!"

Ivan felt deeply upset, but there was no way he could've gotten a single word into Rose's harangue.

"And now you won't take us with you, because, of course, you won't need anyone to make your food, you are going to starve! Be martyrs!"

"Rose!"

That was how they parted. Ivan felt terrible—about the argument, and about the deserted street that stretched before him like a premonition of something that hadn't yet happened but was one day destined to come. And now there she was, right in front of him—happy, smiling, elated. Turned out, Rose had brought their flag. The blue-and-yellow one. Somehow, they had left it behind when they packed. She also found the time to call the rest of the girls in Lviv to tell them to come, because they also had the right to protest and to be here. Yarema started to object, tried to talk to her, but this time she did not even engage with him. She kept smiling, and with Neonila Kryukova's wholehearted endorsement ("The girls absolutely have the right to go on hunger strike and to be here, and you, Rose, will stay with me for the night"), put on the white headband and lay down on a cot. Even then, she looked like stubbornness incarnate.

Someone local brought the first bunch of flowers and put it down on the granite pavement right outside the perimeter. Asters. Their yellow and red blooms burned on the gray stone like flares of alarm.

•

Who knows how Ivan's life in Lviv would have gone had he not found the Twisted Linden. It was, of course, Tymish who had brought him there. The Twisted Linden was not just a watering hole or a café but an alley, a pedestrian shortcut between two streets, Zhovtneva and September Seventeenth. During the warm parts of the year, the alley, a few buildings long, fell almost entirely into the shade of what must have been a two-hundred-year-old tree. Ivan would never have turned into the entrance off September Seventeenth Street, in fact, he would steer clear of it. A one-legged old man hovered at the entrance all day long; he stamped his crutches on the ground and hurled obscenities at passersby, spit flying. The air wafting from the alley smelled of homemade alcohol and something else, ancient filth without a name.

Andriy Groma went there, too, skinny, swarthy, with his aquiline nose like Nikolai Gogol's, a man forever in love with history and its architecture. He'd throw his head back and study the lines, absorb their tempered beauty, and then talk, tell Ivan about the Vienna Secession and urban planning at the end of the nineteenth century. "Look, look up there, the facades mirror each other," he'd say, pointing. "Are they identical? They don't seem to be," Ivan asked. "No, they aren't, just in the same style. They echo each other." Groma gazed with love at the crumbling plaster. Ivan knew very little about architectural styles and nothing whatsoever about secession, but he, too, began to look closer at the pale yellow, beige, and gray facades, the lines of window frames and cornices, and found himself captivated by their elegance. Bas-reliefs—small, detailed human heads—gazed straight ahead from above each window. Branches of the old linden, which was, in fact, twisted, brushed the windowsills.

There was a store there, a common Soviet grocery store, bereft of secessionist ambition, but fitted with an eternally wet flagstone floor and the ineradicable smells of soured milk and low-grade moonshine. People were, as Tymish explained to Ivan, served illegal moonshine here, but only a select few, loyal and trustworthy clients. One of them would keep a lookout while the saleswoman poured under the counter. This was the time of Gorbachev's anti-alcohol campaign, when vineyards in Transcarpathia were being chopped down. Having had their ritual drink, the loyal drunkards would go into the alley to "air out," but the air was full of various fumes; the alley kept smells and sounds trapped, heavy and hovering a long time. The regulars perched on turned-over, empty industrial-sized cans that used to hold herring or seaweed, reached for their cigarettes (some even with filters) or hand-rolled tobacco from several stubs into one new cigarette, whatever luck sent them that day, and smoked. The invalid with his crutches looked hungrily at their mouths but did not come begging—he knew from experience they wouldn't give him anything. He wasn't worried, though, he'd score something later, when a higher-class customer from among the black-market traders swung by the store.

"You don't come here to drink, do you?" Ivan asked Tymish hopefully the first time they went there. Tymish most certainly did not fit in with the rest of the store's clientele.

Tymish snorted.

"Just wait until the rest of our gang show up."

People did show up, trickled in slowly, mostly students but also local artists, poets, writers—you felt an urge to rhyme something with "corpses" about them, more because of the pallid tint of their

faces than their age: these must have been members of the secret
sleepless caste who spent their days watching the clock at work and
came to life at night when they painted, treated carved wood with
horrifying chemical concoctions, and, of course, drank. Someone
inevitably would bring a bottle, and booze in it, not much better
than the stuff the busty saleswomen ladled out. People made alcohol by mixing together whatever they could find: honey, vodka or
moonshine, sugar, the last drops of wine, or even disgusting store-
bought jarred fruit juice, apple or grape. The juice, whenever it
appeared on store shelves, instantly became an object of citywide
pursuit by the needy and the thirsty.

Meanwhile, the actual winos dispersed to nearby buildings, and
the great cans in front of the store now served as stools for musicians
who came to jam. On the nights when the musicians did not come
there was conversation—about writers, philosophers, everything
in the world. A novel by Marquez (Gabriel Garcia, not to be confused with Marx) had come out and those who read it argued about
it until they grew hoarse. Yurko Pokalchuk translated a few other
Latin American writers, and they were subject to similar debates.
The journal *Foreign Literature* printed a bit of Borges in translation,
and the most committed found their way to Carlos Castaneda's psy-
chedelic texts. The world existed, and it was not nearly as gray and
boring as it looked when viewed from inside Soviet reality. It was at
one of these discussions that Ivan met Mysko.

You could not possibly miss Mysko, in any group. He had flam-
ing red hair and a face as expressive as a movie actor's. Later, once
Ivan had seen a few of Werner Herzog's films, he would call Mysko
Aguirre, the Wrath of God in his mind, but sometimes also out
loud. This was not entirely fair because Mysko never did anything
remotely angry or even just ill-considered. Everything about him,
it seemed, was subject to his internal discipline, including his pas-
sions. Ivan would not be able to recall what their first conversation

was about (Mysko would say it was about hallucinogenic mush-
rooms, but Ivan only waved him off—Mysko also had a highly
developed sense of humor.) Soon they became inseparable.

Mysko, as it turned out, was also a student at the Polytechnic,
and yet somehow he and Ivan hadn't crossed paths until then.
Mysko was not a member of the Student Fraternity and seldom
went to any meetings, conferences, or other gatherings. It was
his opinion that one needed no external institutions to pursue
self-development, which he understood as the cultivation of one's
own character. Who knows what books Mysko had read in addition to Castaneda, but he developed his own unique system of
self-improvement.

This consisted of a great variety of odd exercises, some of
which Mysko shared with Ivan. For example, one had to walk to
an intersection with one's eyes closed, being guided by the flows of
energy. Or locate a hidden object at first try. The exercise in observ-
ing people was the most interesting of all: they would choose a person and study him or her—you couldn't follow them, of course,
because that could give an innocent bystander a fright or prompt a
jab in the teeth from someone more suspicious. So Ivan and Mysko
would look for someone who was more or less stationary, in a long,
slow-moving line, say, in which case they would join the same line,
or someone idly sitting on a bench.

The first question they set to answer was about the subject's
profession or vocation, the second about their temperament, and
the rest came rolling like stones from a mountain. Does this person have strong will? Is he (or she) worried, this very moment,
about a pressing matter, and if so, what might that matter be? Are
they capable of a desperate act? What kind of relationship do they
have with their family? Do they read? Do they like music, and if so,
what kind? Do they listen to Voice of America on the radio? And
so on. Ivan and Mysko could spend hours talking about a stranger's

features or a single gesture. Of course, they had no way of confirming or disproving any of their many hypotheses.

One night, Mysko asked Ivan, "What do you think? That dude over there, who is he?" and pointed to the one-legged man of the Twisted Linden. Ivan considered the question. He realized he had never really paid any attention to the man. "I don't know," he said. "A veteran?"—"Of which war then?"

Ivan looked closer. It was impossible to tell the man's age: he slouched, his skin was tough as leather, and he had the dreadful bottomless cough of a miner or a chain-gang worker. He may well have fought in the Second World War, in which case he would have to be over seventy. Seventy! And for how long had he been living the way he lived? Since the forties? Mysko squinted, said, "Look closely. And listen."

The man was swearing at passersby, but the stream of it was not mere profanity, there was another layer there, *fenya*, the criminal argot. There was no way to come close enough to him to see if he had tattoos, but the way he held his cigarette, turned toward his palm, confirmed he had done time. He did not look like a political prisoner, and yet neither did he seem like a petty thief, he wasn't quite so abject. He might have had an education. Ivan looked closer, the man was no more than sixty. His indiscriminate rage aged him—his rage and his graveyard cough.

Now Ivan tried to keep an eye on the one-legged man. He spent the entire evening listening to his cough, to his obscenities and curses that erupted from him like black lava from Krakatoa. The man went on about his miserable life and occasionally swung a crutch at the feet of a passing pedestrian in a paroxysm of impotent rage. Then he would shout something rude at his victim's back. Later, once someone treated him to cigarettes and a drink, he would calm down, find a stone step to sit on, and talk to his benefactor a bit.

"He's very angry," Ivan said to Mysko. "That's obvious. Did you notice he hates women? He keeps trying to hit them when they go by. Why do you think that is?"—"His wife left him? When he went to jail?"

The one-legged man convulsed in another fit of coughing, and the sound of it, what came out of his ravaged lungs, held the story of a life that was terrifying to imagine. The man did not evoke sympathy, or any fellow feeling, but after that day, sometimes Ivan would give him a cigarette or two. He could no longer walk past this vicious, and pitiful, human being as he had before, without a thought.

A bit later Ivan met Rose Voytovych. He saw her first, to be exact, there in the Twisted Linden alley at a jam session. He nodded at Mysko, meaning, *Let's watch this one*, but he was fooling himself. He knew from the instant he'd laid his eyes on her that he wanted no observation of the kind they practiced. He just wanted to stare at this girl in mute admiration. She also went to the Polytechnic, and he might well have seen her during the day, in a classroom somewhere, but if he had, he did not take a good look at her.

Rose was, in fact, extraordinarily beautiful, with her black wavy hair, her bright lips that needed no lipstick, and her white-toothed smile. She was dressed in something similarly bright and colorful: Ivan looked closer and saw it was an embroidered blouse, but reinterpreted from the traditional Ukrainian style, with a pattern of large red flowers. People used to import such blouses from Bulgaria—Ivan knew this because his sister, Christina, in the short interval between graduating from high school and marrying Styopa, was very much into fashion, borrowed *Burda* magazines from her friends, and knew a thing or two about style. Styopa had taken great pleasure in putting an end to this particular hobby of hers.

Ivan could never remember exactly how he and Rose met. Mysko, most likely, simply came up to the young woman and introduced himself with his characteristic Olympian serenity, and then nodded at Ivan, his friend. Neither could Ivan recall what they talked about at first; he only remembered this dazzling, red-hot thing that he felt coming at him. Rose was very much like a scarlet flower, never shy to argue, always ready to defend her opinion or someone else's if she approved of it.

She was full of surprises. She was a regular in the social circles of which Ivan was vaguely aware but never a member, and which were absolutely beyond Mysko, who did not like social gatherings, or Tymish, whose nickname, Gavkalo, reflected the limited range of his communication style. And yet Rose, who was not originally from Lviv, had found these people and they accepted her as one of their own.

These were artists and actors, less often writers and musicians, and the fewest yet, people of obvious but unclassifiable talent (since the Soviet Union had no room for the kind of creativity that would later be called entrepreneurship). These people knew how to stand out in the crowd with their clothes alone, which did not have to mean wearing an embroidered blouse like Rose's, but details were important, and these details usually related to authentic Ukrainian and, more specifically, Hutsul dress. A ceramic pendant or a band of embroidery, a hand-tooled purse or a tapestry *taistra* bag; these people even made their own kind of *kabats*, traditional winter coats, by recutting standard-issue wool army coats. The authentic kabats were felted and embroidered in woolen thread, but even these, made from a uniform and stitched with acrylic yarn from children's scarves, appeared as powerful as magic talismans; and as a direct challenge to a Soviet society that was so focused on erasing differences and devaluing individual nations.

These people wished to socialize within their own circle, and to marry, similarly, among themselves; they had started the trend of silver bespoke wedding bands made by master jewelers from the same circles. Within this community, everyone read samizdat and *tamizdat,* were on personal terms with artists like Sergei Parajanov, held dinner parties at Taras Chubay's, were family, friends, and altogether seemed a bit like a caste rooted as much in their shared customs (Easters and *verteps* together) as in their resistance to the Soviet system.

Rose was welcome to the apartments where everyone got together with everyone else on planned and not-so-planned occasions, and took Ivan with her. One time they found themselves backstage at a tiny theater among the sets and the costumes. Ivan was amazed at how massive the props really were. They could have played hide-and-seek in this dormant kingdom, could make up a performance of their own with themselves as the stars, could dress as a king and a wise peasant woman or a pair of penguins, they could laugh among the waves of the stiff, faded fabric, transport themselves into a different dimension, imagine an entirely different life—or a few of those. Another time, they ended up at someone's suburban house outside Lviv and it took them all night to get back because the buses had stopped running.

Rose was especially fond of poetry and had a circle of like-minded friends. They read out loud poems by Bohdan Antonych, Yevhen Pluzhnyk, and Taras Chubay, as well as Lesya Ukrainka, Shevchenko, Kalynets, Olena Teliha, and Vasyl Stus. They followed contemporary young poets Ivan never heard of: Andrukhovych, Neborak, Malkovych. They read with tremendous passion; the words brought tears to your eyes. At first, Ivan went to these poetry evenings solely because of Rose, but with time he found, to his own surprise, that he had gotten used to hearing poetry, learned the different voices, and was even capable of missing poems if he had not heard any for a while.

> *I am poor in spirit, I am,*
> *an abject, abject thing...*

There's Tychyna, and Rylsky, and Oles'
and no one, truly no one . . . [23]

They frequented the café at the Galician square, the one in an alley that led to Shota Rustaveli Street, as well as the *Chervona Kalyna,* or Red Viburnum, next to the philharmonic, commonly abbreviated as Che Ka and a favorite haunt of poets. Ivan was game for any adventure as long as he could be with Rose. Later, when he married Phoebe, when he attempted to silence her poems forever, he would come to avoid poetry, but it would be too late. One can forget the words but not the rhythms, and the rhythm would remain vibrating inside him, the faithful tuning fork of his true existence.

•

More people came. Many wanted to join the hunger strike. There were Ukrainians from everywhere, Russians, Georgians. The locals kept bringing flowers and warm clothes, and would not stop trying, although much less often, to feed "the children," as mothers and grandmothers called the students. But the students were on hunger strike, they did not accept any food and asked the well-wishers not to bring any. There was a daily medical exam and one was not allowed to miss it.

Curious bystanders kept asking, "Are the students really eating nothing?" Obviously, a counterpropaganda effort was afoot wherein someone was spreading the whispered rumor that the students were but common hooligans and stuffed themselves with bologna sandwiches in their tents when no one could see them, and that they had no political agenda whatsoever, none at all, except

---

23. Yevhen Pluzhnyk, "Galileo" (1926)

their own immediate gain of the kind that was well known to anyone in the land of the Soviets. Yarema tirelessly explained to everyone who would listen that no, no one was eating anything, they were very strict about it, and that's exactly why they had the daily medical checks. If someone missed one, they might let it slide, but if a person did not show up twice in a row, they had to leave the strike.

Volodya Kendzior, leader of the medical team, a fifth-year medical student himself, examined everyone each day and reported the results. In the last two days, Volodya grew concerned, some of the protesters were running a temperature, and many were weak.

"Not all of them will last much longer," he told Yarema, and Yarema, too, was anxious. He asked that the weakest be convinced to stop the strike; after all, people were different, there could be no single standard for everyone. The protesters refused to quit and pursed their lips in defiance. People were losing weight, cheekbones protruded on many faces. It was cold at night, and that seemed to wear them out more than the hunger itself, more than the tension.

Yarema now spent less time at the Kyiv City Council. He wanted to be here, with his people. He stood beside Ivan, and they took in the sight of the square. Ivan could have asked his friend if he thought they would, in fact, get a result, but he did not dare. Let's say he did, and then what? Yarema already had plenty to worry about. Plus, Ivan did not want to sound like a pathetic weakling who could not go on without personal encouragement. After all, who was he to expect to be encouraged?

"Tired?" he asked Yarema instead.

"Not really . . . I've just been thinking," Yarema said. He caught Ivan's concerned look and added, "Not about the Maidan. About my dog."

"Your dog?" Ivan was surprised, he had no idea Yarema had a dog. But Yarema did not live in the dorms, his family was from Lviv. He could well have kept a dog. "What happened to him?"

"Nothing. My brother took him in."

"What kind of dog is he?"

Yarema smiled. The smile did not leave his face for as long as he spoke about his dog.

"Well . . . about yea big, floppy ears," he gestured to illustrate. "He's a mutt, we think he is part Airedale for sure, and something else. Dad found him outside, brought him in, and gave him to me. Said, 'Here, have a dog.'"

"And how's he doing at your brother's?"

Yarema sighed. His smiled vanished.

"He's good. Eats fine and everything. Doesn't miss me."

"And you wish he did?" It was Ivan's turn to smile. Yarema glanced at him and laughed.

"Yeah, I do! You got me there!"

They were interrupted, some kind local soul had brought them a giant can of condensed milk—not the thirteen-ounce one you could buy at the store, but the institutional size, a gallon. If he had only brought it, things would've been easier, Yurko Galaida and his boys had plenty of practice refusing food politely, but this particular gentleman had taken the trouble of opening the jar. Condensed milk was a popular thing; in the gulag people called this food— nutritious, filling, and full of sugars and fats—a "vaccine." A jar like that could save a man's life in Stalin's camps, but here, on the Maidan, among starving students, it was unacceptable.

"All right, get it out of here!" Galaida ordered. The condensed milk looked pearlescent in the light and tempted everyone, including those on hunger strike. Yurko had only one option: to take the can himself and carry it somewhere out of the tent city, where he could pour the stuff down the drain or toss it into a garbage can. It's not like the security squad was going to feast on it while the hungry looked on. Also, it occurred to Ivan, they didn't have any spoons.

Yarema rushed to help. There were rumors that their detractors tried to smuggle poisoned food into the camp nearly every day, which made it all the more important to find a drain to dispose of the milk rather than just leaving it with the trash—someone might go for it if it were just sitting out in the open. You never knew with people and free food.

Rose lay on her cot covered with several blankets. Every day Ivan spent a few hours with her when he was not on duty. He went and sat on the cot next to hers, took her hand in his. Rose's hand was hot; she, too, was running a fever.

"Hey, have they taken your temperature today? Do you want me to go get Volodya?" he asked. His tone upset her. "Let's not talk about it," she said irritably. He did not mind her being sharp with him, he knew a hungry person had no patience. "I'm just worried. I am not going to tell you to stop," he said peaceably. He did not want to cause her any stress. She did not respond. She closed her eyes and just lay there, pale, with her white headband. Ivan put his hand on her forehead, it was also hot. "Damn it!" she said abruptly. "It's not you that I'm mad at, you know? It's me."—"What for?" Deep in his soul, Ivan hoped she would say *For wanting to join the strike . . .* "For being so weak."—"You are not weak."

Except that, in fact, she was.

A bit later, musicians came, bards began to sing. They came every day to support the students. Rose became more alert and even sang along with them. But Ivan could not sing. He opened and closed his mouth and that was it. He saw Rose's delicate fingers against the light, when she fixed her hair, and it seemed to him that the rays of sun shot right through her flesh—a little longer, and Rose would become transparent. That they would all become transparent as if they were made of glass and you could see inside every one of them a slowly ringing bell of light. The days of that autumn were growing shorter and passed without a trace; only a few separate, long minutes were caught in the molasses of time, never to be forgotten.

That night, Ivan went to find Bodya. He told him he, too, wanted to join the hunger strike. "Oh come on, not you, too!" Bodya groaned. Had it been anyone else, he would have growled instead. "Well, why not?" Ivan asked, ignoring Bodya's tone. "Because we need you right where you are. What's so hard about it?" In the dusk, Bodya's dark eyes looked even darker. He was naturally olive-skinned, and despite the season, had managed to develop a serious tan on the Maidan, so that now Bodya's face was about the color of rum. He looked like a Tajik. Or an Afghani. "But why?" Ivan asked again, knowing already he wouldn't get anywhere. "Well, you tell me the truth. Why do you want to do it?" Bodya studied Ivan's face closely, then let his eyes find Rose, the exhausted flower. "Is it because of Rose?" Ivan thought it was best to confirm his friend's guess. You couldn't lie to Bodya anyhow. "Yes," he said.

Bodya spread his arms and sighed. Rose's cot was not far from them, but she would not be able to hear what they were talking about, they kept their voices low, almost to whispers. Bodya looked at the girl for a long time, apparently forgetting about Ivan, and for the first time Ivan wondered what his friend might feel . . . But no, Bodya was too good a friend and comrade.

Ivan broke the silence, "So?"

Bodya seemed to shake awake.

"Listen, I would let you do it if I could. But imagine if . . . if they come—whoever, it could be whoever, there are plenty of options, you can see that, and I've got these grunts on the perimeter. What then? You can't be confused, not anymore, no matter how hard they try. You can't be bought. You see it, don't you? We've got our own professional revolutionaries now . . ."

It was true. In the last couple of days, a lot of people came to join them, and not all of them had the same level of national consciousness. Bodya found two men particularly irritating—new guys, "professional revolutionaries," as he called them. They claimed to be students of a Kyiv university, said their names were Petya and Pasha. Vitya Reshetar, who came from a family of believers (although he declared he did not himself believe in God), called them Peter and Paul, after the apostles. The "apostles" could not be kept away from the megaphone, to which they referred exclusively as a "swear-phone" and talked of their heroics in the field of social protests. How they, for example, staged a sit-in to protest someone or other having been sentenced by a troika tribunal decades ago. Many were beginning to regret letting them inside the camp. Galaida and Bodya kept the two in sight.

"I see what we've got." In addition to his eyes, Ivan relied on his instincts.

"That's it, then. It's an honor. I only have the people I've tested in my security squad," which, in Bodya's world, meant people from Lviv. Ivan had come to Kyiv from Lviv with the rest of the group. Bodya would never let him join the hunger strike, that much was obvious. Even for Rose.

•

Ivan spent his night shift with Oleh the Geographer and his "commandos," as they called themselves. It was a bit cold, but they had full stomachs and kept moving around, while the strikers lay on their cots. In fact, the world lay cradled by a magnificent night, full of crisp autumn scents, starry-skied, and clear. Ivan and the Geographer smoked. The cigarettes were good, Gauloises or something; Ivan did not remember the brands of what people gave them, only the taste. Never again and nowhere else would he smoke so much excellent tobacco as he did there, on the Maidan, under the stare of the granite Lenin.

Earlier that day, a bunch of tough-looking guys they did not know came up to the perimeter to give them a beating, the security squad thought. Bodya rushed to talk to them. Galaida, who apparently never slept, gave orders, but the toughs—well muscled and dressed in good jeans—instead shook hands with everyone, told them they were doing great, dumped a bunch of cash into the donations box, and filled the protestors' pockets with cigarettes.

"Are you scared?" Ivan asked the Geographer. "Scared? What would I be scared of?" he responded, half to himself, and Ivan could hear in the dark that his friend was smiling. "That they'd run us over with tanks, for example?" Everyone in their camp remembered the Tiananmen massacre very well. They even held a rally on May 13, and the students in Kyiv held a one-day hunger strike in solidarity with Chinese students on the Bohdan Khmelnytsky Square, which they called Sofiiska Square among themselves. They wanted to remind people of what happened and to warn them that no bloodshed like that must ever happen in Ukraine.

(*The Kyiv branch of the Ukrainian Student Union calls on you to support the Harvard University initiative to hold an international student solidarity rally on May 13. On this day in 1989, Chinese students began a hunger strike in Tiananmen Square in Beijing to call for a decisive democratization of Chinese society. We all remember the massacre that ended their protest on the fourth of June . . .*)

"I don't know if I am scared of the tanks," the Geographer said as he sucked on his cigarette. He was taller than Ivan and had the massive shoulders of a sailor or a dockworker and light, sun-bleached hair. He turned his face to the sky for a moment, became distant. Then turned back to Ivan. "I'm more afraid that nothing will happen. We'll stand here, and no one will notice. We'll die, and the fact of it will vanish, like water into sand. I want us to leave a mark. That's why I'm not scared of a massacre. And you?" Ivan was silent for a bit, and then said, barely audibly, "I'm afraid that those on the cots will get worse, and I . . . I won't. I might get out of this perfectly whole, and that's not fair." The Geographer was silent for a bit. When he answered, it was in an older, wiser brother's voice; he was, in fact, older than Ivan, having entered the university after he had done his military service. He spoke kindly, the Geographer was never patronizing, "Listen, you know, don't you, what an honor it is to be in the security guard? People like you and me are very important, we have a mission."

"I do," Ivan conceded, downcast. "And then there are my parents . . ." he shared. "Did yours . . . Do they know?"

"They do," Oleh said. "I told them everything, no secrets, and warned them honestly that I might be crippled, or killed. My parents said, 'If that's what you have decided, then you should go ahead.'—"Just like that?"—"Of course. They think exactly what I think about this government. They never hid anything from me. So I don't either."

In their pockets, Ivan and Oleh each had a copy of Vasyl Stus's poetry collection. It had just been published in Ukraine for the first time, there were lines at the bookstores that stocked it, and the whole run sold out at lightning speed, although very soon it became clear that few readers could truly appreciate this poetry. Stus's work was difficult, even for the regulars of poetry readings. Still, at least half of the students on the Maidan bought a copy of *The Road of Pain* and carried theirs in their pockets. If they were arrested, the book would be with them, on their persons. Ivan could feel it, its hot weight, in his pocket. He touched the cover as if the book were a protective talisman. He asked for strength. He asked for confidence.

Stus also went on a hunger strike. Until the end, just as he had decided.

The next morning, as soon as the camp woke up, two people came: Leonid Kravchuk, chairman of the Supreme Council of the USSR, and Ihor Yukhnovskyi, the leader of the Democratic Bloc that constituted the opposition. The latter genuinely seemed to want to help the students, but Ivan was skeptical about how much the man could accomplish. He was too quiet, in Ivan's opinion, spoke too evenly, without any passion at all; if there was ardor in him, he was keeping it hidden or suppressed. Then again, if he hadn't, he would have had to become a dissident, not a politician.

Kravchuk was different; he loved the public, loved the stage. His gestures were well practiced, theatrical. At the moment, he was playing the part of calm, reasonable authority. His cool, however, slipped as soon as he had a chance to speak to Yarema, Rud', and the irrepressible Bodya.

"Boys, please. I am not ordering you, I am asking you to stop the hunger strike." Then Kravchuk lowered his voice as if sharing an intimate secret among the privileged few: "You must understand, don't you, what kind of rumors your protest has spawned. No one understands why you are here; folks think you just want to skip classes. Of course, I know better, I can see you are serious, but you must trust us. We will consider all your demands, I promise you, just as soon as you stop the strike."

"Really, you will?" Bodya could not stay quiet.

Kravchuk glanced at him suspiciously.

"Boys, you must understand, we will do everything that's in our power, but your demands, to be fully honest, are, well . . ."

"Our demands are just," Yarema said. "And not only just but realistic. They can be fulfilled. And we also want to hold a round-table discussion, officially."

"Fulfilled, you say!" Kravchuk made a face and then, apparently to give himself time to think, launched into an unprompted spiel about the Party, and that his membership in the Communist

Party of the Soviet Union was a conscious choice (as if anyone had asked him!), and that he could not make any decisions on behalf of those who belonged to other parties, and they might very well have different opinions on the subject, and therefore . . .

"Mister Leonid!" Rud' interrupted. "Sir!"

Kravchuk's eyes all but popped out of his head at being addressed like this, with a mister and his first name, and not by his first name and patronymic. Later, Rud' would address him in the same manner on live TV and shock not just the Maidan but the entire country. It may well have been that moment when Ivan began to respect Rud', whom he had previously viewed through the lens of Bodya's skepticism. Rud' was skinny as a stick, did not have the primitive, animal power in his body like Bodya, but he did possess his own kind of strength.

"Do you think," Rud' was saying to Kravchuk, "we do not know that there is an opposition in the Supreme Council? And that our demands run counter to the Rukh program? We openly call for new elections to the Supreme Council as soon as next spring!"

"First stop the hunger strike, and then . . ." Kravchuk began, but the young men were no longer listening.

"No, Mister Leonid, first you fulfill our demands, and then we will stop the hunger strike."

Angry, Kravchuk rolled his eyes. Ivan and Tymish were charged with seeing the guests out of the camp.

The Supreme Council, despite Kravchuk's promises of "consideration," reached no useful decisions. The truth was that there had been calls for dismissing Vitaly Masol's cabinet days before the students' revolution: the government pursued such idiotic economic policy that it was a miracle Ukraine was functioning. But now, with a tent city on Kyiv's main square, the Communists closed ranks to protect their own. The infamous "Bloc of the

239"—the Communist majority in the parliament—rushed to rescue Masol and themselves.

The demands regarding the military and mandatory service within the republic's territory were blocked by Moscow. The parliamentary opposition appeared useless. Yukhnovsky came again, asking for a compromise, but Yarema simply repeated to him what he had already said to Kravchuk. Yukhnovsky seemed to be somewhat offended by this, he was supposed to be on the "same side" as the students, and yet he had no progress to show for it.

Meanwhile the crowd around the camp's perimeter churned. The guards had someone talking to them, or wanting to talk to them, all the time. They had a few of the plainclothes cadre approach them (these couldn't be confused with anyone else) and hiss that, well, you know perfectly well how it's all going to end. From the heart of the crowd, old women shouted at them in Russian, shamed them, "Little bastards, freeloaders, send them to the kolkhoz, to work the harvest!" Different, Ukrainian old women came up to them, too, their faces worn by tears and luminous, gaunt, and hatched with wrinkles, and held the students' hands, spoke kindly, wanted to do something for them. People bought flowers, bunches and bunches of magnificent autumnal flowers, that they laid down around the strikers. Something sorrowful and ominous emanated from that mantle of living flowers spread around dozens of bodies on cots.

One day, in the late afternoon, an older woman came. She did not look like a typical grandmother. She moved precisely and held herself with grace and suppleness; she must have been a dancer once. She wore a lilac-colored coat. She instantly caught Ivan's eye in the crowd, and he studied her for a while. She stood listening to Neonila Kryukova while the actress spoke to a group of schoolgirls. "People come here, and in half an hour we've won them," Kryukova was saying. That was true. The woman in the lilac coat listened and shook her head in disbelief. Ivan, not knowing why exactly, approached her.

The woman saw him and his black armband.

"Security guard?" she asked. "Yes."—"Whom are you guarding?"—"Our people," Ivan said with a smile. But she did not care for his smile. She leaned closer to him and hissed just like a snake, "Do you even know how many innocent people have gone to jail because of little revolutionaries just like these?"

In a blink, she vanished in the crowd. Ivan did not quite know what to think, but the encounter left a heavy aftertaste.

On one of their watchful nights, three prostitutes came around, young women in high heels, miniskirts, and short leather jackets. Their eyes gleamed, and so did their lips, lacquered with what must have been imported lipstick. One of them carried—as Ivan would remember this for a long time, if not for his entire life—a huge, heavy bunch of grapes. Elite green grapes, the choicest kind.

"What are you up to, boys?" asked the woman with the grapes. Yurko Galaida answered in low voice; Ivan couldn't hear the words. The women came closer, the one with the grapes raised the bunch as high as she could above her head, held it there like a lantern, tilted her head, and began to bite off individual grapes, grasping each slowly and sensuously with her lips. She moaned a little as she ate. Yurko said nothing. The guys stared at the young woman as if hypnotized. Ivan felt his head spin.

"Would you like some?" she asked, and the charm was broken. Yurko laughed, told her they couldn't be bought just for a bunch of grapes. The young women laughed, too; they weren't offering them grapes, of course. They stayed and bantered for a bit and then left. Yurko Galaida looked at their backs with hot desire in his eyes. There wasn't a single one of them in that squad who didn't dream of grapes that night.

That turned out to be only the first of many strange visits. Next, crazy people came to the camp. One told Ivan his elaborate plan that involved paper displays which, positioned just so, would cause the Lenin monument to collapse. "Well, maybe it's not quite time for that yet?" Ivan said to him, desperately trying to keep calm because he thought that was the appropriate tone to take with a mentally ill person. "Let it stand there for a bit more?" Really, that's the last thing they needed, for that giant idol to keel over, right onto their camp.

Another man came dressed in a white raincoat with a bottle of champagne sticking out of his stylish pockets. He told them he was from "the kay-gee-bee" but was rooting for them, meaning for the guys ("And for the girls, then!" Rose called out from her cot; he came during the day), and wanted to tell them the glorious organization's every secret. He must have misjudged his audience: many of the students knew if not the kay-gee-bee's every secret then enough to stay away from everything associated with it.

Provocations began. Someone called to tell them there was a bomb in the camp. Two guys threw what looked like grenades into the tents—the grenades were fake—and fled through the labyrinth of the underground crossings. Galaida, Ivan, Tymish, and a few of the Geographer's commandos chased after them but the guys were quick, practiced, and must have come from the officers' college or the military itself—they ran with great alacrity. Then one night a whole wall of goons came, hired, perhaps, by someone who did not wish to get the official police's hands dirty. Galaida gave orders calmly, saying, "Get the machine gun, boys, it's time to dance." Mysko and Tymish called back from inside a tent to the effect, "Ready! Will fire on command!" This was pure bluff, of course, they didn't have a machine gun. They couldn't have. But for some reason it worked, and the goons fled. Perhaps what they heard in these mad students' voices was their readiness to die but not give in. Another wave of talk about self-immolation rolled through the ranks of the strikers. The subject mostly came up at night, and Rose was not part of it, she probably didn't even hear anything, and for this Ivan was eternally grateful. Nearly half of those on hunger strike seemed to have given the subject some thought, and Yarema and Bodya had their hands full trying to convince their comrades not to talk about it and most certainly not to do anything to that effect.

"My grandfather's brother was a priest," said Yaroslav, a Kyiv boy whom everyone called Yarko. "He celebrated mass underground. In 1971, he was called to do the funeral rites for Mykola Girnyak. Girnyak self-immolated in Kaniv. He wrote a bunch of leaflets, dropped them around the town at three in the morning, and set himself on fire on Chernecha Hora."[24]—"And no one saw it?"—"No, there were no witnesses."

Ivan shuddered. He pictured the flame in the dead of the night, as if the mountain itself had exploded with grief and fury, the unbearable torment . . . A man set himself on fire. Alone. At three in the morning. Those were some kind of people!

Meanwhile, Tymish Gavkalo perched on one of the cots and prepared to indulge in his favorite pastime, decoding the mind-numbing Soviet lies that constituted reportage in the newspapers people brought for them to read.

"Here, here's a headline, listen: 'An Embarrassment of Riches. A portion of the elected members of the Kyiv City Council declare proudly today that they attended the rally on October 1. But what have they done to ensure the supply of vegetables to Ukraine's capital?'"

There was nothing funny about this, but everyone laughed.

"Vegetables!"

"That's perfect!"

"No, wait, hold on, you philistines!" Gavkalo tutted with affected frustration. "Here, ladies and gentlemen, another one,"

---

24. Also known as Taras Hill, the location where the remains of Taras Shevchenko have been buried since 1861.

and he read in Russian, "'On the Hunger Strike Protest. We, Communists of the Stryi region . . .'" He had to stop reading again because a new roar of laughter drowned out his words. Of course, Communists of the Stryi region did, in fact, exist, just as there were Communists in other regions, even in the most disobedient ones, but the phrase still sounded like an oxymoron. Communists, in Galicia? And they speak Russian? The truth was everyone joined the Party because, pretty often, there was no other way to get things, an apartment, for example.

"Let me finish!" Gavkalo groused. "So, the Communists of the Stryi region . . . will you just listen? 'are outraged by the anti-democratic actions of the so-called Democratic Bloc . . .'" Quit giggling already! 'which in our own town had organized a picket at the city party committee building and demands the liquidation of the Ukrainian Communist Party within the territory of Galicia and the redistribution of its property. To protest the anti-constitutional efforts of the so-called "democrats," employees of the city party committee hereby declare a hunger strike. We call on the elected members of the Supreme Council of Ukraine to show their support and provide legal defense . . .' and it's signed 'V. Boryshkevich, Secretary of the Stryi City Communist Party Committee.' That's how one goes on hunger strike, boys, with the support and 'legal defense' of the Communist Party! We are just amateurs. Can you imagine those people going hungry?"

"Yeah, they must've decided not to go to the special distribution stores for a week!"

"They're plain eating bread and not even spreading butter on it!"

"Right! They're not spreading their butter; they put it on in chunks!"

On one of those tense days, Ivan met Pavlo Dankulynets. Dankulynets was not especially tall and very young, just a bit older than Ivan, but no one would have referred to this man as a boy. There was nothing boyish about him; neither his manner nor his clothes, his face nor his eyes. He had strong shoulders and was built like a boxer—Ivan wouldn't have been surprised to learn that Dankulynets, in fact, boxed. The air around him crackled with electricity.

"So that's what you look like," Dankulynets said without introduction.

"Me?" Ivan was caught by surprise. Who could possibly have come looking specifically for him? A spy sent by Margita? But she has no idea . . .

"You! The guy from Transcarpathia!" Dankulynets explained. "My name is Pavlo Dankulynets."

Now it made sense to Ivan, a Rukh member, a well-known person. Ivan stared at Dankulynets like a ram at the proverbial gates. He thought of people of this caliber—Chornovil, Lukyanenko, Kravchuk—dissidents and politicians, as a kind of demigods, distant stars, yet Dankulynets was one of his own, he might have even gone to the same school in Uzhhorod.

"What's your deal, how come I haven't met you before? Is there anyone else from our neck of the woods? You'd stick out anyway, though," Pavlo teased gently.

"How did you . . . Did someone . . ." Ivan wanted to ask questions but could not put together a single sentence.

"It's okay, first-name basis," Pavlo said. "Why are you so formal?"

Dankulynets spoke without a hint of the Transcarpathian accent or a trace of the dialect. Did he grow up elsewhere? Then why did he make the region his cause?

As if reading his thoughts, or perhaps because Ivan's face had gotten so gaunt his every emotion could be read loud and clear, Pavlo explained, "My mom was from there, but we lived in Kyiv, then I went to Lviv to study, like you, and now I've gone back to Uzhhorod."—"Oy, but can you keep our discourse?" Ivan responded in the dialect, teasing a bit and suddenly comfortable with the idea that this man who was nearly of an age with him, and most certainly a comrade in arms, was truly one of his own.

Pavlo smiled widely, "Sure can! I could've spoke to you like my own kin!"

They became friends. Dankulynets was allowed inside the perimeter and spent a lot of time talking to Yarema, Rud', and Bodya. He laughed a lot, and his laugh, his strength, his movements—like a tamed panther's—emanated something that made them all feel safe. It was as though they'd gotten an extra battery, a new source of energy.

One evening, Dankulynets asked Ivan to walk with him, and they went as far as the Zhovtneviy Palace. They sat on the grass. Ivan felt the quiet of the dusk, dotted here and there with streetlights, the quiet of the faded plants under his palm. They were the only people on this vast lawn in the center of the city because no common mortal was allowed to walk on this grass or sit on it. But they could. They were making new rules. In the middle distance, Ivan recognized the crazy kay-gee-bee man in his white coat, except the bottles that stuck out of his pockets looked different, not champagne this time. Ivan felt like laughing. He pointed to the man who was just then edging toward a new group of people, and Dankulynets laughed.

"Recognize him?" Pavlo asked.

"He's hard to miss!" Ivan said. "Been here since the beginning. Do you think he is still with the KGB?"

"How would you know who is and who isn't if they don't want you to know?"

Ivan shrugged. You couldn't, he wanted to say, but remembered

Yarema's warning not to talk idly, not to repeat useless things, and said nothing. The kay-gee-bee man was not bothering them; he went to sit with someone else, the Geographer, it looked like. There was another Volhynia student there. So let him sit.

"Now, you tell me," Dankulynets began, "why didn't any of you—you, this Yarema of yours, or even Rud'—ever get in touch with us? Why did you decide to go it alone?"—"That's the thing," Ivan answered. "We had to do it like this. Alone."—"But you are now in politics," Dankulynets said. Something inside Ivan's chest contracted then, as if the space of freedom he'd been carrying since the protest began suddenly shrank. Dankulynets watched him, gestured impatiently, and clucked his tongue. Ivan ignored his gesture. "We are defenseless in every sense of the word," he said. "Some of us are on a hunger strike as well, so they cannot, and would not, fight. You say it would be easier with you older people? It probably would, but then we'd have this feeling . . . this feeling, like if I'm going to fall out of the window, someone will catch me. This way, I'm either going to fly or not. There's no safety below."

Dankulynets listened to Ivan's impassioned speech (Mysko would've given Ivan no end of grief for the passion part, as would Yarema, most likely) without interruption, and then said, "Listen, you still don't get it. I've explained this to Yarema, I've explained it to Bodya, and now I've no problem telling you. Look, there may well be older people out there who would be of no use to you guys, but the Rukh is different. It's just different. Who put together the Reunification Act celebration? And the human chain? You were there with us, you supported us. Who recruited people to go to the Baltic Way? And back in July, when we first raised the blue-and-yellow flag in Kyiv . . . We were all there. All your Kyiv friends were there. We must be engaged with you if we are to grow and to win. And you guys, you're just like that guy in *Treasure Island*, you want to do good, but in secret from us. But we share the same goal."

There was truth to what Dankulynets said. The goal was, indeed, the same. But these adults would not have let the students carry out what they had planned. The radicals would have encouraged them to take up arms, and, as Yarema said, what kind of an uprising would that be? With underground weapons caches in modern cities? The conformists would have told them to wait because that's what they do, wait for something, for hell to freeze over maybe.

"Listen," Dankulynets went on. "Did you . . . You must have consulted with *those*."—"With whom?" Ivan didn't understand. "You know who I'm talking about."—"No, I don't."—"Well, the way you are organized, your secrecy, your security squad, your teams of five, and everything else, it must have come from the radicals, the Insurgent Army survivors, those who'd gone to jail?"—"Nonsense," Ivan waved him off. For some reason, he did not feel like talking about this. He looked over the lawn, the kay-gee-bee man in his white coat was drinking from one of his bottles, Ivan could see his throat contract. "We had nothing to do with those people. Yarema threw them out of our meeting once."—"Yeah, I've heard that story, but I don't believe it," Pavlo laughed. "He may have thrown them out that time, but there must have been others. He might have talked to them in secret."

Ivan made a dismissive noise. Whom could they talk to? Their fathers and grandfathers who railed against the regime in their Khrushchev-apartment kitchens? This was a conspiracy theory, being created right before him, yet another thing that Yarema had warned them about. Ivan was beginning to see very clearly how, from their very first days, very first protests, Yarema had drawn a protective circle of acceptable behavior around them, like a life raft. He had good reasons for it. These things were not to be toyed with or else you were liable to start looking for ulterior motives in the words and actions of people you have to trust absolutely, in order for everyone to survive. No, not just to survive. In order to survive and win. Dankulynets just said so himself.

"Anyway," Dankulynets said. "Don't be a stranger. Call me," he wrote all his numbers on a piece of paper for Ivan, his home and work lines. "Do call me. We'll do something together."

•

But the sense of hopelessness did not leave them.

Mysko had to quit the strike; doctors ordered him to do it. After a short stay in a hospital Mysko came back to the Maidan, sat on a cot, made jokes. He was pale. Ivan sat next to him, but could not find the right things to say. Mysko, of course, did not expect to be comforted, that was not his style. On the contrary, he asked Ivan to share what was on *his* mind, to help lighten his burden. "Nothing, I have no thoughts," Ivan answered, glum. Then asked Mysko, "How about you?" He laughed, "Oh, I do! All this, everything that's just happened is fodder for deeper self-reflection in the future. And motivation for self-discipline. Of body and spirit both." He did not say for "deeper reflection on the situation." He said "self-reflection" and "self-discipline" and that was Mysko distilled into two words.

Mysko was hard to convince and harder yet to convert to anything. He was utterly proselytizer-proof. He went to the Maidan solely because Ivan did, as well as Yarema, and Bodya Melnyk (Mysko was friends with Bodya, too). It was an act of friendship, not of ideology. Mysko always said that if he were ever drafted and sent to war, he would give equally no hoots about his own or the enemy command, but would fight solely for the guys in the trench next to him. There's nothing else, he liked to say. He and Yarema disagreed about nearly everything.

"A sacrifice?" he had asked Yarema before the protest. "What sacrifice? What's the point of it?" And told him, plainly, that a sacrifice was only possible when there was something to give up, a means to do it. Their exchange at the group's meeting that time was so tense that Ivan wondered how Mysko and Yarema didn't become mortal enemies afterward.

"What means are you talking about?" Yarema asked. "Material ones. Let's say, a base of operations."—"All right, but what about that guy in front of the tank on Tiananmen Square? What means did he have? Do you really think that's what he was thinking about?" Yarema countered. The rest of the guys made approving noises. "I don't know. He might have been," Mysko said slowly. He was calm but a deep crease appeared on the bridge of his nose. "And I think he was his own only asset," Yarema said, after a pause. Like Mysko, he had nowhere else to be. "And other assets grew from what he did." Here, Yarema could have added, "for instance, we did" and another man absolutely would have done so, if only for the rhetorical effect, but Yarema was different. "And anyway, assets or not, a man in front of a tank is just that: a man before a tank."—"So what about that guy's means? Or the absence thereof? Has China changed much?"—"You can't always measure the effect with straightforward things like that."—"Fine," Mysko went on. "Let's take up complicated things . . . or actually, to hell with complicated things. Say, for example, a man has gone to jail and he learns that the only outcome of his actions is the increased interest shown by the pupils of the Mao Zedong Gymnasium toward the Ming-era arts . . ."

"Do you mean," Gavkalo interrupted, "that they have gymnasiums in China? I thought those were only found in Comrade Bunin's books?"

"How would he know?" Mykyta said. He was also listening to the dispute, but Yarema and Mysko were so focused on the argument that they did not hear these comments.

"Straightforward, simple things," Mysko repeated. "The basics: freedom, an opportunity to improve yourself, a certain level of material comfort."—"You see the world in mechanistic terms. Art, too, is a source of power."—"Art?" Mysko smiled. At that moment he looked very much like Klaus Kinski. *Aguirre, the Wrath of God.* "Yes, art," Yarema repeated. "It's not a prop, not an ornament, not a luxury. It's what molds you into the man you are. Hence the next step, self-sacrifice. That's why it's right to stop eating. It's a gesture: when we don't eat, we cannot fight."—"Cannot fight," Mysko echoed. He, much like Bodya Melnyk, would rather have fought. Fighting came naturally to him. For this reason, he was always quick to support Bodya's proposals. "What if, for instance, this self-sacrificing person of yours defeats the tank. What then? A tank is not just a tank. There's a government behind the tank, good or bad, well run or not, just or unjust—that's beside the point."— "What do you mean, beside the point?" Rose interrupted. "To hear you say it, the Soviet Union and, say, Iceland, are the same thing. A country with a gulag is as good as the one without?"

"No," Mysko said. "That's not what I'm talking about. I'm talking about the fact that a government, a state that had manufactured a tank had also built other things. It had built things like a publishing industry, and the publishing industry produces books, including history books. Not to mention art . . . You keep talking about that Tiananmen of yours like it's the only possible ideal, but why? We could do what Roman Shukhevych did, remember? In order to fund the fight for Ukraine, he launched an advertising agency. He vacationed at the seashore right under the Soviets' noses, didn't he? Honestly, I find him much more relatable than your Tiananmen with Mahatma Gandhi on top."—"But what kind of society produced a man like Shukhevych? It was not the Soviet one, to be sure. If there are to be people like him again, there must first be people like us!" Rose's voice trembled with tension. "And people like us, are we going to change our society overnight? Do we know how to do that? Do we know how to write history textbooks?

Because they'd been making tanks in Kharkiv for decades . . ." Mysko was not arguing with Rose, he was thinking out loud.

And now here he was, Mysko, who did not believe in the idea but took his place among them because he was a loyal friend, sitting pale and ill, and he, Ivan, who did believe in the idea, Ivan whom Mysko did not abandon in his hour of need, healthy as an ox, walking his perimeter beat in the name of security but, damn it, nothing appears to have changed! Ivan felt an urge to punch something, and better yet, someone, he would gladly shoot, hack, tear things with his teeth if only that meant not just sitting there, waiting for who knows what. Well, okay, they did know. They were waiting to be cleared from the square. By force. Christian martyr-like. Heck, even if the Communist Party unleashed on them real lions who would maul them to death right in front of the crowds, who's to say that would be enough to convert the crowd? Or rather, sure, they'll get converted—in a century or three. Isn't that a little too long for them to wait?

And then there was Rose. The medics told the girls they could go without food for four days and no longer, but Rose was not likely to listen, Ivan knew that. She had slipped out of his arms, his embrace with which he had sought to protect her. He had not protected her from anything, and never would, so what was he supposed to do? He suddenly understood why people were talking about self-immolation: that, at least, would be an act. That would feel like making progress.

Ivan second-guessed everything, the usefulness of their protest, their methods, his own willpower, his own presence. He and his fellow guards were like ghosts that haunted the nation's most central square, but have ghosts ever changed anything? They are there and not there, people walk through them as if through empty space.

It was then Ivan missed supper for the first time as a means to punish himself for his uselessness, and for daring to give voice to it, which confused him even more. Not eating turned out to be harder than he thought, he still had to carry out his guard duties. Ivan would feel faint and rage anew at his own weakness, and the more he raged, the less he believed in the ultimate effectiveness of what they were doing. And then he felt guilty.

He kept running inside that wheel like a poor circus animal.

•

Meanwhile, tension grew thicker around them. The parliament went on arguing but made no decisions; the 239 Bloc controlled everything. Who was there to fight for them? The opposition was too weak, and the Communists only listened to Moscow, meaning Moscow and their own guts. They announced plans for a rally of war and labor veterans, and not just any rally, but one "in defense of Lenin." An anti-fascist congress was held at the Ukraine Congress Hall, with the students' camp smack in the middle of the pedestrian route from there to the Lenin monument, which the anti-fascists were sure to visit. The police hinted that provocations were possible. If the boys resisted, the anti-riot units stood ready to respond, with dogs, those shepherds with their show ribbons.

The rank and file were actually quite tolerant. They enjoyed the songs that musicians sang at the camp, and Yurko Galaida's communication talents helped. The police saw him as one of their own, like them, he came from a common family, was not particularly tall or in any way remarkable with his ruddy hair, chapped lips, and scuffed knuckles; a provincial boy come to make good in the city. The cops really came to respect Yurko and Bodya once a group of "internationalist warriors," meaning Afghan vets who'd been sent to make trouble, all to a man came over to the revolution's side after the two young men talked to them.

Ivan did what he was supposed to do automatically. He walked, he talked, he did other chores that felt meaningless. He felt ill, he felt sick to his stomach, and great fatigue washed over him in waves. He saw the girls getting up to speak at one of the city's universities, along with others and Mykyta Kalyniak, their public relations man. But what's the point? He saw Mykyta pick up the phone they had installed on the square, speak to someone, and then heard him announce happily that the call was from Bulgaria; someone there supported them. In Bulgaria? But Bulgaria was so far away. No one there could know that their little show was about to be canceled, the Communist column was marching on as they spoke.

It was October 6, 1990. In the morning, priests came to the square. They unrolled a linen cloth, the name and purpose of which Ivan thought he knew but could not remember, and then a velvet one. They opened the Gospels. They began mass. It had never occurred to Ivan before that the liturgy was, in fact, a conversation with God, a dialogue, which only made it feel worse when one realized that most of the people on the square did not know the words.

He, Ivan, did not know them either.

How were you supposed to speak if you did not know the right words? What kind of a crippled choir were they, when only one out of ten could sing?

•

The afternoon dragged on. Clouds obscured the sun. Ivan missed the exact moment when everything went quiet; it felt as if he'd suddenly woken up to this silence, as if whoever was responsible for the great machine of all existence turned off the sound. He had never heard so many people be so quiet.

After a while, he heard steps and, in time with them, the creaking of musical instruments being carried. A band had been brought to the square.

Of course, how could he forget! The band.

It was there to play for the veterans' rally "in defense of Lenin," upbeat music for the "political zombies," as everyone called the rally participants. Ivan was convinced that when the riot police finally came to clear their camp, there would be music. Something like "Wide Is My Motherland," since the country was indeed wide and, as former political prisoners adjusted the lyrics, "many are its prisons and its camps." Or perhaps "Morning Paints with Gentle Color," since the color of the Kremlin walls from that song did reach all the way down here to Kyiv.

The band stood silent. Now one could hear the shuffle of the veterans' march as they approached down Khreshchatyk. Pavlo Dankulynets, Sergiy Golovatyi, and other members of parliament who sympathized with the students, as well as artists and writers, placed themselves in front of the camp as a human shield against the coming attack.

Never in his life had Ivan been closer to the experience of utter catastrophe. His hands began to shake. His body broke out in sweat.

The conductor raised his baton.

The veterans' march stopped opposite the camp. Up close, it was obvious that not everyone in this rather pathetic march was a veteran. There were your typical grandfathers and grandmothers, some of whom had survived the war and all of whom had paid for it by giving their lives over to the Soviet Moloch. These kinds of people would have worked three shifts a day to earn their Stakhanovite medal. Yet there were also much younger men and women among them who clearly did not belong to the privileged caste: common workers with gaunt faces and calloused hands who had come to the march dressed in badly made Soviet clothes or the striped uniforms of Nazi prison camps.

They carried portraits of Soviet leaders and signs that read BUCHENWALD, NO TO NATIONALIST EXTREMISM, STOP POLITICAL VANDALISM!—that one was obviously about the revolution on the granite. Some signs had been made out in Russian, as in STRENGTHEN INTERNATIONAL SOLIDARITY AND INTERNATIONALISM!—Ivan wondered what exactly the veterans meant by that. He had come to accept that Soviet Communist slogans were all written in a dead language, and no one could translate their meaning into the language of the living. Take one of their own, Bodya the Afghan, and guys like him, who had been *there*, called upon, allegedly, to carry out their "internationalist" duty, but the military fed them bare gruel, made them wear outdated uniforms that had never been fit for the local climate, and kept them silent when the brass sold weapons to the mujahideen. The veterans and so-called veterans stood shoulder to shoulder, looking at the camp with disapproval, almost hatred. They were silent, which was odd; these people usually liked to talk about the great Vladimir Illych, or some such. Ivan could tell they were offended by the students' signs with rhymes such as:

> *Damned Leninism has run its course*
> *and no one thanks it for its work.*
> *The statues that became a shame*
> *are asked to leave their honored place.*
> *This hurts the Party like a knife—*
> *they can't just rule as they would like.*

Or:

> *We will stay hungry night and day—*
> *Illych has made us go this way.*

This is it, Ivan thought. The end. The band will play a march, and then ...

The band began to play.

He knew the piece from its first chords, anyone would. The band struck up a funeral march, Chopin's *Marche funèbre*, performed at funerals all over the world.

These musicians! Who, who were these wonderful people, the best people in the world! Why didn't Ivan at least ask where they'd come from, what institution, what was the name of their band? He should have learned all their names and told everyone, so that everyone would know who played the music!

As soon as the first notes sounded, a great cry burst from hundreds of chests—a cry of relief, wonder, joy, love—and then laughter, Homeric, hysterical, mad. Whatever it was, it was devastating to the veterans' march.

Those musicians!

They beat death with death.

Truly, by death trampling death.

In the same instant, a hot wave washed Ivan's throat, carrying out all the doubt, all the dirt, all the weakness and mistrust of the world.

Things swam before his eyes, and Ivan suddenly realized he was crying.

The crowd swirled, laughed, there was applause.

The veterans turned back.

No one reached the foot of the Lenin monument that day.

•

Rose often cried out in her sleep. Ivan discovered this when she came to visit him one time that memorable summer before the revolution. Margita and Ivan's father had gone to Hungary to visit

Ondia, who enjoyed hosting her kin, and left Ivan in charge of the chickens and the house. Margita fretted that the berries would get ripe while they were gone and Ivan wouldn't be able to manage on his own and would not listen to her husband when he told her the berries would be fine for the three days they would be gone. It was hard for Margita to be away from her little piece of land, her small fiefdom. She'd stay there day and night if she'd had her druthers, holding her cupped hands out to catch every single juicy raspberry, every smooth new plum, every apple, every pear.

Rose came in the evening. It got dark while they walked home from the railway station. Ivan dropped the back gate key, and they had to look for it. Rose laughed at him quietly. At night, when she lay next to him asleep, Ivan heard her cry out, and then again, and slowly came to accept that, in fact, he knew almost nothing about her. Up until then, he did not know how she slept. He really had no idea how she made love, either—all their prior encounters in the dorm had been rushed and happened in someone else's cramped space, among other people's smells and sounds. He had thought she preferred to be quiet and only now realized she was not. She was mute. Rose loved with the overwhelming muteness of her body, her eyes, her inhalation and exhalation. She pressed her skin against his with such intensity it felt as if she were entering him, not the other way around.

Afterward, she fell asleep, and in her sleep, she cried out. Was this a release, a letting go of something, a sob, or a cry of pain? How could her roommates at the dorm not know this about her? In that kingdom of constant disquiet where everyone told everyone else everything, where everyone knew things about each other? And yet no one had said anything about Rose; the girls loved her. Not a single roommate had ever asked or chosen to be moved.

Ivan gathered Rose's hand into his, but she did not wake. When he hugged her, she went on sleeping—and crying out. She lay next to him naked, hot, free. He could feel another wave of arousal rolling through him but did not dare touch her when she was like that, so open and so absent.

On their second night together he, too, fell asleep; her cries no longer disturbed him. As they evidently did not disturb her roommates either. Did Rose's cries have a mysterious rhythm to them, did they mark the gaps and intervals between being and nonbeing, signal her finding a rend in the curtain of existence and looking through it? Perhaps the sound of her voice stabbed at the great Nothing or the great Void that constitutes the majority of our existence, while we, silly people, believe they are merely the vague background of it, the barely visible backdrop for the main drama of our silly lives, these ripples on the surface of eternity? The body does not, in fact, contain the person, or rather it does, but not in the way that people tend to imagine. Much later Ivan would realize he discovered this property of the body—to gravitate toward nonbeing—through a most embodied experience.

"Why do you cry out in your sleep?" Ivan asked, but Rose only laughed at him.

"Who, me? You're imagining things!" she said, and that's how Ivan learned she, too, was capable of saying things that were not true. Until then he seriously doubted that Rose could ever say anything but the honest truth, or what she believed it to be.

"I always thought I'm quiet as a mouse when I sleep," she added later, serious now, once she saw Ivan's eyes. He wanted to share his theory of rhythms with her then, told her that her cries must fall into the lacunae, that they fit into them like gear cogs. Rose listened raptly, as if he were singing her a song that'd never been heard before.

"Do you think you dream of things?" he asked another time, and she thought about it. He waited for her to answer, and then gave up asking any more questions. Why wouldn't he? Perhaps he, just like Rose's roommates, had entered a new era, one of a different, quantum reality, a new plane of existence. Slices of being, its strata slipped and flowed over each other, shadows on the bedroom wall, shadows on the surface of his dreams.

They had three nights together—a drop in an ocean, since they were just beginning to open up to one another. Ivan had no inkling that a person was a locked chest, full of doors, seals, and ciphers, that one needed so much time to open even a few of them, and even longer to remember to leave those inside *him* open. And everything once opened will close again if you don't see each other for too long. If you don't lie in bed together. If you don't caress each other with words and touch.

Ivan and Rose walked around the city, looking for someplace where Ivan wouldn't be stopped to say hello by someone who knew him and who would later inquire of Margita who that pretty girl was they'd seen him with. Ivan did not want Margita to know about them. Margita met Rose when she and Ivan's father had come to visit him in Lviv, but the girl was not to her liking: too independent, too strong. Margita could never share space with a young woman like that. "What d'you want with one like her?" Margita asked Ivan. "She's like a Gypsy or something."—"Mom, please!" Ivan pleaded. He avoided bringing them together after that.

He and Rose found their way to the old Uzhhorod cemetery. Here, on the Calvary Hill, in the center of the city, almost no one was buried anymore. They walked among the graves, sometimes through dense bushes. The sun shone through the green leaves. Ivan knew this place like the back of his hand, he had been here hundreds of times since he was a teenager. There were graves from all eras here: Hungarian, Ukrainian, and plenty of Russian ones, too. The latter often bore sentimental inscriptions, especially if they were children's graves. The Russians had conquered half of Europe, but their babies died just like everyone else's.

Rose stopped at one grave after another, attempting to read Hungarian names. She could read Polish easily but did not know the rules for Hungarian and asked Ivan. He explained that "-ly" was pronounced as "-y" and "-gy" as "d," not "-gi." Nad', he read out loud. Kiray. Migay.

They sat on the grass next to another tombstone. The stone bore an insert with a picture of a thin man and a laconic inscription in Hungarian: his name—surname first, followed by the first name—and the years of life. Gusti Istvan, 1930–1960. He was thirty years old when he died. An entire geopolitical epoch was contained in those years. Yet another partition of Eastern Europe in 1939, then the war, then the Soviets. Istvan died a very young man; it made one wonder what happened. Was he ill? Possibly, he looked fragile in the picture. What was wrong? Rickets? He was nine when Carpathian Ukraine was declared, fifteen at the end of the Second World War. How did he survive the war? With whom? Did he have parents? Extended family? People who cared for him? He was not Jewish and must have thanked his lucky stars for that alone. But did he fit in with the new government? Learn Russian?

People came to a grave nearby, started clearing the grass around it. They did not see Ivan and Rose. Ivan lay flat in the deep grass and reached his arms out to Rose. At first she shook her head—what were they doing, lying down on hallowed ground!—but eventually gave in. She took off her translucent pink necklace and put it around Ivan's neck. Sunlight refracted through the beads, and it looked like the necklace was on fire.

"So what, are we just going to loll around here among the dead?" Rose asked.

"No one can find us here," Ivan answered. Above them, clouds traveled slowly through the sky. A bird sang. Ivan never did learn to identify birds by their songs. "I think the dead are happy to have us," he went on. "We've come to visit them, we are lying here, next to them. We have not forgotten them. Would they really begrudge us this patch of grass?"

Rose smiled, and he kissed her smiling lips. They lay and looked at the sky.

"*When we loved each other old oaks did bloom*," Rose half sang. "That's how the song goes where I'm from."

"Our song's different," Ivan said. "It goes like this: *When lovers hear a bird sing, their love won't come to anything.*"

"That's just so sad!" she laughed.

"Not sad. Just realistic," Ivan did not know what he was saying or why. The old times held no sway over him and Rose. What could prevent them from being together? They'll both graduate, and then they'll think of something. They might both stay in Lviv. Margita's house did not have to be his only home in the world.

"If you say so," Rose agreed, but she didn't want to stay in the grass any longer. They got up and left. Along the way, Ivan picked a handful of wild raspberries, but Rose refused them outright. She did not say anything, only moved her hand as if to ward off an invisible force.

"Do you not like raspberries?" he asked.

"You can't eat from here; the dead are here. This grew straight out of them!"

"Everyone here's long gone, they don't bury people here anymore. The ground is clean."

Later, at Margita's house she said, "My grandfather fought in the war at Leningrad." It was night, and small insects flew into the windows, drawn by the light in the kitchen. The window reflected the set table between them, their shapes. They could see nothing outside, but Ivan knew the vine trellis was there, holding up a cascade of tender new vine growth that reached out and tickled the glass.

"At Leningrad? But why there?"—"They used to live in Russia." "And?"—"Like you don't know what a massacre it was . . ."—"The blockade?"—"No, I'm talking about something different. When they tried to break through . . . half a million people died in that battle. And, you see, nothing grows on that land. It's just weeds and the lumpy ground, everyone knows if you go there, you'll step on a bone sooner than you think. Grandfather went over there after the war; he had a friend who lived there. This man was a field-worker, an illicit archaeologist."—"What's that?"—"You know, people who work for the black market. They dig up graves, then sell the weapons they find to collectors. Sometimes bits of uniform, gear . . . what hadn't rotted."—"I guess people don't eat raspberries from that field, do they?"

Now they looked together into the mirror of the window, silvered by the impenetrable darkness outside. They looked intently as if they were about to see something very important. Rose didn't say anything.

"Is your grandfather still alive?" Ivan asked. Rose sighed, "No, only my grandmother."

Beyond them, far beyond this conversation, beyond the brightly lit kitchen lay the endless blackness, and the flashes of their feelings and insights only made its presence more tangible.

Ivan Chepil. Rosalia Voitovych.

Nineteen-seventy—nineteen . . . Would they be lucky enough to live in the 2000s?

Names and the years of life: Was that a lot or a little?

•

On October 8, Oles' Honchar, the famous writer, publicly ended his membership in the Communist Party.

"My cup of patience overflowed at the meeting yesterday that had been called to discuss the health of the students on a hunger strike. I went to see their camp with my own eyes. In these exhausted, stressed, but extremely resilient young people, so capable of self-sacrifice, I recognized my younger self. Yet our parliament has responded with mockery and scorn to the demands of these young sons and daughters of our nation. The partocratic majority that claims to govern our lives has laughed, heartlessly and cruelly, at these young people's sacrifice. I feel shaken to the core of my being by this unprecedented soullessness. I wish to have nothing in common with the cruel people who respond to their own nation's tragedy, to the suffering of Ukraine's children with scorn and mockery."

Honchar did this the day after Ihor Yukhnovsky had taken the floor in parliament to read the students' demands aloud and speak about the camp. "A hundred and fifty-eight students are currently on a hunger strike," he reported. "These students come from twenty-four cities in Ukraine. The condition of some is quickly deteriorating. A few have been taken by ambulances to ICUs."

Parliament deputies met this report with laughter. The Communist majority, the 239 Bloc, laughed the loudest. "That's great news! Nothing to worry about. It'll all soon be over, with just a pile of corpses!" Mykhailo Bashkirov joked. Another deputy, a Party lifer, commented gleefully that with fewer students around there would be more food left for them, the deputies. One got the impression that whenever they were not assembled in the Supreme Council Hall, these people did nothing but eat, eat their choice provisions from their special stores. Perhaps they saw it as their job. A deputy from Crimea outdid everyone with his suggestion to "Clear the square and introduce martial law in Kyiv." Applause drowned out his words.

Oles' Honchar's exit started a wave of exodus from the Communist Party. While Honchar's step could have been chalked up to his being a particularly sensitive artist, people who followed his example were harder to accuse of extreme emotion. Deputies, journalists, and employees of state television and radio left the Party. Threats rained from Moscow. Coverage came fast and furious. Newscasts from the capital spoke of a "storm cloud of nationalism" in Ukraine and pilloried the students, who, it was implied, had fallen under the influence of outside agitators. Extremism, it was said, raised its ugly head in Ukraine. The local deputies produced an open letter to the students in which they said nothing worthwhile but did attempt to manipulate public opinion just as they accused the students of doing.

> *Our young compatriots! Dear boys and girls!*
>
> *We, the Supreme Council deputies are deeply disturbed by your protest aimed at the supreme organ of our republic's government. An impartial analysis of your demands, as well as the methods you have chosen to promote them, shows them to be inadequate to the sociopolitical situation of the country. This is why your ultimatum-like formulations are widely perceived as an attempt to monopolize the right to the truth. Your protest runs counter to the interests of our people. When young people go on a hunger strike, it is a tragedy. Concerned about your health and your mothers' peace of mind, we ask you, and ask you again: Stop. Be reasonable.*

Signed by deputies Aseyev, Babanskyi, Bashkirov ("As if anyone doubted," Tymish murmured), Bondarenko, Gaisynskyi, Gopey, Dmytruk,[25] and others. There were eighty-five signatures altogether.

The students had a good laugh at the letter. Look, eighty-five

---

25. Herman Aseyev, Yuriy Babanskyi (head of the Western Border region of the KGB), Mykhailo Bashkirov, Anatoly Bondarenko, Yuriy Gaisynskyi, Ivan Gopey, Leontiy Dmytruk.

signatures! And they say no one listens to the students! They say our protest is pointless! Not so.

The camp's leaders hoped to make progress at the next meeting with Leonid Kravchuk and other deputies. Yukhnovsky, who supported the protest, was working behind the scenes to organize the roundtable the students had asked for. Yarema insisted that the discussion be televised. Kravchuk, on the other hand, was clearly against that; a live-air broadcast like that would crack the information blackout around the protest. Then again, a few newspapers had already started to mention the students' protest, but so far only in passing. The students wanted to go live. It would spur more universities to join the protest and perhaps prompt support from the manufacturing sector as well. Yarema believed getting factory workers involved was a critical step.

Bodya Melnyk was skeptical.

"Right, sure. The lumpenproletariat will rise, just you wait," he said sardonically. But Yarema did not give up.

"And are you aware, my friend, that none of us students have ever spoken to a factory worker in our entire lives, unless he or she were our parent?"—"I am not," Bodya answered sharply. "I have met all kinds of people. Who do you think went to Afghanistan? Party bosses' kids?"

The long-awaited meeting took place on October 11. The delegation from the Supreme Council was led, of course, by Kravchuk. The students sent five reps: Yarema, Bodya, Ihor Rud', Mykyta Kalynyak, who was in charge of public affairs, and Viktor Ratyshnyi from Dnieprodzerzhinsk.

The meeting, as Mykyta reported it later, was long and difficult, with the students insisting on having their demands brought up for a vote in the Council and Kravchuk finding ever new excuses not to do so. It wasn't done, and it couldn't be done, and in general . . . The meeting was not broadcast, despite what Kravchuk had seemed to promise earlier. Since his promise was only verbal, Kravchuk said he did not recall saying anything to that effect.

The deputies kept asking the students to articulate their demands; this despite the fact that you had to be blind, deaf, and living under a rock in Kyiv not to know them by then.

Deputy Matviyenko took the floor. He addressed the students with poorly concealed disgust. Later, Mykyta, in his school teacher's glasses, made everyone laugh with his spot-on impression of the man. "As I understand it," Mykyta repeated Matviyenko's words, "you had your demands prepared three months ago. Do tell me, did you send the packet via the proper channels to the Supreme Council Presidium? And if you did not, then what was your reason? Because if you had, we could have had considered it already. But for whatever reason you did not do that and chose instead to start a hunger strike."

At least Matviyenko had asked a specific question. Hostile as he was, he wasn't wasting everyone's time with pointless talk.

Yarema was the one to answer him; he spoke rapidly and to the point.

"I can speak on behalf of the Lviv group. We sent our packet to the Supreme Council in early September. On September 27 we held preliminary protests in Lviv. We did not receive a response."

There were also deputies who wished to join the hunger strike. Levko Gorokhivsky, elected by the Democratic Bloc, said the students had shown the way forward and their actions would awaken Ukraine. Kravchuk, as was his habit, spoke as if addressing an intimate circle of insiders, "Just think about it for a minute. If you also go on a hunger strike here on the granite, as you say, that will ensure that no one believes your actions were not coordinated and that you had nothing to do with the students' protest." He raised his voice then, his baritone vibrating around the room. "No one!" he repeated and slashed at the air with his hand for emphasis.

And yet, the idea perhaps did not bother him as much as he

said it did. Let people think everything about the protest had been planned in advance—it would just disappoint them faster if they did. And he, Kravchuk, the nation's honest leader, would have warned everyone well ahead of time.

More Democratic Bloc deputies spoke; they advocated in favor of the students. Kravchuk could not sit still and took the floor again. "By the way," he said. "I saw there were girls on hunger strike among you. And these are our mothers! Mothers who have to bear children! Do you not understand it? Do you not realize what it means?"

Ivan listened to Kravchuk's lines in Mykyta's interpretation and thought about Rose. What would she have said to that? Compared to Kravchuk, the boys—Yarema, Rud', Bodya, and the rest of them—looked like radical feminists.

Then it was the turn of deputies from the majority to speak. "First you stop the hunger strike, and then we can talk about your demands," they kept saying. This, Mykyta reported, made Bodya jump to his feet. "How stupid do you think we are?" he thundered. Yarema stepped in, motioned for Bodya to cool off, hold his fire for when it really mattered. Because Yarema spoke so little, Kravchuk and nearly all other deputies believed they had a chance to bury him under cascades, avalanches of words—that their sheer mass would keep him pinned down far from daylight.

"First of all, we have no intention of stopping the strike," Yarema finally said. "Second, since you did not keep the promise you made to us—" "I did!" Kravchuk protested, almost shouting. "Since you did not keep your word, we will now escalate. You will have more than students on hunger strike to deal with."—"What do you mean, escalate? Escalate how? What are you talking about?" Kravchuk seemed to lift up from his seat.

Yarema stood up to leave. The other young men did so, too.

"Are you threatening us? How dare you? Do you think we won't find a way to deal with you?" Kravchuk was gasping with outrage.

"We do not threaten. We have warned you," Yarema said calmly.

That night, the camp's Coordinating Committee met, and then a general assembly was called. Yarema conveyed the essence of the conversation with Leonid Kravchuk. "Kravchuk does not want to put the Masol resignation to a vote," he commented. "Others have pretty much torpedoed the rest of our demands, even the one regarding the military."

"F-fat c-cats!" Bodya hissed.

"Kravchuk had promised us that our roundtable would be broadcast, but he did not fulfill his promise," Yarema continued. "Basically, we have to escalate our protest. They are out of touch. New tents come up every day. The city is different. People come here and tell us, we come to talk to you because there's never been anyone to talk to."

That was a fact. The camp in the heart of Kyiv attracted thousands of people. As if to help the students, the weather held unseasonably warm. People could stay and talk out in the open as long as they wanted.

Few were surprised by Kravchuk's failure to deliver. He was thought of as a savvy politician; jokes about him went along the lines of why does Kravchuk never carry an umbrella? Because he's so quick he can zigzag around rain drops and never get wet. Whatever it took, Kravchuk survived politically and followed his ambition. Now he was trying to thread the needle between the old Communist elite and the new people, the Democratic Bloc, Rukh, and the dissidents.

"Yarema, so what are we going to do now?"

"More. We have several days to plan new protests."

The camp buzzed with activity: people were writing leaflets, drafting appeals, and planning events. The Kyiv City Council became their headquarters; Yarema and Ihor Rud' stayed there for hours and returned well past midnight. Teams of organizers, and Rose along with them (thank God, Ivan thought, Rose chose to stop her strike so that she could do more outreach), visited the national university and other schools and spoke to students all over Kyiv. They spent the weekend before the day they chose for the next rally, Monday, October 15, distributing leaflets that said, "Dear Kyivites! Do not let students on hunger strike starve to death at the hands of political corpses!" The "veterans' march" was fresh in everyone's mind.

> *Students! Look around you, the totalitarian system has brought Ukraine to the brink of a political, economic, and environmental catastrophe! The XII Supreme Council, just like every single one before it, has amply demonstrated its inability to solve our urgent problems. We call for a new round of Supreme Council elections, with multiple parties allowed, to be held in the spring of 1991. Everywhere around the world—in Czechoslovakia, Poland, and Hungary—the young people have been the driving force and the spearpoint of democratic transformation. Our time has come! On October 15, we begin a general students' strike. Be at the Maidan at 11 o'clock! Join the strike! Come to the rally! Support the demands of the hunger strikers!*

On the morning of the fifteenth, students from the camp brought out their cots and began lining them up across Khreshchatyk. The barrier, as it were, looked flimsy but no one worried about that. Ivan lost track of time; when he looked up from his work, the sun was already high and the time was 11:00 AM. The square was suddenly filled with people, and Ivan had not seen them come.

This was not the kind of crowd that milled around the camp in its early days, cautious and incidental. No, this human mass roiled and churned like a sea—Ivan finally understood what it meant to say, "a sea of people." Yarema picked up the megaphone and made a speech. Others reached for the megaphone after him. People listened, broke into applause. Ivan saw blue-and-yellow flags in the crowd; there were signs with supportive statements. Someone with a sense of humor brought a homemade funeral wreath with a ribbon that read, FAREWELL, UNWASHED RUSSIA.[26] Students from the camp mixed into the crowd with their banners SHAME ON THE COMMUNIST PARTY!, DOWN WITH MASOL!, and FREE UKRAINE! Above it all floated the giant banner with the slogan FREEDOM OR DEATH. People whistled, chanted "Kravchuk, here we come!" and "Down with Masol and Kravchuk!"

The sun shone. So many young people came—it was clear there were high schoolers in the crowd, along with the college students. They moved out toward the Supreme Council building. Ivan watched employees come out of other government buildings as they passed. They stood on the sidewalks and looked at the march. Someone started collecting signatures in support of the students.

It felt like the hot cathartic wave that had graced Ivan several days earlier now swept through the entire city. People had never seen a crowd like *this*. They were not used to the feeling of solidarity it awoke in them. Up until then, being together in a crowd meant being ashamed of yourself, because you were all there to listen to a bunch of lies that you were expected to accept as the truth and conduct your lives accordingly.

"What's your best guess, how many people are here?" Tymish asked.

26. "Farewell, Unwashed Russia" is the opening line of a widely known poem by Mikhail Lermontov, 1841.

"I've no idea. Ten thousand, twenty?"

"I think there's more. As many as a hundred thousand . . . Look behind us!" But there was no way to look behind, to size up the crowd—it spread in every direction as far as the eye could see.

Deputies of the Kyiv City Council, meanwhile, published their own appeal to the Supreme Council, in which they expressed their solidarity with the students and called on the parliament to meet their demands.

"We remind the elected deputies of Ukraine," their text read, "that the genetic fund of Ukraine has been radically depleted by the terrible Holodomor of 1932–33, the Stalin- and Brezhnev-era repressions and deportations, and, finally, by the worst nuclear disaster the world has ever seen, Chernobyl. We cannot allow any more of our sons and grandsons to die today. They are the flower of our nation!"

At the head of the column that marched uphill toward the Supreme Council, several deputies walked, arms linked. Ivan recognized Khmara in his white headband, Ivan Drach, Horokhivsky. Right behind them, also with their arms linked, walked the participants of the hunger strike.

News reporters surrounded Khmara, he stopped and spoke into the microphones around him in his usual stern voice, "Parliamentary procedure has failed. This is the only way for us to be heard. The Supreme Council has spoken. Now it's the people's turn to speak. Just as they did in other countries, in Czechia, in Slovakia, and in Poland." Finally, newspapers were writing about them, reporters interviewed them as they walked, jotting down notes on the go. Ivan heard several interviews while they were still gathering on the Maidan. A young man from somewhere around Ternopil told journalists that his father, a tractor driver in the local kolkhoz, had been worked to death, and his mother died on the job in the same kolkhoz after she got sick, and now he was all alone in the world and came to join the hunger strike. Another young man, a Crimean Tatar named Kamil, spoke Ukrainian better than most Kyivites. He said little about himself, but said he had spent a lot of time listening to older and wiser people. Those who knew how to listen understood he referred to the deportations in 1944, when Crimean Tatars were relocated en masse. Kamil's "older, wiser people" were either his elders or other dissidents and political prisoners.

A very young girl who came to the march with her father said her name was Nastya, and her Dad's name was Orest, and they had come to defend Ukraine against Russia, just like the Sich Riflemen once had. Suddenly, there were new words being spoken, the banned history brought alive.

•

It was there, in the joyful, excited mass of people, that Ivan met "Sashko Petrenko." "Sashko" told him he was a student, that he was unable to join the hunger strike, but that he came to the march. He did not say where he studied, and Ivan wouldn't have asked, there were too many people. Physically, "Sashko" was utterly unremark-able; Ivan had thought him a schoolkid at first. If only Ivan could have been more vigilant that day, but how? What superhuman effort should he have marshaled? Then maybe there was a chance the man might have made him suspicious. "Sashko" stayed at Ivan's side as if glued, even when they approached the Supreme Council building, and when they stood before its entrance, and when Bodya Melnyk and Yurko Galaida, who had been dreaming of that hour, positioned their men so that they could break the police cordon in two places. "Sashko" was right there when they finally did break the police line, when they climbed to the top of the stairs and sat down, still holding hands.

Then they stood their vigil at the Council. People spoke through the megaphone, Bodya had to intervene to keep away Petya—or was that Pasha?—one of the "apostles" who insisted on expressing his thoughts on the subject of "the struggle," and then Bodya spoke, and the young men whistled their support and chanted, "Knock, knock, Kravchuk! We are here!" The racket echoed over the entire city.

For a long time, no one came out of the building. Later, Dankulynets would tell them that in those minutes the Council was in disarray. Finally, the opposition convinced the majority that they should hear what the students had to say. Kravchuk did not know if he was alive or dead.

What made matters worse was that on that same day, October 15, Mikhail Gorbachev was awarded the Nobel Peace Prize. The message of this was clear: the West loved their good "Gorby," who was showing them miracles of ingenuity as he held together the giant conglomerate of the socialist heaven on earth while illuminating it with glasnost, and even launching a perestroika. It was beginning to look almost like a sort of union of states, this functional federation of fifteen more or less friendly republics. No one was ready to see these republics become independent. Gorby would figure it out, the wonderful good Gorby, and the West would lend him a hand. Everything was going great! But here you go, a horde of deranged students marching on the parliament, like Oliver Cromwell, and with very similar intentions to boot! The riders of the apocalypse!

That was about how the Council members saw it. Moscow was displeased, nationalists were banging on Kravchuk's doors, and the West just had to go and give that award, just to make things worse for Kyiv! And they were left to deal with it.

Finally, the parliamentarians came to a decision. Yukhnovsky came out to the students and announced that they would receive *one*, and only *one* of the leaders to negotiate (the Council particularly emphasized this, as if they feared that if, say, five students went in the building would explode).

"I'll go," Rud' said. Bodya spoke against it, as he always did whenever one of the Kyivites stepped up ("They are not conscious enough, they look for adventures"), but Rud' had a concise counterargument that Bodya could not ignore. "If Yarema goes," Rud' said, "and he gets arrested, it will hurt our cause much more than if I go to jail. Same applies to you."

But Rud' did not get arrested. The deputies, exhausted by their concern with the matters of state, listened to what the students wanted: a one-hour live TV broadcast, a live radio broadcast of the same meeting, immunity for those who were picketing the Council. Kravchuk looked pitiful, he seemed to have spent the last few weeks at war—with the opposition, with these snotty punks, and even with his own friends in the Communist Party.

The broadcast was arranged the same evening, and the five students, utterly spent after the kind of day they had and their hunger strike, finally, slowly spoke into the cameras everything they had so long wanted to say.

Bodya talked about Afghanistan. How, a month after he joined his assigned detachment, he and other young men like him were sent to the front. They had no training, were taught nothing, just sent into the line of fire. Mykyta sat at Bodya's side during the broadcast. He repeated the students' demands and then added that he had faith in the Ukrainian people. Mykyta, in his glasses, looked like a straight-A good boy, and yet this delicate student somehow carried on his shoulders the colossal pressure of managing the movement's outreach and public engagement. His voice, like those of the other students, sounded strained and hoarse—Mykyta, on top of everything else, had caught a cold. But he was smiling.

Outside, in the streets, the crowds roiled. They whistled, the shouted, they chanted, "Free-dom! Free-dom! Free-dom!" The sound of it like a heaving wave that crashed, and crashed again against an inhospitable shore. But it had found its shore.

•

There were now two tent cities, each with its own fight. The new one, in front of the Supreme Council, was at the heart of the public protest. People shouted things through the megaphone; someone was saying he would start a "dry" hunger strike if the Council did not vote on a decision. Lukyanenko spoke through a microphone that had been placed at the entrance to the building. He said the students' cause was righteous and the time for historical justice had come.

The national students' strike had begun; protests flared up all over the country. A few cities had their own tent cities. All universities in Lviv, along with a third of its secondary and vocational schools, went on strike.

In Kyiv, students and other young people marched across the Dnieper to the left shore, to the manufacturing portion of the city. The enormous column stretched from Pechersk to Leningrad Square; Yarema led it. The sun was still warm but gusts of strong wind tore golden leaves off the trees, and back on the Maidan, the wind snatched at the tent ties and spun up what was left of the flowers people had brought, the dried bones of their stems twitched and danced. The wind played with ripped-out petals. The wind blew all night and the entire next day, chased dried leaves and shreds of paper down the boulevard.

Arsenal, the military factory, was the first to announce they had joined the strike. The stern workers, it appeared, had heard the students. "Now the real revolution will begin," Gavkalo said. "Just think, we'll go after the post office and telegraph next. And what's after that? The banks, I guess."—"Right, and we'll have our-selves a new October Revolution!" Ivan said, his best effort at a joke. In Russian, he added, "The ideas of the October Revolution are eternal!"

Next, the Bolshevik plant joined the strike; a few more facto-ries followed. The Supreme Council put the question of declaring emergency back on the agenda. Everything in the city closed, not a single educational institution held classes. People talked about the tanks they heard someone had seen on the outskirts, just like they did at the very beginning of the students' protests. Arsenal's work-ers marched on the parliament as one, in a single column, two days after the students had arrived on its steps.

This became the straw that broke the camel's back. The gov-ernment gave in.

(Or, Ivan wondered later, much, much later, maybe, if there had been time for more factories to join the strike—and the post office employees, too!—and if then, say, the railroad joined, that would have toppled the government altogether. Moreover, it would have been the end of the Soviet state—but as things played out, that state hung on to life for more than another year. The gov-ernment in Kyiv agreed to meet the students' demands because its members suddenly realized what *could* happen.)

In the Supreme Council assembly hall, people were hugging each other. Those who had been on hunger strike took off their white headbands. In the tent cities, too, people hugged, sang, and cried.

"Free-dom! Free-dom! Free-dom!" The sound rose and fell in Kyiv's streets and it felt as if the cobblestones and granite absorbed it, that from then on this call would be the new pulse of their endurance.

•

When they started being *called in*, most of them were not even nervous. So what? They had done what they had done; what could anyone do to them now? Sooner or later, there was going to be a new country with its own new special services. Its own special services—Ivan remembered the idea for the rest of his life; it would never have occurred to him before the Maidan. A country of their own, like Lithuania, where things came to a head in January of '91, when the Soviet troops stormed the TV tower, and people were killed. Gorbachev distanced himself as much as he could, saying no one had told him anything, he knew nothing, he could have done nothing . . . Just like the government "knew nothing" about Chernobyl in '86, when it sent kids out on May Day parades and would have kept sending them outdoors until all of Ukraine was sick or dead if Europe had not raised the alarm about the radioactive cloud they could clearly see coming their way. Lithuania held on. In February, Iceland recognized it as an independent state.

That's when things changed for them, as if someone suddenly remembered Ukraine had its own trouble, right here, a thorn in its side. The city languished in the wet March weather, its air so steeped in moisture that it even smelled like water, the way it smells on a laundry day in a small village house, when women soak the sheets in vats on the stove. Every other day it snowed.

They came in plain clothes. They knocked on classroom doors during lectures, called out names, and asked these individuals to stop at the department office or the dean's office later. They had called for everyone, except Ivan. A few folks were summoned *straight* from class: Andriy Groma, Mykyta Kalynyak, and Yarema.

Bodya responded by taking himself out of the city. He told a few close friends he was afraid he might kill someone. He knew where he could find fellow Afghanistan vets, knew which ones had kept their firearms. Just as likely, he did not even need to know any-one—he might have had his own piece secreted away somewhere. Bodya's father was long dead. His mother was never the same after he got drafted. She was afraid of everything, telephone calls, a knock on the door, her son not being there with her.

Ivan wondered when he would be called. He was not afraid of the university offices. He would, though, feel nervous if he were told to come to an appointment in an investigator's office in the KGB building itself; the building was the subject of many legends. It was not an older building retrofitted for the committee's needs, as had been done with the former NKVD buildings. No, Lviv's KGB headquarters were purpose-built, and as rumor had it, had a network of underground passages and secret rooms. It was there, in the torture rooms, that they interrogated dissidents and poets. The rooms must have been well insulated, so that no sound ever escaped to the street.

Ivan had only qualified for the rector's office. The investiga-tor opened the door as soon as Ivan arrived, which surprised him; he expected to be made to wait in the empty room alone with his conscience, as *the organs* were wont to do. The office, one of the rector's suite, set up with multiple desks and chairs, was deserted. Ivan marveled at that, too. How did they manage to send absolutely everyone out, did they tell people to take a smoke break or go get coffee in the cafeteria?

"Borovik, Viktor Matvyovych," the man introduced himself with a smile. He looked to be in his fifties and utterly without dis-tinction. He had a gray face, gray eyes, wasn't dressed particularly well, the kind of man you see on the streetcar in the morning or pass on the sidewalk without noticing.

On the coat-tree next to the door Ivan saw a gray raincoat and a man's hat of indeterminate color—a Soviet civil servant's uni-form. And the KGB uniform, it appeared.

"Would you like to take a seat?" Borovik said mildly and pointed to a chair. Ivan sat. *Would he like!* The man had a way with words, didn't he?

After that . . . after that, nothing happened. Borovik put himself at the next desk, sideways to Ivan, and began to write something with great focus and diligence. He wrote for no less than ten minutes before he put his pen down abruptly, leaned back in his chair, put his hands behind his head, and smiled. "A smoke?" he asked Ivan informally. "Not for me," Ivan said.

Borovik got up, found his cigarette and matches, went to the window, opened it, and lit up. Now he stood with his back to Ivan, in what must have been meant to be a dramatic mise-en-scène from a crime movie: the wise old detective smokes by the window as he contemplates the brilliant trap he has set for the criminal. Except that Borovik's shapeless, shabby form could only work in a comedy. There was nothing menacing or ominous about him. Ivan held the pause, said nothing. Borovik put out his cigarette, came back to the desk—this time facing Ivan across it—pulled up a chair, and sat. "Well, so, we are breaking the law, aren't we?" he said with a squint. "Which law?" Ivan asked, he genuinely had no idea what they were talking about. It had been six months since the Revolution on the Granite. "The law of the Country of Soviets!"—"Tell me the specific article."—"Oh, so you are one of those . . . What do you call them? . . . Rights defendants?" Borovik chuckled as if he had found Ivan's answer exceedingly pleasant, and then changed his tone sharply, "All right, fine. We don't have to talk about it if you don't want to." Ivan, of course, did not say anything about what he wanted or not. "We can discuss your education."—"You still need to cite a specific article if you want to expel me," Ivan insisted. He spoke evenly, carefully, making sure he enunciated each word slowly. "Expel you?" Borovik made a face. "What young people we have these days, soon as you ask them for a chat, they're off to the races! What's gotten into you?" and he gave another chuckle. His laugh was resonant but intermittent, as if he had a constant pressure in his chest. He had to—he must have smoked a lot. He had a dense chest. He was all of a dense flesh that no crumble of joy could escape, a man like a collapsed coal mine. "So, what about your studies? Are you managing without Cs?"

Ivan said nothing. He had no strategy, just kept silent, maybe just to be stubborn. Let this Borovik tell him why the hell he'd called him out here instead of acting out this polite conversation. Borovik studied Ivan's face closely. He said, "Listen, Ivan. When someone asks you a question, you are supposed to answer. My name, in case you have forgotten, is Viktor Matvyovych. Because some people are like that, they forget a name and then can't speak, because, you know, it's awkward." Ivan listened, incredulous. Where had Viktor Matvyovych met such people? No one cared about names in the Soviet Union. "Did you hear me? When you don't answer, you are being rude? Right? Yes or no?" Viktor Matvyovych chuckled and tutted.

Ivan did not respond. Now Borovik, too, fell silent and remained so for a long time, tormenting Ivan, of course, they were trained to wear out the people they questioned. It was terrifying to be silent like that, together, knowing that you were enemies, that you meant each other ill. It would be easier to scream, to defend yourself. You would know then what to expect, a kick in the face, obscenities, threats. It would be easier to talk. Or did it only seem so to Ivan?

"I see. We are stubborn," Borovik said finally. Ivan felt a small sun light up joyfully in his chest, he didn't let him break him. He had outsilenced this Borovik. Which meant he could do it again. If he had to.

Borovik was smiling. "Actually, you are lucky you got me. This is not an interrogation. How could it be? If only you knew what a *real* interrogation looks like . . . You tell me, tell me honestly, you must have heard all kinds of things about us, that we are hell's own spawn, that we love torturing people. Like it said in *The Aeneid*, have you not read *The Aeneid*?"

Here, perhaps, Ivan was supposed to experience a slight shock at the revelation that a KGB man had read *The Aeneid*; was he, after all, human? Borovik went on, "Whatever people have told you about us is not true. We are people, too. Just people. So we work at the KGB, so what? Do you think your dearly beloved West doesn't have its special services? Of course they do. Everyone does. So you, a citizen of your country, ought to aid and assist your own country's special services in their efforts to defend the country against its foreign enemies. And against the domestic ones, too. The two, as we are well aware, are connected. If it weren't for us—uh-huh!—you can't even imagine what we'd have going on here right now!"

"What would that be?" Ivan couldn't resist asking and gave himself a mental slap as soon as he did, the question clearly made Borovik happy.

"What, what? God only knows!" Borovik wiped his forehead, although Ivan could see neither sweat nor dirt there. Perhaps the dirt was invisible. He paused, said, "Wait for me a bit," and left the room. Ivan was left alone.

After a few minutes, another investigator, lean and sinewy, entered the room.

"Last name!"

Along with this officer, an odd smell came into the room, unpleasant, unnerving, like the smell of spoiled food or long-stored clothes. Ivan's friends, young men, had no clothes put away anywhere, every item they had was alive, was constantly worn next to their warm bodies, did not have the luxury of lying idle and untouched. Ivan thought of the Geographer's real-life tales of the Soviet Army and how he made fun of the Soviet textile industry's brilliant invention: the military footwraps known widely by their

Russian name, *portyanki*. One had to use these dreadful strips of fabric to wrap one's feet so the boots wouldn't rub them raw. The soldiers sweat in them, ran in them, and had no way of adjusting them if they didn't get them right in the morning . . . The smell bothered Ivan. It made it hard to think.

"Last name?" the investigator asked again, louder, in Russian.

Ivan told him. He told him other things, all in response to questions that came out of the man's skinny throat with its large Adam's apple, and the man wrote them down. Every once in a while, he raised his eyes and regarded Ivan coldly. His eyes were cold but a mad, evil fire burned in them.

"And what is your last name?" Ivan inquired in Ukrainian, just to keep being stubborn.

"I'm the one who asks questions here," the investigator snapped. He kept speaking Russian.

All right. Good cop, bad cop. This would be the bad one. He kept asking his clipped questions and giving Ivan sharp looks. Ivan thought he had heard that these people got special training to produce certain facial expressions; they had to practice at home, much like actors, for hours in front of the mirror, miming and aping. Then they had to perform in front of their instructors and colleagues who called out for them to do angry, or disgusted, or a bit of class hatred, and now all of it together, great job, that's an A! The bad cop without a last name looked like he'd been at the top of his class.

The investigator stopped writing. He put the pen down on top of his papers. Ivan expected him to put his hands behind his back like Borovik, to stretch, lean back in his chair, and start the silent treatment. He would not, however, like Borovik, ask Ivan about his studies or let him know he'd read *The Aeneid*—this one didn't look like he even read Pushkin. What's Pushkin to him? With nothing better to do, Ivan studied the man's face, it was severe and lean, with deep lines despite his relatively young age. Ivan wondered if . . .

He did not get a chance to finish his thought. The man got up, leaned low over Ivan, and began shouting at him, spouting choice Russian obscenities like foul water from a fire hose. In Ivan's entire life no one had ever heaved such verbal abuse at him. The words mixed with the smell of the army and prison barracks the investigator had brought in on him. At first Ivan, stunned, thought the screaming would bring someone running—they were in the rector's office, after all!—someone had to come, you couldn't hear this anywhere in the building and not come running at this outrage, this bloodbath, it sounded like a bloodbath, no one screams like that for no reason, but eventually, as he gasped, overwhelmed by the assault of the investigator's shrill, animallike rage, Ivan realized no one would come. They had sent everyone out of the office for a reason; no one was coming to save him, and all he could do was sit there and hold his back straight so he wouldn't hide his face in his hands, wouldn't, for anything in the world, cover his ears, would not bend under the man's viperlike glare, would not twitch a muscle under the machine-gun fire of his abhorrent language, would not . . .

The man stopped as suddenly as he had begun. He sat back in his chair opposite Ivan, picked up his pen, and enunciated very clearly, "Who are your leaders?"

Leaders? Is he insane? *They* knew perfectly well who the "leaders" were, the entire country, along with the Supreme Council, knew who Yarema and the other guys were. They had been on TV. Ivan said nothing. Neither did the No-Name Man, that's how Ivan referred to him in his mind. After a few minutes of silence, the man must have gotten bored with it, it wasn't like he had come to get information, after all, he had known everything he needed to know, better, perhaps, than Ivan himself. For the first time, something that looked to Ivan like weariness slipped across the investigator's face, a real, genuine emotion—slipped like a cloud on a sunny day, too small to rain. It was there, and then it was gone.

"Well," the investigator said. "Looks like your leaders got you into this and lit out for the hills. And you have to answer for them. Don't you? They've framed you. They'll get to go on their way in the world, and what about you? You've got squat. And still, you won't give up your bosses. They've given you up long ago."

On their way in the world? Where? What leaders? What bosses was he talking about? Good Lord, did they send a lunatic to mess with him?

"We do not have 'bosses' as you understand them. No one 'got us' into anything. People do sometimes make their own choices," Ivan said finally. Let the No-Name Man have something.

"Don't you see how they used you? These leaders of yours? This," the investigator peeked at one his papers, "Yarema of yours?" He said Yarema's last name. "Him and those dissidents of yours, your ex-cons ... Looks like it's news to you, isn't it? That you let yourselves be led by former inmates? Yes, they had done their time. And they manipulated you. They've got their sights on ministers' posts, and what about you? You get nothing."

Ivan could not lower himself to contradicting the investigator, doing so would have meant acknowledging that his nonsense had any relationship to the truth. So Ivan kept silent. He marveled at the imagination these people had. Ministers' posts, huh? Would they also go out to buy themselves some felt hats, the better to blend in with Borovik and his comrades?

"So who are they?" the No-name Man asked in a different, softer voice.

"No one. Just our own conscience," Ivan said. He felt wrung out.

The investigator waved him off with a gesture that meant *non-sense*! In his world, things were different, not the way they stood in Ivan's world. His world was orderly, there were leaders who spoke

212 • OKSANA LUTSYSHYNA

to the people only and exclusively from a podium, preferably the one atop Lenin's Mausoleum or another tomb of some kind. They spoke standing on the shoulders of the dead because only the dead fed their power.

It was dangerous to rely on the living; in the No-Name Man's world and all the other no-name worlds, the living were unreliable, disloyal, made, by the very fact of their existence, prone to turn on you, because how could these living—still living, in spite of everything!—not turn when you kept them in cages like animals, and abused them, and beat them, and spit between their eyes, and shoved a hot soldering iron up their anuses, and gave them shit spread on bread to eat? They *had to* turn, these clumps of flesh. Ivan would turn, too, if this were done to him, and the No-Name Man knew it. Now, Ivan had to know it, too. If Ivan had been spared torture this time, it was only because the No-Name Man *had no use* for what torture would have gotten him to confess.

Or the No-Name Man was too busy to bother with Ivan. Perhaps all he wanted was to put the mark of shame on him, with words only, for the time being.

"You're dismissed," he said to Ivan suddenly and waved, as if at a dog. Ivan stood up and left. In the hallway, which was also for some reason deserted, he felt the tears that welled in his eyes. His knees trembled. He could see nothing in front of him, did not know where he was going, did not understand where he was. Ivan got angry with himself. What is this? So what, a bunch of Russian profanity! Why did he feel like crying? All things considered, he had done well, he had not told anyone anything, had not said anything he did not believe, and neither had he betrayed anyone else. Why was he reacting this way—to words? Why? Why did he feel so broken, so indifferent, so . . . so utterly shattered and stained?

Those were not mere words.

That was pure, chemically refined hatred, a real energy weapon, and where it had aimed—the middle of Ivan's chest—a dose of poison now sat, spreading. Ivan grasped at his heart, it was beating so hard that each contraction reverberated in his temples. Suddenly, he could not breathe, as if he had really inhaled a toxic gas.

He recalled Ostapenko, telling them that the KGB was not like a dog that might bite off your finger but a viper that poisoned your entire body. This made Ivan feel a little better; he remembered he was not alone. There were others. His people.

They were.

But he would never be able to tell anyone what had happened to him today.

He would not—he knew it. Never. Not Mysko, not Rose (especially not Rose), not Tymish Gavkalo, not Yarema. Nor Andriy Groma. No one. He pictured the faces of the former prisoners. Those people told them things, but they had not told them everything, and now he knew why, because there was a level of humiliation that was to be forever yours and yours alone. To talk about it meant to consent to your own not-being, because you existed only as long as *it* did not.

So you sealed this terrible fortune, like Chernobyl's exploded reactor, into a sarcophagus and put it in the remotest room of your existence.

A howl. The entire nation was a howl. A howl that you eventually could not hold inside you, so you opened your mouth and screamed—at your children, your parents, your employees, any damn thing that came your way.

It was in Tsar Sergeant-Major's reign
That close-cropped Corporal One-Arm

> *And drink-besotted Long-of-Arm,*
> *Two N.C.O.s, ruled the Ukraine . . .*[27]

I am the one asking questions here!
You scum!
Dis-missed!
What did I just say?
Shut up!
Pig!
Vermin!
Bandera's spawn!
Shut up!!
I am the one asking questions here!!
Shut up!
#$%^&*!
. . .!
. . .!!
. . .

Ivan did not remember how he found his way outside, where the cold sun blinded him, did not remember who offered him a cigarette, who clapped him on the shoulders, did not remember anything; he was seeing himself as if from outside his own body, that body that had been *yelled at*; he did not remember what he said, only saw his own lips move, watched them slowly shape themselves into a smile (he had to hide what happened there *in the rector's office*, hide it at any cost, erase it from his mind, forget it once and for all!), saw himself finally reach out for that cigarette and put it in his mouth, where he kept it lest anyone saw how hard his hands were shaking.

---

27. Taras Shevchenko, *The Half-Wit*. Translated by John Weir. https://taras-shevchenko.storinka.org/poem-the-half-wit-taras-shevchenko-translated-by-john-weir.html

On August 18 of that same year, 1991, only a few months later, everything changed. That morning, Mysko shook Ivan awake, it was just before seven.

"What d'you want so early?"—"Something is happening. It's nothing but *Swan Lake* on every channel!"

Ivan leaped out of bed. He and Mysko got dressed in record time, wolfed down a couple of stale rolls—the only food they, eternally hungry students, had left over from the day before— and ran out into the streets. Glyboka Street, which led to the Polytechnic's main building, was already busy, packed with people. By eleven, they knew nearly everything there was to know; people came in from different parts of the city, bringing reports of strategic assets. No one said this out loud, but everyone expected Russian tanks.

There had been a coup in Moscow.

However, rumor had it that it was limited to Moscow. In Leningrad, Sobchak was making speeches straight out of an apartment-block window. No emergency had been declared, he said. There was no coup in Leningrad. People were barricading the streets, and this was a good sign; without Leningrad, Moscow would achieve nothing. If the military failed to take Leningrad . . . which they just might . . . Russian politicians, like feudal lords, each had their own fiefdom, without Sobchak's say-so, they could not have Russia, never mind the other republics.

Someone brought explosive liquid to blow up the tanks. That there might not be any tanks did not even occur to anyone. Sunlight splashed like waves into open windows, the noise of the big city swelled, a fire engine sounded its siren, the streetcars rolled on their rails, the wind carried the sound of a train whistle from the distance.

How could the clatter of the tanks fit into all this? Metal on cobblestone? Soviet tanks had gone through Prague, they had gone through the peaceful streets of Budapest . . . They had been to Vilnius, and now they could very well appear here, in Lviv.

After many phone calls, the activists finally set out for number 23 Shevchenko Avenue, the building that used to house the city Komsomol committee and had been given over to youth organizations. Now Lviv's Student Fraternity, the Lion Society, Postup, and the Carpathian Skiing Club had their headquarters there. They pulled together whatever equipment they could find. Bodya the Afghan brought an army-issued radio that could receive broadcasts from both Russia and the West. They printed some leaflets, and a few of them went to scatter and post them around the city.

They laughed because it was not that long ago that Gorby had obviously tightened the screws, which was why the KGB went after them. Earlier in the summer, American President George H. W. Bush had come to Ukraine and made his infamous "Chicken Kiev speech" in English in which he had called for keeping the Soviet Union alive. He said an independent Ukraine was not the best idea. Well, maybe for him it wasn't, the students joked.

•

On one memorable day that August, Vyacheslav Chornovil and other Supreme Council deputies came out to the crowd on the square in front of the building carrying the yellow-and-blue national flag. In December, Ukraine's independence became a fact. Few, however, took note of the monthslong fires in which the KGB burned their archives, the columns of black smoke that rose into the gray sky. A fire, people mused to each other, no surprise there, who knows what those KGB people were doing, must have been smoking next to a stack of case files, and there you have it . . .

That winter, the snow melted long before Christmas. Ivan spent a very short time at home despite the fact that he loved the holidays and the warm domesticity while the indefatigable Margita worked her magic at the stove and the smell of the Christmas tree mixed with the aroma of sweet cookies. Being home was like stepping back into his childhood. He was free to spend his days in bed, reading books. Yet something urged him back to Lviv, to the frigid dorm where he lived after his freshman year in a shared flat, in a room without the slightest hint of the comforts that were his at home. Home, however, muddled his thoughts, muffled what he felt. Home wanted to engulf him entirely.

He found Lviv still snowless but dusted with white—the temperature had dropped the night before and everything was frozen. Streets turned into skating lanes. The cold wind got under one's skin, and Ivan was chilled to the bone as soon as he stepped out of the railway station. It was so cold it hurt to put one foot in front of the other. When Ivan finally made his skidding, shuffling way to the dormitory, it seemed to him the epitome of luxury, like a warm hive of cave dwellers.

Rose had been waiting for him. Laughing, they got into the bed she'd warmed while he made his way from the station (whenever Ivan's roommates were gone, she came to spend the night with him). They caught up on what had happened in their lives over the last few weeks, it had been a while since they last saw each other. "I've brought treats for you!" Ivan remembered; Margita, as always, packed all kinds of food for him. Because of all the political upheaval, it had been a tough year, and growing your own food was a big help. Ivan jumped out of bed and realized he had felt warm in the dorm purely because he had come in from the freezing air outside, the radiators were barely tepid. He carried the bags with homemade delicacies to bed, and the two of them dined, reclined like Romans, on pies and other bits Margita had wrapped.

Later, having laughed themselves silly and more or less shaken the crumbs off the comforter, full and a bit sleepy despite the early hour, they listened to the murmuring in the room next door. The family that had moved in there appeared to belong to a Christian sect; they were reciting prayers, probably reading from their books. It was hard to tell exactly what kind of Christians they were.

At the moment, they were reading aloud, or rather, one person was.

"Let's listen to them," Rose said. "Shh! Be quiet!" Ivan spoke loudly, just to be contrary, and tried to sing. "What's wrong with you?" she said. "Shush, I'm curious, and it's a sign, too: whatever we hear by accident around New Year's Day will come true."—"What's accidental about it?" he laughed. "Do you ever hear anything surprising in church?"

The people on the other side of the wall paid no mind to their talking and laughter, although, surely, they must have been able to hear it. They kept murmuring, and Ivan listened, despite himself, because Rose was listening intently. He was so sleepy he no longer knew if he actually heard someone reading or if he was dreaming it.

"And Cleopas was one of the disciples to whom the Lord appeared after His resurrection, on the road to Emmaus. On the third day following our Savior's death, Cleopas and another disciple, Luke, were going from Jerusalem to a village called Emmaus. The Lord himself came and walked along with them as they talked about what had happened in Jerusalem, the judgment of our Lord, and His death on the cross. The Lord asked them what they were discussing and why they were so downcast, and Cleopas told this traveler, who was our Lord, about Jesus of Nazareth, and his powerful deeds and teachings, His suffering and His death on the cross . . ."[28]

Ivan and Rose fell asleep for an hour or two, then woke up, made coffee, and sat drinking it and looking out the window at the gray city frozen hard as a bare bone.

---

28. Luke 24:13–35

•

On January 19, 1992, Sashko Reva fell out of a speeding train. According to the police, he got up for some unknown reason in the middle of the night, went to the end of the carriage, opened the door, and stepped out. The inquest confirmed he was drunk, but the problem was that Sashko Reva did not drink. At all. No imagination could picture him in the cheap-seat train car, in the company of intoxicated pals, gathered around the basic drinking kit of pickles and slices of salted pork fat. Sashko had abhorred such eating as much as he had abhorred drinking. And if he had, somehow, managed to be drunk, he would have gone to sleep, not walked the length of the car to the exit.

Ivan did not know Sashko well but remembered him from the days on the Maidan. Sashko was tall and athletic. He was into sports. Cross-country, was it? Ivan did not remember for sure. Guys in the dorms nicknamed him Rakhmetov, after the character in Chernyshevsky's *What Is to Be Done?* Sashko, unlike that character, did not sleep on a bed of nails, but he did get up at five in the morning and wash in cold water. He did gymnastics. He went for runs. He did not smoke or drink. He was studying English.

And suddenly he had fallen out of a train. Rumors varied wildly, but one thing was clear: he could not have fallen by accident. Someone must have pushed him. Sashko was an activist, he was forever involved in one cause or another and might have crossed someone, but how could anyone find out who had finally had it in for him?

"He traded currency," the police said. Sashko? Foreign currency?

"A turf thing among criminals," the police explained. That theory held no water either.

Had the KGB called him for an interview? Of course they had. They would never have missed him.

"Did you know he had family sent to the gulag?" Tymish asked. "No, I did not," Ivan said.

For one, how would he have known? And two, was there a single one among Ivan's friends—never mind his friends, was there a single person in Ukraine—who had not That seemed unlikely.

•

They sat in the Twisted Linden, dazed. They were not intimate friends, but still, they all knew Reva. The day was not unbearably cold, but it was still too chilly to be outside for long; they had to find somewhere indoors to be. On that day, Tymish talked the saleswoman into *pouring* for them from her special reserve under the counter. Things were looking bleak: following Bodya, several more people removed themselves from Lviv, some, like Bodya, in the middle of the semester, abandoning their studies.

They went to the home of a young woman painter who had known Reva; they sat on the floor there, drank wine, talked about their lost comrade, the way he was, and who had been the last to see him. "Are you sure it wasn't suicide?" someone asked and was met with a chorus of protests: like hell it was, few people loved life as much as Sashko had, few cherished every single moment of it the way he used to. "It was as if he knew something like this was coming," the painter said. Ivan never did learn her name. People nodded in agreement. They talked about the funeral, which would be held in the village where Sashko's mom and dad lived, about his parents, and his sister (at least there was his sister, the bereaved parents would still have another child).

At that point Ivan fell asleep for a spell—he would have sworn he never closed his eyes, but one couldn't dream with one's eyes open, could one? He thought of trains, and the time he and Gavkalo went to smoke at the door of their railcar on their way to Kyiv, on the first day of the hunger strike. Things got muddled after that, there was a dark railcar, the noise of the wheels, the door that then flew open onto a place covered in snow, and then he was flying, headfirst, and thinking that the snow ought to soften the impact, but suddenly he knew there was no snow, nothing like that, just an abandoned quarry where his body landed hard on the sharp stones, and . . .

Ivan woke up to someone shaking him by the shoulder. "Hi! Do you recognize me?" the man asked. Ivan, befuddled by his nightmare, shook his head, "Can't say I do."—"We met at the Maidan! I'm Sashko!"

Ivan shuddered. Sashko? Another one? Slowly, the fog in his head lifted and he remembered the man. Yes, he had been there, had marched to Bankova with them. But what was he doing here, wasn't he from Kyiv? Before he had a chance to ask, Sashko was telling him he had just moved to Lviv, literally the other day, and had rented an apartment. He told him other things, too, but Ivan stopped listening, he was thinking about Reva.

By the time he and Rose left it was dark. They slipped on the icy spots, no one bothered to put sand on the sidewalks, but did not talk as they usually did, just held hands in silence, squeezed each other's palms as if to say, I've got you, don't be afraid, I'm still here, and my hand is warm.

•

"Sashko" called Ivan at the dorm the following week.

"Ivan, hey! Hi!" Ivan heard the voice in the receiver say. "Remember me?"—"Who is this?"—"Sashko! We sat on the pavement in front of the Supreme Council together, remember? Hey, I've got a thing for you, come downtown, let's go for a walk."—"I'm busy at the moment," Ivan lied. He did not feel like going anywhere. Sashko, however, insisted, and eventually Ivan gave in. They agreed to meet at the Neptune fountain.

The square around the town hall was crowded as usual. "Sashko" rather informally grabbed Ivan's elbow and steered him through the square.

"How did you know where I live?"—"One of the guys told me."—"Which one?"—"I forgot his name. Let me think, it'll come to me ..."

That was weird. But okay, maybe it would come to him.

"Where are we going?" Ivan asked. "To a studio. I want to show you something."—"What exactly?"

What "Sashko" referred to as the "studio" was not far, near Halytska Market, a tiny apartment on the ground floor. There was no kitchen, only a very tight room and a miniature bathroom. The air inside was moist; there had to have been mold everywhere, hidden behind the Carpathian rugs hung on the walls. Another smell, repulsive, mixed with the smell of mold, but Ivan could not identify it. A table, a couch, and two chairs had been squeezed into the room, just barely, there was physically no space for any other furniture. If indeed it was a studio, you were left to guess at the art or craft practiced there.

"Sashko" invited Ivan to sit down, rustled things in a wall cabinet, and produced a bottle of liqueur and a pair of small stemmed glasses. The liqueur had an unattractive red color and Ivan refused curtly, "I won't have any." He did not want to drink; the smells of this place were making it hard to breathe. He would have much rather got up and left, but that would have been rude. Instead, he asked "Sashko" questions: When did he arrive? What did he intend to do in Lviv? Did he have family here? "Sashko" answered cryptically: yes, he had come to stay, no, he had no family.

"And what is it that you do exactly? Do you paint?"—"Yes, I

paint. But I don't have my paintings here yet, I still have to move them."—"What do you paint? What's your style?"—"That's exactly what I wanted to talk to you about! I do portraits, posed in interiors. I'm starting a new series and I need some Hutsul clothing, but it has to be authentic, you know how people are, they think embroidery is just there for decoration and put twentieth-century pieces with nineteenth-century outfits, like they don't know the whole ensemble has to work. Or they put an embroidered shirt from Bukovyna with a waistcoat from Kyiv. I want things to make sense together. Would you know anyone who could help me find the stuff? You have so many friends, and I just moved here."

Ivan was taken aback. What friends? Did he look like an art collector to "Sashko"? He knew less than nothing about Hutsul clothing, he'd be lucky if he could tell a *keptar* from a *gunia*. "I don't know anything about such things," he told "Sashko" honestly. "Well, maybe you don't, but could you introduce me to someone who might?" "Sashko" looked at Ivan with genuine supplication. "Well," Ivan said and tried to think. Who would know anything like that? Rose?

He promised "Sashko" he would work on it, but then got busy and forgot all about it until several days later, when he remembered his promise while he lay in bed listening to the murmurs on the other side of the wall. He remembered it for about two minutes before he fell asleep. He told himself he should ask around, so as not to be rude . . .

". . . but we had hoped that he was the one who was going to redeem Israel. And what is more, it is the third day since all this took place. In addition, some of our women amazed us. They went to the tomb early this morning but didn't find his body. They came and told us that they had seen a vision of angels, who said he was alive. Then some of our companions went to the tomb and found it just as the women had said, but they did not see Jesus. We do not know, said Cleopas and Luke, if we are to believe in Christ's resurrection . . ."

Ivan most likely would have forgotten the entire episode, but a few days later—classes had started again—"Sashko" reappeared. This time he found Ivan at the doors of his building, in the heart of the campus.

"Hey there! I was starting to wonder if you forgot about me!"—"I'm sorry, I kind of did," Ivan said. He did not feel like lying. "It's my last semester, lots to do . . ."—"I get it! Look, I'm going to a party, and I was wondering if you could come with me. Would you? Please? There will be people there I'd like to meet, and I'd be more comfortable if you could introduce me, you know?" "Sashko" pleaded. In that instant, looking at his face, Ivan felt a bit sorry for him, and asked, "Do you have any sketches or anything?" Because, really, could a person who insisted he was an artist not have brought a single piece of paper with him when he moved to a new city? "Sashko" looked deflated and told Ivan again that all his stuff was in transit, and was supposed to have gotten there already, but was held up.

•

At the party Ivan brought "Sashko" to meet a man he knew, Mykhailo Malyi, whom everyone called Mike. In contrast to his last name (which meant, literally, "small"), Mike was a tall, powerful guy, well known in Lviv as an art historian and a tour guide. Back in the Brezhnev days, Malyi was labeled a "social parasite" and police occasionally busted him for trading in banned consumer goods, but he always got off easily since, as many suspected, he also procured antiques for the Party bosses. It was rumored, rather cautiously, that Mike maintained a staff of interpreters, all young and very attractive women, but no one knew this for sure. Ivan did not know Mike very well, which made him nervous; the underground trader could very well just tell him to go to hell, why would he ever even want to talk to a random student?

Besides, Ivan thought, he really did not want to talk to Mike about "Sashko" at all. For the first time he faced a basic fact: he did not like "Sashko."

"I wonder if I might ask you a question," Ivan said to Mike by means of opening. "What kind of question?" Mike asked, looming above Ivan. One of his eyes was bigger than the other, and this bigger eye sat under a heavy, twitching eyelid. The twitching had a certain rhythm to it. "A . . . an acquaintance of mine . . . This one guy I know, he is looking to buy some Hutsul clothing."

Ivan wanted to say "friend" but could not.

Mike squinted as he always did when conversation concerned business.

"It's not cheap, you know," he said. "Where is this . . . what did you call him? Acquaintance of yours?"

"He's here," Ivan nodded at "Sashko" in the crowd. "He's come with me."

Mike studied "Sashko" for a beat.

"That one? Are you sure he has the money?" He asked. There was a tinge of mockery in his voice, he, unlike Ivan perhaps, could tell a *client* from a common loser. "Well, he said he did," Ivan said, defensive. Mike had asked a very good question indeed. What little "Sashko" told Ivan about himself included the fact that he had inherited a bit of money from his grandmother, but it wasn't going to be millions, was it? There were no such grandmothers in this country. He could well have been lying about who he was, couldn't he? Mike wasn't one to be taken for a fool—he wasn't, like Ivan, young and gullible. "Sashko" did not bring any sketches, no one Ivan knew had heard of him before . . . A man from nowhere.

"All right, go get him. We'll talk," Mike said, finally.

As soon as they exchanged a few words, Ivan left them, feeling a bit easier; the two were discussing points of craftsmanship, something about seams, patterns, villages and localities, and what came from where. Ivan knew nothing about these things, but "Sashko" definitely sounded like he did, which was a good sign.

"So how's that new friend of yours doing? Sashko, right?" Rose asked, with a squint.

"Seems all right... He said he wanted to paint portraits of people dressed in Hutsul clothing."

"I've heard worse ideas. Ask him, maybe he could paint me, in exchange for your services?"

Rose would look divine in a Hutsul outfit, Ivan had no doubt. Yet he could not fathom her going to that so-called studio where "Sashko" had taken him.

He wondered about the man again. Where would he put his easel in that den? And where would his model stand, or sit? There was no room.

And that smell!

A few days later, Mike found Ivan in the Twisted Linden.

"Well, there was a reason I asked you if that guy of yours had any money. I was right, had a feeling about him!"

"What happened?" Ivan asked.

"Nothing special. What often happens," Mike laughed. "Meaning, nothing. He disappeared like he dropped off the face of the earth. I thought he might."

"Did he make an arrangement with you?"

"He sure did. And I found what he said he was looking for. But he did not come to collect the goods."

"I do apologize!" Ivan blushed, he felt terrible. Also, he was confused. Why would "Sashko" have asked for contacts, for an introduction, if he did not have the money to pay for the clothing he had arranged to buy? Why would he have said he wanted to buy it in the first place? Why didn't he keep his arrangement with Mike?

"You don't have to apologize," Mike said. He spoke to very few people and almost never first, everyone came *to him*, waited for their turn. The fact that he sought Ivan out was another big sign. Had Ivan paid more attention that day, he would have seen or heard something that was meant as a warning. That's what Mike was about to do, warn him about "Sashko," and in no uncertain terms, it was Ivan who did not know how to hear the warning. Or could not.

Or perhaps none of it would have made any difference.

"Ivan, listen to me," Mike said firmly, and his eyelid twitched harder. "Get rid of this guy. Get away from him, do you hear me?"

"I do. Thank you. I will."

•

Two days later Ivan saw "Sashko" waiting for him outside the building, just as he did last time, and felt, for no apparent reason, alarmed. This seemed odd.

"Ivan, hi! Well, yeah, here I am again . . . I was wondering if I could ask you for a favor. About Hutsul clothing."—"Not anymore. I've made the introduction for you."—"Oh, don't be like that! So there was a misunderstanding . . . but we are buddies, aren't we?"

Really? Ivan felt his eyes bulge. How the hell could they be "buddies?"

"Ivan, hey," "Sashko" whined. "Didn't we stand together against the regime? Please help me . . ."—"Listen, pal, I'm sorry, but I don't even know who you really are. You tell me you are Sashko, but you could be anyone. And you don't own an easel."— "Me? I'm Sashko! I'm . . ."—"And your last name?"—"Last name? Eh . . . Petrenko."

Was he really mocking Ivan, or did it only feel like he was? He hustled to keep up with Ivan, who was walking away, saying something. Ivan stopped.

"Look, what do you want from me?" he said. "Let's be straight, I barely know you plus you just stood up a friend of mine. I won't be introducing you to anyone else. And that's it, do you get it? And one more thing, we are not buddies, and never were."

In the next instant, he saw "Sashko" transform into a different person, the man's eyes flared with malice. It lasted only a moment, and then he said, quietly, "Not buddies, eh? So you are saying we are not buddies?"

Ivan waved him off and started walking again. "Sashko" caught up with him and grabbed him by the shoulder. Ivan jerked himself free, turned to face "Sashko," and—

—and realized this was not the "Sashko" he had been talking to two minutes before. It was hard to believe a person could slip on a different mask so radically. It was no longer the nervous, shabby "buddy" with rapid gestures and his head forever sunk in his shoulders that stood before Ivan, this was a foe: strong, upright, broad-shouldered. His lips curled in a nasty grin, and now Ivan understood why the man's presence had been bothering him all this time. Back at the Maidan, he never saw "Sashko" smile; some people look more beautiful when they smile but this man turned downright repulsive. And even when Ivan had gone along with his "Hutsul clothing" story, "Sashko"'s smile, at some instinctual level, repelled him.

(Later, much later, Ivan would wonder about that smile. *They* had seemed so powerful, so invincible, and yet somehow none of "Sashko"'s colleagues, bosses, mentors, or runners ever realized they should have told him not to smile because the smile gave him away instantly? Why didn't they? They could have taught him to smile differently . . . They really *could not* see themselves as others saw them, could they?)

"Well, well. Now you get it, don't you?" this new "Sashko" said. "That's one thing I've always liked about you, you are a very smart boy."—"Who are you?"—"You can keep calling me 'Sashko.' I've gotten used to it, and it would be easier for you. We won't trouble your mind with another name."—"What do you want from me?"— "Just what I told you, I'm new to the city and all alone." Whereas before "Sashko" had delivered his tale of woe with tears in his voice, now he sounded sardonic. "I need a friend. I like you, I really do. Let's be friends."—"With the First Department? Will you tell me your rank, then?"

"Sashko" merely shrugged.

"Sure, why not, if we are friends. You be a friend to me, I might get you a rank as well . . . Oh no, don't!" he pleaded in a new voice, seeing that Ivan was about to walk away. "That's not what I meant to say!"—"Really? So what *did* you mean?"—"I can see you won't suffer lies. Fine, let's not lie to each other."—"I never did."—"Yes, of course. I'm sorry, I should not have said that, just got carried away. I'll tell you the truth. But you also tell me the truth, okay?"— "What are you talking about? Are you insane?" Ivan felt suddenly so angry he could barely breathe. "Well, I'm not exactly from the First Department. That department stayed in the other country, and I don't work with them. Not exactly. See, I'm telling you the truth, everything I can . . ."—"Go to hell!"

•

Ivan came back to his dorm, collapsed on his bed, and instantly fell asleep, in the middle of the day. He felt mortally tired. Only Hercules, he thought, could have been as tired after he had defeated the Lernaean Hydra.

But the hydra Ivan had fought wasted no time growing new heads.

About a week later "Sashko" appeared at Ivan's dorm. He had not come there before.

"Let's go for a walk," he said. "Go fuck yourself," Ivan suggested. "I would, but. I have to talk to you about a woman."—"Go fuck yourself with your women. Go and do not come back here, do you hear me?"—"This woman's name is Margita. Margareta Iosefivna Chepil, to be precise."—"The hell?"

"Sashko" was referring to Margita, Ivan's own mother.

"Leave her alone!" Ivan yelled at the man.

"I would, happily, but . . ."—"So what do you want? You want me to be a rat? I won't. You can tell them as much."

"I wondered," "Sashko" said coyly, "how it is that your mom still doesn't know anything about your Maidan adventures. Or about the people her son chooses to spend time with. That's quite a bit of not knowing!"—"You want to tell my mother about the Maidan, be my guest! I'll take you to the station myself!" Ivan shouted. "To the train station, eh? I see you're a fighter! Don't see that every day. You really growl! A growler then, and not because you guys from Transcarpathia bring growlers of wine everywhere you go. An actual growler, someone who growls . . . All right fine, we'll drop it. Things are not so simple, and I am not from the First Department. But let's just say there are people who are interested in you. And then there's this: I really like you. I actually want to be your friend."

The street in front of the dormitory was still covered with snow, only the road itself had been cleared. The asphalt lay bare and black under a dusting of fresh, white snow, and closer to the trash bins, fat black crows hopped around on it.

"What the hell do you want with me?"—"Talk to me, and I'll tell you."

Still, "Sashko" said nothing whenever Ivan asked him direct questions and instead steered the conversation onto another tangent: the Maidan, Ivan's heroism there (What heroism? He stood guard, so what? Plenty of others did too!), how honored he was to make friends with such a cool guy. And every time "Sashko" finished by saying, "I want to be your friend. That's what I have decided."

All Ivan could do when he came home was fall on his bed— the mortal fatigue never left him. He recalled his conversations with Ostapenko and Hnativ, what they told him about people who lived in anticipation of being arrested: the tension wore them out, they could not get out of bed, and when they could, they could barely walk, but he had never imagined he would experience this himself. And now, after Independence! How could it be? He second-guessed everything he had done, looking for that one error: if only he had not picked up the phone, if he had taken a different route home . . . He knew, rationally, there was no point in this—once they'd decided to find him, they would have found him one way or another. He lay on his bed, incapable of getting up, and equally incapable of sleep, and words from the other side of the wall wove themselves into the twists of his thoughts. "Then he said unto them, O fools, and slow of heart to believe all that the prophets have spoken: Ought not Christ to have suffered these things, and to enter into his glory? And beginning at Moses and all the prophets, he expounded unto them in all the scriptures the things concerning himself. And they drew nigh unto the village . . ."

Who were those people on the other side of the wall? Ivan got up (he felt dizzy), slipped his bare feet into shoes, and, shuffling, made his way next door, where the people with those voices lived. He knocked, and no one answered. "Open up! You've got mail!" he shouted the first thing that came to his mind. Then knocked again. Silence.

The door never opened.

•

Now "Sashko" appeared everywhere Ivan went, he caught up with him in the street, at lectures, and at home. There was no way to tell where he would pop up and when. He would just slip around a street corner or loiter at the dorm like a ghost from a bad horror movie. He'd touch Ivan's elbow in the street or in the cafeteria, with "Here I am, your friend Sashko Petrenko, how are you?" He spoke slowly, spreading his words like honey, and pulled his lip into that terrifying smile of his, fit to scare children. Ivan wanted to start a fight with him or at least make him angry, anything to make the man tell him what it was he wanted. The way he threatened Margita, so casually, unnerved Ivan, just as much as his own apparent impotence—he had no clue what he might do to protect his mother. Even if he were willing to become a traitor and an informer, "Sashko" had given him no chance; Ivan could not make out what information was wanted and by whom.

"I can see you don't believe me. About Margareta Iosefivna, do you? Well, let's try this. Go call her, right now, and let her tell you about the little dog she found dead in her garden."—"About what? What dog?" They never had a dog. "Well, I could have played with artifacts a bit, but . . ."—"Arti— what?"—"Nothing, never mind. What I mean is, I could have arranged for one of her, say, rings, to come into my possession and then I could have brought it to you as proof. It would be like something out of *The Three Musketeers*, very romantic. But men don't care about things like that . . . can't tell one ring from another . . . A husband sometimes doesn't recognize his own wife's hand . . . But you should go call Margareta anyhow, just to make her happy, you don't do it often enough . . ."

Ivan wasn't listening at that point—he was running to the post office to make the call.

•

Margita told him disturbing things indeed. When she went to work in her vegetable garden, she found a dead dog in one of her beds. A long-dead one, and there was no way that the dog had gotten into the garden and died there unnoticed. Who could have done such a thing? Leave a rotten carcass for her to find!

Ivan came out of the telephone booth angrier than he had ever been in his life and spent a long time crisscrossing the city with the aim of finding "Sashko" and beating him up. His mind raced through the list of people who went to the house and knew Margita's habits. The neighbors? The girl from the village who brought milk to sell? The mailman? Volodya, the chimney sweep who was always drunk and long ago fired from his job but kept plying his old route, collecting change for a drink? One of the family's friends?

Ivan did not find "Sashko" that day, but that mattered little because the next day, his "buddy" met him on campus. "Did that convince you?" "Sashko" asked.

"Who is spying on her?"—"What difference does that make? I just want you to know that we know everything."

"What do you want from me? What!" Ivan screamed at the man the next time he saw him, days later. "Where is this kay-gee-bee of yours?"—"There is no kay-gee-bee anymore, haven't you heard? The Union is gone."—"That's my point!"—"But you have to realize the people have not gone anywhere. So many experienced people!"—"Yeah? All right, let's go see your boss, I'll tell him myself where he can put me, I don't mind, anything to get rid of you, you lunatic!"—"Lunatic, eh? Some words you've got," "Sashko" said, grinning. "And what has a lunatic ever done to you? Do you even know what kind of people get called *lunatics* in the camps? You don't, do you? Next you'll tell me you haven't read Solzhenitsyn!

Like I'm going to believe it, that you, with all your smarts, missed Solzhenitsyn! You can buy his book anywhere, you know that! It's only sometimes smuggled . . . weapons, drugs, Solzhenitsyn, they go together. I can't believe you, Ivan! You know too little about life on the inside, way too little."—"And you? You are an expert then?"—"I'm from the right side of the fence!"

And yet the smell "Sashko" carried on him, Ivan finally identified it, the same smell the No-Name Man had brought into the room, was just it, the smell of prison camp barracks.

What if, Ivan wondered, "Sashko" was rogue, and no "organs" sanctioned his improvisations? What if he had escaped from the loony bin? But then Ivan remembered tales of just such young men, with all their faculties quite intact, sent on special missions, such as, for example, to "pick up," in their official car, a dissident's wife off her red-eye train, put her in the back seat in the textbook configuration, with a man on her right and another on her left, like the thieves on Golgotha, with another pair of beefy boys in the front, and go drive the poor woman around the city for several hours, squeezing her thighs with theirs and shouting dirty jokes. So that the whole crew would laugh.

"I just want you to be my friend. Are you really not going to be my friend?"—"Like hell I will!"—"But why?"—"How about because you are a rat and work for the KGB? Is that good enough for you?"—"All right, all right . . . you have good intuition. Still, you are mistaken. I am an informant and a KGB man, but a *former* one. An ex."—"Right, like I'm going to believe that. Just arrest me."—"There you go again! Why can't you believe that I actually, genuinely respect you and want to be your friend. Back at the Maidan, I talked to people there, and met you. Do you not believe that people like me can change?"

"What people did you talk to? And what do I have to do with anything? We didn't even speak!"—"Ah, now you remember. You say we didn't speak. Are you sure? Margareta Iosefivna Chepil, your mom, would she be sure? Or your dad? Speaking of, we used to have a file on your grandfather, too . . . But, listen, it's all pretty simple, really. You are correct, I am not with the organs. I mean, not with the organs you think of as the organs. Rather, those that can, push comes to shove, take you apart into organs . . . But don't worry! We don't want Margareta Iosefivna, she is too old. We'll just . . ."

Ivan wanted to throw his hands around his head. He wanted to knock this "Sashko" down on the ground and stare down into his bloodied mouth. But he could not do that. He was afraid. Not for himself, for Margita. He hated himself for being afraid.

He started avoiding his friends. He acquired new habits. Now he spent long stretches of time silent, not adding a word to their shared conversation, not joking. Not laughing. He had never appreciated his own laughter before, had not realized what a treasure it was, and had laughed easily and enthusiastically, never counting the happy moments when he lost himself (and laughter, like sleep, could refresh him, take him out of the flow of time, help him be born anew). Now Ivan slid over the surface of things, knowing all the while that the surface had its own depth beneath it, and it was this abyss that would swallow him whole. He listened to his friends and marveled at the ease with which they spent their energies on jokes and how not funny these jokes were. He used to retreat into laughter, it was his refuge, his haven. He used to laugh even in difficult circumstances. Especially then.

Ivan's laughter was the first thing he lost. Clarity of thought followed. Before, he felt he looked at things logically. When emotions overwhelmed him, he did his best to do as Mysko had taught him: acknowledge his feelings but also put them aside. Now all logic was gone. Except the logic of fear. He listened to his friends and realized he was looking for secret, covert meaning in their words as if everyone around him was suddenly speaking in clues and this was a test he had to pass. Could he, Ivan, identify those who really *knew* (Knew what? He asked himself. What could they possibly *know*? See, you can't even answer your own stupid questions!), or not, in which case it was, as the local saying went, the wrong side of the grass for Ivan.

He was lost in a dark forest, and the forest was growing so dense and frightening that Ivan felt like a small child, a Hansel or Gretel, a child running straight into the thick of the giant dark trees where the path disappeared. Who did he have to blame for this misadventure? Not an evil stepmother, surely. No, it was "Sashko Petrenko" who was responsible, said the resilient voices of clear thinking in Ivan's head. They were still there, hidden in the deep folds of his self, but they, too, were growing weaker, it seemed, day by day. Ivan, and only Ivan himself, was to blame for everything. He had felt guilty before, of course, and Margita was an expert at pulling that particular string, but he never knew living with a constant sense of guilt was such a tremendous burden. The guilt might have been worse than the fear. It exhausted him, sucked him dry, shattered him. He had no reserves left. He could no longer tolerate waiting for anything and fled from lines in the cafeteria or at the post office, where he had to go to call home. He could not focus on his books, lines of text fanned in every direction before his eyes.

And "Sashko" was there, again and again. Always, they had essentially the same conversation.

"Listen, leave me alone or I'll tell everyone who you are."

"But what about Margareta Iosefivna?"

"Especially since some people already know who you really are."

"Do they?"

"Mike knows you're up to no good."

"Mike? Ha! He's been with us for ages."

"You're lying."

"Why, did he say something to you?"

In the heat of the moment Ivan almost blurted that yes, he had, but if "Sashko" was not lying, and Mike really did know what he was doing, then ... then maybe that time when Mike talked to him in the Twisted Linden he wanted to give Ivan a clear and fair warning?

"No."

"Ivan, come on! Don't worry. We won't touch Mike. And I know he'd never have said anything directly, he would've hinted, like, such and such, meaning me, did not keep the appointment. You're just so naive you didn't get the hint, right? You really are not very good at people."

"Oh yeah? Well, I know the way you talk, and it doesn't take a doctor to diagnose you."

(How? How did he still have the energy to snarl at the man?)

"Yeah, right, you're a linguist now!"

"Shut up already! Shut up! You're a walking loudspeaker!"

"No problem, happy to. We can be a pair of silent friends today."

•

The worst was how things ended with Rose.

Things ended: hanging out together in dorm rooms, lounging together in bed, their endless laughter that had seemed to need no reason at all. The laughter vanished. Ivan could not yet tell what he was becoming but he knew this: a person without laughter was a pathetic doll, something with a mute and repulsive body. He could not stand being this way, neither with Rose nor with himself. He could not hold up his end of the conversation; he found a hidden attack in every word, even when he was talking to Rose. Rose would say it had been a while since they went for a walk in the city, and Ivan would hear, *We haven't gone in forever because you only go with Sashko Petrenko these days.* His immediate instinct was to defend himself, to deflect the blow, even at the cost of a misunderstanding. He'd agree curtly, yeah, so what, while other words popped up at the back of his mind, like subtitles, "I never went anywhere with Sashko, he was the one that met me at the streetlight, and what the hell are you doing spying on me anyway?" Ivan had to be grateful he wasn't yet far gone enough to say them out loud. "You must have met someone else!" Rose would say, desperate to get anything out of him, a conversation, if not an apology. She kept asking, "Did you meet someone? You have to tell me, why are you torturing me?" Ivan, meanwhile, heard *Sure, you've no time for me because you've decided to become an informant, with your Sashko's help!* In his heart, Ivan fought back: "Me? A rat? How dare you! Why can't you just leave me alone? Do you think it's easy, fighting him off every day like this? You're making it worse!"

One time she did actually ask about "Sashko"—she knew nothing about the way things had gone between him and Ivan. Rose asked if Sashko ever found the Hutsul clothing he was after, and if he was working on his paintings. She might have thought this would remind Ivan how they had laughed about her sitting for one of the portraits, and cheer him up. Instead, Ivan turned pale and threw his arms in the air. Rose must have thought he was about to strike her because she drew back sharply and covered her face with her hands. To have him paint Rose! If only! That guy only knew how to roll shitballs, he'd never seen a brush. Then again, maybe he had, they say Hitler was a talented painter. But Rose! To imagine her in front of "Sashko," that bastard! And "Sashko" with a brush in his hand?

"What's wrong with you?" Rose was scared; Ivan stared mindlessly into the air. "Are you seeing a ghost?"

Lines from another, different life came up unbidden in Ivan's mind, an existence where his laughter was still alive, *My lord the spirit, we are not up to any fuckery.*[29]

"Don't you ever mention that name to me again!" Ivan burst out, unable to help himself. Rose, utterly shocked, just stood there in the middle of Ivan's dorm room as he bolted into the hallway, slamming the door behind him. Where could he go now?

He went to the neighbors' door again. He knocked. As before, there was no answer. Ivan pressed his ear to the door to see if he could hear the worshipful reading that had lulled him to sleep so many times—if he were able to sleep at all—but heard nothing. He lowered himself to the floor then and attempted, contrary to the laws of physics, mechanics, and basic human anatomy, to press his ear against the narrow gap between the door and its threshold. He pushed his body hard against the door, but still heard nothing.

Where the hell were those apostles now, when he needed them? Where was their God?

He did not realize he was shouting these things at the top of his lungs.

Rose came after him, helped him to his feet, hugged and soothed him. She made him many cups of tea and he mumbled that yes, he was feeling better now, and no, nothing was wrong, he was just anxious, because, you know, if they could throw Reva off the train, they could do it to any and all of them, and the idea really bothered him, he did not want to be thrown out of a train onto the hard gravel, not yet, he wanted nothing of the kind, just to be left in peace, left alone . . .

"Of course," Rose said. "I understand."

. . . he wanted to be left in peace, and also to know why all the doors were always locked, he wanted to know what happened in

---

29. From Les Podervyansky's absurd short play *Hamlet, or the Phenomenon of Danish Katsapism.*

Emmaus ("Where?" Rose asked, very confused), he wanted peace, peace and to be let in when he knocked.

That night, he finally fell into a dreamless sleep, like a baby. Words came at him, words he could not understand but on to whose sound he held, his thread in the labyrinth: "As they approached Emmaus, Jesus continued on as if he were going farther. But they urged him strongly to stay. So he went in to stay with them. When he was at the table with them, he took bread, gave thanks, broke it, and began to give it to them. Then their eyes were opened, and they recognized him."

•

Ivan could no longer live like this.

He came up with a plan. He would go with "Sashko" to his, as he called it, studio—he kept inviting Ivan, didn't he?—and once there, he would put him into an armlock Mysko had taught him long before the Maidan, and finally make him spit out what he wanted from Ivan.

He just had to be sure not to kill the man outright.

The idea haunted Ivan. He dreamed anxious dreams. He dreamed he decided to murder "Sashko." He dreamed he was contemplating his options. He would never get his hands on a firearm, that went without saying. He did not know how to handle a knife, so would likely botch the job. He was similarly unlikely to manage to poison the man, unless he were to treat him to ground meat or liver sausage from a government-owned store before a holiday. What did that leave?

A hammer.

A hammer, the weapon of the proletariat.

He thought of the Arsenal factory. Of Knight Molybogovych.

(Did his sense of humor, Ivan wondered at that point, not leave him so much as turn bitter?)

He would go to "Sashko"'s "studio," come up with an excuse to have him turn his back on Ivan, and then—crack!—take him out. Waste him. Except he wouldn't be able to clean up afterward; it wouldn't do to drag the body across the city, which meant Ivan had to get in and out without being seen by "Sashko"'s neighbors. Come to think of it, Ivan had never caught any sign of the neighbors. They might well have bought out the entire building and populated it with their valuable employees, all in *footwraps*. In Ivan's dreams, these men swarmed around him, so sharp and real within the netherworld of his sleep that later Ivan could not forget their faces, the way they moved, details of their dress. Outside, he started nervously every time his eye caught anything resembling the things in his dreams: someone's black purse, someone's well-worn boots, the yellow shadows under a person's eyes. A man's gray hair that billowed like a kicked-up heap of down feathers, seeming to grow out of thin air . . .

So, "Sashko" would turn his back on him, and then Ivan could step up smoothly and clock him on the top of the head. In his dreams, Ivan had perfected the blow he would deal "Sashko," and "Sashko" acted as if he wanted to help: he kept turning his back on Ivan, again and again, as if to say, "Here, why don't you try again," as if they were not a victim and his murderer (and which man was which?), but a pair of privates in base camp. Go ahead, the dream "Sashko" would nod at Ivan, but he hesitated, until "Sashko" turned back to face him, terrifying as a troll ("my lord the spirit!"), and whispered the name of Ivan's mother. Then Ivan would strike.

He brought his hammer down again and again, but "Sashko" refused to fall. He stood straight as a post, more alive than ever. And yet in his dream Ivan knew that "Sashko" was, indeed, dead, alive and dead at once, and that he, Ivan, was to blame, and people were already looking for him—and there the worst began. In his dream, Ivan ran through the city, gasping for breath, his heart bursting out of his chest. He had to escape. He ran into buildings, leaped over roofs—he could fly in his dreams, but only briefly, and then he began to fall—hid behind street corners waiting for the angry mob of popular retribution to run past him. Sometimes he hid below the counter in the grocery store in the Twisted Linden. Sometimes he positioned himself so that Mike's large body would hide him. He turned himself into the small plume of smoke that rose off the cigarette being smoked by the one-legged beggar (Who was it that said the man looked like Long John Silver from *Treasure Island*? Whoever did was absolutely right, only the story got garbled somehow and the quartermaster ended up on the margins). Sometimes, Ivan had to catch a ship sailing from Lviv's port that had never existed. Except, perhaps, if the River Poltva, now locked underground, still carried her boats with her own cohort of Charons to steer them.

Eventually, he was caught. Of course he was, he was no good at murder. He had no criminal talents—no talents at all, perhaps. Ivan would then dream he was in jail, in a cell with Chornovil, Ostapenko, and Stus. But he did not dare approach them and they looked at him disapprovingly. So the KGB boys finally figured out how to hurt him! They found his soft spot: these three pairs of eyes. They were to be his undoing. He could bide his time among his friends, he could lie to Rose, he could be sure Mike would never say anything because he only cared about his business, but these three men would not keep silent. And would be right to judge him.

Ivan woke up covered in cold sweat. No. He must not even contemplate murder. No. He'd just visit "Sashko" in that so-called studio of his, he would just . . .

. . . What? What would he do next? Did he even remember how to make that armlock? Or should he check with Mysko first, to refresh his memory—never mind that he now avoided Mysko even more assiduously than he avoided Rose?

Ivan did find "Sashko" but the meeting did not go at all the way he had imagined. There were to be no armlocks. "Sashko" dealt Ivan a preemptive strike by saying, as soon as they entered the apartment, "You must be badly wanting to find out why I've been following you around. So I'm about to tell you. No more secrets. I have to become a member, a trusted member in a specific organization."—"So, go and join!" Ivan answered. His heart was beating so hard that his temples hurt. His legs felt like they were made of cotton. Calm now, he told himself he had to hide what he felt, and for heaven's sake, not break out in cold sweat. Could "Sashko" have sensed danger?

"Sashko" named the organization he was interested in; it was Yarema's latest endeavor. He said, "I need someone to introduce me to Yarema as one of you guys. As someone who could be trusted."—"And you must be thinking," Ivan answered in the same pointedly mocking voice he always used with this enemy of his, "they are like the Masons or something? Let me tell you, there is no secret handshake. Go and tell them you want to join."

The fact that "Sashko" gave no sign of having registered Ivan's shock lifted his spirits. And still, it would've felt so great to murder the bastard!

"No, that won't work. I can't do it without you."—"Why me?"—"You are loyal, an old friend to Yarema and the others."

It was at this instant that Ivan remembered that Sashko Reva used to belong to the same organization. There was nothing clandestine about it, just another youth group, and yet . . . Oh, Reva, did they do to you what they were now doing to him, Ivan?

"I might run with the plurality bloc, if I joined now," "Sashko" went on. He spoke of his scheme directly, with no apparent pangs of conscience, as if it needed no justification. Ivan asked, "But why? They are not a political party."—"Precisely. That's why I would run with the bloc."

Ivan thought for a moment, and then asked:

"Did your people shove Reva off the train?"

"Sashko" gave a start: "Re . . . who? Oh, yeah, that associate of yours. No, what are you saying? This has nothing to do with that!"—"So he fell out of his own free will, did he?"—"Listen, Ivan," "Sashko" grew grim. "I don't know. But I do know this, if you don't help me, something bad will happen to Margareta . . . Iosefivna. We respect family values. To threaten you personally, that would be obsolete technology."—"Obsolete what?"—"Technology. Why?"—"I see. So it was you. You tried this with him, and Reva did not play along, so you got rid of him. With me, you're being more sophisticated. But there's one thing I still don't understand," Ivan paused, intentionally mimicking "Sashko"'s slow speech. "I still don't understand why you needed to bother with following me around, all these talks. Why couldn't you just come out and say what you needed? You already threatened me. Which meant you wanted something. But you wouldn't tell me what it was."

Ivan was lying. He understood everything. He doubted "Sashko"'s people had any real need for him or his contacts.

What they needed was to perfect their "technology."

But then again, he wondered, weren't they already experts?

For the first time that day, "Sashko" smiled, gently, with the corners of his mouth alone, the way an adult smiles at a child.

"Don't be a child. I had no illusions; you people would never believe me, so I had to find another way. To blackmail you right away wouldn't have worked. You didn't know who I was and would've thought I'm some kind of thug. You would have told the other guys. And this way, I have created a certain . . . atmosphere, have worn you down a bit, run you through that little skit with Mike . . . And here we are."

Both were silent for a bit.

"You are a rare piece of shit," Ivan said. He put the full weight of his—not hatred, "Sashko" didn't deserve that—his abhorrence behind it.

And for some reason, it hit a nerve.

The smile vanished from "Sashko"'s face. In fact, for what had to have been the first time in their entire acquaintance, his face reflected a spontaneous emotion, a whole cocktail of uncontrolled feelings: anger, shame, and something else, something hard to describe—Ivan grasped it on a cellular level, he recognized, to his astonishment, that "Sashko," despite everything, wanted to remain in Ivan's eyes a *good person.*

"Sashko" spoke again and there was genuine reproach in his voice:

"You say I'm not a friend to you, you don't believe me, but think, if I weren't a friend to you would I be wasting so much time on you? I told you everything."—"But what do you want Yarema for?"—"What does anyone want him for? He is the leader of the uprising."—"All right, fine, but what's your problem with our uprising?"—"What, you think I don't care? I'm a Ukrainian, too."—"Like fuck you are!"—"I've told you all my secrets. You should appreciate that."—"No, I won't! What do you want with the group? What do you want with Yarema? Who are you working for?"

"Sashko" took a moment to think. Ivan doubted he was considering his answers to these questions; more likely, he was scheming to turn the conversation so that he wouldn't have to answer at all. For whatever reason, "Sashko" did not want to end it.

"Well, what would you be more comfortable with? Say I work for organized crime. Because you are right, the country that had coughed us off its conveyor belts is no longer there. But we are. And there are playgrounds, and apartment buildings, and in some of them guys come together, real fighters, not like you, and sooner or later, they will go to war. They are the ones I work for." Sashko said all this in a monotone, in a single breath.

"War? With whom?" Ivan asked after a bit, since "Sashko" seemed to have stopped mid-point.

"Sashko" snorted. "With whom!? Like in the old days, the Nazis! As if. Don't be naive. You know who we were up against in Kyiv."—"But we won."—"Not so fast, soldier. Winning a battle is not the same as winning a war."

Why, in God's name, was Ivan still there, with this scum, why was he still listening to his putrid nonsense in his disgusting "studio"? The devil's den, that's what it was! The church taught that to despair was a sin, and here, right before him, was an expert, a man who made his living driving others into despair. And he, Ivan, was still listening. To this kay-gee-bee man. Wait, not KGB, it was called something different. But the tradecraft, that was vintage. An old trick. "The agent is a person, too; talk to him." Or "The agent just wants what's best for you; you should share what you can."

He would just have to kill the man.

Ivan felt his face burn hot. He got to his feet.

"I don't think so," "Sashko" said and blocked Ivan's way out. "We aren't done yet."

And, smiling broadly as he always did, he started talking about Margita.

•

Never in his life did Ivan feel more humiliated, not even when the No-Name Man screamed at him.

From "Sashko"'s apartment, he ran straight to the bus station. There, he shoved the change into the ticket window, which—miracle of miracles!—did not have a line before it, said the name of Bodya's hometown, and within minutes was riding a bus, broken-down like everything else in his country, along the bad roads to see Bodya. Why hadn't he thought to do this earlier?

The bus took Ivan to the edge of town, but the place was small enough to cross end to end in half an hour. The bus station was dirty and in the open square before it, where the buses parked, wind tossed sheets of dust into people's faces. Ivan felt sand crunch in his teeth. The large park he was now crossing was also dusty, but in the shelter of the trees, the dust did not rise into the air; it lay in a thin crust on benches and even on the young spring leaves.

Beyond the park, there stretched a long street, also dusty, and full of thundering cars. There was a military base nearby, and large tarpaulined trucks deafened Ivan each time they rolled by. Eventually, he came to a foul river where the entire town had been throwing its garbage for decades. The black water stank. Beyond the river lay the market. All manner of goods were laid out on metal tables, from pasta to clothes. Small-time cross-border trade supported the entire region.

Up the hill, Ivan could see the remnants of the old city walls, and on top was the center of the town itself, with a church, a cathedral, and a few stores. Bodya, however, lived at the edge of town, close to the bypass and almost next door to the hospital, a tall building near the Jewish cemetery, except it was not, in fact, a cemetery, but the burial site for the Jewish residents gunned down in 1942. The actual *kirkut*[30] was farther away, and the stones that still stood there (locals were not above carrying them off for their construction needs) were overgrown with grass. Cattle grazed among them in summer.

Bodya and his mother lived in an old three-story building, in an apartment on the second floor. Much like many buildings around the Polytechnic in Lviv, this must have once been a wealthy resident's suburban villa because the current layout of the apartments made no sense. The old wooden stairs creaked with menace

---

30. Galician Polish for "Jewish cemetery."

under Ivan's feet. Ivan rang the doorbell, and in a minute, Bodya opened the door. Bodya had put on some weight and seemed to be less anxious than he was in Lviv. Things must have been going well for him here, in his small town.

"Hello!" They embraced.

Bodya had Ivan come in. They sat in the kitchen; Bodya's mom came and put food on the table. She, too, appeared calm and content. Bodya was working as a night guard and intended to get a job at the local candy factory, despite the fact that with his education, even incomplete, he could do better than that. Going into business was another option, but he said he couldn't see himself as a trader.

"I didn't know you were coming," Bodya said, making them tea. His mom went back to her own room; she had a small TV in there on which she watched movies and the news.

"Neither did I," Ivan said softly. Since the moment he entered the building and saw Bodya, he had been feeling better. It was almost a physical pleasure just to sit and talk like that, without torment, without fear.

They talked about this and that, then went downstairs to get the mail, and sat some more at the sandbox full of little kids, then, when it got dark, went back to the kitchen. Life in this town moved slowly. The residents returned at dusk from their jobs in bigger towns, took care of their livestock, if they had any ("We only have a cat, although there's a chicken house downstairs, it's ours, but we don't keep chickens. Mom's not up to it, and I don't have the patience"), made dinner. Bodya opened the window; the spring weather was gloriously warm. They could hear noises from other open windows, the homey sounds of the province: the tinkle of spoons, a ringing of water falling from the faucet into a steel sink, the low mutter of televisions, then a train whistle and the clatter of the evening train. Ivan felt sleepy. This place brimmed with serenity, with quiet, full of lulling whispers. But that's not what he had come for.

He had to bring himself to talk about "Sashko Petrenko."

"Why did you leave Lviv?" Ivan asked, gathering his courage.

"I told you. I was afraid I was going to kill someone," Bodya said. (I'm afraid, too, Ivan thought).

"Did they pester you much?"

"Not really . . . but then again, I'm not like . . . like most of you. I could never again be like you after Afghanistan. When I get really angry, I can kill. But you go ahead, tell me what's going on. *Them* again?"

"Yes. Did you hear what happened to Reva?"

Bodya sighed.

"I did. A bloodless independence, right?" he said, mocking someone, possibly Kravchuk. Much was being made of the bloodless independence, how Ukraine managed it, without military conflict, without losses. Right! Did anyone bother to count people who fell off trains?

"Did they threaten you? Like, the same could happen to you?" Bodya asked.

"Not me. My family," Ivan said and instantly wondered if he was being incautious, saying these things out loud. What if Bodya's apartment was bugged? Should they have done as Kyiv's dissidents did and sat at the table silently and exchanged notes they burned in an ashtray right after reading?

But no. Bodya would know. His face was untroubled, his movements smooth and calm, so there was nothing of the sort. Bodya was like a litmus test, if *they* were anywhere close, he got very anxious.

"Would you like my advice, Ivan?"—"Of course, I do."—"Listen, I'm not sure what's going on and how things are going to evolve because we did win our independence. But this scum is still around. You can think me a coward . . ."

A coward! Bodya Melnyk! That was unfathomable. The man

sitting before Ivan was nothing less than the field marshal of the Maidan.

"I do believe," Bodya went on, "things will change eventually. But they have not changed yet. You need to graduate, just make it happen, I couldn't, but I've got the Afghanistan stuff, and Mom really can't cope on her own, things are different. Dad's been gone ... What I'm saying is, graduate and go back home. And until you can do that, you just have to manage, come up with excuses, promise him ... them—whoever's after you—rivers of gold. You'll do what they ask, but tomorrow. Or the day after. We'll come back to Lviv yet. Our job right now is to survive."—"Don't tell anyone about this, okay? The guys don't know anything."—"You should tell them. It's better to speak these things out loud."—"No, I can't. Not yet."

"Well, then," Bodya exhaled loudly. "I won't either. That's your business. Enough about that. Let's talk about something fun for a bit, and then I'll make you a bed on the couch. Tell me, how . . ." he tripped up, but quickly regained his composure, only his voice faltered as if stopped short by an invisible wall, "How's everyone doing?"

It's Rose he wanted to ask about, Ivan thought. Wanted to, but did not.

•

Back in Lviv, Ivan went to see Rose.

"Listen," he said. "I think we should go back to my people after we graduate. It's not like we're going to get job assignments, like in the old days. What do you say?"—"You mean, like, for a break?" Rose was confused. "Or what?"—"No, to live."

Rose did not say anything. Ivan saw a whole array of emotions in her face.

"I don't want to go to Uzhhorod. I . . . I don't like it very much there."—"But I have to go back, don't you see? Please don't ask me why. I'll explain it later. Let's just go? Just trust me on this one. It will be for the better."

"Ivan," she said firmly (very firmly, he never expected such firmness from her.) "I will not go to Uzhhorod with you. Do you not realize you are telling me about it as if it's already done? Have you asked what I think? What I want? What made you think you have the right to make decisions for both of us?" Her voice vibrated, tense with offense.

But Ivan, too, felt offended. Betrayed. Of course she wouldn't understand that he, too, was making a sacrifice! He could have just packed his things after graduation and left, and then, in fact, made her choose, as in, *Either you come live with me, or . . .*

But no. Rose cared too much about her own stupid independence! What an egotist!

"And besides, if you want me to come with you, you need to explain why. What's there? Another woman?"—"Would you quit with that!"—"Please don't raise your voice at me. I can see that you are not yourself, I can tell something happened. You cry out in your sleep. You frightened these," she waved vaguely, "evangelicals. You were gone yesterday and the day before without a word. And now you ask me, mysteriously, to pull up stakes and go with you and to not ask any questions."—"But aren't you," Ivan started to say with urgency, and then stopped, looking for the right word: "Aren't you . . . a feminist?"

Rose went pale.

"A feminist? Do you even know what that means?"—"I don't and I don't want to."—"I have no doubt. Let me tell you anyway. It means I want to have *my own* life that's not life as an appendage to your mother."—"Don't talk about my mother like that!" Ivan shrieked. What the hell! Why are they all going on about his mother? "Sashko" first, and now Rose, too! "When she sends honey bread you eat it just fine!"

He was lost now; Transcarpathia was talking. Such a generous place, it always knew how to present its bill when it needed to.

Except now was not that time.

Rose took a long look at him. She sighed.

"Until you explain to me, in detail—do you hear me? In detail—what happened and why you are being the way you are, and where you went the other day, and why on earth you suddenly want to go back home and want to take me as well, and until you apologize for the nasty things you have just said to me, I won't be speaking to you. And now—go!"

Ivan could not say a single word, he was so angry. Some thanks he got from her for everything he'd done to keep her safe from . . . from . . . And now it's his fault!

"I have nothing to apologize for," he said.

And then he left.

•

That night, he was so miserable he felt like beating his head against the wall. Against a mute and silent wall, the evangelicals next door had made no sound since the week before. Ivan got up, felt his way to the door in the dark, ran to Rose's floor, and knocked on her door. She opened. Her roommates were asleep, but she still let him in. He apologized, said he would tell her everything, just not right this second (Bodya's advice came in handy!), asked her why she did not want to go to Uzhhorod, and she whispered passionately that she wanted to be the mistress of her own fate, that she could not imagine living by Margita's side, that she did not wish to relive the fate of a typical Soviet woman who got married just as soon as she had her university degree. That she had been promised a job at a local radio station and she would try to get Ivan hired there as well. That she wanted to live a free life, not one circumscribed by the triangle of "home-work-kindergarten." That she did not know yet if she wanted to have any children at all. That she loved Ivan, but she also loved herself—and this was true, and fair, and he could not object to that. Later, he would remember crying.

He promised he would do anything to make all of this happen. He would work it out, and she did not have to worry. They would stay in Lviv, and everything would be fine.

It was nearly five in the morning when he left.

Yet how? How was he supposed to make things work for everyone?

. . . even after that party, after Ivan committed his crime (he could not, was not able *not* to bring "Sashko" into the group, he was forced to introduce him to the other guys because—Margita, and (much as he was afraid to admit it) Rose!—"Sashko" did not let him off the hook. He kept close to Ivan and when asked what he wanted replied invariably with his usual vacuous list. He said he was still after some Hutsul clothing, he wanted to be Ivan's friend ("I admire you!"), and again and again, as if Ivan had not done anything, mentioned Margareta Iosefivna . . . Ivan could not buy his freedom even at the cost of betrayal, but he, Ivan, had gambled everything on this one move, and lost it all. He would not be allowed to leave the game; he should have left at the very beginning, should not have played at all.

But there was Margita.

And Rose.

Ivan could not look Rose in the eye. He had done what he had to do—what he thought he had to do!—but it was not what was needed. Guilt lay heavily on his shoulders.

He dreamed of "Sashko" again, a black phantom this time, devoid of a physical body. "Ha!" The phantom laughed. "Of course

I'm without a body, you killed me, and now I am a hungry ghost, like in Japanese myths, remember?" Ivan knew nothing about Japanese mythology; it was Mysko who explored such things, and he, Ivan, could never have kept up with Mysko. "I am a hungry spirit," screamed the ghost of "Sashko Petrenko," "I must be fed," it screamed and came inside Ivan, seeped in as a dark vapor, and laughed again, now from the inside, from its nest within Ivan's own guts.

There was a moment then when Ivan suddenly realized that the high-rises around him, these many-chambered birdhouses, were all full of unfortunate souls just like him, people who also had *this* living inside them.

How was he to free himself?

"And it came to pass, as he sat at meat with them, he took bread, and blessed it, and broke it, and gave to them. And their eyes were opened, and they knew him . . ."

"Sashko" was always there, at Ivan's heels, like a shadow, and they kept having the same infernal conversation without a way out:

—When are you going to leave me alone?

—Eventually. But not yet. I still need your help.

—With what?

—I'll tell you later.

—So you are driving me crazy as part of that plan?

—No, I'm just practicing my tradecraft . . . Like in that movie . . .

"Sashko" named a spy film Ivan had never seen—he had no interest in spies. He only had the misfortune of running into them when the First Department called him in.

—What, you haven't seen it? Your high-minded organizers never showed it to you? Only screened that bullshit about Carpathian Ukraine . . . Yes, indeed—I do know about that, too.

—Did you come to see *that*, too? Did you watch from the balcony or did you crawl up the ventilation shaft?

—Carpathian Ukraine, my ass! Might as well be Chinese Ukraine.

—I can tell you really do admire us.

—What do you mean, "you"? Whatever makes you think I am not a Ukrainian? The fact that I do not serve this . . . er . . . Ukraine?

—Of course not! You sat with us on the Maidan, didn't you? You are friends with the heroes!

"Sashko" would shut up at that, but only for a moment, after which he would start again, on his Margareta Iosefivna script.

Ivan said little. "Sashko" wouldn't give up, and would then turn to his part about friendship.

—Why are you being like this with me? I took a risk when I didn't treat you like the others from the start. I'm your friend.

—Do you think that if you keep saying that, you will eventually stop being the rotten motherfucker you are?

—Ivan, listen to me: I am your friend. Why can you not believe me? Because you don't believe me, do you? You keep telling me I'm a kay-gee-bee man, a rat, that I am incapable of loving Ukraine. But I am capable! Why do you think that these things cannot coexist in the same country?

—What things?

—That what you call a rat and a kay-gee-bee spook is true. But at the same time, I am your friend. I told you right at the start: I would like to be your friend. I did genuinely admire you at the Maidan. You guys are nuts! You think a man can only be one thing. But it's not true. What am I, Dzerzhinsky's[31] grandson? I am a person, just like you. And my soul is withering.

---

31. Felix Dzerzhinsky, a Bolshevik revolutionary. Born into Polish nobility, from 1917 until his death in 1926 Dzerzhinsky led the first two Soviet state security organizations, the Cheka and the OGPU.

—Okay, fine. I still don't understand who you work for. So, cut it out, stop following me.

—Wait!

"Sashko" touched Ivan's hand, and he jerked away in disgust. How did Ostapenko put it? It's not a dog that bites you, it's a serpent that poisons your blood.

—Be honest for a minute! Here you are, walking and talking with me, and you could have told me to go to hell long ago. It makes me wonder . . . You don't see the other guys much, do you? I know you've neglected your girlfriend. I know why . . . you can't . . . You did not tell them the truth and now you regret it. But you still have to talk to someone. At the moment, you see, I'm the closest person you have. I am the only one to whom you do not have to lie.

This was the paradoxical truth. Ivan froze on the spot.

The hardest thing was to look at "Sashko"'s face and not murder him.

Even if he did, the bastard probably wouldn't die, just like in Ivan's horrific dreams.

. . . "Sashko," however, looked miserable. Hard as it was to believe, he might have cared quite a bit about him. Ivan, in a certain sense, was the center of his universe, an embodiment of something that was, for "Sashko," vitally important: he was his perfect and unattainable friend. The two men were like a pair of mirrors that faced each other, the only choice they had was to look into the depths of the endless rooms opening one from another in their reflections, multiplied by themselves, and discover no possible way out.

It was then Ivan started laughing.

He laughed, he guffawed like a madman. He slapped his thighs and "Sashko"'s shoulders, only to rub the spot he had just hit, he leaped and bent at the mercy of this laughter, this intolerable burden. He squeezed his head in his hands. He shouted something.

He made it home, but it was not Ivan who walked across the city, it was Ivan's despair, the only passion still capable of spurring his body into battle.[32] He put down his books and went to the evangelicals' door. He knocked. He knocked quietly, not the way he had before. He knocked again. Now. Now he could at least ask them if God existed. And why He was silent. Let them tell him—perhaps He talks to *them.*

Finally Ivan heard a soft, "Who's there?"—"It's your neighbor!" he said. That's who he was and he was sick of lying. "Can I help you with something?"—"I'd like to meet you. Please, open the door."

In a moment, the door creaked, and the person who unlocked it stepped out into the hallway. It was a boy no older than twelve, with very large eyes and black hair. Ivan stood there stunned. A child? What was a child doing there? Then he remembered that Lviv's many student dorms had become a source of income for university bosses—those who had enough pull to rent out most of the rooms to whoever could pay.

"Are the adults home?" Ivan asked.—"Mom's at work. It's just me and my brother." Another, younger boy, about eight, appeared. "What about school? Don't you go to school? And the after-school program?" Ivan struggled to think of what a typical tween would be doing.

The boys were silent. He had to ask another question.

"What is it that you read aloud? What book is it from?"—"Mom brought it," the older boy said. "And . . . is it about, er, God?"—"It's about apostle Cleopas and his life," the younger boy answered, for reasons of his own. He seemed a little more sociable. He had the same large eyes as his brother, and was more delicate; the two looked very much alike. "So, is it the Bible?"—"We

---

32. A quote from "De Profundis," an 1880 poem by Ivan Franko, known also by the alternative title "The Eternal Revolutionary."

don't know."—"Do you, like, go to church?"—"We go to meetings. Everyone comes together and prays. You can come, too. Will you come?"—"I don't think I believe in God."

"That's okay. We will pray for you. Cleopas said it's most important to pray for those who cannot pray for themselves because they have no faith."—"No, that's the other Cleopas!" the older brother interrupted. The boys laughed.

Then the older boy said, "Mom will be mad at us. She doesn't like it when strangers come over. If she finds out that we opened the door for you . . ."

They went back inside. Ivan heard the lock click.

He went back to his own room and lay down on the bed.

No one will give him the answer. He had to solve his problem himself. How was he to break free? How could he shake off the damn "Sashko Petrenko"? And stay in Lviv? And ask for Rose's forgiveness?

And how on earth could he forgive himself for everything he'd done?

Ivan closed his eyes and lay there flattened by life, squeezed under its heavy wine press. He wondered about the boys next door. He must have fallen asleep because the wall that separated him from them became transparent, and he could see the older boy come to a table, pick up an open book, settle his brother next to him on the bed, and begin to read. Words and images came to Ivan easily in this dream because that was exactly how words were supposed to come to people, and Ivan listened and listened, and felt like he understood something in this dream, something he would forget as soon as he woke up.

"So he went in to stay with them. When he was at the table with them, he took bread, gave thanks, broke it, and began to give it to them. Then their eyes were opened and they knew him and he vanished out of their sight. And they said one to another, 'Did not our heart burn within us, while he talked with us by the way, and while he opened to us the scriptures?' And they rose up the same hour, and returned to Jerusalem, and found the eleven gathered together, and them that were with them, saying, The Lord is risen indeed, and hath appeared to Simon.

"And they told what things were done in the way, and how he was known of them in breaking of bread."

PART THREE
THE CHOIR

EVEN THE VERY OLD PEOPLE COULD NOT REMEMBER AN APRIL AS COLD
as this. A few deceptively warm days were enough for the buds on
the trees to open and the sakuras to bloom, only for the blossoms
to be washed off by rain and blown away by wind. Rain carried pink
streams of battered petals down the city streets, and at night fog
hung low above the river. This was the time of rampant logging in
the Carpathians. When great rains came, the water, which no longer had the thick old tree trunks to sate, could not be contained in
the ground and the clay. The river rose several times and threatened to flood its banks, and each time, soldiers came out to pile up
bags of sand along the shores. The pedestrian bridge was closed.
The river came high up to its defenseless belly, currents wrapped
like serpents around its footings and rocked it so hard that its entire
body groaned. Life in the city came to a standstill. The military
brought spotlights and put them on the banks; they cast white circles onto the yellow water, full of old snows, and the circles rode
the current into the unknown.

People came out to the riverbanks and stood there, in the bluish gray dusk, among the heavy smell of the great mass of water,
under the chilled ancient lindens, and waited for one of the bridges
to give. What held them up? The stone they were built of? The
people's prayers? A secret angel of engineering? The bridges had
stood firm, these taut lifelines between the shores, bandages over

the wound that was the river. Gods, if they had come to earth and walked masked among the people to study this city and its sinners, would have forgiven the city for its bridges alone and spared it.

Yellow waters filled the city with the cold and the dark; power cuts became frequent. When Ivan walked home across downtown, he was surrounded by tired people with umbrellas hurrying home. Except for the stores, everything was dark, and only the shopwindows glowed in different colors, human shapes in suspended animation inside. Ivan would come home (which was, like the rest of the city, cold and dark), pick up his baby daughter, who had been born the year before, sit down on the couch, and close his eyes for a moment. From the darkness women assaulted him, Phoebe or Margita, fraught with woe like goddesses of the underworld, they reached for the child, took her away from him, and launched into their endless lament, their song of anxiety and hatred.

Ivan's father in those days drank harder than ever before, barely got out of bed, and lay there coughing, and the sound of his cough itself was enough to tell how deeply drunk he was. Margita would yell something at him, he would respond with a long, coarse wail and turn in his bed to remain still for a time, his face up to the ceiling, and the quilt thrown off—he felt no cold. Ivan knew his father's face in those moments burned fire-hot, turned to the heavens, no longer a supplication, though, but a slap, a silent protest, not against the government or its policies, but against existence itself, the great burden of it he could no longer push on.

Ivan would hide his face in his hands. There was nothing but the wall of his own palms to look at. Darkness crept at him through every crack. Margita did not like to have more than one candle burning, and she and Phoebe would take it to the kitchen. Rain came down all night, and in the morning, everything was iced with a thin coat of frost. Mornings like those were eerily quiet, as if time itself stopped and was on the verge of turning back, of flowing backward, into the clean slate of nonmemory, the deep slumber of childhood. In the mountains, great masses of snow still loomed like prison walls.

Whenever the power returned, everyone suddenly came alive, a short-lived euphoria ruled. Margita feverishly worked in the kitchen. Ivan realized, to his own surprise, that he would rather not see her work. That he would rather have the dark. Under the light, it was easier to hide the true nature of things while in the dark it emerged undeniable from every molecule. Ivan wished he could go outside and wander there until the small hours, looking at the melting snow, the thin ice on the river that shifted and departed somewhere, wished he could touch the chilled water, commune with its mystery.

Where was the water going? Was it really only to join the near and familiar Tysa?

•

That spring, Styopa came over almost every day, wanting something from Ivan, wanting something from all of them. "You are asleep," Styopa would say, like their own family prophet.[33] "Asleep! Wake up already! You are not hearing the voice of the times!" If Styopa knew how many other voices I have to listen to, Ivan thought, he might take pity on me and leave me alone. Styopa was, once more, full of plans, and went on about the restaurant he would open imminently, its grand dining room, the menu, the tables, and the tablecloths, this description of the nonexistent establishment delivered with the single-mindedness

---

33. Styopa appears to be riffing on lines by Oleksandr Dukhnovych (1806–1865), a Transcarpathian writer, priest, and educator. Dukhnovych authored "The Anthem of Carpathian Ruthenians" which included the call, "Ruthenians, abandon ye deep slumber!"

of a man obsessed—the restaurant would herald the dawn of a new era, for Styopa personally, and for the city more broadly, and Styopa went on and on, about Ivan's duty to his family, about their traditions, about *bográc* and goulash, and the great cast-iron cauldron out in the open air where these would be cooked, and the firewood he would need to keep the fire going, about baked potatoes and the delicious Transcarpathian *salo*—pork fat smoked and cured with salt and paprika.

In the last three to four years the number of new restaurants opening in the city was truly astronomical, nothing like in the old days, when places of any style served only smugglers and police officers. The city had changed. Beyond that—the country, in less than two years, had become unrecognizable. Politicians of all stripes spoke from TV screens. The Kuchma era began—for some reason, Ivan felt it was going to be nothing less than *an era*. A new mayor was elected, Semen Ulyganets, once a principal of a second-rate trade school, but with a father who used to be high enough in the Communist Party to have access to its coffers, which had to be filled with the money stolen from the people, from the State Savings Bank, when the Soviet Union fell. The money vanished from the meager savings accounts of people who had put away pennies for years, denying themselves a set of new teeth for the sake of having money "on the book," of having something to give their grandchildren when they turned sixteen, grandchildren who were just as likely never to touch that money as women in the villages were never to touch their trousseaus, the delicate nightshirts adorned with yellowing ribbons.

People had been abandoned to fend for themselves, and they panicked like shipwreck survivors do in the open water. Those other ones, the ones in the boats, rowed as far away as they could while their unfortunate compatriots drowned. They were terrifying, these people, with bulging eyes and a mouth that gaped in the sudden void of their world like the maw of hell. What did they know in their lives, what could they believe? That their thrift would be rewarded? But with what? An automobile, a television set, a washing machine at the end of their lives, when their turn came, because there was a waiting list for everything, there were never enough of these simple blessings for everyone in the Soviet Union? And now they were left to live out their lives robbed of the only hope and faith they had ever known. Everything they had done in their lives was vanity, vanity of vanities.

Ulyganets, who was commonly referred to as Senya (a born and bred Transcarpathian, he was, for a mysterious reason, a Russian-speaker), wasted no time in opening an entire chain of stores filled with brand-name goods that no one ever bought—of course, everyone understood that the goods were never intended to find new owners. Their point was to launder money. Senya shook his prizefighter's fist at the regional television cameras and insisted that a normal person cannot be a Communist, because no one is born with his hands flat. It was hard to argue with that. Caravans of trucks filled with contraband rolled into Slovakia, and just as many came back. Business became politics, and politics turned into a business. There was no longer any room in either endeavor for people like Ivan (and perhaps there had never been!). A former colleague of his mother's, one fat, squat man named Zhenia, suddenly became elected to parliament to represent the village he used to supply with Chinese-made shoes and buckwheat.

The former dissidents, now referred to as "democrats," were being displaced by a different, never before seen class of moderately rotund, arrogant moguls. People got rich and went broke abruptly, with nothing in between. They hustled hard but also appreciated a chance to relax, to spend a good night at a pleasant "spot," eating and drinking. Day traders—shuttlers—crossed the borders with bags of consumer goods, most made in Turkey or China. These people did not sleep at night as they waited for their turn to cross, then caught naps over their wares during the day, under the hot sun. There was nothing they wouldn't carry: shoes, clothes, chocolate with peanuts, cutlery and cooking pots, bed linens. One could find just about anything one wanted in the stores or at the market. The era of chronic shortages had given way to a plague of things.

That spring, Ivan did not have many places he could escape to. Yura Popadynets had not yet shaken off his obsession with the Ruthenians and kept talking about a "Carpathian prime minister" who would lead a new government, and about ministers with portfolios already done and decided, just waiting in the wings for the opportune moment. Ivan had seen that prime-minister-in-waiting, he was a deeply confused university professor. Margita knew him, too. It was impossible to tell if he really believed in the Ruthenian state or had gone totally nuts and could no longer tell black from white and the real from the imagined.

"Whatcha gonna do when your kid grows up?" That was Styopa, incessant like a bumblebee (and there the resemblance ended), buzzing in Ivan's ears, circling around him, dogging him. "Come, let's do business with me, where else will you get money? Do you know what they rip you off for daycare these days? And your parents' place, you gonna finish it or just let it sit like that? D'you know this joke I heard?" and, not waiting for an answer, Styopa would tell a typical joke of the time, the kind that wasn't particularly good or funny, something like, one Georgian asks another, his pal Gogi, Hey, Gogi, where d'you keep your deposits these days?—In a jar under my bed! And would go on, again not waiting for Ivan to respond, "You'll go dead broke at that bank of yours! Because do you know what's going to happen next? Shit'll get worse!"

Ivan made excuses: the house—yes, sure, they'll work on the house, but in summer, when the weather's warmer, and the bank

. . . "There are banks, and then there are banks. The ForestBank did just collapse, but it's a totally different story," he would say to Styopa, and not quite believe his own words. The writing about the bank was, in fact, on the wall: it would not last. Nothing did.

And as far as him being a father went, Styopa was the last person he wished to talk to—and he did not know what to say anyway, how to articulate how desperately he loved his daughter. He had not expected to love her like that. He thought he had prepared himself for her arrival, but when she came, he was not ready, not at all. He had no words for this. How could he say, and to whom, that Emilia turned out to be exactly, precisely as he had pictured her the moment the maternity ward called to report the birth, delicate and exquisite. Even as an infant, she cried very little and always woke up in a good mood. She learned to smile very quickly. And now she was the center of Ivan's existence, the core of his existence, because when he was not thinking about her, his every action and every thought reached back toward her.

There was another thing, harder yet: how to speak about the fact that he shared his parenthood with Phoebe—Phoebe about whom he could not imagine talking to anyone at all.

When they picked up Phoebe from the maternity hospital, the family came together, they celebrated. Christina and Styopa came. Margita set the table. "A new person is born!" Myron Vasyliovych toasted, and everyone drank. Everyone, that is, except Myron Vasyliovych himself, because he was driving, and Phoebe, because she was nursing. Phoebe sat there, distant. "What shall we call our little girl?" Margita asked. "Emilia," Phoebe answered. Everyone talked at once: Was the name in the church calendar, or had it been in the family before? They suggested other names. Phoebe listened in silence, and then said, "She will be Emilia." Margita asked, "Why that name? What does it mean?" Phoebe raised her head (slowly, so slowly that for a moment Ivan was terrified—what if there were serpents where her eyes should have been?), looked at Margita and then at the rest of them, everyone who was at the table, and said this: "I will tell you what it means. It means I have chosen her name."

The terrible truth was that Phoebe came back from the maternity ward seeming deranged. She spent all her time in the armchair with the baby in her arms when it was time to nurse. She only came downstairs when the power was cut; otherwise, she just sat there and cried, sometimes quietly and sometimes out loud, which drove Margita up the wall and made her yell at her daughter-in-law (thank goodness, the neighbors' houses were not close enough for them to hear), "Let your mother come help you! Whaddya doin', sitting lazy all day, doing nothing? Should've thought of that when you made the baby? You won't go partying in the city now!" As if Phoebe had ever done any such thing! "You have a child now, so go put her in your pocket!"

Kateryna Ivanivna was not too keen to come over—she did anyway, of course, and always brought something for the baby or for her daughter or some money. She did not neglect them, by any means. But she would not stay long with Phoebe and entertain the baby, Margita was just too much: never leaving her in-law alone, rushing to do every task, picking up her granddaughter as if to show, beyond any doubt, that only she, Margita, was the sovereign mistress of the house and ruler of all. Kateryna Ivanivna would grow downcast and leave, telling herself that everything was fine. Like everyone else, she was determined not to notice the state Phoebe was in.

And Phoebe went on sitting in her armchair. Around her, as if around the red sun of despair, spun the planets: her infant daughter, Margita, Ivan, Kateryna Ivanivna when she was there, local pediatricians—women who uniquely combined self-sacrifice with being utterly nasty—guests who came to the house for every significant occasion, and sometimes also for dinner on Sundays: Christina, Styopa, the Raptors.

And she still sat. She got up only when it was absolutely necessary and walked around the house as if unseeing. She nursed her baby, changed her diapers (Margita, furious, threw out the Pampers Ivan had bought, because what would all those chemicals do to the baby?), ironed what Margita laundered. Phoebe had to force herself to nurse the baby; she had found the process repulsive from the beginning, could not stand all that hungry smacking.

Ivan resented Phoebe. For some reason he had become convinced that with the baby's arrival Phoebe would become, like all his friends' wives, a happily bustling homemaker who would have no more time for him (or her poems!), concerning herself instead with mashed vegetables and the color of the infant's excretions, Bifidobacterium, measles vaccinations, and lullabies. When guys at work asked why he did not bring Phoebe to a corporate party, he bragged to them that she *stayed in, stayed in and would not go out.* And so she did. On the second floor of the house, his and Phoebe's apartment was in chaos—things scattered everywhere, toys, dirty sheets that even the ever-vigilant Margita did not get to, and in the middle of it all, Phoebe, like a broken mast. Every night, at the first hint of dusk, at the same hour each day, she began to cry as if someone had wound up a new, peculiar clock inside her.

Ivan dared not touch her. She would tense all over and become hard as a rock, and then cry again, and if she did not, she would start talking, saying things of which he could make no sense, something about her poems, best he could tell, that she wanted to write, that all her words had turned into a torn wound, that she is a poet, that life should not do such things to poets, that she did not know how to tell him what tormented her. Ivan listened—and did not hear her. What did she want from him? Why did she let all these words of hers loose on him, like ferocious dogs?

The only chance Ivan had to play with the baby was at night, when he came home from work, but even this small window of time snapped relentlessly shut; another trap set to spring on Ivan. He thought that Margita, at least, would be on his side, that he could count on her because what could be more natural than for the grandmother to enjoy her granddaughter and wish the same for the baby's father? He was not permitted to participate in bathing the child, changing her diapers, or even helping with the laundry, and now they didn't even let him hold the baby for very long. Ivan might well have made a great father, but he was not going to have the chance. He realized gradually, to his surprise, that Margita yearned for her granddaughter's company no matter how much she later complained of being tired. These were equations too complex for him to solve, tangents and cotangents of flesh and blood—Phoebe, Margita, and the little Emilia, and who knew, perhaps the two women, with some help with Kateryna Ivanivna and her horses and goats, were teaching his child how to speak that women's language of theirs, where everything was said with a twitch of a shoulder, a quiet laugh, a silence, and, what was the worst for him, tears, their eternal, implacable tears.

Styopa was aware of none of this, and even if he was, he would not, in a million years, be interested in knowing the details. That's the kind of man he was: he knew things about rebar, was competent with plumbing, and was discerning about lumber and flooring. He knew how to count money, and he knew how to work like a draft horse, with veins bulging under the skin of his neck. What did he care about women's language? Let them mind their own business, and when they, as Margita did, outworked him on a job, he just gave them an offended look and muttered something under his breath. He had to mind Margita, no question about that, but at the moment, no one was building anything—they were waiting for the summer. So for the time being Styopa worked on Ivan, trying to convince him to go into business together, to open a restaurant, to buy an old house somewhere, even on the edge of the city, all the rich now had cars, the regular citizenry would follow soon enough, and they could serve the bandits, and the police, and . . . "Yes, who else?" Ivan would ask. "Whom?" And this would trip Styopa up. "How am I supposed to know right now? Once we start feeding people, we will see!"

And Styopa would go on talking, saying that not everything in this city could be replaced with plastic siding, that they had to pre-serve their traditions. The new restaurants served all kinds of dif-ferent food, but it was mostly foreign: pizza, something called hot dogs, Italian-style meat, faded-greens salad, and the waiters were young, with no proper schooling, not like the ones in the old days. Ivan knew what Styopa meant there, knew that even in the Soviet times table service was the exclusive province of middle-aged gen-tlemen, the knights of silver and napkins with impeccable manners, solicitous and aloof at once. Such gentlemen with their heavy eye-lids were at home as they shuttled noiselessly across grand dining rooms where cigarette smoke coiled into the curtains and stayed forever.

Those were the last outposts of the long-dead Austro-Hungarian empire—the restaurants with Roma music, those wait-ers with exquisite manners.

•

And the rain kept coming down, for days and weeks, washing away roads, soaking the houses of Maly Galagov with their inhabitants huddled inside. Tree branches bent lower and lower under the weight of the water. In the park around the People's Council the paths got so muddy you had to wear rubber boots to have any hope of getting through. The city's fountains, dry for years, with their chipped bowls and splinters of rusty pipes poking from their bottoms, now filled with dirty yellow water. Near the market, streams ran down the terraces where flower sellers stood, carrying off to the sewers the smells of faded petals and blackened, rotting stems. On the left bank of the river, in the new developments, roads cratered into countless potholes and a layer of silt covered the sidewalks. Above the old, neglected cemetery next to the library, the giant trees that had not been trimmed in ages locked their branches into a single laden dome that threatened to collapse any second into the blackness beneath them. Styopa talked and talked, paying no mind to Ivan's silence, and the weary Ivan listened and listened, thinking that perhaps, eventually, some kind of truth would hatch from the tangle of Styopa's words, but the truth did not come.

PHOEBE'S SECOND MONOLOGUE

And you don't know what happened there. I'll try to tell you now, right now. Now. I gave birth to a child. No, not like this, this is wrong. I have to be calm. If I get nervous, you won't believe me. Okay, calm now. Bullet points, short theses, that's better, so I don't break up. So I don't cry, but, actually, if I'm honest, I don't want to cry. Because I don't want to cry the way most people cry, like they cry for a while and then they feel better. I do not feel better. I need a hundred years to cry all this out, and I don't even know to whom.

Let me begin again. When did I find out? I don't remember, it's all in a fog. I just remember when I went to the ob-gyn clinic for prenatal visits, it's on this noisy street, and the office is set back, in an orchard, there's an orchard around it. An old building, almost without windows, very low, and they had cockroaches. The street was very loud. No one sees me because people don't look at pregnant women at all. What's there to look at, nothing there, nothing to do with her, can't even take her to the sauna like a chick. No clothes for the pregnant anywhere. You have to have them made on all these sewing machines, the heat in the tight Khrushchev apartments, women's sweat, and the metal of the machines. I did not make my own. I just wore whatever I had, and when nothing fit anymore I did not want to leave the house. No, there was still that one pair of pants. Autumn began, everything faded, the cold blew in. That's how it was.

Here I have to go fast. No, I can't go this fast, I'm going to breathe for a second, and then write it down, later, once I've had enough air. From here—fast. It would be better not to tell at all, but I'll just write it down here and then it won't be anywhere else, ever. It cannot be allowed to be heard. No one can find this note, I'll make sure no one ever does.

Okay, from here, fast. Quickly, quickly. I am writing very quickly. It is confusing. Why can I not make it go fast? I have to explain the prestory, explain that all stories are connected. When a girl, still a child, is beaten until (crossed out) And the whole city thinks (crossed out) No, I can't talk about that. And no crying, I promised myself I would just write down everything the way it went, that's right, in simple words, and no digressions. I am not trying to write about it. I am not writing about it—just writing it down, that's all. Putting it down. I just want to put down how I gave birth to a child.

They decided to put me in the hospital a week before I was due. Aaaaa, it hurts to write hurts so much. Quickly now. My back hurt a lot, and it was hard to breathe. They took me to the hospital, Ivan and my mom. Ivan drove. The doctor on duty happened to be the one that Mom had talked to. Half the city worships him, he is very good. He smiled a lot and ate onions. Well, they have to eat something, don't they. The smell of onions—for some reason, I remember that. What do onions have to do with anything? I just wanted to tell how I gave birth.

Now, short and to the point. And very quickly, very. Come on, you can do it, short and fast, so you don't have to talk about it for a long time. On the first floor, they separated me from Mom and Ivan. From there I went alone, at least they let me keep the nightgown I brought, they took the rest of my clothes. They took me to the ward, it was night, there were four other women there, all older than me by, like, fifteen years. They had been there for months, and I had to be with them for a week. They turned the light on, and all of them lay against their wall, pale, and the light was pale. They saw I was frightened, asked me if it was my first time, I said yes, and asked about them—It's our second round, they said and laughed, you see how it is, hard, but we came back anyway. They turned the lights off and I was told the doctor wanted to see me. Wanted to see.

Quickly now. If only I could write this down in the dark with invisible ink and it all vanished right away. Or squeeze my memory shut as you shut your eyes, let it write things down without me, I'll come back later. Write, write quickly, or the flywheel will catch you. Don't forget the flywheel, you are just leaving your testimony, for the history, that's all. There will be no process, no one will stand judgment except you, so you are not betraying anyone.

The doctor's exam. He took me to a very small room, not even a room, I think, but a small space behind a screen, there's only room enough for a cot. Don't cry, don't cry, you must write. Fast. Lie down and take your undies off, he says in the dark. That's when I see we are not alone, a tall young man is there, eyes glistening in that half-dark, he must be younger than me, a student. I want him to leave, I say to the doctor, but the doctor presses lightly on my shoulders and I am down. My belly won't let me get up. God almighty, this is where I freeze, I always do, I can't run this film to the end in my head, but I have to write it down. I don't have to analyze anything; I don't have to curse anyone. They think I do this because I was not born "a real woman" but a monster. A woman is always a mongrel, a not-quite human. Do not think about this, you promised yourself, come on . . . You are not saying anything to them, you are not talking to them in your already crowded head, you are just putting things down, damn it, goddamn it, can I not just write things down. I just want to write things down, that's all.

Okay, the doctor pushes his hand inside me. Let him leave, I beg, because the student comes closer. There is no one to protect me. The doctor turns his hand inside me, my belly won't let me get up, and the student stares right where the doctor's hand is. Now the student avoids looking into my eyes, too. That's what they teach future doctors. That's what they teach men. Do not look the woman in the eye. Do not analyze, now, come on, write it, faster. Yes. I am down, my belly won't let me get up, and Now you, the doctor says, and the student puts his fingers inside me, so many fingers, nails me to the cot, Let him leave, I scream, and for the first time they look at each other and say nothing. The belly won't let me get up. I have no legs, no arms, no head, no mouth, only the belly, and it won't let me get up. Weakness makes them hate you. It's like smoking at a gas station. Now I know why they are like that. I will never get up. The doctor takes off the bloodied glove, and the student's hand is still in me. Okay, I almost got this part down, very good, let's go on. Just breathe, you are not saying anything bad about anyone, you are just writing down how things went. A document, you are just putting things down, I don't know what for, for history. When the student finally finishes, the doctor claps me on the shoulder and says "Oy, Marichka, you just gotta have some sense of humor 'bout these things. That's your women's lot." The doctor smells like onions.

They would not let me call out of the hospital. And whom would I call? Ivan would not listen to this stuff, and Mom most certainly would not. Who to call? And what would I say? That the doctor examined me? No, I am in this alone, alone. That night, I go into labor. A document, this is a document. There are several women in the delivery room, two I think, I'm the third. It's a small room, there's a cot there, too, there are chairs. The doctor is there, and a nurse, and someone else. They tell me to lie down, then to walk. Then to lie down again. When I lie down, I pass out with pain, and they wake me up. No one gets anything for the pain. When you pass out it's a blessing. Too bad it does not last, and the contractions are not as strong. They wake me. Then—the chair, all of them there: the doctor, the nurse, there must have been someone else, my entire body hurts with effort, they laugh, look, a black head is coming. Everything was quick, they put the baby on my belly, and then took her—and that was it, they messed about inside me and left. They all left because it was the end of their shift.

I was there on my own for two hours. On that chair. My legs spread apart and blood trickling out a bit. Not a lot, thank goodness, or I would have died. I did not die. For two hours I looked at the concrete wall outside the window, that was the view. Later, I read up on all this stuff, psychology and physiology, I read up on it, later, when I had the time and time to read, because I did not have it then. About the euphoria, the need to have a close person there, in the first hours after the delivery, about the care needed, not just for the baby they had taken away before I could even see her face but for the mother, too. Well, I did not have anyone with me. Only that concrete wall. At first I cried from happiness and relief. They say it's physiological. I told the wall about myself, "You know, wall, I gave birth to a child, can you imagine it, I had a child, I did it, isn't that awesome?" Then I felt worse, so sad, and so cold, and I could not get up. I just shook so hard my body rattled the chair, and kept talking to the wall, "Oh, dear wall, I am so cold, would you hold me, would you hug me, dear wall?"

And about the ward, quickly, I just have to pick up speed and rush through it, because I might not make it, the flywheel is there, quickly, about the way they yell, yell (crossed out) at you, the custodians, for the blood on the floor, how they crash your thermos on the floor because your kin downstairs had sent you hot food but did not pay and I don't have any money so the custodian breaks the thermos so there's glass in my soup. You can still eat it, just with glass. Maybe I should have. Now I have to wait for the flywheel to stop turning. But it's okay to write it down . . . just as history . . . At home they yell at me for not being a Madonna and not being happy. At home I spent a long time (crossed out) in the armchair and Margita yelled at me. My mom . . . no, not about this, skip this, I never want to have children again. But when I say it like that, never, no one believes me, because how could a twenty-year-old woman know something like this, what is she going to do with her life. Quickly, quickly I put it down and now (illegible) No do not reread it there are no right words (then illegible.)

•

Kreitzar, too, had come into misfortune. He got married. The marriage was not for love, because Svetka had disappeared from Kreitzar's life. Once that happened, he stopped caring. For a while, momentum remained the only force that still made the machinery of his life spin. He went to work and tended his goats, but all of it now with a permanent moronic grin on his face. There's a phrase for people like that: as if boiled. No one realized at the time that those were the last good days in Kreitzar's life.

His sister, Yerzhia, had her own heartbreak to endure. Sanya had left her a few months earlier. She became distant. She would not talk about anything and locked herself in her room, where she ran and ran her sewing machine with its machine-gun sound, as if she could halt life's assault with a barrage of threads and bits of fabric, for lack of any other weaponry. She had many more clients now, and no friends to speak of. That's when Kreitzar's mother had the fatal idea to get him married. Doing so ran, in fact, counter to her own interest: her son, once he had a wife, would take his money and his heart's affection away from his mother and sister, but what was she to do? Yerzhia protested, but her mother was implacable. "Once a man gets hitched, there'll be a way to put his head in order," she said. "But what's to put in order if there's naught there?" Yerzhia answered.

Still, Kreitzar's mother made her determined rounds of the neighbors, to whom she praised her son and denied the fact of his drinking. He was so hardworking, and in construction, too, and a gentle soul to boot . . . She knew how important it was not to end up with a mean husband who would throw cutlery at his wife— you wanted one who cared a little bit, and felt sorry for his wife, and bore her well—and yes, the neighbor women nodded their wise heads for they, too, knew very well what a treasure that was, a man who did not drink, and had good manners, one who would not use his fists and paint his wife's face black and blue. "Sure, they're all nice when they hang under your windows," one neighbor said. "Right, but have you seen a perfect 'un?" the others answered. Still, they did not want their daughters to marry Kreitzar.

Kreitzar's mother would go home and weep. "Get married," she told him, "have yourself some kids."—"But Svetka won't have me," Kreitzar answered, resigned now, a man with a spring broken inside him, who spoke like a classical tragic hero who had accepted his doom. Someone like Ulysses, say, would not have gone down yet, he'd be slapping the waves around him and cursing Poseidon, but what could a simple mortal do? He, Kreitzar, was the simplest of mortals. Kreitzar went to the kitchen, poured himself a drink, and then feared nothing. Death? Let it come. If life would not give him Svetka, it was all the same to him. Bankruptcy? Then at least he could stay home all day, thinking and thinking about Svetka, spinning out longer and more demanding fantasies in all of which Svetka fell in love with him once and forever and the two became one flesh.[34]

Sometimes he imagined that first she left him, just like she did in real life, but then she came back, tearful and regretful, and said, "Please take me back," begged him to take her back, and he just lay there on the couch and went on smoking his cigarette, because that's what happens when the goat comes back to the cart! He knew he would get up, he was moments away from jumping to his

---

34. Mark 10:8–10

feet with a new lease on life, reinvigorated by her confession, but he kept lingering—not just yet, in a second, just so he could enjoy this moment—but then his mother would come, stand there above him, and blast his castle in the sky to pieces, the life he so carefully imagined for himself. "Get up!" she yelled, and he leaped off the couch as if bitten by a snake. And his mother droned on, one ridiculous thing after another. "Get married already," she told him. "And then loll here all you want, let your wife look after you, I'll let her have you!" At first he wondered if he really ought to get married, but then he stopped. His mother's words became just something he lived with. And that's when Alisa came.

She was unattractive, a woman made of mismatched parts. Her long, puffy face always wore the same unhappy expression. She lived with her mother, grandmother, sister, and her sister's son; her stepfather, thank God, died recently. There was nothing; they had nothing. Alisa was nothing to look at. If only she had looks, she could have gone somewhere where she could have been taught the tricks of life, at the very least, how to smile at rich men. But people's eyes slipped right off her face. Kreitzar did not look at her twice either, but Alisa heard from her mother, who knew Kreitzar's mother, about the plan to marry him and found him one day while he was herding his goats. "Listen," she said, "marry me, I'll be a good housewife."—"No way!" he laughed. "That's just what my old woman says, that I should marry."—"Your old woman, eh?" Alisa worked on that for a while, and next day went to see Kreitzar's mother, with a story of how Kreitzar had courted her, and how they became intimate, but he is in no rush to get married, and Alisa had pinned her hopes on him. She sat in Kreitzar's kitchen, crying all but straight down into the plate of cookies set out for her, while the foolish old woman rejoiced. Yerzhia bolted out of her room then and shouted to Alisa, "He's a drunk! You should know!" Yerzhia's mother chased her away with a tea towel, saying, "Don't mess with your brother's life when you can't sort out your own!"

Eventually, the day came for Kreitzar to stand there before family and guests wearing his moronic grin, as if, having gone irreversibly nuts, he was now ready to be made a public spectacle. The light-colored suit he wore would have looked great on him—if not for his holy-fool face. His mother put a white kerchief into the breast pocket of his suit coat as fashion once dictated—this was a bit of outdated knowledge she dug up from a deep stratum of her memory, like an archaeologist. Alisa's family was there, too, a whole clan of unattractive women worn down by life. The bride's sister—skinny, with her hair dyed very black—bit her lips in impotent rage, Alisa—just think it!—this wet rag who was never even in the running was getting married! Caught herself a catch! The bride bit her lips, too, smearing her lipstick so that the red of it was on her cheeks and on her teeth like the masticated flesh of a mauled small animal.

They meant to put up the canopy in front of the house but never got around to clearing the yard, and the pile of dirt sat where it always had, colossal as the Tower of Babel. Pieces of broken pots lay around. They managed to fit the canopy behind the house, where there was nothing, not even a vine trellis, and decided that since the guests were few they wouldn't mind too much. Kreitzar's mother and Yerzhia cooked up a feast and had Alisa's mother over to help with the baking—which was a waste since all Alisa's mom did was steal whatever was not nailed down, from bits of ham to matches. She hid things in the sleeves of her blouse.

"The old woman's gone off her rocker," Yerzhia whispered into Ivan's ear when he went into the kitchen to get a drink of water. "It's one thing to get you married off, but why'd we have to have it all here, when we have naught!" Indeed, the wedding was a public disaster. It started to rain. The flimsy tent filled with water and leaked. The food got soaked, water dripped everywhere from above and from the oilcloths that covered the tables for lack of proper linens. The goats got loose and wandered between the benches and old chairs, bleating and picking off soggy lettuce from salad plates. Kreitzar and his drinking buddies laughed and raced paper boats in the puddles. Ivan found Phoebe at a table, entirely soaked and ready to leave.

Everyone could see how foolish it had been to host a wedding with as little as the family had—since Kreitzar spent everything on drink—and with in-laws like that to boot, but Kreitzar's mother, the ascetic zealot, believed in the power of the ritual. An invisible messenger from the halcyon days of her childhood whispered as much into her ear. It told her the wedding would justify everything, and fix everything, and her son, once married, would turn to householding, for that was how things always went, that was how the world was ordered. There was no shortage of those who were keen to enlighten her, to tell her that a piglet had never yet turned into a fiery steed, but she had no ears for other people's voices. She would have to see things with her own eyes. Soon it became clear as day that her son was not changed. Everything was the way it had been before, only worse. The old woman woke up from her dream.

But what could she do? Alisa had moved in with them, as covetous as her mother and with a face as if after the great flood, never warm nor clear. There was never a moment when Alisa was not ready to cry or at least be downcast. The woman did not seem to know what a smile was. A mask of disappointment was fixed permanently onto her face—not the kind that comes from snobbery, but the kind that is born of black misery, utter desperation. Kreitzar's mother just kept her head pulled down between her shoulders. What could she expect of this daughter-in-law of hers? Who knew, she was liable to come out to the kitchen one morning with an axe in her hands. Yerzhia, meanwhile, stayed in her room and sewed.

Alisa spoke little and did not move much; her joints hurt, they learned, she'd had this malady all her life. And yet, before the end of the year, she was pregnant. Kreitzar grew somber and even went to work at some sort of a job, if you could call it that. His uncle, the construction crew foreman, could barely tolerate having him. A daughter was born and filled the house with crying. Her cries woke them up now and again, shocked their souls out of the deep, sightless slumber in which they had all become mired. The baby would cry in Alisa's arms, and for an instant, Alisa's eyes would brighten and she would look around the kitchen, and shudder; what was this place and why was she there? The spoon with which Alisa stirred the porridge for the baby would then stop and hang for a moment in midair. Her mother-in-law would also wake, as if pricked with a magic needle. Behind her door, Yerzhia would wake, too, stop her sewing machine, and listen to the hum that came, it felt, from the very center of the earth. Something down there shuddered and turned, and Yerzhia would suddenly become aware of all the many strata below her, their heavy tectonic life. Even Kreitzar, at the jolt of his daughter's cry, would grunt and put away his drink. And then everything would go quiet again, and invisible dust would settle back on these people.

Ivan had come to visit once or twice. It was an odd experience. Alisa barely spoke and looked past Ivan, past her own life. Kreitzar sat on the couch with that same not-quite-there grin of his, even when he was comparatively sober. Yerzhia did not even come out of her room. Only the old mother showed some feeling, she called Ivan into the kitchen and cried to him there, whispering her sorrows through the tears, poured out her heart to him, a stranger— but no, he wasn't, he was Ivanko, the one who'd grown up with her, Ivanko, good as her own, so let him at least listen, let him know if the world would not how things were in this house, what misfortune they had, what burdens—and wiped her eyes with her tea towel embroidered with tiny roosters. It was an old, handmade towel, embroidered with red and black roosters and yellowed with time and frequent use. Ivan knew the objects in Kreitzar's home as if it were his own. He used to sit in this same kitchen, doing homework with his friend. Kreitzar's mother would feed them whatever she had on hand. These days, she only brightened when she took her granddaughter, the little Beatka, from Alisa's arms.

But then she would glance at Kreitzar and tears would roll down her cheeks again.

•

Styopa showed up in the middle of the night. Ivan had to take him out into the street, in the rain, and call a taxi for him. Styopa breathed in Ivan's face and spoke urgently, "Yeah, yeah, I got it, I'll go, but listen, tomorrow! Tomorrow you are coming with me to the restaurant!"—"What restaurant?" Ivan asked. For a moment he feared Styopa had bought one. "The Urbino! Listen!" Styopa yelled. "You know the one, on Tolstoy Street! I'll show you everything . . . I'll explain. I got it all figured out because a man must provide! I, man, have to find something I can lean on! I found a way to provide!"—"All right, fine," Ivan said, relieved. He did know the place, it was actually in a basement but for whatever reason was considered high-class.

The Urbino's sign was hard to spot and the doors were locked from the inside. The guy who opened the door, a big one, wore an apron the color of military fatigues—in fact, it could have been army-issued. They shook off the rain and handed their umbrellas to the dude. In the low light of the dining room, a man was waiting for them at a table. Ivan did not know him, but Styopa obviously did, very well, judging by the way they greeted each other, the way Styopa's back was slapped—they must have done business together. Ivan looked around. The dining room was very dark, darker than one would like, and all the tables were placed against the walls. Dark shapes sat around these tables, most of them male, all very focused on what they were eating, bent low over their plates. The waiters—well built and broad-shouldered—produced the same impression as the guy who opened the door.

"This is Lotsi, and this is my brother-in-law, Ivan," Styopa said. Lotsi had sweaty hands and a restless face, but spoke very rapidly, in a low voice, almost at a murmur, so Ivan and Styopa were forced to all but lie on the table if they wanted to hear him. They ordered food, meat baked with cheese, a new trend, never mind that the cheese was all the same whether you ordered sandwiches or a plate to go with wine or a baked dish—nominally Dutch (or rather, pseudo-Dutch) due to how it was made, but sold, for some reason, as "Russian." On top of the cheese, local chefs usually poured ketchup or mayonnaise, so the result was peculiar. The cheese would melt and stick to the meat, which would remain raw on the inside and scorching hot on the outside, under the crust stained with ketchup or mayonnaise. While they waited, they were served the appetizers: a bit of *salo*, some sauerkraut, pickles sliced lengthwise, and, of course, vodka. Ivan decided he would not drink tonight.

As it turned out, Lotsi wanted Styopa to buy a house in a village just outside the city to convert into the restaurant Styopa dreamed of. The house, allegedly, belonged to Lotsi, but it was at this point that Lotsi's story stopped holding water. Ivan had no idea a person could talk as much as this Lotsi did and say absolutely nothing. Styopa, however, listened very attentively, acted politely, asked clarifying questions, and every so often glanced at Ivan, as if to say, Well? This is a good idea, isn't it? Lotsi sat across from them, and it was now he who leaned in, hovered in front of them with his fleshy face and his big nose, and blabbered on and on about how fine the house, the neighbors, and the roads there all were.

The food arrived, and Ivan realized he had misjudged this establishment. However little experience he had with the various cuisines of the world—he was expert in Margita's cooking only—it was enough to tell that what they had been served was not, in any way, poorly cooked meat with cheap, bad cheese. The chef at this place was superb. Meanwhile, Lotsi and Styopa drank. Then they drank some more. They praised the food and the restaurant more generally. They praised themselves. If someone had bothered to translate everything they were saying to each other and each of them to themselves, the total would amount to something along the lines of, "I am feeling really good right now." Their hearts sang in thrall to the pure and undiluted alcoholic euphoria. "Foso!"[35] one man would declare, full nearly to tears with well-being and sentiment. "N-no!" the other would instantly respond. They would pour another round and lean to each other to clink their glasses. They forgot about the chaotic times they lived in, the politicians on TV, about their wives and children for whom they had to provide, and the houses they had to build and rebuild. They were on their little island of joy.

"Well," Styopa said, as a way of finally getting down to the business of the evening. "Here's to you!" He turned to Ivan and added, "Our manager!"—"What!" Ivan nearly choked on a piece of meat. "Styopa," he said, once he cleared his throat. "Could we talk about this outside for a minute?"—"No, wait, I don't get it!" Lotsi piped in, instantly much louder. "What's this talking about? Who'd I come to talk to here? We had a deal! The deal was you are buying it, you and him," Lotsi pointed at Ivan. "Together!" Ivan gave Styopa a sharp look, but Styopa either did not see it in the damn dark or pretended not to have seen it or, possibly, was by now, considering

---

35. An all-purpose Hungarian pejorative, here translated as "It's the shit, man!"

the amount of vodka he and Lotsi had drunk, too intoxicated to see it. "Calm down!" Styopa said. "I've got it under control." Ivan only shook his head and said nothing. This, however, was not enough to fool Lotsi. Somewhere inside him a switch had flipped. There was no logic to this, because, if you thought about it, what difference did it make who bought what as long as money got paid. But for Lotsi, apparently, there was a big difference indeed. His euphoria evaporated. "There's discord 'mongst the comrades!"[36] he half said, half sang, before jumping to his feet and facing Styopa. "You fucking cheat!"

"Who? Me? You gonna be sorry you said that!" Styopa growled, getting to his feet himself. This was the moment Ivan had been afraid of. He leaped to his feet, but before he could get to the two men, Lotsi swung his arm wide and hit Styopa on his ear. Styopa, who somehow managed to stay upright, punched Lotsi in the face so hard that Lotsi's knees buckled and he sat back onto someone else's table, possibly directly in someone's plate, like in a bad American comedy. After that, Ivan could only remember separate snippets of action. He was just trying to get Styopa's hands off Lotsi's neck when the men on whose table Lotsi had landed jumped to their feet as well and went to break up the fight. Neither Styopa nor Lotsi was about to give up so easily. A waiter came running, and then another, big guys used to seeing scenes like this, but then something exploded either out in the street or in the guts of the building above them, and the lights went out.

Now there was no way to tell who was pummeling whom in the various nooks and corners of the restaurant. A mass of invisible clay had come alive and battered Ivan from all sides. He ducked and sidestepped blows instinctively, as best he could, all the while

---

36. A line from Ivan Krylov's fable "Swan, Pike, and Crawfish" (1814), a staple of elementary school curriculum.

acutely sick with the sharp smell of cologne that had suddenly filled the air, cologne mixed with sweat. The cologne must have been expensive, and quite appropriate somewhere in the reception rooms of Europe, but here, in this subterranean eatery, everything became something different, mysterious compounds bound onto the perfume and made the smell intolerable. God, what next? Ivan managed to think. What came next was very simple: someone hit Ivan on the head and he fell down.

He came around minutes later; the lights were back on. Ivan sat. The room spun around him. He felt sick to his stomach. He could smell that cologne on him, it seemed to have saturated his shirt and his hair to the roots, it would stay there for the rest of his life. That was the last thing he needed; people would think he got a male lover, a real dreamboat who adored him, and waited for him faithfully at the bank or at his house's garden gate. What would Margita think! Actually, she might just take this boyfriend in, he is a man, after all, could come in handy with the jobs in the garden and such. This happened to Ivan: in the most disastrous moments of his life he thought of random things that made him laugh. The fight raged around him, Lotsi and Styopa shouted things at each other, waiters ran to and fro, yanking tablecloths from the wine-splattered and food-smeared tables, and even the owner of the establishment himself made an appearance. None of this concerned Ivan. What was it Styopa had said? A man has to find something he can lean on. Ivan rose to his feet, put his hands on the edge of the nearest table, and stood there, leaning on it, while the world rocked and swayed before his eyes.

•

The new people came to their bank on an afternoon, read out a document, announced who in the accounting office would keep their jobs, let the rest of the staff go, and called everyone who functioned as a manager to the boss's office. Ivan's official job title was Head of the Computer Department. The new crew consisted of three people. The oldest, with his shaved head, could have been taken for a real tough, but his eyes told a different story. The toughs were drunk on their newfound power, but at the same time, profoundly scared, and this man moved steadily, sharply, and his eyes were just as sharp, focused on their aim. His name was Nikolai Nikolaich, and he spoke Russian.

Nikolaich's younger associate, Vasya, wore a pair of glasses and a suit that was too nice for the occasion, as if he were trying to look older and more respectable than he was. The third man said nothing and took notes. Nikolaich did introduce him, but Ivan forgot the name immediately. Nikolaich made a speech about the need to expand to Kyiv, to open branches there, first a local branch of the automotive parts business he himself managed, and then the bank. Everyone made approving noises. Vasya chirped something about their sophisticated business plan. Ivan could barely control his scorn. He knew it was all bullshit, knew what the market looked like in Lviv, and enough about Kyiv. The essence of what he knew was that these "branches" were about to swallow up modest provincial banks in peripheral cities, meaning all of them. They would chop them into kindling, sell them off, and use the money to ensure the survival of their business in Kyiv. And, for instance, this Vasya. And Vasya knew it. Nikolaich also knew it but was putting on a show for them, telling them a fairy tale, and they were happy to hear it, because a man wants to believe a happy lie, to be fooled. He must. They would buy themselves another six months, thinking all the while they had caught the tiger by the tail.

"Well, let's get to know each other," Nikolaich said with a smile, and his smile annoyed Ivan even more than the rest of this schemer. Everyone introduced themselves: Mytio Mytiovych, whom everyone knew anyway; Myron Vasyliovych; Volodya, the chief accountant; Diana Semenivna, his deputy. "And this is Ivan," Volodya said, noticing that Ivan, when his turn came, said nothing. Ivan just nodded, as in, *howdy*. "Excellent," Nikolaich said in Russian, smiling even more coyly. "It's a pleasure to meet such pleasant people. We'll do some good work together, shall we? We'll fight our way to Kyiv! What do you say, Vanka?" And he looked Ivan straight in the eye.

"Ivan," Ivan said. "My name is Ivan." He made the correction and it surprised him. Did such silly things really happen? Could a man really feel so angry just because some redneck calls him "Vanka"? This was something from village tales, from stories written "for the people," from jokes no one took seriously because, really, was language the problem? Could they allow, in this difficult time, for language to separate them? Ivan remembered a young man from somewhere in the Urals who stood on the Maidan with them, remembered others like him. Remembered the soldiers who deserted to escape abuse. He would have been happy to speak Russian to them, even though he never learned that language well. He could not pronounce Russian words correctly and had an ineradicable Ukrainian or, more specifically, Transcarpathian accent. And here he was.

As if he could pretend he did not know that this Vanka plunked into one cup of the scales meant the other one held his little Emilia, Margita, and Phoebe, his home.

Things got worse after that. Nikolaich, they found out, planned to cut their salaries. Only temporarily, of course, until his partners in Kyiv could get the business going, and as soon as they did, they would, of course, repay everything and more. They just had to hang on for another day and last another night, as the old Soviet war song went. At this news, a shadow crossed their boss's face. Myron Vasyliovych, immaculately turned out, as always, moved impatiently in his chair. He, for one, had long ceased believing anyone,

God and devil included, and now sat watching the unfolding com‑
edy through the ironic eyes of the man whose house is being lev‑
eled to the ground right before him. Things come, and then things
pass, as Ecclesiastes said, because everything passes. Let it be, then.
Myron Vasyliovych knew there was no one here with whom to bar‑
gain, that all he could do was endure this meeting until its end, so
that he could start asking around for a new job elsewhere. Neither
was this worth an open confrontation; one never knew when one
might need this Nikolaich on one's side. A poor peace, they say, is
better than a good fight. Or an open war. Or is it?

"Why so little?" Ivan heard himself say. "Why do you need
more, Vanka?" Nikolaich said, squinting at him. "I have yet to see
how things go. If we like you, we'll give you a raise, move you to
Kyiv. You'll move your wife . . ." Ivan felt his muscles spasm again.
"Ivan!" he said. "My name is Ivan, not Vanka." The boss breathed
harder, and Myron Vasyliovych sighed.

"Aha!" Nikolaich said and suddenly switched to speaking
Ukrainian. "You're a proud one. Proud you might be, but you're
not thinking with your head. Fine, *Mister* Ivan," he put mocking
emphasis on the formal address, that profoundly Ukrainian piece
of grammar, absent altogether in Russian. "Have it your way." He
kept Ivan in the crosshairs of his gaze; the man's eyes pinned Ivan
down like a bug. Nikolaich was openly, shamelessly mocking him.
His eyes waited. The man waited for Ivan to make his next mis‑
take. He still thought Ivan had made a mistake, that he had spoken
out of impatience. Just a bit more, Ivan would do it again, and then
Nikolaich would be completely within his rights to break his ribs.

Ivan stood up. He had no intention of handing over his aces. He
had no intention to lose, either; he would just stop playing. Let them
sort their mess out without him. Ivan had already lost everything,
and he knew it, but they did not. Myron Vasyliovych would proba‑
bly kill him later, but better it be his father-in-law than these thugs.

"I quit," Ivan told Nikolaich.

For a moment, a quick moment, Ivan saw panic in the man's eyes, it was as if a snake swam underwater and troubled its surface. In the next instant Nikolaich regained his composure and said, "And what are you going to do, Mister Ivan? You think you'll just get hired somewhere else?" There was a threat in his voice, he must have already installed his people throughout the industry. "Don't rush into things. Let's figure something out for you . . . Sit down, let's take another look at your contract," Nikolaich kept speaking. "Just take a minute to think things over . . ."

And with that, he revealed himself, utterly and completely. Nikolaich did not know how to lose, he only knew how to keep on playing the game, like all the other ones like him, *those men* whom Ivan could now recognize without error a hundred miles away regardless of the guise they came wearing. It did not matter if they had actually served in the infamous *organs* or had just grown used to the matrix, they kept playing, forever, and sucked others into their games, lured them with fake bait, to keep them entangled. Forever.

But not this time.

Ivan went to the door, turned the handle, and left.

•

He walked down the street and felt his fury burn high and bright inside him. He walked slowly, he did not want to spill any of it, he wanted to stay like that, brimming with fury, his sacred fire. He would not speak to anyone, did not want to run into anyone he knew, he was too busy—it was hard work to guard his tall flame of rage. The blaze was pure and any interruption, any conversation would only have polluted it. Ivan walked and, it seemed, began to smile; he held his shoulders wider, and his head rode proudly upon them, never mind that it hurt ferociously—he had felt a drilling ache in his temples as soon as *they* showed up at the door. He did get hit on the head during the brawl in that restaurant Styopa had taken him to, and now suffered from headaches regularly. Ivan wondered if he had walked off a concussion instead of taking the time to recover properly. But let it hurt. He would pay it no mind. He walked bareheaded, and the air around him vibrated with the promise of summer—spring had finally arrived and every living thing burst with happy, genial noise.

Where to now? Nikolaich would find him wherever he landed, even if he chose to bide his time. Ivan did not wish to be found. He did not even want to think about it, did not want to go on looking over his shoulder. He remembered well what he had experienced in Lviv, remembered what it was like to see a pursuer behind every corner. Ivan shuddered. He was a computer programmer, an experienced systems administrator, and knew enough accounting to get by if need be. He knew the banking business. Which meant that's exactly where they would look for him. He would go elsewhere. He would find a menial, physical job. Why not? Let Margita yell at him, let his father-in-law be offended all he wanted. The dissidents, when they came out of the camps, could not get good jobs either. So neither would he.

Ivan's schoolmate and his best man at his wedding, Seryi, aka Serhiy Kovach, had an autoshop or, more precisely, a service garage. Their friendship was sporadic, they did not see each other very often, but when they did, they sort of plunged, immediately, into a different time, into their shared childhood and schooldays, and the bond between them renewed itself. Serhiy did not concern himself with things like the nation, oligarchs, or even elections. He operated in tangible, particulate dimensions: here was a space, here was a way to lease it, never mind that there was no formal lease, here are cars that need fixing, and here are guys who know how—Dyusi,

Shoni, and Misha—and they have able hands, and here is cash, and cash can buy this thing and that, and pay off a "cover" if the need arose. But Serhiy's uncle worked for the police, so he had no particular troubles on that front.

The garage was close to the edge of the city, a fair distance from Galagov, where Ivan lived. Beyond Galagov lay Slovakia, and on that side of town people with money snapped up land along the highway to build hotels and spas. By the time Ivan reached the garage it was midafternoon. Seryi, who was not averse to getting his own hands dirty, was helping one of his mechanics. He was happy to see Ivan, wiped his hands on a rag, and came out to greet him. They embraced.

There was no office per se, only a partitioned-off corner of the garage where Serhiy had his desk, buried under a mountain of paper. "Are you not cold here?" Ivan asked. "Are you kidding? I'm never here, I have no time. And summer's just around the corner!" Seryi said, laughing. He had gray eyes and a ruddy face. He wore a dress shirt to work, but then forgot to put on his coveralls when he went to help, and his shirt was dotted with oil stains. He took Ivan in with a single look. "How are you?" he asked. "I need a job," Ivan said, not bothering with a preamble. "Well," Seryi said, hesitant. "I don't employ an IT person . . . I should, really, to keep up with the times, but . . ."—"I know," Ivan said. "I want to work as a mechanic. I am not as good at it as your guys, but you said you could always use another pair of hands."—"That is true," Seryi said, considering. "But I don't pay the kind of cash you get at your bank . . ."—"There is no bank anymore."

Ivan had been helping his father with their car since he was a boy. At Seryi's, however, he quickly realized that the work was too much for his concussed head. Things would spin around him: when he bent down or when he climbed under an axle, when he inhaled the ubiquitous gas fumes. Whenever it happened, Ivan had to stop whatever he was doing and take a break, step from the garage out into the street, also noisy and very polluted, but the air outside felt heavenly. In the evening, he would walk home across the entire city. He enjoyed that. This was his time to clear his head. Time to rekindle the fury that went on burning inside him. This fury was different from impotent rage, it had no bitter aftertaste. It purified and elevated him. He could sit with the smallest flame of it, and it kept burning, giving him strength. It must have been a little flame like this that warmed the Mother of Cossacks, Oksana Meshko, when they exiled her to the Sea of Okhotsk and the snow buried the hut she lived in.

Summer came, unexpectedly hot after the cool spring. Greenery climbed the walls of the gray uniform buildings in the neighborhood where Ivan worked. The verdant green was this impoverished place's only adornment—it could hide the peeling walls, the dirt. In the evenings, the heat held on, refused to subside. Walls that had absorbed the blaze of the sun during the day slowly leaked it back to the streets. People's kitchens sent the heat of cooking and the smells of vegetables out through open windows. Ivan's headaches got worse. Heat, physical effort, or just being tired at the end of the day sent circles of light swimming across his field of vision, made it feel like something was squeezing his temples, and, somewhere above his left ear, roused a pain as sharp as if someone was cutting into his flesh with a knife. The garage smells made him constantly sick. Once, Ivan spent three days in Margita's darkened living room, he did not let the curtains be parted or open his eyes. After this, Margita took him to a doctor. A migraine, the doctor said, and prescribed something that did not help very much. As soon as Ivan went out into the street, under the sun, pain leaped back at him with fresh strength.

But the fury, Ivan thought, where is my fury? Why can I not subsist on that alone? Will it not pull me out of this misery? He searched for the precious flame inside of him, and could not find it. The small light was being doused with waves of pain and nausea. The pain reduced him to his physical, common body, stripped of its magic, robbed of its special skills. Pain overpowered everything else. It pushed him out onto the porch of existence. Pain mocked him. He would have liked to respect himself, to think of himself as a keeper of fury and fire. But the space inside his head hummed like a great struck bell, and he had to lie down, defeated, annihilated by life, defenseless against it and the pain it brought. How quickly everything ended! How simply. He could do nothing. He dared nothing. His rebellion in the name of justice turned out to be short-lived, and no organs, no "kay-gee-bee" were required, nothing of the sort. Pain was enough.

Up until then Ivan had not known what pain was. Even his arm, when his father so carelessly slashed it a week before his wedding, hurt no longer than about two weeks, and never so much he could not live with it. He just had to keep it still and take his pills. Now the pills did not help. That, before, was a mere sign of pain, and this, in his head, he could touch, it was as thick as shortening spread on a piece of bread. Perhaps providence had known things about him back then, and sent signs to warn him, but he failed to read them.

And what if he had had to show up for interrogations feeling like this? What would "Sashko Petrenko" and Borovik have done to him? What if he had had to go to the Maidan? How could he have been a guard? Would he have lied to his comrades that he was not feeling well and laid down on a cot to join the hunger strike? And what then? Would he have died of pain? Pain fired shots above his ear, there and above his eye, a barrage of terror. He held his head in his hands and did not know how to go on living, how to be, how to think. He knew nothing and whatever he had known before turned out to matter not at all.

He now knew what it meant to be utterly defenseless.

It was also becoming clear that he was going to remain unemployed for a while.

Andriy Groma called from Lviv. He asked if Ivan felt like coming to visit. Ivan packed his backpack the same night, told his family he was going, and went to the railway station. He bought a ticket for the overnight train that arrived in Lviv early in the morning, too early, really, if you thought about it, and it cost more than taking the regional connector during the day, but it ran in the dark, and that meant Ivan did not have to worry about his head; it did not hurt in the dark.

Lviv Station in the morning was a buzzing hive. The mechanical voice overhead called out arrivals and departures. Ivan left the building and crossed the square to the streetcar stop, but they were not running yet, so, after sitting at the stop for a while and getting bored, Ivan decided to walk. He didn't have anywhere in particular to go, really—he hadn't talked to anyone about staying the night. He just walked, letting his instinct take him down the streets he had so ingloriously fled a few years earlier. He loved every stone under his feet, the bulging cobbles, the rocky maze of it all. He knew his way by heart, he could have walked blindfolded.

He called Andriy from a payphone downtown. Told him he would wait at the Neptune. This particular fountain, in the city's old Market Square, traditionally served as a landmark for romantic and casual rendezvous, and there were always plenty of people sitting on its rim. God, how long it has been! How could he have lived for so long without this city? The sun shone brightly, but the air was still cool, laced with the freshness of the morning. The streetcars now ran, rattling across the square, and the square shook under them. Ivan knew everyone who lived in the apartments around it could feel the ground shudder as well, but he also knew it was something you got used to.

Andriy came running after about twenty minutes. He ran up to Ivan, leaped at him, crumpled him in a bear hug. They went to Andriy's place first, and later to a café that bore the popular nickname of Mausoleum—the voluminous shadowbox tables, made of dark wood, brought to mind coffins with glass lids. Inside, the boxes held miniature rock gardens, pebbles, plants, and small unidentifiable objects, all manner of things, except, thank goodness, the relics of the Great Leader himself. Tymish Gamkalo joined them at the café, and the three of them went to see Yarema. They had more coffee in the famous "Armenian Place"—each cupful boiled in a tiny cezve set into hot sand. Yarema now ran an arts center he had opened in an ancient residential building with fortress-thick walls.

Finally, they had a chance to be together, all of them, and to catch up. Tymish worked as an IT programmer and spent his evenings writing prose (essays, he said), which he was planning to publish. Andriy was in the tourism business, he led walking tours and put in hours in the city's archives. He had no interest in national politics; he had made Lviv his politics. He protested whenever the city administration attempted to raze a significant building or issued a permit for reshaping a historic facade—Andriy was doing this long before anyone began to listen to people like him, wrote petitions, talked to people, convinced, and cajoled. Still, just as in their earlier days on the Maidan, there was not a pinch of aggression in him.

Yarema spoke little, as always. He smoked a lot. He talked about the defeat of national-democratic forces, about Rukh, which, he maintained, was bound for collapse. ("And then what? Who will follow us after that?") About fabricated scandals. About assassinations. The way various student organizations disintegrated from the inside. "You see," he said, "in our movement, somehow everyone got along: nationalists with other -ists with people who were just Castaneda fans—everyone stuck together, these things didn't get between people. And now everyone's at each other's throats, and fighting to the death. The cut each other down." Ivan had heard a little about this, but that only made it worse to hear Yarema say it. Nationalists were at war with the liberals, liberals with the democrats, and democrats—with the feminists.

Yarema talked about the oligarchs, too. The oligarchs rode in on a flood of money, unimaginable and unimaginably dirty, made in the arms trade, made on death, stolen from the people. What did the National Democrats have to show against that? What, besides their idea, their stubborn endurance, their physical sacrifice, and a few clean shirts? Oligarchs negotiated with organized crime. Oligarchs dressed in Paris. Their pocket change bought an apartment in Kyiv, or a few in the province—many of the dissidents didn't have a permanent roof over their heads. "What should we do now, be afraid of the oligarchs?" Gamkalo asked and laughed, and they all laughed, except Yarema, who barely smiled with the very corners of his mouth. "We should keep doing what we do," he said. "Hold the perimeter." That was what he, Yarema, did. He held the perimeter. Inside, many finally learned what it was like to feel safe. He supported rock bands. Poets. Painters. In the evening, they went to Lyalka, a venue of legendary reputation.

Inside Lyalka, people stood along the walls—there were not enough seats. Ivan marveled at this crowd that was not, in the true meaning of the word, a crowd. Each person here was expressly an individual unlike any other. A different, new kind of young people, a different life, even though it had only been a few years since they—Yarema, Tymish, Ivan himself—thought of themselves as the young people. Girls were dressed in black and wore exquisite coral-bead jewelry, the kind never seen in the Soviet Union. People listened to the kind of music that had not existed before. That night Dead Rooster were playing. Ivan felt as if every nerve in his body had been stripped naked, and now every sound, every gesture, every pluck of the bass string sent echoes reverberating through his limbs. Mysko Barbara, the frontman, was saying something in the intervals between songs; Ivan could not hear individual words, everything came at him as a single wave, the music, the words, the poetry, the people's faces, the joy of recognition.

•

The band took a break. Ivan went out to the street with Yarema to smoke. Time, Ivan suddenly thought, is what made the difference. Time that had passed. That's what explained why the steel hand that had gripped his throat all these years now released. Time had freed him from his chains more effectively than any heroics would have. He had sat out the worst on the shores of *his* river, in Maly Galagov, like a child who hid under a blanket. He mustered his courage and asked Yarema about Rose. Yarema looked at him, was silent for a moment, and then said, "She got married to Bodya. They are expecting a child. They all live in that small town he's from." Ivan asked no more questions. Now he knew. Well, what else could he expect? He just vanished back then, disappeared, and never talked to her as he should have. She knew nothing. And now it was too late. It was good she married Bodya. Bodya loved her; he would never abandon her, unlike Ivan. He had to believe they were happy.

Ivan closed his eyes. His head spun. Rose. The red rose on the black earth. The pregnant Mother Earth who carried life inside her, but also took in the dead. He shuddered—why did he think about death right then?

"How would you like to move here?" Yarema asked. "We could use you." He named a few friends of theirs who had started their own business, and always had a need for educated people, especially someone they knew from the Polytechnic. Ivan breathed in—very slowly, because his chest suddenly hurt.

He did not know what to say. Or rather, the trouble was, he did know. He would not move without Emilia, and Phoebe would not come with him, and even if she did, they would have to bring Margita, too, otherwise they would have to look for a nanny because a woman who barely got up from her chair could not manage being a mother, a partner, a quiet harbor for her husband while he searched for something he could apply himself to, meaning a big, important undertaking. Actually, the truth was even worse. Phoebe, if they came to Lviv, would eat Ivan alive. Or she would leave him—of course!—were she, too, to get access to this environment. She would start wearing all black, curve her lips just so, wear those magnificent necklaces . . . She, too, would go to Lyalka, attend book launches, listen to others read their poems, and lose her mind because what did she have at home? Little Emilia, the daughter she sometimes could not even see, and Ivan, the husband she—Ivan had no doubt about this— abhorred. How would he live? How would they all live? And what would happen to the baby?

Ivan sighed. "I'll think about it," was all he could say. There must have been stars in the night sky, but the streetlights were too bright to see them. Ivan could see nothing except the electric lights around the square, only these yellow flashes and the black cobblestone under his feet.

•

He returned home in two days, again by the overnight train, and again walked from the railway station. The entire time he was traveling and drinking and going to noisy places, with the straps of his backpack pressing into the muscles of his shoulders, he never once had a headache. But now, in his own city, at home, he could feel the pain that had dozed off for those few days stir and come awake. Ivan let himself into the house quietly; he had the keys. He climbed the steps to his floor. Peeked into the bedroom, looked at baby Emilia. He went out on the balcony and lit up a cigarette. He felt a great wave of gratitude wash over him: for his home, for Lviv, for this trip. He thanked his pain for giving him the gift of freedom for these few days. Lviv had poured new strength into him. All he had to do was find where he could apply this energy. Invent the script of his own life. He had to do something—he just did not know what it was.

•

In the fall, the old Paikosh died. He was in the hospital for a while and stayed brave. Every day, Christina called Margita to report the news: what tests the doctors did, and which one came to see him, and which other one, and that they had asked Dr. Migalina himself to check in on him—Migalina was the best cardiologist in the region, and the old man had known his father—and that Dr. Migalina came, and took a look, and prescribed drugs that Styopa went to buy across the border in Hungary. The old Paikosh was lucid and, most of the time, in good spirits; he was not a man to feel sorry for himself. He overlooked nothing, and reviewed his will one last time. Christina went to see him, and the Raptors came, and the old Paikosh looked at his grandsons for a long time, and a tear burned in his eye. He asked Christina, "What about Ivan? Why doesn't he come?"

Ivan came, and the old Paikosh propped himself up on his elbows, and with a great effort, sat up. The other patient in the room was asleep. "I wanted to speak with you, Ivanko," the old man said. "Sit here, with me. You mightn't know this but back when I was a director, I had this gift of making peace between people. I could talk to people, there were some who'd die before they saw each other, and then the head of the district committee would call me and ask me, 'Mykolaich, would you give it a go, I've tried everything.' And I did, and it worked. There are lots of things I can do, all things, and I can recite poems in Latin by heart. They taught us in the gymnasium. They taught us well! I was in the same class with Yuri Shkrobynets', the poet, d'you know him?"

Ivan started as he did whenever someone mentioned poetry, because it made him think of Phoebe.

"You didn't know, did you?" the old man said.

"No," Ivan said.

"Well . . . I want to speak with you about your wife. I am an old man, and, as you can see, 'bout to die, and don't tell me nothing, because I know it. But my heart aches for you and your wife— how is it no one's taking care of you, not her family, nor your mom? Ask your wife to come here, too, I'll speak to her yet. I've heard you don't live so well. Is that true?"

"No," Ivan said. "It's not true."

The old man studied his face for a long time. He breathed long, labored breaths. His skin had a bluish tint to it and shadows lay under his eyes.

"Why do you lie to me?" he said finally. "I know well how things are. You are in a bad way. I'll have you know this, son, you're same as my own to me, and before I go lie in the raw old dirt, I want to see to it that things are good with you. And family, mark my word, son, is the biggest thing. Your job won't dry your tears or hold you at night. Look at Christina and Styopa! Have you seen how they are?"—"I have," Ivan said honestly because, in fact, he had. And Paikosh had not. But then again, we all have our blind spots. "Then why don't you tell me the truth? Speak to me, I won't tell anyone. Speak!" the old man said, almost begging. "Speak to me, let it all out, maybe I can counsel you, I've lived a life, and not an easy one! Don't be afraid, tell me how it is. Why are things the way they are between you? What crossed you? Does she spend too much money? Do you not make love in bed? Speak to me, it'll take the weight off. What is it?"

Ivan said nothing. Their bed! What is this man talking about? He had to tell Paikosh something, to satisfy him, tell him something that wasn't true. "We get along fine," he said. He touched the old man's hand, not knowing, really, how to speak to someone ill or dying. He had never been taught. He stood up. "Maybe you are tired? You should rest."—"I don't need no rest!" the old man was angry now. "I'll rest when I'm dead!" Ivan sat back down. The old man had a point. "It's just that we are doing all that remodeling," he said, the first thing that came to mind. In fact, they weren't doing much at all, only small touch-up jobs when Margita asked her cousin to help paint or put a new coat of varnish on the stairs herself. "Everyone's on edge when remodeling."—"I want you to live well. To be happy, a man of your own home."

Ivan had to smile. Since the time the Soviets collectivized this country there had not been one man happy in his own home. Those who took up husbandry had to learn anew the love for the land and ownership—and, on top of that, to fight everyone around them: the stupid parliament with its idiotic laws, the police who did not enforce even those, the stupid taxes, the stupid gangsters in their little leather jackets, and the stupid oligarchs . . .

"I'm happy as I am," he said. Old Paikosh looked into his eyes steadily as if trying to read something in there, and he must have seen what he was looking for; his expression changed. He had seen that Ivan would not tell him anything, would not unburden himself. That Ivan, no matter how soft he appeared, was, in fact, hard as a flint inside. And that was the way he ought to be.

Old Paikosh saw that and gave up. His own life was now exhausted, his last strength rustled and fell, like so many wings of dead butterflies. He had done much, and had not had the time to do even more, but a human life is not without its limit.

"Fine," he said. "Fine, Ivanko, let it be the way it is. I never forgot that you stood up for Ukraine. Ukraine needs standing up for. And your wife . . . Maria . . . Be good to her."

The old man fell silent for a while—he was tired, he had spent the last dregs of his strength on this conversation. He squeezed Ivan's hand and said, "Keep them safe," and made a sign for Ivan to leave.

Whom did old Paikosh have in mind? Whom was Ivan supposed to keep safe—his wife and daughter, or Ukraine? The old man might have wanted his last words to Ivan to be solemn, memorable, but they were ambiguous. A man like old Paikosh was not likely to intend ambiguity.

He died three days later. They buried him at the old cemetery, on Calvary Hill, because he had relatives there (in addition to his distinguished service to the city). They dug a hole beside a grave that already held someone from his clan, to add another Paikosh on top. Steady fall rains had started a few days before and the ground opened its muddy maw to swallow everyone it could catch. The old Paikosh lay in the coffin, and the rain drops drilled hard into its lid, slowly chipping through the wood to reach the dead but still recognizable flesh. When everyone left and darkness fell, once the rain, like spit, softened the wood and the bones, the earth would begin grinding the old Paikosh in its old yellow teeth.

Ivan made himself shake off the vision. It wasn't right to think this; the old Paikosh had lived a good life. He had not been afraid to die. He only feared leaving Ivan alone, but he, Ivan, had not wished to burden the old man.

•

After the old man's death, a stinging shame took root in Ivan's heart. Stand up for Ukraine, but did he, Ivan, stand up for it? Petrified by "Sashko Petrenko," he lay at the bottom of life like an ancient catfish, waiting for things to pass.

Ivan went to the post office and called Pavlo Dankulynets from there. He called his office number and the voice that answered was Pavlo's own. "Hi, it's Ivan," he said. "Ivan?" like old Paikosh, Dankulynets grasped things instantly, no need to explain which Ivan was calling. If he did not recognize the voice on the line, no matter: Dankulynets was attuned to the vibrations of cosmic energies. "Come, come to our office, I won't hear anything, come on, here's the address," Pavlo spoke quickly, and his words stumbled into one another as they had never before.

Ivan wrote down the address and got up to go, but found he could not move, gripped by a sudden fit of despair. Where did he think he was going? What for? He, the unemployed, he the eternal revolutionary, spurred by passion into battle? Nonsense! Nothing spurred him to anything, nothing urged him, nothing compelled him—he was forever being tossed to the very bottom of life, the only place where he seemed capable of surviving. So what, he had gone to Lviv and his friends cheered him up! Add to this the old Paikosh, whose loss Ivan hadn't even begun to comprehend. He might never comprehend it, actually, it would be easier that way. He could just tell himself that Paikosh was alive and well, and had merely gone somewhere. Abroad.

After a few days of not being himself, Ivan mustered his courage and went to see Dankulynets. He had not kept up with the papers for the last six months and did not know what was happening with Rukh. He heard it said that democratic forces could never figure out how to unite and wondered if the stereotype, in this case, was true. There was a time when Dankulynets had an office downtown, in an old villa on the riverfront that was slowly falling apart around its residents. They had moved far from there, to Labortsi, deep in the guts of Old Galagov, where not a single person ever cared for politics. Why there? They rented rooms in a privately owned building—a brand-new one this time, recently finished.

The tight hallway that led to the office hummed with activity. People sat on new couches along the wall, people ran to and fro with papers to be signed, a printer buzzed in another room. Ivan went straight to the office, but people stopped him; the line shouted at him, just like in the good old Soviet days, that no one skipped ahead, and everyone had to take a number. In the distance, obscured by the roiling swarm of the visitors, Ivan saw the receptionist. She was the one who gave out the numbers.

"What are you talking about? I was asked in!" Ivan said. He shook off someone's too-insistent hand, grabbed the doorknob, opened the door, and stopped still. The room beyond was not an office as Ivan had anticipated, but a negotiations room. In the large space, he saw Dankulynets and two of his people at the long oval table, recognized a couple of others, political figures, and took in a few Orthodox priests beside them, including the notorious Father R., a rotund character whose cassock all but burst at the seams. Dankulynets saw Ivan and his face lit up. He sprang up, came close, and whispered in Ivan's face, "Hey, come back a bit later, I gotta run this meeting. Come back in two hours. I'm thrilled to see you!" and closed the door behind Ivan.

Ivan waited for four hours to come back, but when he did, the meeting was still going, albeit with a somewhat modified cast of participants. He peeked into the office, a plate of wilting sandwiches sat on the table, and he could smell coffee. Ivan sighed and sat down. The only difference from before was the number of visitors in the hallway: the crowd had significantly thinned. In another hour Dankulynets saw his guests out, closed the front door behind them, mimed wiping sweat off his face, laughed, and embraced Ivan.

The office still smelled of coffee and what was left of the sandwiches. "Take a seat," Dankulynets waved. He was clearly tired, but his eyes were bright. Ivan found himself basking in the familiar but forgotten feeling of energy and spontaneous joy that being in Pavlo's presence gave his visitors, friends, and, let's be honest here, voters. It was called now by a fashionable word, charisma.

"What a day," Pavlo said, laughing. "Sorry, it's been a really long one. What took you so long? I expected you last week."— "Well, I . . ." Ivan muttered. He thought he could have told Dankulynets about old Paikosh's death, but that felt like a first-grader's excuse, as in, *Oh I didn't come to school because my grandpa died.* So Ivan said nothing. Dankulynets studied his face. Then he asked, "How are you doing? Do you have a job?"

"Not yet," Ivan said. Dankulynets seemed happy to hear it. "Great!" he said. "I have a job for you. Come work for us, at the campaign office."—"Rukh's campaign office? Me?" Ivan laughed. "But I'm no agitator . . . or a Rukh member for that matter." Dankulynets frowned. "I see," he said in a moment. "You are living on a different planet entirely. I'm not a Rukh member either."—"I've heard that, I have," Ivan said, affecting President Kravchuk's manner as a joke. "I've heard there is no Rukh."—"No, you have not. I'm not with Rukh because I'm finished with them. I left that party."—"Wow! So what's all this?" Ivan gestured to the office. "This? This is my new party," Dankulynets said proudly. "And what is it called?" Ivan asked. Dankulynets answered, the word "Christian" was part of the party's name.

"Aren't you an atheist?" Ivan asked, just to ask something.

"Hey, I forgot!" Pavlo said. "We can have a drink." He called the secretary, and she came in with a tray bearing two cognacs and sliced lemon on a saucer. Only the smoked Baltic sprats were missing.

"Cheers!" they drank. Ivan surreptitiously studied the furniture: the table, the nice chairs, the armchair in the corner. Everything was expensive, a far cry from the Komsomol days of particleboard painted black. He wondered where the furniture came from. And who paid for it? Dankulynets was silent for a while, and then said, "I'm not an atheist. There are no real atheists in Western Ukraine. Only believers who are very frightened."—"Fine. But what do you need Father R. for? Don't you know who he is?"—"Do tell me, who do *you* think he is?" Dankulynets said, suddenly almost hostile. "You know. A Ruthenian, a separatist, a Moscowphile, a traitor. You know as well as I do that they all had rank back in the Soviet days. What did he make? A major, at least?"—"That's a lot of labels for one man," Dankulynets laughed. "The Father, to hear you say it, must be a very busy person."—"That's the point."—"No, the point is, he is nothing of the kind. Actually, if you don't mind, I would rather not talk about myself and my party . . ."—"Oh yeah," Ivan mocked in Russian, "you have a party?"[37]—"We had a party, have a party, and will go on having a party," Dankulynets said, picking up the joke. Old Soviet jokes, that's all they had now, the only thing at which they could laugh together.

"You see, Ivan, people need values. Politics must have its foundation in values."—"Is Ukraine itself not a value anymore?"

Dankulynets thought for a moment, then asked, "Why do you twist my words?"—"I'm not twisting anything," Ivan said. He shrugged. "I'm just asking. Is it not?"—"People want something tangible, you see? Faith is a great value. Faith helps us show people who they are from a perspective that brings out what's best in them."

"We are a Christian nation," Dankulynets went on. "And what

---

37. *There is such a party!* is a catch phrase allegedly uttered by Vladimir Lenin on June 17, 1917, at the First All-Russian Congress of Soviets in response to the thesis of the Minister of the Provisional Government Irakli Tsereteli. In Russian, the joke is a pun on the two meanings of the word "есть," "there is" and "to eat."

are the Christian values? Honesty, hard work, family. Moral rectitude. That's what I highlight in my platform."—"Right. And the Father, he must be helping you with that? Like, supplying the highlighters?"—"What's he done to you?"—"No, the question is, what's he done *for you*. Does he bring money?"

Dankulynets did not answer. Finally he said, "You just do not understand how politics happens."—"Clearly! Because I never touched it."—"How can you say that? You stood on the Maidan!"—"I was there for Ukraine!"—"Good lord, spare me the pathos!"

Now they were both silent. Dankulynets tried again, "Listen, how did you think things were done? You must know, it's the same everywhere—enthusiasm can only take you so far. Common sense, yes, it's not sexy, because it means compromising. But we remain true to our core, we do not give up our positions. We just add fuel to the fire. Our democrats do not see it either. They're all strife and discord today, and they'll be gone tomorrow. They will destroy themselves."—"And their other option, as you would have it, is to sell out?"—"Why 'sell out'? Like it's the end of the world. Look at other countries, look at the States—politicians have donors!"—"Donors! So this pig in a cassock is a donor?"— "No," Dankulynets said, now angry. "He merely knows people who might become donors. Or already have."—"And what does he want for his matchmaking?"

Dankulynets stood up, opened a window, and lit up a cigarette. Ivan had never seen the man smoke before; did he start recently? Ivan got up and lit up as well. His last cigarette. Dankulynets saw it and offered him his pack, Here, this'll tide you over for a bit. Ivan could have refused to take it, to make a point, as in, *I don't accept your views and I do not want your cigarettes.* But it would've been a cheap gesture, trite, even funny. Cigarettes had nothing to do with anything. Cigarettes were a universal currency, an indulgence he was due after a tense conversation. He took a few.

"I don't know," Pavlo said. "I don't know what he wants for his matchmaking. I am working on this. But you, I need you. I know you are loyal, and I know you and I stand for the same ultimate goal. It's just like this, you see, one can't be Jesus and Machiavelli at the same time. Someone has to be the Machiavelli. Maybe me. Have you considered that I could very much use your support, under the circumstances? You could watch out for me."—"And do what? Save your immortal soul?"—"If that's how you want to phrase it. I need you to remind me that I'm not alone in this. You must know, I, too, bleed for Ukraine. Nothing else!"

Right. He would become this man's hostage. Someone to remind him about Ukraine at his banquets with high-placed church functionaries, all from the Moscow patriarchy. He would be the token Maidan hero, the unblemished battle flag, the living trust deposit. And the worst thing was, Ivan thought, that Dankulynets might very well be right. That politics does not happen any other way. Compromise is everything. It's not the revolution anymore. Bohdan Khmelnitsky did not negotiate with the Seim, Adam Kisiel did. How was he supposed to live with that? What was he to do?

Ivan had a desperate urge to hide, to go into the heart of the forest and dig himself a one-man hideout, climb in there with a gun or two and never come out, and if someone suddenly knocked at his door, he'd fire first and ask questions later. An anarchist—that's who he was, and that was nothing to be proud of. A grown man does not dare be an anarchist: it's too easy. Even Pavlo—the Paul who would very much like to turn himself back into Saul—knew that much.

"I'm sorry," was all Ivan said as he stubbed out his cigarette. "I'm sorry about all of it."

•

Styopa took his father's death very hard. At the funeral, he stood with his fists clenched and muttered at the grave, more angry than sad, "I won't let you down, Dad." Ivan feared Styopa would launch into another spell of furious activity, but he did not rush out to buy or do anything. And yet, something did happen. Styopa grew obsessed with Lotsi. He hunted everywhere for scraps of information about that deal that had fallen through. He talked to countless people and called in favors from friends who worked in the right places—the city had always run on networks. One day, he asked Ivan to come with him for a drive out to the country to see the village house he had failed to buy.

Ivan spent almost the entire autumn at home. Ever since that conversation with Dankulynets, he did not feel like seeing people. He played with Emilia. She crawled over him and laughed, and it made him happy, he wanted to be with his daughter.

He still had savings from his old job, but Margita nagged at him about why he wouldn't go out and get any kind of job at all. We still have money, Mom, he would say, but Margita would not be rebuffed: Here today, gone tomorrow, she droned, and what if something happened? She looked at him, and he could see fissures to the heart of the earth in her eyes. Illness, death, bankruptcy—these were Margita's visions. She would talk about this or that neighbor and count off the many misfortunes that fell upon their untroubled heads. She lived expecting the worst. Women are afraid of the future.

Phoebe said nothing, only skewered him with her eyes. Ivan's wife stood at the ironing board ironing the cloth diapers Margita had washed—no one in the city used cloth anymore, but Margita demanded it, and insisted on the diapers being ironed because the hot iron, in her opinion, properly disinfected the fabric. It was useless work, for Phoebe and Margita both. But Phoebe was broken and Margita implacable. Phoebe, silent, drew the iron across the fabric, and the damp fabric hissed.

Ivan and Styopa drove out to that village. It was already December and the ground froze hard as a bone. The day was windy, and Styopa's car leaned hard out of the curves on the poor, unmarked roads. They turned into a village, not the one Ivan thought they were looking for. "Why are we going here?" he asked. "I thought Lotsi's old house was . . ."—"Lotsi's old house!" Styopa growled. "I'll show you his old house! Damn Mongols!"

"Damn Mongols" was what Styopa sometimes called anyone Hungarian who happened to be a source of frustration for him. The Hungarian thing was complicated: those who lived in Transcarpathia took great pride in their roots and, in fact, did sometimes look down on the "Rusnaks." But then Hungarians from Hungary itself were just as likely to turn their noses up at their Transcarpathian brethren—the *Russianized*, or *Ukrainianized* ones. The Transcarpathians had their own word, *Madyaron*, for those local Hungarians who, they felt, were too invested in their sense of superiority vis-à-vis Ukrainians.

Styopa's "Mongols" was, in turn, considered outright rude since it evoked the Central Asian origins of Ugric tribes and made them sound no better than the Tatar hordes. Styopa, at the moment, did not care how rude he was; he was apt to shout to the whole world that Hungarians were savage ogres. The tragic part was that Styopa himself had Hungarian blood in him, and even if he did not, his wife and children most certainly did, as did Ivan, naturally, since Margita was half Hungarian and her own dearly departed Hungarian mother, although she knew other languages as was common for all inhabitants of the region, where one had to be fluent in four or five tongues, spoke to her children exclusively in Hungarian.

The street they drove down was pleasantly tidy. It led to a dead end, convenient for an ample old homestead, now refurbished into a restaurant and a small hotel. The place was called At the Fish. Ivan failed to work out what the name meant, and Styopa could not care less. In front of the restaurant stood an old horse cart, painted brightly and filled with dirt, dwarf fir trees, decorated for the holidays, grew in this rustic planter. Ivan knew this trend; there were carts and wheelbarrows like this all over Hungary, planted with flowers. It looked very nice. The building itself was freshly whitewashed; the whole place was very well maintained.

"Do you want to go inside?" Ivan asked Styopa.

"Are you nuts? Inside!" Styopa yelled back as if Ivan had insulted him. "What do you mean, *inside*? What the fuck do I want the inside for? I just wanted to show you. You know who keeps this? István Syipesz! Fucking Mongol. He lives the next village over. Can you imagine what business I'd've made here? Can you?"

"Actually, I can't," Ivan said truthfully. "But you know . . ."

"Do you know what I learned? That Syipesz, he wanted to buy the place, but the owners were asking too much. So he thought, let them sell to a stupid *Rusnak*, and that's when Lotsi, his best pal, found me. Then when things went south, Syipesz would swoop in, all rescue-like, and buy the place off me for pennies. Do you see!"

"Sure," Ivan said. He felt a headache begin to pulse above his eye. "But what difference does it make who wanted what? You didn't take the deal, did you?"

"But just look! Look at this!"

"I don't think it was a *Rusnak* thing at all . . . I don't think the nationality mattered," Ivan said, but Styopa was not listening.

"Just look at this! He's got a fucking sanatorium here, a spa! He's got a store, too, and all his daughters-in-law work there, he got his three sons married as soon as they were of age, and this hotel, and restaurant, and he has a field, too, and a vineyard! The grapes are not sour enough for Hungarian taste, but still! Do you get it?"

"Yeah, yeah, I got it," Ivan said. He was losing his patience, Styopa's growling was getting on his nerves. "And can you see how much work it all is? You wouldn't want it!"

"I'll kill him!" Styopa howled. "Fucking Mongol!"

Ivan could not fathom how Styopa would manage in this fucking Mongol's shoes: the man clearly worked around the clock, rising with the sun to inspect his holdings, the restaurant, the fields, and the vineyard. The ribbed soles of his sturdy boots never stopped treading the ground. He must have had the entire police department drinking here at his place, on the house, of course, but they kept him safe.

Styopa, meanwhile, jumped out of the car and ran to the cart with the trees in it, intending, by all signs, to cause some serious physical damage, kick it perhaps, but Ivan ran after his brother-in-law and stopped him before he reached his aim.

"Fucking Mongols!" Styopa cried, shaking his fist at the cold windy sky.

They were lucky no one came out and saw them.

•

Next Styopa decided they had to go to a talk by visiting American experts. The visitors had rented a space from the Scientologists, because the latter gave them the best deal. The hall was large, in a building in the very center of the city. The Americans sat along a table on the podium. There were three: a gray-haired man with a droopy nose, a young guy in a leather biker jacket he kept taking off and putting back on, and a middle-aged gentleman—smiling, white-teethed, and very well dressed and groomed. There was also a young woman interpreter, in a green dress, and a moderator.

Bit by bit, the room filled with local entrepreneurs. Ivan recognized Mr. Galchynski, an engineer who had reinvented himself as an owner of a modest firm, a pair of brothers who he knew dreamed of going into tourism, and a handful of young people from the market. There were a few people from the country, as well, including

Styopa's bête noire Syipesz, with his three sons in tow. He had long, slim legs and stepped lightly in his sturdy boots, exactly the kind Ivan had imagined, cleaned and polished on the occasion of the Americans' visit.

The moderator, a professor from the economics department, stood up, pulled down on his suit jacket, and began, "I have the great honor of introducing our guests. This is Judge Bredfield from the state of Texas." The gray-haired eminence stood up and greeted the audience. "This is Mister Milkesz, a motivational speaker," the moderator pointed to the perfectly groomed and smiling guest. "He is actually of our own Hungarian blood . . ." Styopa moved in his seat. The moderator went on, "And from the University of New York itself, here's Doctor Richard . . ."

Ivan did not catch the last name, and perhaps there wasn't a last name to catch, just this code: Dr. Richard from New York. Or Newark? The moderator stretched his words mercilessly and the ones he managed to get out unmangled were distorted by the microphone.

"Professor Richard," the prof consulted a piece of paper, "is teaching business planning at our university."

Professor Richard looked to be about thirty-five and had a long, thin neck. He had finally settled his biker jacket on the back of his chair.

The judge spoke first, but the audience did not get much out of his speech. Whether the interpreter had only a vague notion of Texas state law or the judge did not actually have much to tell them, either way, everyone was relieved when he finished and sat down. Dr. Richard got up to speak next, and Ivan thought of the bit of gossip passed around by the city's DJs, that more than one had heard the man complain he was desperately tired of the women with silicone breasts who surrounded him back at home.

"Business is a hard thing to do," the doctor declared. "And it is impossible without a plan."

He went on to educate the stunned entrepreneurs in the room on the many varieties of business plans, about the break-even point, and other subtleties that meant something entirely different to them than they did to Dr. Richard himself. He, for one, did not have to pay off the local gangsters, keep shadow accounting in a second ledger, and treat the police on the house to buy their kindness. People in the audience showed their reaction in different ways. Galchynski, in his suit and tie, pulled out a leather-bound notebook and wrote things down with great gravitas. The market crowd, being less sophisticated, exchanged murmured remarks, arched eyebrows, and sneered a little.

"All right, a question!" one of them finally said, out of patience. "Let's say I write this business plan like you say, plan everything just so, and the government up and raises the taxes?"

The young interpreter relayed the message, stuttering, and nervously ran her hand over her hair, which was very white and cropped very short.

"What do you mean, raise taxes?" Richard said, confused. "They can't raise them so much that you can't pay, can they? You have to pay taxes. It's the same everywhere in the world." He spoke in the tone of an adult explaining to a child why it was not appropriate to drop trash in the middle of the street. The entrepreneurs made a collective noise. Had Richard been just a touch wiser, and paid attention to body language and the faces in the crowd, he would've judged it prudent to flee the room posthaste, biker jacket in hand.

"They raise it twofold, and the toughs take as much! Enough's enough!" someone shouted in the back. The interpreter struggled through it.

"That cannot be," Richard insisted. "You have to explain to your government that it is not acceptable. You live in a democracy!"

"No, doctor, it's you who lives in a democracy!" several voices shouted, all but in unison. In the hubbub, Ivan forgot to watch out for Styopa, and this was a mistake, because Styopa just then leaped to his feet and hollered so loudly that the founding fathers of Scientology themselves must have heard him wherever their souls abided, "How can you call your bloody government a democracy if you're dropping bombs on Yugoslavia!"

Everyone grew quiet. The silence lasted exactly long enough for every single person in the room to feel very uncomfortable. What if the speakers got offended and left? The talk was ticketed. It wasn't expensive, but still. They couldn't just make the speakers stay and go on; it's not like anyone would force them. They didn't come all the way here to be offended.

The speakers themselves must have thought the room was on the brink of an armed uprising and also sat quietly. That's exactly what happened when you went out to enlighten the barbarians.

And then nothing happened. A few folks turned, as if on command, to Styopa and articulated the collective sentiment. "Hey, leave politics out of it, pal!" they said. "We have enough problems." Styopa sat back down.

The motivational speaker stood up. He took the microphone, walked around the table, and began pacing back and forth in the front rows. "You must think like a rich man!" he shouted. "We must all learn to have a millionaire's mindset! How does a millionaire think? Look, we all have a certain amount of money in mind, for a year. What do you have in mind? Who wants to tell me? A hundred thousand dollars? A hundred and fifty? No less than that, because if you just think, fifty, that's all you're going to get!"

The room rumbled, but the speaker must have taken it as a noise of comprehension, the awe of a collective epiphany.

By the time he started on the benefits of regular visualization, the room was getting wild, people giving in to anger and hysterical laughter. *What* was this man talking about?

"You must think like a rich man!" Milkesz shouted after every two sentences. Ivan, and he felt he was not alone, started hearing *think like policeman!* instead, which made a lot more sense but also shook his insides with laughter. Jokes about traffic cops popped up in his mind.

The motivational speaker knew none of this. He went on telling the audience they needed to repeat the rich-man affirmation to themselves. Ivan pictured the men in the room practicing the affirmation, out loud, and folks looking askance—we live in tough times, you know, lunatics are out of the bin! The speaker said they had to have values (Sure, Ivan mocked in his head, and we even know what those are already! Everyone here is full of value!). "The rich socialize with the rich, and the poor with the poor!" Milkesz shouted. (How else? Ivan thought. Take Margita, for one. She's proud, she'd never go to a rich person's home to *socialize*. What would she *socialize* about? Her favorite Bergman film?)

"The rich rise above their problems, and the poor spend all their time complaining!" (Again, what else would they do? Of course they complain. At least they can hear each other out, find some consolation . . .)

"The rich know how to receive gifts, and the poor do not!" (Margita put presents she received away at the back of her deepest closet: ancient perfume, tubes of lipstick so old it would be unsafe to use them. She could not bring herself to throw these treasures away. And there were also gold-rimmed shot glasses, and things of Bohemian crystal dark with time, sets of never-used dessert spoons and forks, yellowed linens, the kind of stuff a mother gives to her daughter, and no one ever touched it, wouldn't even think of touching it . . .)

"It is all up to you!" the speaker pronounced. "Together, we can defeat the scarcity mindset!"

Scarcity mindset! The man was so hopelessly wrong, and no

one could tell him. Scarcity mindset! No, theirs was not poor people's mentality. Theirs was the mindset of trenches and cellars: the kind you have when you sit in a trench or a cellar and pray for the next thing to miss you, to fall elsewhere. Moments like that, a man does not think about constructing his own reality and exercising his agency, because that man knows the only thing he can choose is the manner of his own death. It can be sudden and instantaneous, provided you have a chance to leap out of that cellar into the light of day and take a quick bullet to the chest or fall under a piece of an exploding building, or you can wait for death cowered, you can rot slowly and painfully in that very cellar, or in your trench, or wherever, and there would be no one around you who was not terrorized physically, with their entire body, terror incarnate, carnal—all experience reduced to the shocked mass of tangled nerves. You would be hungry and there would be no food. You would be thirsty and there would be no water. You would want to press yourself down into the earth, become one with it, lie in it until the end of time.

Think like the ground. Think like the grave. That was something the men in that room would have understood.

Ivan could not keep listening after "the scarcity mindset" came up. He abandoned Styopa to fend for himself and escaped out to the street. The day was windy, he could tell it was just about to snow. The wind whipped the air down the stone corridors of the streets. Ivan tried to light a cigarette—this required turning to keep the wind at his back, then turning again. Spinning on his spot, he did not see when a stranger approached him.

"Hey! Wait up a sec, I'd like to talk to you," the man said. Ivan made a quizzical face, eyebrows raised, but kept working at his cigarette. "You used to work in a bank, didn't you?" the man said and then named Ivan's old bank. He pulled out his own pack, put a cigarette in his mouth, and started lighting it. "That's me," Ivan said.

He took a drag on his finally lit cigarette. He did not bother to add, So what? He was used to speaking very little lately. Whatever people had to tell him, they would if they wanted to. "I have a job for you," the man said.

Ivan wondered if Nikolaich had somehow neglected to speak to this individual. Then he thought what a coward he was! A worm of pain stirred in Ivan's soul. Nikolaich might not have bothered to do anything at all, and still Ivan did not even try to look for another job, went straight to Seryi's garage instead . . .

"I don't give a shit about your Nikolaich," the man said, having apparently read Ivan's mind. Aha, then. Nikolaich had, in fact, spoken to him. "Do you know who protects me?"

"Who?" Ivan asked.

"The Holy Spirit!" The man was clearly very pleased with his answer.

"I see," Ivan said after a pause, because it felt like he had to say something but he couldn't think of anything.

"Whatever Nikolaich says, we do the opposite," the stranger said, punctuating his words with puffs of smoke. "The Social Democrats are now in, and there's no love lost between them. Watch, they'll have the whole region soon. Ready or not, they're coming! They've got Irshava already. Surkis and Medvedchuk, heard of them?"

Ivan had.

Margita read about them in her newspaper. Viktor Medvedchuk, it said, met with any citizen who asked and helped them all. Like a messiah on their local scale. He gave away bags of money. Such a nice member of parliament! "Right," Ivan had said then. "He's just a nice guy."—"So! Maybe there are good ones, sometimes!" Margita retorted. She was irked that her son could not find it in himself to agree with her even once in his entire life. That he begrudged her this one fantasy: the idea of a nice, caring parliamentarian. Was that too much to ask? "A nice one, Mom, is the one that pulls his voters' pants down before he screws them!" Ivan said. He couldn't, and didn't want to, choose his words.

The same was true now. Obscenities seemed to be on the tip of everyone's tongue. They fell out of the *body politic* like innards from a gutted pig.

"So come work for me. You need a job, don't you?" the stranger said.

How did he know? Did he follow Ivan around? What did he think, that Ivan would give him some secret dirt on Nikolaich from the computer? All these people who had no idea how to turn on a PC firmly and sincerely believed that programmers and system administrators were demigods and that there existed a whole class of secret, magical buttons they could press.

"What for?" Ivan asked.

"What do you mean, what for? Do you not need money?"

"Sure, I do. But what do you need *me* for?" He realized he was addressing the man with an informal you. His future boss, possibly, but Ivan did not care.

"I know what you can do. I'm godfather to Volodya's kids."

Finally, things were clear! Ivan barely ever saw Volodya anymore, and yet his friend did not forget about him.

"Do you know what people call the local religion we have in Transcarpathia?" the man asked.

"What?"

"*Relative*-ism!" He was apparently the kind of person who laughed at his own jokes.

"What's the job?" Ivan asked.

"I've got my own company. I'm Vadik, by the way. I know, you're Ivan."

They shook hands. Vadik then added, like an afterthought, "The job's the same as anywhere else."

Ivan did not need to ask specifically what it was that, in Vadik's opinion, *anywhere* required; he could guess. Vadik needed help with his shadow books. The official ones, of course, also needed looking after; the accounting in them had to look real.

"I see," Ivan said. Before he could ask about the salary, Vadik named his offer. It was not exceptionally high, but perfectly acceptable. A portion of it would be paid tax-free, cash in an envelope. Margita would be happy. Also, Ivan could rid himself of Styopa. At least for a while.

•

Vadik, nicknamed the Ripper,[38] began his career as a Komsomol leader. Later, he spent some time organizing beauty pageants—this was after the collapse of the Soviet Union. He would find sponsors for a pageant among the local members of parliament, who would then either be offered a seat on the jury or just a seat in the front row, so they could choose a new babe for themselves. The babes strutted around the stage on legs extended by the high heels of expensive shoes. The swimsuit contest was always the most popular. The swimsuits themselves, along with the shoes and stage-worthy hose, had to be bought in Slovakia—remember, it was the nineties, the decade people later called *furious*, a word that meant wild in Russian, and downright evil in Ukrainian.

Vadik put his heart into the job. Before each pageant, the babes were thoroughly groomed, taught to move to music, tilt their hips at specific angles, wear charming but not provocative smiles, mind their manners, and apply makeup like Western women so that they did not look like clowns. The makeup was also procured by Vadik,

---

38. After Andrei Chikatilo, "Ripper of Rostov," a notorious Soviet serial killer.

as an in-kind contribution from the show's sponsors. Say what you wish about Komsomol, but it had taught him to hustle, and to hustle things up, under the most desperate circumstances. Under Vadik's creative oversight, everyone was happy. The babes were happy because they got a whole sack of happiness embodied in lipstick, mascara, eyeshadow, hose, and new shoes. The parliamentarians were happy because each got a sweet new babe they could play with for months and, if they were lucky, years; and the audiences, meaning everyone who was anyone in a given town, were happy because they got an occasion to go out to the theater and show off their best outfits in the marble-walled foyer.

With time, however, the pageants lost their luster. The babes got older and needed to be paid more than a bag of face paint. The new babes aspired, if not to a career in modeling, at least to a serendipitous marriage to a member of parliament, of which there was going to be a dire shortage. When the first modeling agency opened in the city, the youngest babes flocked there. They had new goals.

The older generation, however, still demanded bread and circuses, ignorant of the changes around them. At their invitation-only parties in expensive restaurants, they, ex-cons and ex-con wannabes, drunk, would shout to Vadik out of their wide-open mouths, "C'mon, Ripper, get one to rip it for me!" but the truth was that hardly anything titillated them anymore, they had everything, except meaning in their lives, and wanted Vadik to produce whatever never-before-seen entertainment could fill that hole. These statesmen were experiencing a great tedium, and on the far side of this tedium, the doors of death creaked open. What could poor Vadik possibly do for them?

These days, however, Vadik was in luck, he had reliable *cover*. Vadik's company sold and distributed the output of a new household cleaning products plant. Vadik's office was furnished according to the latest Komsomol business trends at the time, with particleboard desk and chairs painted black. By the time he recruited Ivan, Vadik was just over thirty. He smoked constantly, lighting the next cigarette off the stub in his mouth, spoke in a low, rather theatrical voice, and dressed, as he imagined it, to appear cool and open-minded: one day he would come wearing a somber black suit over a black shirt, as if he were expected at a Hollywood afterparty, or, better yet, a funeral, and the next he'd be attired head to toe in distressed denim. He thought nothing of wearing a tie with a plaid flannel shirt. When he went out to lunch at a next-door café, Vadik would tuck his linen napkin into his collar like a perfectly mannered boy from a picture in a Soviet cookbook.

Vadik was actually pretty good at business. Of course, no one would ever know for certain how he made his money: the city was surrounded by three national borders, and across these borders people ran any number of things: cigarettes, vodka, drugs, weapons, and even other people. Vadik's company did not appear to be short of money; in fact, there was more than could possibly have been made in the household cleaning product business. Ivan tried not to think about that. He set up the computer and the printer, sometimes lent a hand as a driver or even at the warehouse when a truck needed unloading. If they needed him to call around to the shops that retailed the stuff, he picked up the phone.

If he'd wanted to, Ivan could have found out what else Vadik was trading; you could sniff things out if you put your mind to it. But Ivan did not want to know.

Vadik often brought in people he referred to as clients, showed them around the office, pointed out his furniture, of which he was rather proud, and Ivan, of whom he was also proud. "Here is my office," he would tell them. "And here's the young man that works for me, an IT guy." Vadik's guests looked approvingly at Ivan, who, often in need of a haircut and a shave, looked like a typical IT guy. Clearly, the company was solid and kept up with the times.

•

Meanwhile, the end of Kreitzar's life began. He stopped eating, stopped working, and stopped getting out of bed. Alisa could not take it and moved out to live with her mother and sister. Kreitzar, however, was no longer concerned about her. He no longer cared about anything at all, not even about Yerzhia, who had once been for him the most important person in the world. Such was his rebellion against life. "I am done," he told his mother back when he still left the house to work. He would come home and fall asleep, drunk, on the couch. Sometimes he peed himself while he slept there.

Yerzhia and the old woman scraped together their last cash and hired a cab to take Kreitzar to the drug clinic, where they paid yet more cash for the doctor to see him. "Too late now," the doctor said. "Rehab won't help. All his organs are shot."—"Dear Lord!" the old woman cried. "What are we to do?" They could hear ominous noises from the patient rooms, as if someone there was methodically breaking and splitting furniture. The doctor saw the look on her face and rushed to say, "We're renovating here." Then he added, "Nothing you can really do, my dear. All his insides are shot." The doctor was a small and nervous man. He could do nothing more for them.

Kreitzar lay on the couch for two more months, not eating, only chirping like a cricket when he got thirsty and wanted a drink.

"How can you drink again!" the old woman would cry. "Give me wine or give me booze, I'm all a-hurting," Kreitzar would plead, and she would get him a drink.

"My friends are coming, we'll have fun," Kreitzar would say every time he got drunk. "You ain't got no friends," his mother cried. "Should've thought of that sooner!"—"My thorny thoughts, *bazmeg*[39] thoughts, you bring me only woe!"[40] Kreitzar would moan. "I'm on a diet, I am! Ain't you heard what the doctor preached?"—"There ain't no doctor for you!" The old woman wept. "You'll only see one on the other side!"—"No, I won't! I won't need any there—I'll cure myself!"—"You mean you'll keep drinking in heaven?"—"That's the word. What d'you want me to do, play the harp?"—"Be quiet already," Kreitzar's mother cried, heartbroken. "If I'd only known what I'd borne you for!"—"What for indeed? Did you think you could pop a pauper and have him turn into a man?"— "Shut up already! Where d'you have it in you to talk such talk?"

It would be quiet for a while, until Kreitzar's barely audible voice cut in again with, "Don't just sit there! Pour me a drink," and she would pour him one. Yerzhia no longer entered Kreitzar's room, which smelled of urine. He did not ask about her. He drank and smoked. He dropped the ashes straight onto the floor, not bothering with an ashtray.

Kreitzar's mother was happy to see Ivan when he came to visit. But what could Ivan do? He wanted to take his friend to see other doctors and made arrangements through Christina to see the cardiologist who had treated the old Paikosh, Dr. Migalina. But Kreitzar would not hear of it. He squealed and fought when Ivan and his mother tried to get him dressed and take him to the clinic. He was shriveled and weak, but still they could not overcome him. Eventually, later, they finally got him into a taxi and took him to the hospital. Migalina took a look and shook his head. He refused to take Ivan's money. "What's wrong with him?" Ivan asked. The doctor shrugged. "The drinking. His heart. I don't do transplants." Ivan said other things, asked other questions, but it was all in vain.

---

39. An all-purpose Hungarian curse word.
40. The opening line of Taras Shevchenko's canonical poem "My Thoughts," here as translated by John Weir.

They had once lived in another era, the time of their childhood. It was the time when people were only born and no one ever died. And now, it was as if a great big gate had opened. In every home there was someone ill or getting worse. People rotted alive, became a clot of deep wrinkles, and soon after that passed away. They grew old, every one of them, and walked the slippery streets bent over like hundred-year-old ancients, with their heads bowed, and their arms weighed down by the pathetic plastic bags in which they carried home whatever sustenance they had found. Only Ivan's home was as it had always been: warm, tidy, and orderly, and the same air filled its cracked but still strong vessel, and Margita drained shredded beets at the sink as she had always done.

Ivan would go over to Kreitzar's and sit with his friend; he could do nothing else for him. Kreitzar was the last close friend he had, because Korchi had disappeared somewhere, and so had Mysko, and Tymish and Andriy lived too far away. Yura Popadynets had finally given up his obsession with the Ruthenians and got serious about photography, so he spent all his time in the mountains. Guilt tormented Ivan; he had spent too little time with Kreitzar to have had a chance of saving him. They were all boys from Galagov, and now Kreitzar, the last of them, lay dying. Ivan himself was a different man. He had had Lviv, and the revolution. Kreitzar only had his Galagov, his roots, the land of his mother and grandfathers. And Galagov had not kept him safe.

Kreitzar died at the beginning of April, as cold as the year before. Ivan was not there; the old woman reached him when they needed help retrieving the body from the morgue—the funeral was to be the next morning. Kreitzar's mother kept Ivan at her side the whole time while the relatives sat around the body. She had to talk to someone, and the relatives were a handful of tipsy men, distant relations who drank energetically in memoriam. Yerzhia did not speak. They buried Kreitzar in Barvinkosh, of course, the more distant, newer cemetery that grew by the day. The day was rainy. The grave site they were allocated was poor, in a hollow. You could tell the grave would flood in every storm. Kreitzar, of course, did not care; he would just laugh from his place in heaven as he watched his bones circle the muddy pit like small boats.

Kreitzar's mother could not bring herself to leave the closed grave. She keened over the black earth. "Oh," she sobbed, "oh why'd you leave me?" No matter how poor a son he was, she wanted him back, because how could it be that her child was gone forever and she was left to go on living? Who did she have to live for? Why did not Death take her as well? The old woman spoke, many words, but Ivan could not untangle her speech, could only hear the sound of her weeping and her loud, desperate *Oh*s like black exclamation marks in the white fog of life. He could not comfort this woman, did not know how, and what would he say to her? That he had loved her son? That he was his friend? Lord, did I even know him? Ivan asked himself. Did I? What would I say about him if anyone asked me? That here lies Kreitzar, Ivan Farkash, Ivan the Wolf, who was never for a moment in his life a wolf?

Ivan recalled their childhood together, random snippets of the past—only snippets came to mind now, moments that refused to cohere into a story: Kreitzar's smile; their neighbors' garages and the narrow spaces between them where they crawled; trees; pebbles and bits of glass they picked up at a construction site before the guard chased them out; someone else's windows one of them might hit with a hard, inedible green apple or a rock to hear his missile make contact with something hard, to hear the ruckus inside, glass crack, cups or vases shatter, water spill out of them onto papers or the polished floor, to hear this particular office or room turn into ground zero for the end of the world, an utter dissolution of all matter that would now rip, like a fissure in the earth's surface, along the equator, along every meridian and parallel. After a stunt like that they would run far away from the windows, to the Black Lakes, where they could cannonball into the dark water and swim, and laugh as the white clouds floated above them and somewhere else, behind them, the universe collapsed and renewed itself.

What did Ivan Kreitzar, the poor wretch, have to say to the world? What would he tell Ivan and anyone else who would listen? That he was in love with one Svetka, a mortal woman? That he believed he died of his love? He thought he was to carry his love like a cross. And no one reached out to him, no one told him it would get easier, no one offered a helping shoulder like Simon of Cyrene. There were no legionnaires around him, no crowds, no glory of the resurrection to come—not even a Pontius Pilate. He had no one except his sister and his old mother, and now everyone will forget him, and his sister and his mother, because there will be no second coming, no resurrection, no recollection at all of the fact that there had been such a man, Kreitzar—and he was now gone. Behind the many fences of the city, new generations will be born, new flowers will bloom, and new grass will get long on the lawns, and last year's grass will be gone because it will have died and dissolved into the ground, become the ground, and the only thing left of it will be an impotent word—its name.

•

Days came after days, weeks came after weeks, and they dragged Ivan's life along to points unknown. Everything repeated itself, ran in circles: the routes he walked, the people he saw, the things he did, even the words he spoke. There were Vadik's uncomplicated business schemes and Margita's simple joys—Margita with her crumbling teeth and flaking skin, who spared no penny for herself—and Phoebe's eyes, red from crying. All this was once upon a time, when the king was wise and people carried land in their pockets, in the olden days when the king was gray and the earth was flat all around. Life had become flat as if earth did indeed rest on three whales atop a turtle, rested like a pancake, and there was no mystery in its depths, no depths themselves. Ivan did not give a damn who was around him, who took up and allocated the little time he had: Margita, Phoebe, or Vadik, they were all the same to him, he didn't care. *Let the sun beat its drum*, he realized he was humming—a popular song. *I shall march to my tune.*

Edelweiss, edelweiss—Transcarpathia blooms, Kreitzar would have sung along. No, don't think of Kreitzar. Kreitzar died and was buried. Ivan wondered if he should go visit the grave. He could bring a bottle of liquor with him, drink it there, with Kreitzar. That, of course, would require him to pretend to believe that Kreitzar sat somewhere on the other side, like Swedenborg, in a circle of angels with white wings attached to their backs, and smiled, touched by the proper commemoration: Ivan on the slippery dirt of the eternally wet cemetery, with a bottle of bad moonshine, eyes wandering and his throat singed, his stomach ready to expel into the mud all the tasty things Margita had fed him that morning. If the dead could die all over again, Kreitzar might just do so after a wake like that.

Ivan now had internet at home. The connection, however, ran through the phone line, so Ivan only logged on at night. Margita got very anxious if the landline was tied up during the day; she was used to relying on the phone, its loud rooster-like noises, she had to have the line open and clear like an escape route. Christina called her, her grandsons talked to her on the phone, and her neighbors rang if they wanted to stop by for a slice of pie and a chat over coffee—a few happy moments in the lives of these permanently overworked women, homemakers retired from their full-time jobs who barely went anywhere except the stores and the market. All they had were their girlfriends, as aged as they were, as scared of the inflation, price hikes, unsanctioned pop-up markets filled with leather jackets, jeans, cheap Turkish clothes, vodka, and gangsters. But they never lost the habit of greeting each other with a smile, and their eyes shone brightly after a sip of superstrong coffee and the egg liqueur they had with it. They nibbled on the pie and soaked up the smell of cinnamon-laced apples.

Ivan, therefore, connected to the internet at night. At first he searched for things, looked for things as if someone else's experience might somehow help him, as if he could stumble into a chat room for people whose entire lives had gone upside down. He had a job, he had a family, but neither felt meaningful. It felt like his life was over before it had even begun. His friends never stopped by even for a shot of liqueur—he had no friends, they had all left. Styopa terrified him, Yura Popadynets was about to marry, Korchi disappeared, Volodya the accountant and Tolya had jobs clear on the other end of the city and no time to hang out, and Kreitzar . . . At this point Ivan always had to stop and take a break, because the screen blinded him, the white light of it, the kind, they say, people see when they are dying. To lose himself he would go off on tangents, wandering, wandering among random websites, page after page, books of other people's lives.

At dawn, a sudden morning chill would creep through the window Ivan kept open. He could hear Margita get up and walk across her room. Ivan would turn off the computer, unplug the modem, and free up the landline, never mind that no one ever called Margita at such an early hour. He fled to his bed and pretended to sleep, but of course he didn't; he got up and went to work. Drank buckets of coffee. His back hurt, his neck ached, and that was all he could feel as he walked across the waking city. Several times per day (sometimes a dozen) Ivan would drop off, fall asleep wherever he was, even walking, sinking into a dead place without dreams or memories. Then he would return and automatically go on doing whatever he was doing, making phone calls, and even driving—it was a miracle he didn't get into an accident.

•

Vadik the Ripper, meanwhile, acquired a mistress. He was married, but that did not stop him. Then again, he might have started the thing because he felt he had to; the other men of his circle had mistresses, so he could not be seen falling behind. He called her all the time, spoke to her in an endless low rumble, believing, perhaps, that he sounded passionate. It did not bother him that Ivan could hear him and that Ivan, squirming, could only just contain his disgust: If this moron thought he sounded passionate, it was going to take a real idiot to go to bed with him. That's what Ivan thought, but then a wave of yearning would come over him, and he would be just as disgusted at himself. His own wife had long stopped going to bed with him and Ivan had to admit he knew about passion only as much as he had read in books.

Vadik went to see his mistress every two days, about 5:00 PM, and went home afterward. The hours between five and seven, like in Paris, were his hours of love. Vadik told his wife he was working late and sometimes asked Ivan to hang back in the office and answer the phone if the wife called. "Hello, yes, Vadik is busy at the moment, he's in a meeting, yes, some people can't schedule any earlier, what are you going to do, customers out of town, can't turn them away, of course I'll tell him, he'll call you back on his cell." Then Ivan would call Vadik on his cell. Vadik would answer out of breath—he would be hard at work already in his mistress's bed, and who would have thought the man could be so prompt—thank Ivan for the heads-up, and that would be that. He might call his wife later, when he caught his breath, might even go out on the balcony to talk to her—he would be shameless, like all of them, the men who paid their mistresses handsomely with clothes, cars, apartments, or trips abroad. Just another strange man on the balcony of an apartment that belonged to a young single woman, a man in striped boxers. Or perhaps plaid ones (with Vadik, who could know!). A strange man in his underwear, with a potbelly and a cell phone in his hand, so that no one would have any doubt as to what he was doing there.

Ivan always knew when Vadik was going to see that woman. Vadik would get this catlike grin. He would douse his shoulders and ears in trendy cologne. His eyes gleamed. Ivan would wish him a good evening. Vadik would laugh, tell Ivan that his evening would be not just good but awesome, and leave. Ivan would stay at the office for a while and then go home and sit at his computer.

One night there was a power cut. It had been quite a while since they had one. The greedy, chatty prime minister lady promised the country's pensioners mountains of gold and assured the public that their comfort was her own personal accomplishment and that she would personally take care of the electricity supply. Margita and Phoebe had long since gone to bed. Ivan alone stayed up on his vigil to watch the ceaseless motion of the universe.

Well, not quite. First, he went upstairs and lay in bed next to Phoebe. He could not remember how long it had been since he slept there last—he had all but moved downstairs, into Margita's domain, and did not spend any time near his wife. His unused side of the bed pricked him with a cold sting. The bed felt like a two-person coffin. Ivan lay quietly in the dark. Suddenly, he realized that Phoebe was not asleep; her even breathing had stopped and she now lay there, like him, waiting for something. He could not make himself touch her. He wondered what she was wearing. A shapeless pair of pajamas? He remembered the lines she once wrote: *Sunlight falls, a lacework / but no longer for me . . .* what did it say next? Phoebe used to wear lace, actually might still wear it, only he did not know.

Whoever that sun was making lace for, it was certainly not for Ivan.

He might have been able to overcome the cold. But he could not step over the words. Not her poems. He went downstairs and lay down on the couch. He wanted to forget Phoebe.

There he lay, stretched out, as if underneath the current and invisible to the anxieties and labors of life. Somewhere above him life raged like a horde of invading Huns, but he had found a good place to hide, and flat on his back there in the dark, he realized how great it felt just to lie there. What made him fight himself for so long? What made him afraid to fall asleep? It felt so good to stretch loose. To surrender to the darkness. The darkness could be trusted, it would not betray him. Faces spun in a kaleidoscope before Ivan's closed eyes: there was Rose, her full lips; then the damned "Sashko Petrenko," the terror of his life; then Vadik the Ripper in his denim suit; and Kreitzar—separate and apart from his death that stood alone like a period on a page of text. In another moment, the soft hand of darkness shooed them all away, and Ivan fell into a deep slumber.

He slept so deeply that, in the morning, Margita could not wake him and eventually left him where he was. The office called, and Margita politely informed Vadik that her son was unwell. Vadik was stunned but behaved like a human being. He wished Ivan to get well soon and Margita to have a good day, and let them be. Ivan slept until evening. When he woke up, it took him a while to figure out where he was and what time it was. Margita called him to come eat, and he went, sleepy and, he suddenly realized, desperately hungry; he scarfed down a plate of her signature cheese balls drizzled with sweet cream, and went back to sleep.

He woke up at dawn. The day was one of those gloomy

springtime affairs when it looks like it's about to rain but never does. The sky hung low and gray, no sunshine could get through. Ivan went to the office but found he could not really work. For the first time in a very long time his body, rested and content, did not hurt—but his soul did. Up until then it had hid behind the physical suffering as if behind a shield, and as long as Ivan lived with the pain in his back, as long as he struggled through a migraine (whose assaults were no longer as acute and intolerable as before), his soul remained quiet because it was not her time or her turn. And now, all of a sudden, Ivan's soul peeked over the rim of his body, saw what she had no particular desire to see, and lit up with pain.

What was he doing there? Why was he where he was? The simple tasks of his job that did not require any thought stood out like welts on his skin. The meaninglessness of it all, the contentlessness. The absurdity. Ivan drank several cups of coffee, which made his heart race, and chainsmoked several cigarettes. After that he felt like he could go on. After yet another cigarette, Ivan noticed that Vadik, too, was in low spirits—which was the opposite of normal, since it was Thursday, a day when he saw his mistress without fail.

Turned out, Vadik had houseguests. Actually, Vadik's wife did, and he had to go straight home from work. Vadik found Ivan in the large room where they stored excess inventory.

"Say, are you super sleepy today?" he asked casually.

Ivan knew his boss very well. He blinked at Vadik, and then looked back down at the packing slips in his hands.

"Why?" he asked after a moment. "Do you need me to do something?" Ivan addressed his boss with the informal you—had been doing so since the day they met, and Vadik never objected. Vadik deserved some credit, he never called Ivan *Vanka*.

"Well, someone needs to be picked up."

"From where?"

"I'll leave the car with you, my wife is coming to get me. Go to the Transcarpathia Hotel, they have a sauna in the backyard," Vadik told him the address. "You have to pick up a ... a person. Right after five if you can. I promised I would, but I'm all tied up today. Family time!" He laughed.

"Okay, what does this person look like?"

"You know ... you'll see," Vadik said, suddenly shy.

"Actually, I'd rather you told me who it is, what they look like, etcetera. You know? Or else I'll show up and say what, 'Vadik sent me'? What if, like, half the people in that sauna get into the car, then what am I supposed to do?"

Vadik saw Ivan's point.

"Milena," he said. "Milena ... er ... Mikhailivna. There. I'm asking you to pick up Milena Mikhailivna."

"So, like, I go there and ask if Milena Mikhailivna is available?"

"Come on, man, don't be a child!" Vadik said, angry. "Which part do you not understand? You go to the sauna," he told Ivan the address again. "There's Milena Mikhailivna, damn it, you pick her up, and you take her here," Vadik told Ivan another address. "Dammit! I've explained it a hundred times and you still don't get it!"

"I got it," Ivan said. What a day. Now he had to go pick up his stupid boss's stupid mistress from some stupid backyard sauna. Run an errand for the former Komsomol star. Is that what he, Ivan, sat on the granite in Kyiv for? If the Lviv guys could see him now ... holding the goddamn perimeter ...

Ivan drove to the address he was given right after five, as he had promised, and parked the car. It never did rain. The sharp tang of moisture hung in the air, strong enough to make one feel intoxicated yet not filled with a sense of well-being, like after good wine, but full of concentrated impotence, the apathy that comes with late-stage drunkenness. The sky was a stage for a battle of titans: massive gray clouds crumpled the blue-black ones, and below them, light-colored smudges glowed white like an unmade bed.

Ivan went to the small building that was an extension of the hotel. He knocked, but no one answered. He cursed his own stupidity then. Who would knock on a sauna's door? It's not like it was a literary salon. Milena fucking Mikhailivna. And he, Ivan, was freezing his ass off in this godforsaken street to give Vadik's paramour a ride home, where she would probably change into tiger-striped lingerie so as to look more appealing for her lover, because Vadik himself might just talk his way out of his house, might lie enough to his wife and her relatives, tell them an urgent shipment came in—pink elephants!—and needed unloading. He'd ring Milena Mikhailivna's doorbell and wrap his hefty paws around her waist when she answered.

Ivan yanked at the door handle. The door was unlocked. The entryway was dark. He reached back to open the door wider and let in more daylight but could not feel the door. He moved forward and instantly stumbled into a piece of furniture, a desk perhaps, but why would there be a desk in a sauna? Was this room an attendant's or a cashier's office? The visitors, in order to enjoy the good life, would have had to pay money, wouldn't they, for a chance to lie on a wooden bench laced with someone else's fungus.

Ivan was already stewing, and the thought sent him into a rage. Another moment and he would have trashed the entire disgusting place, in the dark, no matter what he broke, furniture, people, or hidden monsters! But a switch clicked softly and the lights came on. The woman who stood in the other doorway, the one that led inside the building, made a startled noise and covered her mouth with her hand.

"Are you Milena Mikhailivna?" Ivan asked sharply.

"Oh, yes," she answered. "Did you come to pick me up?"

"I did."

"Oh, could we possibly just wait a moment here? There's a pipe burst inside, and all my stuff is already there . . . I was promised . . ."

"What?!" Ivan growled. Milena Mikhailivna showed no reaction to Ivan's tone.

"I mean, it's just that . . ." she trailed off and moved back into the depths of the building. Ivan thought about it for a moment and followed her. The next room was a locker room, there were lockers and a large bench. Milena sat. Ivan sat, too. He had no idea what (or why) they were waiting, but it's not like he could just drag Milena Mikhailivna out to his car and take her to Vadik, or wherever, by force.

Milena made another one of her half-sighs, half-yelps—Ivan could not interpret it. She pointed to the door to the sauna itself. Water was slowly seeping under it. Milena pulled up her long skirt, lifted her feet off the floor, and sat on the bench cross-legged.

The water kept coming.

"Listen, miss," Ivan said, choosing his words very carefully. "Why are we sitting here? It looks like the sauna is not working. I am supposed to take you home."

"Well, it's just . . . I left something in there," she said anxiously.

Ivan finally took a good look at her. Milena had dyed blond hair that was going dark at the roots (How did a sugar daddy like Vadik allow such imperfection?), large brown eyes, and a serene, almost sleepy expression. In a few years, this dreamy look would be history; life would speed up like crazy, people's faces would become anxious and only prompt unease in anyone who looked upon them. The woman had large breasts, her sweater stretched over them. Her legs, evidently, were not particularly long or shapely since she hid them under a floor-length jersey skirt. Ivan caught a glimpse of a thick ankle and a plump foot with a surprisingly high arch. The arch of her foot was the only thing he really liked.

"Where are your shoes?" he asked. He did not—because he could not—take his eyes off her feet in their black nylons. Milena gestured in the direction of the sauna. "Did you leave your shoes in there? Are you even allowed to wear shoes in there? I don't understand, did you go in there fully dressed and with your shoes on?"

Milena shook her head.

"I only went in for a second," she said. "And then the pipe burst. And that's it. I can't find anyone. My shoes are in there. Floating, I suppose."

Ivan stood up. Her shoes were floating! All right, fine. Now he felt like a hero of folktales. All that raging energy he had just mastered, so as not to punch holes in the walls and break furniture, returned.

"All right, come on, then. Put on your coat," he told Milena. She made to get up, but the water was already on the floor between the bench and her locker. Ivan bravely stepped in, pulled out her coat, and gave it to her. Then he picked Milena up in his arms and carried her out. He crossed the yard to the car. The day had grown darker, and the sky had inched closer—it felt as if they were alone on the top of a mountain and could touch the clouds if they stood on tiptoe. Ivan carried Milena Mikhailivna to the car, then put her down so that she stood on the top of his feet since she was shoeless, and the thought of her soles stirred him again. He opened the car, helped Milena inside, got in himself, and started the engine.

Milena lived in a building not far from the embankment, on the left shore. The neighborhood was relatively new, and the apartments there did not come cheap. Vadik must have paid for the place. Although, come to think of it, even Vadik might not have been able to afford it. She might well be sleeping with someone else by appointment. As he drove, Ivan kept glancing at Milena in the passenger seat. She sat quietly, and her large, docile eyes looked serenely ahead. Ivan thought the men must like her eyes. A sensible girl who did not make a fetish of her own weakness, did not pitch fits, and just knew her place. A real man could not simply walk past someone like that.

At her building, Ivan did not dare carry Milena inside, the neighbors would have seen them, but asked for her keys and went upstairs to her apartment to get a pair of shoes.

The apartment was small, a one bedroom, but the window had a view of the river. A beautiful spot. The only thing that would make it feel less cozy would be a flood. It was on the fourth floor, but still, it would be scary to look down upon the rising water. You never knew if the ground floor would hold, if the foundation would hold. Ivan remembered the flooded sauna and smiled. This woman was haunted by water. Come to think of it, so was he—haunted by rains, floods, the deluge.

In the entryway—the layout of the apartment had been modified—Ivan saw a couch with embroidered pillows on it. He wondered if Milena did the needlework herself as she had been taught at school or if there was a dynasty back in the country, mothers and grandmothers. Ivan peeked into the bedroom purely out of curiosity—he had no business in there—and saw a neatly made wide bed, pillows (no embroidery this time), a floor lamp, a rug, and a wardrobe. The wardrobe had to be holding that tiger-striped lingerie he had imagined, he was sure of it, and felt a strong urge to root around in there, find what he expected to find, and press the things to his face, like a trophy.

"Here you go," he said, handing a pair of shoes to Milena in the car. She bent low and put them on while he looked steadily on; Ivan could not deny himself the pleasure of looking at this woman, of taking in her every small movement. The shoes locked away her small feet with their high arches. It was over. He could leave. It was time he gave the space back to its lawful owner, that peacock named Vadik the Ripper who was just about to roll into her neat, small apartment, turn on the soft light of the floor lamp, pull off her underwear and nylons, open her knees in the dimly lit room, and look there, in between them, at her most secret place, hidden from

344 • OKSANA LUTSYSHYNA

the world during the day. He would become very still, held fast in his adoration of that precious vulnerability.

Such a vulgar woman, with her dyed hair, and such beauty.

"I'll go up with you," Ivan said and helped her out of the car by her elbow. Milena Mikhailivna did not object. In the elevator, he pressed number four, her floor, and then carefully, not letting go of her arm, turned to face her. She raised her serene, just slightly surprised eyes at him. Ivan touched her lips with his fingers. Her eyelids trembled. No, she could not, would not belong to a Vadik today—not to Vadik, and not to any other man. Ivan leaned in and kissed her, and it was his turn to be surprised because she fastened onto his lips with such desire it made him moan. When he regained his senses—in a pause between bolts of lightning that ran through his body—he realized he was still standing next to her in the elevator, which had stopped quite a while ago and opened its doors, but they did not use them, so the elevator closed the doors again, and if someone now pressed the call button they would just ride who knew where and to whom— perhaps Vadik the Ripper himself. Ivan freed himself from their embrace, pressed the button to open the elevator doors again, and led the woman out.

Once in the apartment, she whispered something to him, something about Vadik, that it seemed he could turn up banging at the door any minute now and Ivan had to run and come back tomorrow or the day after and that she would wait for him. Only one word out of her impassioned pleas wormed itself to Ivan's comprehension, *wait*, but he could not possibly wait any longer, what did he have to wait for? Here before him was his entire life like Gulliver trussed by the Lilliputians' threads, like a patient in a coma, about to die, there was no time and nothing to wait for. Ivan, crazed by this word, *wait*, squeezed Milena Mikhailivna in his arms ever harder. He had no idea he had so much desire amassed inside

him, so much pain and fury. In the bedroom he asked the woman—
no, ordered her, all but forced her—to take all her clothes off but
then put back on just the black hose, the nylons that titillated him
back in that locker room, the dump they had fled. Ivan tore them
apart along the seam, against her soft-spoken protests, laying bare,
in an instant, her loins and a part of her stomach, and all but fainted
with arousal, so sharp was the contrast between the black of the
fabric and the paleness of her body.

Then Ivan closed his eyes and did what he had imagined himself doing.

What he could not do with Phoebe, whose words stood
between them like a suicide squad. Soldiers who would die before
they let him into her body or soul.

Or whatever it was she had inside her.

•

Ivan ran into the man one day as he was leaving Milena's. The man
got onto the elevator on the third floor, pushed the button for the
ground floor, and glanced at Ivan. He was small, sharp-nosed, and
sharp-eyed, not a man easy to ignore or forget. The elevator filled
with the tear-inducing smell of his cologne, so strong that Ivan had
to take a step back. Why was everyone dousing themselves with
this stuff? For a few seconds, the man watched Ivan. Then he asked,
as if he had a right to know:

"Which apartment are you coming from?"

"I'm a courier," Ivan answered with the first thing that came to
mind. He tried not to meet the man's eyes.

"A courier? Wow. Who on earth could have a courier like
this going to their place?" the man said. He was having fun. Ivan
thought the man winked at him. "I know everyone in this building,
but I don't think I have met you."

This made no sense. How could one person know every courier who ever delivered anything to the building?

"Do you live here yourself?" Ivan asked, working hard not to breathe through his nose. The elevator stopped, and the small man left without answering. The trail of his cologne hung in the air behind him. Musk? Sweat? Spices Ivan did not recognize?

Who was he? A neighbor? Does Milena Mikhailivna really have such inquisitive neighbors? Had it been an older woman, one of those unfortunate Soviet grandmothers wracked by rheumatism, abandoned by their children, and uncared for by anyone else, who spent their days on benches in the yard like a volunteer neighborhood watch and knew absolutely everything about everybody, Ivan would not have been suspicious. Such old ladies craved a chance to talk and couldn't resist chatting up the objects of their endless gossip. Men, on the other hand, especially relatively young men, would never do anything like that. They might have their opinions, naturally, might feel jealous if they were honest . . . but to ask questions? That was unthinkable.

What if the man was Vadik's spy? Could Vadik have suspected Ivan? And sent this character, who, by the way, made for a poor spy with that distinctive face of his? You needed a man whose own mother would not recognize him, a man everyone would look past . . . But if he were a spy, would he now be reporting to Vadik that Ivan had visited Milena? So what? He couldn't know what they did together, could he? Or did he listen from next door, or rather, his apartment below, with a glass jar pressed against the ceiling? He could have, of course, gone down a floor before getting into the elevator, just to confuse Ivan.

Ivan felt his breath getting faster. His breath and his heartbeat. He knew what this meant; this was always how his panic began, his fits of paranoia. He willed himself to dismiss the thoughts that were shaping his current version of reality—he knew his mind interpreted all inputs the same: as signs that Ivan was under threat. No one was watching him. And even if someone were, Ivan, most likely, would not have noticed the tail. He wasn't worried about such things anymore, he would have ignored a whole posse, let alone a single spy, because he had gotten used to feeling safe. No one had followed him in years. No one wanted him.

Still, Ivan thought, he ought to remember the sharp-nosed man.

Just in case.

•

He kept seeing Milena.

At first they barely talked, he would just come and remain in her bedroom for a certain amount of time. She was neither conventionally beautiful nor conventionally smart. That look she had that Ivan had originally interpreted as docile was just absent. Not hostile in any way. It was just that when she did show interest, it felt like the kind of interest a space alien might show at her first encounter with a human. She met humans and she would soon forget them. Perhaps there was really nothing special about them, nothing worth remembering. Or perhaps her kind of aliens did not even have the concept of memory. They experienced things as drifting upon the surface, and then disappearing.

After a while, Milena began to ask him questions. Who he was, why, and how, who he was married to, and whether he had children, and how many women he had been with, where he had met them, and what they were like in bed. Ivan did not know what to say. Milena had quite an imagination. He said nothing or joked his way out of an answer. Or he would start kissing her, the entirety of her, from her large eyes to the tips of her toes. Never before had he kissed a woman so totally. With Rose, they were always at the dorm or someplace inconvenient, they had no time to explore each other's bodies. They only had those three days at home, but three days was too short, not enough time to achieve such complete conjugality.

Phoebe . . . He could not think about her. Not about her, and not about her family. They were a monolith in his mind, that cabal he had tied himself to for God knows what reason. Their singing, landless clan. No, that was wrong. They were decent people. He was the one who let them all down, who had ruined everything. He destroyed Phoebe's disk; he lost Myron's trust.

But it wasn't like he could speak of these things with the bovine-eyed Milena Mikhailivna. Confession, self-revelation, the highest currency of love cost too much to be spent on another man's mistress. Ivan had protected himself, but he could not tell from whom or from what. He stopped, made the idea go away. What was it that Yarema used to say? "Fear is an idea."

How many times did he need Yarema to rescue him in his one single lifetime?

Milena was not satisfied. She lay next to him and lazily stretched her taut body on her fragrant, freshly laundered sheets, on her bed in her apartment, which was, by local standards, exceptionally comfortable and well furnished. Ivan thought Vadik must have had her furniture shipped from across the bor-der along with the cleaning supplies; they most certainly did not come from Vadik's own factories—the Ripper's shampoos left you with a ferocious itch and his shower gels made healthy skin welt and rot. Or, perhaps, the furniture did not come from Vadik. It could have been paid for by someone before him. Or someone else Milena was seeing at the same time. Milena probably would not have minded at all if Ivan asked her about this. She saw the two of them as something like accomplices: Ivan, just like her, was a servant of other men, an errand boy. He was in a worse position, in fact. Unlike Milena, he had no power over those he worked for. She had power. What she did not have was understanding, and that was why she was so determined to find the key to Ivan's mind. She wanted him to fill this lacuna in her life and make it, finally, full-blooded and real.

Or, perhaps, she just wanted to wield her power over him, totally and irrevocably, and was waiting for him to fall in love with her. To love her. Why not? People fell in love all the time. People loved other people. Why could this one particular man not love her? "Tell me something," she said. "Anything. Just tell me about yourself." She twisted to look in his face, and he turned away. He had to avoid her eyes, the way they looked at him, the questions they had for him. He worked so hard at this that he eventually caught himself not looking at her face at all and nearly unable to remember it.

Unlike her feet with their high arches, which he would have known out of a thousand.

It was at the same time that Ivan got into the habit of walking the city at night. He would leave Milena's and wander through the streets. The weather finally turned warm. He loved walking along the riverfront and would circle back to it again and again, walking quickly past the medical school, and the court building with its naked caryatids, past the ancient Café Penguin (Ivan remembered it being there for as long as he remembered himself) to the school, then to Theater Square, over the pedestrian bridge, and again along the Kyiv embankment. The city reciprocated. When he was tired, he would dive into the narrow welcoming streets on the right bank, not far from where he lived. Later, he would dream long dreams about the city at night, full of architectural details, and as he dreamed, the details, almost fantastic and suddenly larger than themselves and even the buildings they were a part of, revealed to him new and unexpected meanings. The trees around the court, across the street from the officers' club, whispered kind things into Ivan's ears. Their kindness was like nothing he could ever hope to find among people. In the mornings, Ivan woke up smiling—to himself, to his walks, and to his dreams. Then his day would begin, with Vadik's clockwork tasks and his nasty shampoos, with Phoebe and her black eyes, and Margita and her black eyes, the terror of it all. Ivan could not make himself go back to this terror after work, even on the days he could not go see Milena. What would he be doing at home? Staring back at his merciless women? He fled from them, but the other side was full of no less merciless men.

Ivan's father always waited eagerly for his son to come home from work. There was something he wanted to tell him, something he had never told him before, but the old man was impossible to listen to. Out of a half hour of his talking—random details, unfamiliar names, suppressed feelings—Ivan could not pull a single coherent thought. His father talked about how he first came to Transcarpathia, the bus depot where he got off, then about his childhood, then about the bus depot, and it was impossible to tell where he had gotten lost. Somewhere in the foothills, under the rain, with mud under his feet, or later, here in the Silver Land?

Ivan knew every home had an old cricket-like man like this. They chirped and chirped, together and individually, talked until they drove their families out of their minds, especially their wives, who also had quite a lot to say but whose turn never came because who would then be starting the dough for *varenyky*, who would chop the beets for the borsch, who would look after the children and hold the four corners of the house together? So the women went mad with rage, and beat the old men into whom their husbands had so precipitously turned, and shouted at them to go to bed or keel over already, and even from the dark of their bedrooms the old men still muttered and rustled with their unmanly, inhuman noises.

•

As soon as Ivan got used to Phoebe's nonpresence in the daily reality of his life, she suddenly started to get better. One day she confronted him about her poems.

"Where is my floppy disk?" she asked, her fists on her hips, furious and terrifying like a Gorgon. Her chestnut hair spilled wildly over her shoulders. Ivan started to open his mouth to remind her that she was, first and foremost, a mother and had to look after the baby when Phoebe exploded into sobs, but sobs unlike any he had heard before, not worn out and apathetic but angry and resolute. She launched into a long monologue then—also unlike anything he had ever heard from her—about how he had ruined her life, that he dare not, dare *not*, contradict her, that he failed to feel the most basic human empathy because his life had not been changed at all by their marriage, or by them having this baby—he was living in his family home just like he used to, well tended and well fed, he went to work just like he used to, while she lost everything she once had: home, freedom, work, love. She lived in lovelessness: Margita hated her, Ivan hated her—he destroyed her poems, didn't he?—she had no doubt he did (Who? Who could have told her? Ivan knew no one had seen him that night . . .), but she remembered every last word of them, even if they weren't written down, she found a way to recover almost all of them, and would find a way to publish them, without his help and despite him, and let him not, for an instant, hope for a quiet family life, let him not dare speak a word to her about their child!

Ivan stood before her thunderstruck and could not muster a response. This new affliction cut through his measured, nearly new life with Milena and his nocturnal wanderings like a knife plunged between his ribs. The shock of it made him mute. He had thrown everything against this woman—against his conscious will perhaps, and who could ever know why?—everything he had and the heavy artillery as well: Margita, a lioness scorned. And what came of it? Nothing. He might as well quote that Russian who said manuscripts did not burn.[41] Even when they were manuscripts of poems by a provincial girl, a girl Ivan should have run from, far and fast, the moment he met her. But he had overlooked things; he had missed the fact that she was dangerous.

Margita came running to the sound of her daughter-in-law's shouting and joined in with her own grievances. She shouted that this entire family did nothing but fuss over this *poetess*, while she broke her back keeping them all fed and clothed, that her children did not honor her as they should, and that Phoebe was a terrible mother, and hopeless around the house, and her mother was the same. And yet, Ivan noted automatically, Margita said nothing about Phoebe's father, the handsome Myron Vasyliovych. He could not quite shake off the shock of this sudden maelstrom and instead found himself focusing on small absurd details he had never noticed before. Margita kept on shouting that Phoebe had come with nothing, couldn't buy her own bread, earned no wages, and nagged at her husband, when suddenly Phoebe raised her voice so high Ivan was sure the neighbors would call the police. Phoebe screamed at Margita to shut up about her stupid son, who did not sleep with Phoebe, and fled from her bed and from her herself as he had always done because he was always afraid that any moment Margita could come into their bedroom without knocking and give him a job to do, as if they were her bonded servants. This sent Margita into a whole new rage.

Never! Never did anyone dare raise their voice at her the way this daughter-in-law of hers had just done, this fifth wheel, foundling, whore! How dared she speak of their bed, had she not been taught such things were not spoken of! Especially by a woman.

---

41. Mikhail Bulgakov, *Master and Margarita*.

"Well, here they are!" Phoebe thundered. "And I write poems and will keep writing!"

"Whore!"

"I write and I'll keep writing!"

"Beggar!"

"I write and I'll keep writing!"

"*Poetess!*"

"I write and I'll keep writing!"

"Calm down, both of you!" Ivan shouted but was brushed away like an inept protester in the path of the water hose. He could only just manage to exhale before he ran down the stairs out of that apartment, hearing behind him "Whore!" and "I write poems and I will keep writing!" The two statements locked together like a pair of wild beasts coiled in a mortal duel, fast at each other's throats until they both tumble off the edge of a cliff.

From that day on, his home was hell. Margita only spoke to Phoebe by means of her back. She threw the accumulated force of her life against Phoebe. She possessed several vocal registers, from affectedly kind to poisonous, from calm to explosive, and she worked them all against Phoebe, all day, every day. Instinctively, she knew that if she stayed in one mode, even her most terrible, she would wear herself out. On the other hand, nothing demoralized an opponent as much as the constant change, endlessly random responses to the same thing. *That* was how a person was trained to always be afraid. And indeed, Phoebe was afraid. But not for long, because once driven to desperation she forgot she was supposed to be afraid and then exploded, like that time upstairs, with terrifying force, and then it was Margita who became afraid, and cowed and complained that she did not feel well.

Phoebe got into a new habit of taking Emilia for long walks around the city instead of staying in Margita's yard, as her mother-in-law insisted. She was gone entire afternoons; she had friends who invited her over. At dinnertime Margita furiously called her to come eat, but Phoebe would just say she'd eaten already and carry first the baby and then the stroller up the stairs as if she had never been incapacitated. Margita muttered things under her breath and washed the dishes in her yellowed sink with black spots on its ancient enamel. While the water heater hummed in the background, she spoke with her back to Ivan's father, the old cricket, and tears crawled down her cheeks and dropped into the soapy water. Ivan was prepared to stay at the office until midnight to avoid seeing any of it. He preferred to stay there until the small hours of the night and would then go to Milena, and then wander, wander around the city he had never loved as ardently and achingly as he did that spring and summer.

As if I would never see it again, Ivan thought sometimes, and the idea would scare him, and he would wander, wander deeper into the quiet streets that opened themselves to him more fully than any woman in his life—as much as he wished.

•

Styopa, meanwhile, was still moping. He picked up odd jobs here and there, and worked a bit as a taxi driver, but none of it was right, none of it made his heart sing. He still invited Ivan over, but he no longer lectured him or nagged him to get on the right path; he just sat there with his drink, in a cloud of cigarette smoke, poured rounds for Ivan, himself, and his friend Shoni, the painter, who had loyally stuck by Styopa, and asked "What are we to do? Eh, guys, what are we to do?" He was a sorry sight. Gone was his cockiness, all that sense of moral superiority; gone as if he had locked it up and lost the key after his business plans collapsed and, what Ivan guessed was more important, after the old Paikosh died. Ivan realized he had forgotten how much Styopa had grated on him, that he no longer resented the well-fed Raptors who continued to invade and occupy Margita's, and by extension his, territory, or the fact that Styopa had broken Christina's will. Styopa was now the closest thing Ivan had to a friend, a fellow traveler; he was his helpmate and his comrade in arms, that brother in the trenches who would die for you, and for whom you would lay down your life.

"Styopa," Shoni said, "start up a place at home. My brother-in-law did. He sells shashlik in his backyard, and plenty of people come. Remember that little French guy? He used to work for him . . . Wanted to make cheeses . . ."—"Where would I come up with cheeses? Or shashlik?" Styopa shook his head. He had only two pigs, and he was not Jesus to feed the capacious local public with only two pigs. Shoni did not give up. He told Styopa that his brother-in-law was working with suppliers, guys who bought grown pigs from the country and did the butchering, as many as five a day. All day long that crew cleaned carcasses, stuffed sausages, and sliced the meat into retail portions to be dropped off at a store at the Pyany market that was, consequently, never out of fresh pork. Styopa listened and did not interrupt.

"Uh, well. That could be," he finally said.

"That's what I'm saying," Shoni nodded, satisfied. "You see? And you've got your own wine, so you can serve that. D'you have your own brandy?"

"I do, some."

"And slice up some cheese to go with the wine, that's the trend now. Goat cheese."

At this, Styopa sat up straight. Something obviously clicked in his mind, a puzzle solved itself.

"Cheese?" he cried. "Where's that damn Frenchman? Let me have him!"

So they went to look for the Frenchman. They found him at a friend of Shoni's in a new neighborhood. The Frenchman had students there that he tutored in French, but seeing how he did not know the grammar, all he did was teach the kids to sing various French songs. The apartment reverberated with the bellicose *Au clair de la lune / mon ami Pierrot*, sung with the enthusiasm that it could have given Styopa, in his patriotic Raptors day, a run for his money. The Frenchman was very happy to see them and so touched that they had thought of him that for a moment he could not speak in any language at all. "You're coming with us. I've got a proposition for you," Styopa said. "Why're you standing there like that? Don't remember me? I'm Styopa."—"Je m'appelle Jean Paul," the man said. "Yeah, yeah, fucking Pierrot with his kisses!" Styopa responded. He appeared to be regaining his confidence. The four of them went back to Styopa's where Christina, when she saw all of them together, let out a loud groan. Having both the Frenchman and Shoni around Styopa at the same time did not bode well.

Christina began muttering her objections and then launched into a full-out protestation. "Why'd you have to up and bring them here? We've enough trouble as it is!" she all but sobbed. "I brought them because I'm gonna open a restaurant!" Styopa snapped back. He was feeling emboldened. Christina could not take this and howled, "You done lost your mind, man, what are you talking about? You just want to drive us all into the grave, the sooner the better, all we have is this here house and you won't finish it!"— "Right here, in this house!" Styopa yelled back. "We are not even close to the street, you lunatic!"—"I'll open the gate!"—"So that people can rob us clean?!"—"No, they won't. C'mon, wife, enough of this, my ears hurt!"

Styopa was trying to hide his own fear, his wife, always so quiet, was at the moment hurling at him every single thing that terrified him. She would not stop. "You're all drunk senseless! You nasty bums!" she shouted and then ran out to her vegetable garden to cry out there. Ivan went after her. He tried to hug her, but Christina pushed him away—even him, her only brother, who had always stood by her, or at least felt like he had, he certainly had, a long time ago, but when? Ivan tried to stop thinking about this because someone had to hang on, to keep going, men had to keep going— men like him and Styopa, his newfound friend who cared about all of them and right that instant was developing his new Plan for Saving This Family. Give us a few million Styopas like that, and no one could hurt us! Ivan said this last part out loud, several times; it gave him confidence. "Who are you talking about? What could they do? When this moron bankrupts us with his ideas, where am I gonna go with the children?" Christina shouted back at him. It was so strange to see her face contorted by fury, her tears—all of her who was always so mute, so docile.

Where would she go with the children! Ivan suddenly felt angry. Wasn't that what everyone was thinking—starting with the country's corrupt presidents and down to the smallest land- holder here in the Silver Land. Silver it was, the Land of Thirty Silver Pieces, where everyone looked out for themselves and no one cared about the country. People like that, they couldn't give a hair off their slick heads for the sake of the country, they only cared about themselves. "You are wrong," Ivan said to Christina. He was smiling, he realized suddenly, a foolish smile, the smile of a peace- ful lunatic. "We must look at things more broadly!" He kept try- ing to hug his sister, but she kept pushing him away until he gave up and shambled back to the house. He could hear Christina still wailing out there among the vegetables—who knew she had such a powerful voice? Who knew any of them ever had a voice?

In the kitchen, Styopa looked for glasses to pour everyone a round of brandy, but could not find any, since he had always relied on Christina managing the place. He gave up and drank straight from the bottle. He handed the bottle to Shoni, the next man in the circle. "I won't have any," Ivan said, but after Styopa, Shoni, and

Jean Paul all took a swig, yielded and held out his hand for the bottle. Perhaps, he thought, if he were drunk, he would not be able to hear his sister screaming.

After a certain number of drinks, Ivan forgot about his sister entirely. From that point, he remembered what happened in fragments. The four of them did a crawl of the city's bars, then Styopa and Jean Paul, whom Styopa stubbornly continued to call Pierrot, looked in one of these dives for a bathroom that, of course, did not exist, and the owner of the place made it clear to them that their business needed to be taken outside. To this Styopa yelled that by law (he was very concerned with laws these days) there had to be a bathroom, and the bar would get an inspection presently because he, Styopa, would make sure of that. Shoni barely managed to drag Styopa, suddenly in the throes of righteousness, out of there, while Ivan tried to get a hold of the Frenchman, who was swaying so hard that he kept slipping, like a giant fish, out of Ivan's grasp.

"So you'll put up a john at your place, right?" Ivan asked Styopa outside in the filthy courtyard, after the four of them, lined up against a wall, finally relieved themselves.

"Heck no," Styopa said, zipping up. Then they thought of the cheese and the goats. "Where do you get some goats?" Styopa asked and scratched his head.

"Kreitzar, a pal of mine, he used to keep some," Ivan said. He thought of Kreitzar. No, that wasn't quite right, he never stopped thinking about Kreitzar, not for a moment. He wondered what became of his goats. The old woman would have sold them, surely, now that there was no one to look after them? Yerzhia wouldn't do it.

"I remember him," Styopa said. "Where are they now?"

"Hell knows."

"So go to his old woman and ask. Maybe they just ran away."

"Nah, guys," Shoni said. "That won't work. For the cheese, you need special goats. They are hard to find, maybe up around Lviv somewhere."

•

Afterward, they went to drink some more in Shoni's studio. The studio, to Ivan's surprise, was in a stately old building, near the city center—Shoni would eventually sell it for a boatload of money. Ivan wondered how Shoni had come in, possession of the place. Ivan by then had sobered up enough to look at a few of his paintings and find that Shoni was also a decent artist. He painted landscapes—fantastic ones, in lilac and purple, abstract places evocative of the sea or the sky, and always full of motion and, for that reason, captivating. Shoni was familiar with Vlodko Kaufman's work and used to be friends with the now-deceased István Molnár. He had been to many European museums and was fanatically in love with the paintings of Fedir Manailo. All this took Ivan by surprise. To hear Christina tell it, Shoni was nothing but a hack and a freeloader. Margita would not like his paintings either. She wanted her art to be well executed and relatable, a painting of a winter landscape, for instance, with village wives in white sheepskin coats, mountains, and churches on distant hills. Both women were wrong about Shoni, he was neither a hack nor a freeloader. He was also a loyal friend—he was at Styopa's side in his time of need, wasn't he?

They finished the plum brandy, the drink scorching their insides. Jean Paul was the first to succumb. He collapsed right there in the studio, onto a pile of dusty, paint-stained rags—old curtains, maybe, or something smaller. This son of France was now sound asleep far from home, among very questionable characters, like a modern-day de Custine.[42] If only his mother could see him now, in the company of a hapless entrepreneur and a hard-drinking artist. And Ivan's, too—the company of an ex-revolutionary.

"He's a weak one, our Frenchman," Shoni said. "Let him sleep, leave him lie, tomorrow he'll have to go catching goats."

Styopa laughed. By the time they left the studio, the sun had gone down.

"Dark, eh?" Styopa said. He could not drive home; he had left his car at the first bar they hit, but that was okay, a good pal of his lived near there, he would make sure to move the car to his own yard.

Styopa invited Ivan and Shoni to dinner at his place. Ivan, now almost entirely sober, thought about what Christina would do when they showed up and mentally crossed himself. She would, however, feed them. Ivan would eat, and then he would have the energy to go home and present himself to Scylla and Charybdis, meaning Phoebe and Margita. Ivan felt a rush of odd giddiness produced not so much by the alcohol but by the absurdity his life had reached in the last couple of weeks. No, months! He started a ditty under his breath, something about Scylla and Charybdis that he was composing on the spot, but then something important happened—an event that, as is customary to say in American movies, would change the lives of our heroes forever.

The three of them were crossing the street in front of the university building that housed the chemistry department and the rector's office. A heavy flatbed truck rolled up to the intersection and stopped at the red light. On its bed sat an old, beat-up bus, or the body of one. Even in the dusk (night came quickly), they could see

---

42. Astolphe-Louis-Léonor, Marquis de Custine (March 18, 1790–September 25, 1857), was a French aristocrat and writer famous for his travel writing, especially his account of a visit to Russia, *La Russie en 1839*.

the bus was white, with a faded and chipped red stripe. The metal of the body had rusted here and there, and rust showed through the paint. Styopa stopped dead, right in the middle of the pedestrian crossing, turned to face the driver of the truck, and raised his arms and waved them above his head, shouting, "Stop! Where's this here bus going?"

Shoni and Ivan tried to move Styopa off the road but failed. The light, meanwhile, flipped to green for the traffic and they were no longer safe in the crosswalk, but Styopa ran up to the driver's door and shouted something at the man. They could not hear the words, but the next second the driver's door opened, the driver stuck his head out, and he hollered so the whole street could hear, "You fucking lost your fucking mind!"

Styopa did not give up, he went on shouting something back at the driver and other people in the truck's cabin, pointed to the bottle of brandy, now an empty one, that dangled from his belt, and gesticulated wildly until he seemed to reach some kind of an understanding, because the driver turned on his long-overdue turn signal and instead of going straight ahead, as he had intended, turned left onto Styopa's street, across another lane and in clear violation of traffic rules. Ivan rubbed his eyes to make sure he was seeing things right. Styopa jumped up onto the step below the driver's door and rode on the truck like Superman, held aloft, for all intents and purposes, by the air itself.

Shoni and Ivan were left behind. They looked at each other and followed the truck; it was clearly headed for Styopa's house, provided he would still be alive when they got there. It took them about ten minutes to walk to the house, it wasn't far. Indeed, the flatbed stood in the street before it. Styopa, the driver, and the driver's partner stood smoking together on the sidewalk. Apparently, they had been waiting for Shoni and Ivan. Styopa came up to them and launched into a confusing explanation of how he was about to move the bus to his vegetable plot, put chairs and tables in it (Tables? Chairs? Ivan's mind reeled under the accumulated weight of their day. For whom? Mice? Moles? The Raptors?), and that would be his eatery, just like so, he already knew what he was going to call it: Transcarpathian Bus.

"Transcarpathian Bus?" Shoni asked, also stunned. He, like Ivan, was failing to grasp the brilliance of Styopa's plan.

"Sure thing! I done paid these dudes; they were taking the bus to the junkyard anyway, so they'll help us put it in here."

"You mean you want to turn this bus into an . . . eatery?" Ivan asked, just in case. He fully expected Styopa to tell him to go to hell with this stupid idea. It sounded really, really stupid, but Ivan could not come up with a different way to make sense of what Styopa was saying.

"Finally, you get it! Only took you forever," Styopa laughed. Ivan thought that they should not have been drinking all day. Some of them, apparently, had gone nuts, and, if he thought about it, he was barely holding on to reason. A café in a scrap bus? Ivan remembered their conversations about the toilet and imagined what hell Christina would raise when Styopa's customers started urinating and more on her vegetables. Or in her greenhouse, where she tended to her prized cucumbers and tomatoes.

They opened Styopa's gates and unchained the bus from the bed of the truck. Styopa produced a jack and a few small wheels from children's bicycles which quickly proved useless. The easiest thing, it seemed, was for all of them to lift the bus together and carry it. So that's what they did. There were five of them—Ivan, Shoni, the two drivers, and Styopa himself. They moved the bus to the vegetable patch and set it down on the beds of something. "Your wife has stuff planted here," Shoni said, but Syopa only cared to steer clear of the greenhouse. "That's eggplant," Styopa said. "There's plenty at my in-laws', no worries. This a good spot for my café." The eggplants did not agree and turned sad immediately, except for the lucky plants that ended up inside the bus—the floor had long rotted away, and the thing was reduced to its basic skeleton. Now the eggplants rose proudly in the very heart of Styopa's bus.

"Well," Styopa said. "We'll paint it a little. And here, you'll paint me a sign, okay?" he asked Shoni.

"No problem," Shoni said. "But if it's too rusted, it'll still show . . ."

"It'll be fine," Styopa said. "Or we'll find some plywood or something."

"You want me to put it like that, Transcarpathian Bus?" Shoni asked, to be sure.

"Yeah, what else?"

While they maneuvered the bus into its spot and fussed around deciding where to paint what they also trampled the carrots, and that made Styopa really worried. They smoked together for a bit longer and said goodnight.

Ivan had the terrifying mental picture of Christina waking up in the morning, going out to water her vegetables, and finding instead the body of the bus that looked like it had been brought up straight from hell. At least Shoni hadn't had the chance to paint the sign yet . . .

.

When Ivan came to work on Monday, he found Vadik at his desk, looking ominous. When he saw Ivan, he stood up and then sat back down again. Ivan had a good idea what was coming, but he had to play along to the end.

"Take a seat," Vadik said and nodded at the other chair. Ivan sat. Vadik got up, walked around Ivan, and locked the office door. Here we go, Ivan thought. He wondered what Vadik would exact from him in retribution, a pound of flesh? Years of free labor?

Vadik appeared in no hurry to exact anything. He sat back in his chair and remained sitting there. He looked down. Ivan did not say anything either, because what would he say? He could have asked what the problem was. He should have, in fact, and someone better at lying than him could have managed the whole thing to his own advantage, but Ivan was no good at lying. Moreover, he didn't want to lie. The only thing he wondered was who had turned him in. That sharp-nosed character in the elevator?

Finally, Vadik raised his eyes to Ivan.

"I know that you, bastard, slept with Milena," he said quietly. He might have intended to sound menacing but ended up being pathetic. Vadik was suffering. Ivan surmised from his tone that being betrayed by Ivan was not, in fact, the main cause of this suffering. Who was Ivan? Nothing. Only Milena mattered, and she had chosen Ivan.

Ivan said nothing.

"Well, say something," Vadik asked in the same sad voice. He sounded almost pleading. Perhaps he wanted Ivan to confess to him, to ask for forgiveness, to tell him the devil had made him do it, anything. That he hated Vadik. That he loved Milena and wanted to marry her, and would like to ask for Vadik's blessing, because things are the way they are, and what are you going to do, that's life, c'est la vie, or whatever other stupid thing people say in such situations—anything to protect themselves.

To defend themselves with bare hands against a knife.

Ivan said nothing.

Vadik leaped to his feet, grabbed a heavy paperweight from his desk, and hurled it at Ivan. Ivan ducked and got to his feet, too.

They stood facing each other. Vadik breathed heavily. Finally, he caught his breath and yelled, "Fuck you, you son of a bitch, you slept with my Milena!"

Ivan started laughing. He laughed for a long time. When he

stopped, he asked, "Is that it? That all you got? You won't even shoot me or anything?"

Vadik looked at him askance.

"You won't hire a hit man or something? And why not?"

"I'll think of something," Vadik hissed.

Ivan wondered if maybe he shouldn't have mocked the Ripper. What a stupid nickname. But the man was no ripper, he was just a Vadik from this town. A coward, a fool, a man who got cheated on. Sure, he could complain to Surkis and Medvedchuk. Medvedchuk was already known to get even with dissidents by getting himself hired as their lawyer and then sinking them. Sure, mighty politicians were going to come after Ivan to punish him for having slept, while being married to another woman, with Milena Mikhailivna, who had previously also slept with Vadik What's-His-Name, who was likewise married to another woman. Well then. It would be an honorable kind of punishment, the righteous thing to be done by their social-democratic, or national-chauvinistic, or whatever kind of party they had. Every party needs to have a few heroic pages in its history. They could put this in their party-colored leaflets.

"Get out," Vadik said.

Ivan paused for a moment at the door as if he could not quite believe that death, again, had decided to spare him. Then he left.

•

He walked; his legs felt like they could buckle under him at any moment. Ivan had to sit down. He got up again and couldn't quite feel his legs. He thought of hailing a cab, but none were in sight. At the main road, he waved down a *marshrutka* that was going to Styopa's neighborhood. The driver shook his head, but let him on anyway. "I'm late for work," Ivan lied by way of pleading his case. "'T's not like the rest of you are off to a circus!" The driver shrugged. The van was packed. Ivan barely squeezed in. The ride was long. Each red light took forever. Perfumes mixed with the smell of sweat and together seemed to cover another smell, a terrible one, but Ivan could not identify it.

"See here, let me read you . . . the stuff they write . . . it's a funny paper," he heard a man's voice saying. The man began to read, "*A true-bred Rusyn, once he cellars his apples, sets to sort them after about a month. Any that are marred he'll take to peel for meat, and the best ones he leaves. In another month, he turns them again: the dinged ones he eats, and the sweet ones he leaves.*"

Ivan heard someone, a woman, laugh.

"*He turns back another month, and then another . . .*"

Laughter.

"*In this manner, with his cellar full of sweet, fine apples, our good man partakes all winter of blighted fruit and marvels to himself, What's so good about these apples that others praise them so?* That's Mykhailo Chukhran wrote that. Nicely done, eh?"

Ivan willed himself to stop listening, but just as soon as he did, he registered another conversation, similarly pointless. Pointless because it was about people who were absent and things that could not be remedied: "A world of grief, it was! Her poor mother, God forbid, you'd never seen such grieving!"—"And what about him? Did he come back from the Czechs?"—"Sure did! Been gone long and what he done there, why he gone, no one knows and he won't tell."—"He cheat on her?"—"No doubt. Must've. She had such a hard time without him."—"She sure did! Such grief, and the baby so little . . ."

His limbs gone numb, Ivan worked his way to the exit and as soon as the marshrutka made its next stop, got off, or rather, fell out onto the road dust, which looked to him white as snow. The world shifted and slipped before him. Ivan covered his eyes with his hands and stood like that for a minute or two.

Where to go now? Who did he have left in this world?

The answer was plain: Styopa. The Transcarpathian Bus was due to open any day. The sign was up, and the meat marinated. Styopa and the Frenchman were in the yard, fixing chairs. The chairs came from the university—the law school had thrown them out, and Styopa found them. A good deed, that. All lawyers should have new chairs to sit on, and their old chairs could still serve the great enterprise of keeping the general public intoxicated. Which would, in turn, ensure, the lawyers did not run out of work. A virtuous cycle, you could say.

"Pour me some plum stuff," Ivan said instead of a greeting as soon as he was close enough.

"What's wrong?" Styopa asked. Ivan glanced at the Frenchman. "Pierrot doesn't understand a thing . . . spit it out."

"I got fired," Ivan said. He told the truth, and he hadn't wanted to. Styopa would now tell Christina, and Christina would tell you know who, Margita. Margita would then marshal forces effable and ineffable, from Myron Vasyliovych up to the saints in the church where she offered a tithe along with her humble prayers. The news of Ivan being fired from Vadik the Ripper's business would travel through hell and heaven, and back, since it wasn't the kind of news they'd welcome in heaven!

"Fuck me!" Styopa said and slapped his thighs. "You'll work for me then."

"Done."

They went and got some plum brandy. Christina was home, so they had to be circumspect. First, Ivan went in to say hello and asked for a cup of coffee. Then he asked Christina to show him something in the greenhouse, and while they were there, Styopa, quick as a weasel, sneaked the demijohn out of the kitchen.

They drank until noon. Then they took a break, finished the chairs, and drank some more. The Frenchman, naturally, drank with them—What else would they have done with him? Jean Paul had sort of moved into Styopa's, there was plenty of room and he was handy. He even learned a handful of obscenities and dialect words from the Raptors (Styopa's characterization of him as not understanding a thing was somewhat exaggerated). "We'll make a man of you yet!" Styopa said to the Frenchman, slapping him on the shoulders. It was evening, but not dark yet. Ivan managed to get upright and told Styopa he was going home. He asked him to keep mum about his getting fired, but knew his brother-in-law would not be able to keep mum for long. Ivan had to use what time he had wisely.

·

Only when Ivan was already walking down the street did the full recognition of what he had lost hit him. It was over, another chapter of his life. Milena was over. At that very moment he could have been on his way to her apartment, to her bed, her embrace, where he could find some sweetness to mix into his miserable life. He knew, didn't he, that it was miserable, he didn't have to be afraid of the truth, he could just be honest with himself: his life was miserable.

What was it that Yarema used to say? Fear is an idea. Ivan repeated the words to himself and kept mumbling under his breath, Fear is an idea, fear—an idea, fear-idea, fear—an idea, an idea—fear, until fear and thinking about it got so tangled in his mind he no longer had any hope of pulling them apart.

Then another thought stopped him: What about Milena? What would happen to her? He, being the bastard he was, hadn't even thought about her until then. He was the one who had put her in jeopardy, and now she would have to find a way to make up with Vadik. She could have lied to Vadik, told him that Ivan had forced himself upon her, that he had stalked her, but she did not. If she had, Vadik would've made sure that the vigilant police cuffed Ivan and packed him off to rot in endless pretrial detention.

Or, perhaps, she didn't have to tell Vadik anything. She might not even be aware of what happened to Ivan. Vadik had spies, and his spies could have done their quiet job, and now he, Ivan, was forever barred from Milena's while Vadik ruled supreme. There would be no scene, no excuses to be made. Ivan was simply no longer a part of Milena's life. "I fired one of my knuckle draggers," Vadik might say to her, "you know the one, he picked you up from the sauna that one time. Yeah, I fired his ass. Yep, the usual, stealing from me. He's lucky I didn't put him in jail. That's right."

There would be nothing for Milena to do but smile and hide her tears and keep playing her role. Once there was an Ivan and now he was gone. That was it. Both of them ought to be grateful to Vadik. Ivan for being cut loose relatively easily and Milena for not losing her keep, Vadik not abandoning her, not even making a scene.

Vadik the fixer. Say what you wish about Komsomol, they did produce well-rounded cadres.

Or should he have run? All the way back that day, from that elevator? Should he have grabbed Milena and fled with her to Lviv, things were over between him and Phoebe anyway, they'd never let him have Emilia, and even if they did, what would he have done with a baby alone? Perhaps he should have . . . And now—now what? He'd think of something, Ivan told himself, he still had his brains, all he needed was a few days to think, for Styopa not to blab to Christina about him being fired, anything could happen in a few days, he would think of something, fear is just an idea, or was it that an idea was simply fear, everything would be fine, just hold on, Ivan, hold on . . .

Against all reasonable expectation, the Transcarpathian Bus did just fine, as if the old husk of the bus were a magic talisman whose forceful emanations had touched the chakras Styopa held open on that fateful night. People came in droves to stare at the exotic setup, and thirsty police soon followed. Styopa's crew fashioned a bar and kept a few tables outside the bus in the yard itself. The sign Shoni had painted was large enough to be seen from the street. They kept one half of the gate open and marked off a portion of the large yard for parking. The butchers who supplied fresh meat were easy to deal with. They grilled fish, too, since Styopa's neighbor fished regularly. They had their own wine, their own vegetables, and their own plum brandy. "Pierrot" went on living at Styopa's; he helped with the meat and lent a hand to Christina in her greenhouses, for which she came to love him like her own son. He served wine and could talk to the guests a little. Styopa bought him a toque in Hungary, and the French chef was now part of the place's appeal.

"Well, what are you gonna do when it's cold?" asked those who envied them. "Put a cauldron out and make *bográc*, of course! Bake some taters!" Styopa answered. "Grill 'em, no oil!" Styopa made up a jingle on the spot. He had many plans, to bring in a wood-burning stove and space heaters, like Jean Paul had told him about. The Frenchman had grown up in a village, but had been to Paris, and told them that cafés and restaurants there kept right on through the winter with outdoor seating. They could figure out how to keep people warm.

And so it was that while the rest of the world stood still, the Transcarpathian Bus rolled on and on. Ivan lied to Margita and Phoebe; he told them he went to work at Vadik's office but worked at Styopa's instead. He waited tables, served the meat, and poured vodka. Skewered pork grilled on an open fire, and the welcoming smoke rose above Styopa's yard. Glasses clinked, although so many were broken in the first month that they had to switch to plastic. Styopa did not throw out used plastic plates and cups, he had put Christina to work washing them in warm water in the kitchen sink. He read somewhere that the water had to be warm, not hot, lest the plastic crack.

Shoni usually came in the afternoon, after they were done with lunch and could take a break. They'd sit together—Shoni, Styopa, Ivan, and the loyal "Pierrot"—and drink, especially Ivan. They were four comrades, tired but full of newfound confidence. At least that's what Ivan preferred to think when he drank. So what, he was just sitting there, inside the old bus, with these three guys who looked the worse for wear, their hair spiked with grease, their eyes red; no one could see him there. Not Mysko and not Yarema. Over these few weeks Ivan had had a chance to learn what wonders plum brandy worked on a man who had lost everything. Even drunk, he could keep himself upright, or so he thought. Especially if he didn't try to wait on anyone.

At home, he and Phoebe kept having their long, dull, terrible conversations. She kept up her complaining, her crying. She would not be quiet. None of them would. Margita yelled at Phoebe, Phoebe yelled back at Margita, and the two of them together yelled at Ivan. But Phoebe got him the worst. She had the bitterest words for him. He had gotten used to her words, and for a while could convince himself that they no longer pained him, no longer touched him. That he was just a man who went home to this woman who expected something from him. Or had expected, once. This was worse because it meant he had failed her. But nothing said he had to respond to her; he could just let her grievances fall on deaf ears, he could ally himself with Margita, who, however many complaints she had of her own, could be relied upon to take his side against her daughter-in-law and unburden herself, in a furious whisper, of everything she thought about Phoebe. For a while, that was exactly what Ivan did, and it seemed almost enough, right up until he realized his strategy was getting him nowhere, and that Phoebe's accusations had taken on a life of their own, nested in his mind, and needled at him from dawn until late night, until he fell asleep. Her words poisoned his days, and even the plum brandy was no match for them.

Phoebe in the flesh, the physical Phoebe, could be ignored or yelled at, but against this fury in his head Ivan could do absolutely nothing. She did not have to care when he was rude to her, did not have to listen to his arguments, and ignored him when he begged her to please for the love of God shut up just for a minute and leave him alone. He wrestled her like a chthonic monster that kept changing its shape, again and again. Whenever he stopped, exhausted, to wipe the sweat of this righteous labor from his brow, the monster rose taller before him. It did not burn in fire and did not drown in water. Ivan covered his ears with his hands, squeezed his eyes shut—and would, if he could, squeeze his memory shut, too—and walked away, walked without purpose just as long he did not have to see anything, hear anything, feel anything.

•

A great heat wave hit the city. Styopa put up portable fans around his bus. He and "Pierrot" built trellises to shade the tables. The customers liked that. Ivan went on working for his brother-in-law. Early in the mornings, dew lingered on the grass and gossamer threads flew in the air, but steadily, the sun rose high above the earth like a blazing torch and scorched the fabric of earthly life in halves. The sun shone straight into the essence of things below and burned off all things superfluous. It brought pain with it, but how could it have cut so deep into the earth otherwise? Noon came, and then sultry afternoons of condensed heat, a time when there was no memory, no torment of the past because the essence of man was the same as the essence of the earth, and that heart of hearts was in the hands of the best doctor there had ever been. The best and the cruelest. If one could spend one's corporeal life in this sunlight, blinded, that would have been a wise choice.

But the Transcarpathian Bus had to keep rolling. Ivan came back every day to the smells of meat, the drunken conversations. The drinking. After lunch, the guys would sit down to talk. The talking, as usual, was mostly done by Styopa: he had plans to share, always new plans, and this was good, Ivan thought, it was good that someone had plans. Plans and money. Mysko used to say that money was a fetish whether you loved it madly or abhorred it altogether, while, in fact, money was neither (he'd laugh here), neither an idol nor a demon. Money was just a loyal friend.

That used to make Ivan smile, too; he couldn't quite picture it: money as friends, banknotes walking down the street with him arm in arm. But Mysko had a point. So did Styopa. And Ivan had neither a point nor any plans. Perhaps he never did.

He was afraid to think ahead and to ask himself if he would ever have plans again. For the moment, he lived day by day. If someone refilled his glass, Ivan drank, so what if he did, it was something to do, to sit there for a bit longer, under the trellis, in the shade, hidden from the sun and from life.

•

Finally, the other shoe dropped. Margita personally came to confront Ivan; someone had told her the truth. She found him in his refuge at Styopa's and had a terrible argument with her son-in-law. She yelled that Styopa had made her boy (that's what she said, "my boy") quit his job in order to come slave away there at Styopa's. Styopa's eyes nearly popped out of his head; he was many things, he could be mean, but he would never have done what Margita charged him with doing. He would never force anyone to do anything, never make anyone a slave. Margita screamed at Christina, too: Why hadn't she told her, why had she kept it from her, and Christina could only mutter her excuses. How would she have known that Ivan got kicked out of his job? All she knew was, her brother was with them, working for Styopa; she had no idea why! Styopa only told her when he saw Margita walk through his gates.

"What do you mean, *kicked out*?" Margita spiraled into a new level of fury and the words she screamed fell now, like knives, onto Ivan's head.

Christina, meanwhile, decided she had been wronged and screamed her own things at her mother. What was she doing, coming here, making a scene before the neighbors, what'd the boy (she said it like that, too, "the boy") done to her, why'd she act like she owned his soul, so what he doesn't turn down drink, he can think for himself! "And I," Christina yelled into her mother's face, "am not your handmaid to keep track of everyone. I don't run a detective agency here! He's a grown man, he can do what he wants. And actually, Mother, why don't you just turn around and leave, you're scaring off customers!"

"Sure," Margita answered, wounded to her very heart. "Sure! So you can go about your business getting a man to drink himself to death!"—"A man wants to drink himself to death, he don't need no help, he does just fine quiet in his own home!" Styopa said with menace. It was the old man, Ivan's father, he was talking about, as in, *If you are such a fine woman then why does your own husband come home on all fours?* Margita could only hiss at this.

She and Ivan went back to the house together. He started up the unfinished stairs that still did not have a railing to his floor to see baby Emilia.

Margita stopped him.

"No use looking," she said. "Your wife done gone from you."

Everything got very quiet. Then Ivan's heart dropped out of his chest and fell onto the stairs. It fell and rolled down, like a stone, heavy, clanging, all edges. He had no idea the human heart could be so heavy and so jagged. All he could ask was, "Where?"—"What d'you mean, *where*?" Margita said, less stentorian now that she saw how white Ivan's face had turned. "To her parents. Where else?" She was getting angry again. Did she have to explain this to him, too? He was the one that let his life go to hell! "Told me she would swallow pills, a right hysterical fit she had here, said she didn't want to live anymore, that she'd cut herself dead. And what am I supposed to do—Am I everyone's keeper? If you can't live together then get divorced, and none of this pills and cutting nonsense! They came for her, and I left. Let her cut herself dead at her own folks.'"—"How?" Ivan exhaled. "What do you mean, cut?"

"And where have you been?" Margita asked him. It was not a rhetorical question. Where had he been? What had he actually been doing? He thought of spending all his energy on wrestling the Phoebe inside him, the beast that tore at his heart. On Vadik, on Milena. On his own freedom. On walking. On God only knew what.

"Oh Lord," he said and came down the stairs, set to run to Myron Vasyliovych and Kateryna Ivanivna, good Lord, what would he say to them, what . . .

"Where d'you think you're going!" Margita said. "Just look at yourself," she commanded, and Ivan, anxious to obey—obey *her*, since his own judgment had failed him—looked in the mirror. He looked like the devil himself, an unshaven mess, intoxicated, short on sleep. The stubble on his cheeks was as blue as a dead man's. His T-shirt, the rest of this clothes were wet, his hair and all of him rank with grease and sweat. Where did he think he could go?

Margita was right.

She was always right. All this time she had been right.

Ivan sat down on the stairs—the stairs without the railing in the house he had failed to finish—dropped his head into his hands, and moaned. What had he done? What had he done to all these lives, his own included, all these lives someone had entrusted to him? Things had been different once, hadn't they? He had once been strong, hadn't he? When he was with his friends, there, on the granite in Kyiv—he was strong then, he was like a cup filled with all the strength of the world that flowed into him as easily as it poured out of him. And now all he had was his stone heart, and it no longer held fast in his chest. That and his life that he kept carrying, carrying somewhere, pushing it before him not knowing where and why.

•

Phoebe herself came to the door. Good lord . . . it was just like in the old times, when he used to come over like that, to see her after work. It was only a few years ago, but it felt as if a century had passed. A shadow slipped across Phoebe's face. Ivan, who a mere week ago made every effort not to see Phoebe's face, now could not get enough of it, he thirsted for it, for its every feature—he wanted to know what she was feeling. He needed to know that she was alive, that she existed.

They went into the living room. Kateryna Ivanivna, eyes puffy with tears (Of course she loved her daughter! She always had; it was Ivan who couldn't stop doubting her), was already there, with baby Emilia in her arms. Ivan reached for his daughter, and she reached back. He took her into his arms, kissed her. A quiet light illuminated his soul. Emilia wanted to be stood up on the floor, so he did that, and she ran around him, laughing. Babbling. Everything about the child was real and true—her little body had not learned to lie, to keep things hidden. She loved, she was happy, or she cried.

When did she grow so big? How much of his life had he missed, like stretches of a bad movie?

Myron Vasyliovych came in. Now they had the quorum. A line from a folk song came into Ivan's mind, something about poor ne'er-do-wells coming back together in their mother's house. Except, of course, no one was singing. Myron Vasyliovych, Ivan thought, might well still be singing in that church, but Ivan no longer went there to hear the choir. Myron sat down. Crossed his legs. Ivan thought of all the times he had come to this apartment before, the times he listened to Myron Vasyliovych, all his stories. The silence now was awkward; no one was sure how to begin, what, exactly, they were there to talk about. Divorce? Reconciliation? Alimony? Ivan simply had to speak with Phoebe alone. He said so, she agreed, and they went into her tiny bedroom where they used to . . .

They stood there, face-to-face, not daring to sit down.

"I don't know what to say," he said finally.

"Neither do I," she echoed. Once, they used to have so many words for each other: first, the words of love, and later, words of bitterness and resentment, and now they had none. Perhaps this was the pinnacle of human communication: talking without words, with one's breath alone, with being present? They no longer loved each other, but there was no sorrow in that. No, not like that. They were no longer in love with each other, no longer ardent, but love couldn't care less about ardor, it couldn't care less about their pleasure or choice. Being there, their presence was a form of love, wordless, tearless. The space they occupied was like a frozen arctic sea, featureless yet full of life.

"It's hard for me to be here, with my parents," Phoebe said.

"It's hard for you at my place, too," Ivan said.

"I'd like to go somewhere, leave, but the baby . . ."

"I know."

They spoke and understood each other like captured soldiers of the same eviscerated army who had no more time to squabble because they were about to be taken somewhere else, and they had to tell each other where and why, had to come up with a shared plan—for escape, or an honorable death. Ivan was afraid Phoebe would start crying, but she did not cry.

"Come back," he said finally. "I'll talk to my mother."

Actually, why not? Let her live with them, he would no longer hate her, they could become friends, comrades, until the time came for each to go their separate way. Ivan did not know how to be friends with women, but he would learn. For Emilia's sake, he would learn.

They went back to the living room.

"I'll go back there," Phoebe said. Myron Vasyliovych shook his head.

"Why would you do that?"

"Well," Phoebe said, "what am I doing here?"

Kateryna Ivanivna kept quiet, thinking perhaps that the goat had come back to the cart, or something along those lines involving horses and goats. Or hares. The hare would be appropriate here—the one that was supposed to but didn't have any use for the stop sign. Myron nodded to Kateryna. She took Phoebe and the baby out of the room, to give Myron Vasyliovych and Ivan a chance to speak alone.

Ivan studied his father-in-law as if seeing him for the first time. The man had gone gray at the temples, and his eyes over the last year or two had become sadder, radiated more lines.

Myron stood up, reached into the inside pocket of his sport coat that was draped over a chair, pulled out a piece of paper, and gave it to Ivan. In the same uninflected tone he had once used to ask Ivan whether he was going to marry Phoebe, he said, "Go to this address. This is a friend of mine, a counselor. He does marital

stuff, sexual, too. He'll be waiting for you. I heard you have issues."
Ivan was surprised. Who could have told Myron such a thing? Not
Phoebe, surely? And then he thought of how he spent these last
few years, months . . . He gave no sign of what he thought to his
father-in-law, though, and instead asked sharply, "What do you
mean, issues?"—"How should I know? Just go, talk to the man."

Myron made it clear that until Ivan went to see this counselor
at least five times, they would not give Phoebe back to him. Same
for helping him find a new job, although Myron Vasyliovych had
his eye on a place. Well . . . This family, apparently, was not as hopeless as Ivan had believed. All right then. He'd go along with their
plan. If not for his own and Phoebe's sake, then at least for Emilia's.

•

Ivan looked up at the dark building at the top of the hill, one of the
local hospital's facilities. Below it, the hill was dotted all around with
many freshly built homes called the "Tsars' Village"—one of those
developments where Kreitzar used to work construction. Kreitzar.
The houses were garish and clumsy, like pieces of a birthday cake
left over after the party. Some were still uninhabited, and their awkward heft loomed in the dark. He could see the sixteen-floor high-
rise on the far side of the bridge, its many lit windows.

Ivan stepped into the hospital's building and found himself
plunged into another darkness. Weird, he thought, there had to
be doctors and patients here somewhere, and yet there were none.
Nothing except these dark hallways, dark stairwells, and black railings along the stairs. It was as if the entire large building had been
erected for the sole purpose of being filled with emptiness. Still, it
smelled like a hospital: of urine, cloying medicine, insulin perhaps,
and cheap laundry detergent.

Finally, Ivan got to the floor he needed. There was more light here. A nurse distributed pills to the patients, voices came from behind the doors, a TV set's monotonous mutter. In the dim light, through a half-open door to the nurses' room Ivan glimpsed a metal container full of steaming syringes, a nurse had just taken it out of the autoclave, probably to go give someone a shot. But these syringes were unsafe, Ivan thought, the plunger came loose with time and was no longer hermetically sealed in the tube. Air could get into the vein. A vein or an artery? But did they ever inject anything into arteries?

Ivan passed patients' rooms. No one stopped him, no one asked him anything. Faces flicked past him as if in a silent movie, fixed into masks of pain or laughter. Then it was dark again—he had left behind an island of life. The doctor Ivan had been sent to saw patients late in the evenings, practically at night. Leave it to a shrink to be different. At the very end of an endless hallway, Ivan located the door he was looking for. He actually had to use his lighter to make sure it was the right place. He wondered how anyone who didn't smoke would find their way to this doctor. And then answered in his head, in Myron Vasyliovych's voice: Those who did not smoke did not have the problems he had. Actually, neither did he. He had a different set of problems altogether.

Ivan knocked. A muffled "Come in" came from the room.

A man sat at a desk inside, a wall of darkness behind him. A mirrored wall, a vast, floor-to-ceiling window without a curtain. Ivan recalled what newspapers once wrote about this building: that Soviet central planners decided to build a bunch of glass cells and never stopped to think about the local conditions, meaning the winter cold—in winter, the building was impossible to heat. The hospital must have rented some rooms out to private practices.

"Myron Vasyliovych sent me," Ivan said.

"Yes, I see," the doctor answered and smiled. "Serhiy."

Serhiy looked to be in his midthirties, was lean and very

tanned. Does he actually go to a salon, Ivan thought at random. Or does he just put something on, a fake tan? Serhiy extended his hand, and Ivan shook it. Serhiy's hand was knotty and strong.

"Please take a seat. What's the problem?"

That felt too fast. What was his problem?

The problem was that life had fallen apart, unraveled down to the last thread. And, while they were at it, might as well add the politics to the mix. Whoever said politics did not affect the mind was stupid. The country, it seemed, had fallen into oligarchy. Assisted, as needed, by various special services. At the very top, it was all special services and oligarchs. That was the new social order. Ivan wondered what would happen if he said all this in response to Serhiy's question. Would the shrink pack him off to the asylum in Berehove right away, or would he be shocked at first? People usually acted shocked when they heard such things. They accused whoever voiced such views of believing in conspiracy theories, of being paranoid. And perhaps they had reasons to do so—in Ivan's case, especially. But he was not paranoid at the moment. Not at all.

He was not paranoid, but he could sense the special services. They were there. He could feel them with his skin.

"You see . . . it was my wife's idea. That I come see you."

"I see. And what made your wife insist that you come? Tell me about your relations with your wife."

"The sexual ones?"

"Whichever you wish." The doctor spoke calmly, evenly, as if he had not heard the hurt and challenge in Ivan's voice.

Still, Ivan thought. What a moron.

Ivan looked into the accidental mirror of the window. Two men, sitting, talking . . . a serene picture, it only lacked a fire in a fireplace. With a fire, it would look downright cozy; a pair of friends in a hunting lodge, after a good hunt. Just about to smoke their cigars. Ivan wanted to keep mocking the doctor in his mind, and yet Serhiy's words had unlocked something in him. About your relations, he said. And not just the sexual ones. There was hope in this.

"You see, my wife and I . . ."

"Yes?"

Ivan thought of a line from an old Cossack song, "The woman does me no good . . ."

"Physically, you are healthy?" the doctor asked.

"I am," Ivan answered, not at all certain.

"Do you have reasons to believe your wife is being unfaithful to you?" Serhiy asked.

"I don't know." Phoebe, unfaithful? That would take an incubus materializing in her bedroom on the second floor, because the first was guarded by the vigilant dragon, the hundred-armed and hundred-eyed Margita, the Hecatoncheire of the Ancient Greeks who would not let Phoebe leave unnoticed. "I don't think so." And what did he, Ivan, care about Phoebe's faithfulness or lack thereof? "My wife, if you wish to know, is also healthy, has no symptoms . . . No problems with her . . . er . . . cervix, whatever those are called." Ivan wasn't sure what made him talk about *that*. "Like, erosion—I remember. But her cervix is hard to reach. You have to check it with special tools. I personally haven't."

"I did not think so," the doctor said evenly, without mockery. Even sympathetically. Ivan felt something shudder and move inside him, as if a mountain began to slip off its foundation, down into the sea.

"Do you mind if I smoke?"

"Not at all," the doctor said. "I'll smoke, too."

He studied Ivan for a while, puffing on his cigarette, and then said, "Just tell me. What's bothering you?"

•

Tears filled Ivan's eyes. He took an intentionally long drag on his cigarette, then exhaled, let the smoke hide his face. The counselor (or whoever this Serhiy was) said nothing, looked at Ivan. Ivan coughed to hide the sobs that tore at his chest. Could anyone imagine the pain that tormented him all this time? Phoebe, Margita, his job. He fought the urge to cry like it was his worst enemy. The smell of cigarette smoke summoned a picture from his past, his childhood, when he and Korchi Vash used to go to the courtyard of one of the Party apartment buildings on what used to be Sverdlov Street, now Rakotsi. The courtyard was connected to the yard next door, where Roma families lived, including their friend Edik, and Edik's mother sat out in her improvised loggia and smoked, exhaling straight into the wall of wet sheets hung out on the laundry line.

There was nothing dramatic about this memory, nothing particularly significant. But it was proof of Ivan; proof that he had a life separate and distinct from other lives. The idea crushed him.

The doctor continued to look at Ivan steadily. Ivan managed to control himself and finished his cigarette in silence.

"Here is the thing," Serhiy said. "You have no reason to be anxious about what happens with your wife. Or with other women, which is not something I have asked or, going forward, will ever ask you about. It doesn't matter. You are mentally exhausted. And have been for a few years at least. There's a lot going on right now. It's the time we live in. But no one has ever asked you, not in a very long time, just, How are you doing? What are you feeling? Right?"

The words brought on another urge to cry. This time, Ivan could not even pretend to be coughing, and just sobbed, silently, for several minutes.

As earlier, the doctor said nothing.

•

They made arrangements. Ivan kept seeing Serhiy. It did make things better. He felt relieved. He had forgotten what that felt like, he had gotten so used to carrying his impossible burden. Now that someone had lifted a part of it, he felt like he'd grown a pair of wings. Perhaps everything would, in fact, turn out all right—Ivan did not know how, but things could be all right. Things had a way of sorting themselves out. For the first time in a very long time he felt he was not alone in the world. After all, Myron had taken pity on him and Margita stopped screaming at him. She promised not to nag her daughter-in-law either. He and Phoebe could speak to each other, although Margita shook her head skeptically at that.

Margita did, because she, his mother, knew life better than he did. She knew that bitterness did not leave a soul easily, that it was easier, as the saying went, to find a hermit who survived on leaves alone than a man who could endure. She knew how hard it was to traverse this desert alone, without even the consolation of sweet lovemaking. She knew Phoebe would not find peace, that pain erupted from a human soul like fire and lava exactly when the person thought she had conquered it.

Ivan wanted to believe things would be better. Why not? It was so easy to be at peace, he just had to stop worrying about things, stop being anxious. Everything was all right, everything was fine, and would only get better. No one had died, no one was sick, and even if (if!) he, Ivan, took some time finding a new job, it's not like he was going to starve in the meantime. He had his family!

The family you are supposed to support, not the other way around, spoke the voice somewhere deep inside him, but Ivan shushed it. He had to stop thinking like that.

Serhiy told him it was in his power to replace a bad thought with a good one.

•

That's what he was thinking that day, walking along the street, when all at once a great big hole yawned before him. An empty cube. The sidewalk on this quiet street Ivan walked nearly every day had been excavated. Inside the hole he could only see thick rusty lengths of pipe, like the earth's own naked bones. The hole cut the street in half. Ivan thought he could jump over it and that, perhaps, it wasn't the best idea to do so. He turned around; he knew these streets like the back of his hand, knew the way around. When he turned the corner, however, there were two police cars and two regular ones in his way, an accident. Not a crash, really, just one car bumping into another, but the drivers had called the police, and everyone was making notes and arguing. Ivan had no desire to go through the scene, even though no one would probably have stopped him— he had that marrow-deep instinct of someone raised in the Soviet Union, in the world full of No Entry signs as if forever subject to an endless curfew.

Where then? He knew other ways around. Any of them would take longer, but he was not in a hurry. Ivan walked on. On the third street he tried, a city crew was cutting trees—of all the times to do it! And whatever for? With zeal like that they would turn the entire city into a concrete desert in no time . . . Thick branches fell onto the pavement. He could have gone through, the crews would have paused to let him pass, but a sudden idea struck Ivan: the city was putting up walls before him. The city, his city, which he loved and had loved him back, for some reason, was not letting him go home. It turned itself into a labyrinth, put up dead ends before him, pushed cars together to block his way.

He had experienced something like this in his dreams— dreams of which he could remember little other than that he was wandering through a city that was both like and not like his own, that he got lost in a maze of narrow medieval streets, or walked down a familiar street only to discover suddenly that it was jointed with another that was far away from it in real life. He would go into a particular neighborhood, and find himself somewhere else entirely, and fences would sprout in his path, right in the middle of the street, odd barricades of loose rock, of cobblestone, and felled trees with giant trunks of a kind he could only have seen in a book on exotic botany. He could stand at the top of the Witches' Stairs that led downhill from the cathedral to the bus station downtown, not far from the university buildings, could look down at the city from there and see a sea where there had never been and could not be one. Zamkova Street, in his dreams, wound up the hill and ended at a humongous metal structure, something like the Eiffel Tower, but unfinished and rusty, like those broken water pipes in his city's ground . . . Streets dropped off suddenly into deep crevasses, and Ivan wanted to look over the edge to see what was at the bottom, but never could.

Or sometimes, the dreams had him going into the new neighborhood where Phoebe lived, along Kapushanska Street, which was noisy and chaotic with holes in the pavement, but also dotted with whimsical private homes, some adorned with turrets, and ancient, sunken cottages whose windows flashed at him like weary eyes. There were also abandoned houses here, and Ivan liked peeking into them. They held the air inside them the way a cracked cup holds water, water that had not yet realized that its home was ruined and it should go find another. Ivan would see the caryatids he had passed so often on the embankment, but in his dreams, they would be under water. This was a river, not a sea, Ivan could touch the pebbles it washed up, he would have known these pebbles, gray and grainy to the touch, anywhere, there was only one river in the world that worked them into this texture. In his dreams, Ivan would lower himself into the current, and the light and water flowed above him, linden trees on the shores whispering. He would sleep there like a strange amphibian beast, a hibernation so real he would feel cold and the green lindens above him would flare into golden-and-orange torches, their flames alive as ginger manes, while the last roses still bloomed under their canopies.

This, however, was not a dream. The city was not letting him through. Something happened, something, somewhere was happening. Ivan turned into the next street, the fourth he tried, and his heart boomed mad in his chest. Cold sweat broke out on his forehead. He knew he had to hurry, had to run. He knew he was already too late.

He was not far from home when the goats blocked his path. The surprise of them brought Ivan to a sudden stop. There were eight of them, maybe seven, he could not get a count of them. The goats milled about, picking off leaves from bushes and trees, they left no room for him, and whenever he came too close to an invisible line they seemed to be guarding, the goats lowered their horns and aimed at his stomach. Entirely confused, Ivan could only stare. Two gray ones, one black one, two rusty-colored ones ...

He looked closer. Could these be—could these be Kreitzar's goats? So that's what became of them! The old woman must have lost them, let them loose, or forgotten about them, and these escape artists now roamed as a troop. A troupe. A choir. Singing lamentations for their dearly departed master, a man no one had ever understood.

As if they could hear Ivan's thoughts, the goats formed themselves into a line and raised their little bearded faces. And then they sang.

"Maah-maah! Maah ..." rolled the goat noises down the street. "Maah! Maah!"

Some started, like the leading tenors or sopranos, and others picked up the song. Every so often, they gave Ivan a content glance. They nodded their heads to the beat of their song. They seemed to be having fun. To be challenging him.

No, these could not be Kreitzar's goats. Kreitzar's were quiet. These were the spawn of hell itself! They seem to be mocking Ivan: Here you go, mister, a choir for you, the kind you really deserve, serves you right. Stand there and take your "maahs" for there weren't words left in the human language to tell the story of Ivan's forsaken life.

Ivan looked behind him, half expecting to see someone, something, big and scary there. What abyss, what crack into the underworld spat out these goats? Or were they summoned by Kateryna Ivanivna's many sayings? Poets had always said words came true.

"Shoo! Shoo, you beasts!" Ivan waved his arms at the goats, broke through their line of defense, and, no longer able to control himself, ran home as fast as he could.

•

When he came, gasping for breath, to his home, Ivan could hear a great ruckus in the yard. Margita saw him as soon as he reached to open the gate; she was running across the yard to the house, her face scared, streaked with tears. "Mother! What's gone wrong?" Ivan asked coarsely as he turned his key in the gate. He braced himself for the worst.

"Oy, a hog of ours fell into a pit, broke his legs, so we had to kill it." She glanced at her son and added, "Styopa's here," and ran into the house calling out, "Styopa?"

Right, of course, someone had to help kill the hog at this random time, no one in their right mind would butcher a pig in summer; they only did it after the weather turned cold, so that the meat would keep longer. Ivan had been gone all morning to an appointment with Serhiy, and on a bunch of errands before that. Whom was Margita supposed to call for help? Styopa, of course. Ivan had not spoken to his brother-in-law since the day Margita came to make her scene at Christina and Styopa's place. He owed Styopa an apology, at least. But he was waiting for the hurt to dull.

Well, no more waiting then.

They had already slaughtered the hog. Blood trickled into the drain next to the garage. The air was thick with the smell of pig guts and burned bristle. Ivan's father was right there, hosing blood off the concrete pavement. The hog's head sat impaled on a post and surveyed the yard with its dead eyes. Ivan came closer. He looked straight at it.

Normally, when they had to butcher a pig, they called for the man who did it for a living and had a special gun. It was complicated business, because as soon as the bullet hit the pig's brain someone had to cut the animal's throat and drain the blood before it poisoned the meat. It took several people to hold the pig—they never looked at it and did their best not to hear his screams. The hog knew what was happening, pigs were intelligent animals, you couldn't fool them. Ancient tribes knew the right way to kill an animal, knew how to ask for its forgiveness: Dear beast, forgive me, the hunter, for taking your life so that I may go on living mine.

When he was little, Ivan asked Margita if she didn't feel sorry for the pig. "Oy," she said, wiping her eyes with the hem of her apron, "of course you're sorry for them, but what to do?" He knew his mother loved every living thing, and when the family bought its piglets, Margita could not resist—she petted them and scratched them behind the ears, but only for a week or two, and then tried hard not to do it. She did not want to get attached to the pigs. So the piglets grew up in the dark, crowded sty, without human affection or company in the midst of the riotous luxury of Margita's garden.

Forgive us, dead animal. Forgive all of us together, and me, Ivan the coward, in particular, for not having my hand on your head in the hour of your death, for not putting my body next to yours to absorb your agony. Or did he? Was he always feeling it, the agony, the throes, because it had come into his own flesh—death, so that he could go on living? Ecclesiastes was wrong, and the living dog did not fare any better than the dead lion.

There was justice in that. Why should the living be better than the dead?

Ivan marveled at his own thoughts. He felt he could converse with the dead now. He smiled at the dead pig's head and nodded to it, like an old friend.

"There you are!" his father said, happy to see him. He did not notice Ivan's communion with the dead head, but wanted to tell his son all about what happened, and his tale, as always, scattered into small fragments, disconnected from each other, and Ivan worried: wasn't this how old-age dementia began, the confusion that would sooner or later take his memory (or most of it, anyway) and, with his memory, reason? The past, it would appear, was what held everything together inside us. Let it go, like a balloon, let it leave you, and you enter nonexistence. What would become of his father? Ivan thought of the very old people he had seen, their bird-light bodies, their need for warmth, the need to lean on the shoulder of a younger, still-robust man.

Styopa must have gone to the cellar already. He would be cutting the meat into portions or setting up to make sausages with Margita and Christina.

Ivan went down to the cellar, bent into the low door. Styopa was indeed there, behind the coarse table knocked together out of scrap wood, grinding or cutting something—it burned red in his hands, and the red flame of blood burned around him, blood burned on the shelves and on the boards, blood stood bottled in the great carboys around him. They would mix the blood with ground-up innards and rice, and fry the lot for sausage. Styopa was a little drunk, as the occasion required, and his mouth also glowed red like an oven fired up on this hot summer day, and the blaze of him seemed to send shadows and flares dancing upon the cellar walls.

"Well, look here! There's our man of the house!" Styopa jeered, and the fire inside his mouth turned malicious and flashed like dark rubies. "Here's our great man of the house, he who builds, and fixes stairs, and slaughters pigs!"

Margita, who ran into the cellar behind Ivan, made her anxious noises and started asking Styopa questions—random ones, just to distract him from the fact of Ivan's presence. But Styopa would not be thwarted. He stood tall behind the coarse table and looked taller still, as if he had grown an inch or two since he finally got his restaurant and became his own boss. All of his furious might had not only come back to him, but grown, massed larger like a dragon's neck. He filled the small cellar. His words thundered; he hurled them at Ivan, read him, the traitor, the coward, the riot act for hiding behind Margita's apron, him who was the reason Margita had raked her omnipotent son-in-law publicly over the coals, and then came calling because her own son was shit at husbandry and would never learn. Styopa insulted Ivan, he called him names, but Ivan barely heard the words, and only saw the blood—burning, burning.

"What d'you got to say for yourself, man?" Styopa shouted. He railed at Ivan but also against the very nature of betrayal and cowardice. Why were people afraid? How dare they? And Styopa, seeing that his words had very little effect on Ivan, shouted louder, stronger, so that the whole cave of the cellar shook. "I heard, didn't I, that your wife done left you? That you were no more good to her than to your house? Too good to work at it, like anyone else. You done ruined everything you had so what are you gonna do now? Go into politics, eh? Ha!" Styopa squinted for a moment and suddenly stopped shouting. "Nah! You no good at that either! I betcha I know what happened: the wife didn't just leave you, she left

you for another man! C'mon now! Did she? Fool around?" Styopa
had said this in a low voice, with his eyes narrowed, and the poison dripping into the blaze from the narrow slits between his lids.

Something then exploded in Ivan's concussed head. Styopa
could say whatever he pleased about him—was welcome to
curse him out in the most obscene terms imaginable, could say
that Phoebe must have found someone else, because the woman
might very well love another man, seeing how he had never
become one. But Styopa had no right to accuse Phoebe of anything, could not be allowed to use the phrase that men, in this
land, hopelessly mired in its seventeenth-century morals, in the
categories of "people" and "wives," spat at a woman. He, Ivan, a
man, did, in fact, fool around, sometimes literally, when he went
on his long walks instead of going home, but the phrase "fool
around" did not have the same power over him. Someone else
paid for his sins. Because someone else had always paid: for love,
revolution, even his food.

He no longer saw Styopa. Perdition itself had opened its scarlet maw at him, and it was to fight this perdition that Ivan grabbed
his father's ax from its nail at the door and lunged. He saw nothing but the red fog, the blood that now spurted from everywhere
around him as he swung his weapon. He did not see, only heard the
breaking glass and wondered, in the fog that possessed him, Was
Styopa's head made of glass? Who could tell what really was under
that hair; what if Styopa's soul itself had burst into a million shards,
that sacred vessel filled with the essence of life?

And the rhythmic tapping—as if on wood, tap, tap, tap-tap-
tap—could it be the metronome, counting the days and hours of
our lives, or was it, finally, that Someone who comes sometimes to
remind us of the most important things and Whom we can never
see, calling all to come to Him, with his wooden fingers tapping out
in Morse code a single message: be free be free be free . . .

•

Ivan ought to have come back still there, on the floor of the cellar, amid the fragments of wood and glass—the glass of those jugs of blood that had stood there like glowing lanterns and were now extinguished. But he found himself upstairs, in the house. He was laid out on Margita's eternal couch, as old as the world itself. He lay there and slowly woke up, and in the intervals of being almost awake fell again and again back asleep, as if a powerful hand dragged him each time under the surface of the river. He dreamed that he was in a forest, there were tall trees all around him, and the trees sang, but those were not trees, he knew, those were people: Margita, Mysko, someone else, and were not trees but sky-high lit candles. This dream then faded and another began, about smoke and gunshots, and he had a machine gun in his hands and was about to shoot at the enemy he could not see but hated with every fiber of his being. Whoever sends us the dreams we dream, Ivan thought, has it easy—*he* knows how things are going to end, but we don't, and at this, he woke up.

Why am I here? was his first anxious thought after the few sweet moments when his body, while already in possession of itself, remembered nothing. Yes, he remembered, and instantly, Ivan's sarcasm kicked in, unwanted and bitter in his mouth: I fought for Ukraine and in the process smashed my brother-in-law's skull. For Ukraine's freedom, no doubt, and its people. Ivan worked himself upright, sat. Margita or his father would have called the police already. Or Myron Vasyliovych—he is, after all, both a lawyer and family, he could advise them which way to lie. They could get away with it yet, tell the authorities it was self-defense. But not likely. Ivan would go to jail, and the newspapers would print something in the indomitable style of Transcarpathian news (à la "and then a bear came out of the forest and robbed the local farmer of a bottle of vodka") that a former employee of a such-and-such bank murdered his kin. Ivan wondered how much time he had before people came to arrest him? Could he have tea?

And fell right back to sleep. In the next dream he had, a tall, scary-looking man beat a small boy, and then turned around and patted the child on the head and gave him candy; the boy smiled with gratitude and loved the man because he had to love someone. The boy's face was the most terrifying thing. The faded memory of the beatings he had endured only showed in fragments under the mask of joy and the boy's need to trust. The boy was both Ivan and himself, and beyond that, the play of meanings and identities turned so elaborate that Ivan had no hope of putting it into words.

He woke up for the second time in the dark, at night. He could not read the clock that ticked on the wall, because it was old, made in the Soviet time, without any regard for life's actual needs, and the digits on its face did not light up. The designers might well have thought that a Soviet person had no business looking at clocks in the middle of the night. At night, people were supposed to sleep in order to be ready for work in the morning.

Why, why wasn't anyone coming to arrest him? And what had his parents done with Styopa's body? Asked his father's goddaughter, Valentina, who worked as a pathologist, to hold it in her morgue for a bit, just until they sorted out their story? And gave Ivan a chance to flee?

Ivan got up quietly. It was good he was where he was, in that particular room. There, in a drawer, was his passport. His winter jacket was in the wardrobe, carefully folded and stored for the season. It was summer at the moment, yes, but winter would come. Winter always came sooner than you thought. He had some money in his pockets, enough to get to Lviv. His shoes. His backpack. That's it. He needed nothing else . . . he wasn't about to fool around packing, making sandwiches for the road . . . Ivan ran his hand through his hair. He felt bits of glass.

The jars of blood. That's what he broke. His hair and clothes must have been covered in blood, too. But he hadn't killed anyone. The house was quiet. He did not dare go stand by Margita's door and listen to the sounds of her fitful sleep (if she ever slept). If he had killed someone, there would be people all over this place. What was he thinking! If they wanted, they could find him. He had to go. He would buy a bottle of water at the night kiosk, pour it over his hands, head, and clothes.

Ivan left the house, locked the door behind him. He opened the gate, closed it behind him, locked it, thought about it for a moment, and dropped the key into the mailbox. Still. It wasn't right. He found a notebook in his backpack, tore out a page, grabbed a pen, and wrote in the light of his pocket flashlight: "Mom, I left."

Should he write where he was going? But she would know anyway. There was only one place he could go. And he would call her as soon as he could, he would make sure to call her. And would keep calling, regularly, her and his father.

It was true. He was not the person he used to be.

Ivan walked down the dark street. He wanted to look back at his home, see it one more time. He could not do it. Instead, he stopped and just stood there, taking in the stillness of Maly Galagov, the stillness of his birthplace. He tipped his face to the sky.

The sky was dark, and only in one corner of it there was a glint of a tiny star, a pinprick of light that blinked bright and then stayed steady, hard and round like the head of a nail someone had hammered into the darkness.

AVAILABLE NOW FROM DEEP VELLUM

CHARLES ALCORN • *Beneath the Sands of Monahans* • USA

SHANE ANDERSON • *After the Oracle* • USA

MICHÈLE AUDIN • *One Hundred Twenty-One Days* • translated by Christiana Hills • FRANCE

BAE SUAH • *Recitation* • translated by Deborah Smith • SOUTH KOREA

MARIO BELLATIN • *Mrs. Murakami's Garden* • translated by Heather Cleary • *Beauty Salon* • translated by Shook • MEXICO

EDUARDO BERTI • *The Imagined Land* • translated by Charlotte Coombe • ARGENTINA

CARMEN BOULLOSA • *Texas: The Great Theft* • translated by Samantha Schnee • *Before* • translated by Peter Bush • *Heavens on Earth* • translated by Shelby Vincent • *The Book of Eve* • translated by Samantha Schnee • MEXICO

KB BROOKINS • *Freedom House* • USA

CHRISTINE BYL • *Lookout* • USA

CAYLIN CAPRA-THOMAS • *Iguana Iguana* • USA

MAGDA CÂRNECI • *FEM* • translated by Sean Cotter • ROMANIA

MIRCEA CĂRTĂRESCU • *Solenoid* • translated by Sean Cotter • ROMANIA

LEILA S. CHUDORI • *Home* • translated by John H. McGlynn • INDONESIA

JULIA CIMAFIEJEVA • *Motherfield* • translated by Valzhyna Mort & Hanif Abdurraqib • BELARUS

MATHILDE WALTER CLARK • *Lone Star* • translated by Martin Aitken & K. E. Semmel • DENMARK

SARAH CLEAVE, ed. • *Banthology: Stories from Banned Nations* • IRAN, IRAQ, LIBYA, SOMALIA, SUDAN, SYRIA & YEMEN

PETER CONSTANTINE • *The Purchased Bride* • USA

TIM COURSEY • *Driving Lessons* • USA

LOGEN CURE • *Welcome to Midland: Poems* • USA

ANANDA DEVI • *Eve Out of Her Ruins* • translated by Jeffrey Zuckerman • *When the Night Agrees to Speak to Me* • translated by Kazim Ali • MAURITIUS

DHUMKETU • *The Shehnai Virtuoso* • translated by Jenny Bhatt • INDIA

PETER DIMOCK • *Daybook from Sheep Meadow* • USA

CLAUDIA ULLOA DONOSO • *Little Bird* • translated by Lily Meyer • PERU/NORWAY

LEYLÂ ERBIL • *A Strange Woman* • translated by Nermin Menemencioğlu & Amy Marie Spangler • TURKEY

RADNA FABIAS • *Habitus* • translated by David Colmer • CURAÇAO/NETHERLANDS

ROSS FARRAR • *Ross Sings Cheree & the Animated Dark: Poems* • USA

ALISA GANIEVA • *The Mountain and the Wall* • *Bride and Groom* • *Offended Sensibilities* • translated by Carol Apollonio • RUSSIA

FERNANDA GARCÍA LAO • *Out of the Cage* • translated by Will Vanderhyden • ARGENTINA

ANNE GARRÉTA • *Sphinx* • *Not One Day* • *In Concrete* • translated by Emma Ramadan • FRANCE

ALLA GORBUNOVA • *It's the End of the World, My Love* • translated by Elina Alter • RUSSIA

NIVEN GOVINDEN • *Diary of a Film* • GREAT BRITAIN

JÓN GNARR • *The Indian* • *The Pirate* • *The Outlaw* • translated by Lytton Smith • ICELAND

AVAILABLE NOW FROM DEEP VELLUM

GOETHE • *The Golden Goblet: Selected Poems* • *Faust, Part One* • translated by Zsuzsanna Ozsváth and Frederick Turner • GERMANY

SARA GOUDARZI • *The Almond in the Apricot* • USA

GISELA HEFFES • *Ischia* • translated by Grady C. Ray • ARGENTINA

NOEMI JAFFE • *What Are the Blind Men Dreaming?* • translated by Julia Sanches & Ellen Elias-Bursac • BRAZIL

CLAUDIA SALAZAR JIMÉNEZ • *Blood of the Dawn* • translated by Elizabeth Bryer • PERU

PERGENTINO JOSÉ • *Red Ants* • MEXICO

TAISIA KITAISKAIA • *The Nightgown & Other Poems* • USA

SONG LIN • *The Gleaner Song: Selected Poems* • translated by Dong Li • CHINA

GYULA JENEI • *Always Different* • translated by Diana Senechal • HUNGARY

DIAA JUBAILI • *No Windmills in Basra* • translated by Chip Rossetti • IRAQ

JUNG YOUNG MOON • *Seven Samurai Swept Away in a River* • *Vaseline Buddha* • translated by Yewon Jung • SOUTH KOREA

ELENI KEFALA • *Time Stitches* • translated by Peter Constantine • CYPRUS

UZMA ASLAM KHAN • *The Miraculous True History of Nomi Ali* • PAKISTAN /USA

KIM YIDEUM • *Blood Sisters* • translated by Jiyoon Lee • SOUTH KOREA

JOSEFINE KLOUGART • *Of Darkness* • translated by Martin Aitken • DENMARK

ANDREY KURKOV • *Grey Bees* • *Diary of an Invasion* • translated by Boris Dralyuk • UKRAINE

YANICK LAHENS • *Moonbath* • translated by Emily Gogolak • *Sweet Undoings* • translated by Kaiama L. Glover • HAITI

JORGE ENRIQUE LAGE • *Freeway: La Movie* • translated by Lourdes Molina • CUBA

FOUAD LAROUI • *The Curious Case of Dassoukine's Trousers* • translated by Emma Ramadan • MOROCCO

MARIA GABRIELA LLANSOL • *The Geography of Rebels Trilogy: The Book of Communities; The Remaining Life; In the House of July & August* • translated by Audrey Young • PORTUGAL

TEDI LÓPEZ MILLS • *The Book of Explanations* • translated by Robin Myers • MEXICO

PABLO MARTÍN SÁNCHEZ • *The Anarchist Who Shared My Name* • translated by Jeff Diteman • SPAIN

DOROTA MASŁOWSKA • *Honey, I Killed the Cats* • translated by Benjamin Paloff • POLAND

BRICE MATTHIEUSSENT • *Revenge of the Translator* • translated by Emma Ramadan • FRANCE

ERNEST MCMILLAN • *Standing: One Man's Odyssey through the Turbulent Sixties* • *Kneeling* • USA

LINA MERUANE • *Seeing Red* • translated by Megan McDowell • CHILE

ANTONIO MORESCO • *Clandestinity* • translated by Richard Dixon • ITALY

VALÉRIE MRÉJEN • *Black Forest* • translated by Katie Shireen Assef • FRANCE

FISTON MWANZA MUJILA • *Tram 83* • translated by Roland Glasser • *The River in the Belly: Poems* • translated by J. Bret Maney • DEMOCRATIC REPUBLIC OF CONGO

AVAILABLE NOW FROM DEEP VELLUM